Self-Reliance

D1570780

Also by Michael Brownstein:

Fiction

The Touch (1993)

Music from the Evening of the World (1989)

Country Cousins (1974; 1986)

Brainstorms (1971)

Poetry

Oracle Night (1982)

When Nobody's Looking (1981)

Strange Days Ahead (1975)

Highway to the Sky (1969)

Behind the Wheel (1967)

Translations

The Dice Cup: Selected Prose Poems of Max Jacob (1979)

Self-Reliance

A NOVEL BY MICHAEL BROWNSTEIN

COFFEE HOUSE PRESS :: MINNEAPOLIS :: 1994

Cover art, *Witness (B.E.)*, by Jane Dickson reproduced courtesy of Brooke Alexander
Back cover photograph by Mary Gearhart
Excerpt from "I Only Have Eyes For You" (Harry Warren, Al Dubin) © 1934 WARNER BROS. INC. (Renewed) All rights reserved. Used by permission.
Excerpt from "People" (Bob Merrill, Jule Styne) © 1963 (Renewed) CHAPPELL & CO. & WONDERFUL MUSIC INC. All rights administered by CHAPPELL & CO. All rights reserved. Used by permission.
Excerpt from "The Sun is Shining" (Elmore James), reprinted with permission, © 1960 (renewed), Arc Music Corporation. All rights reserved.

The author wishes to thank the editors of *Between C & D*, in which part of Chapter 12 first appeared.

The publishers would like to thank the following funders for assistance that helped make this book possible: Dayton Hudson Foundation on behalf of Dayton's and Target Stores; The Lannan Foundation; The Andrew W. Mellon Foundation; Star Tribune/Cowles Media Company; The McKnight Foundation; and the Minnesota State Arts Board, through an appropriation by the Minnesota State Legislature. Major new marketing initiatives have been made possible by the Lila Wallace–Reader's Digest Literary Publishers Marketing Development Program, funded through a grant to the Council of Literary Magazines and Presses.

Coffee House Press books are available to the trade through our primary distributor, Consortium Book Sales & Distribution, 1045 Westgate Drive, Saint Paul, MN 55114. Our books are also available through all major library distributors and jobbers, and through most small press distributors, including Bookpeople, Inland, and Small Press Distribution. For personal orders, catalogs or other information, write to:
Coffee House Press
27 North Fourth Street, Suite 400, Minneapolis, MN 55401

Library of Congress CIP Data
Brownstein, Michael, date.
Self-reliance : a novel / by Michael Brownstein
    p.   cm.
   ISBN 1-56689-018-7
   1. City and town life—New York (N.Y.)—Fiction. 2. Journalists—New York (N.Y.)—Fiction. 3. Men—New York (N.Y.)—Fiction. I. Title.
PS3552.R79S4 1994   93-23690
813' .54—dc20   CIP
10   9   8   7   6   5   4   3   2   1

Printed in Canada

For my father

PART ONE

PART ONE

ONE

I started to lose control in the days of Jerry Ford, a time of transition not long ago but already far away. After terrorizing the populace for years, the two-headed monster of Vietnam and Watergate finally slouched off into history. In 1976, a presidential campaign took place which meant nothing to me or anyone I knew. Jimmy said that if elected he would never tell a lie, while Jerry banged his head getting out of a helicopter at the Bohemian Grove. Here in New York, the city was broke and seedy, slated to go bankrupt. Thousands of cops and firemen were laid off and the crime rates climbed. In SRO hotels on the Upper West Side cat food suppers were becoming fashionable, while bantam Mayor Beame clung stubbornly to his own pet project, the Second Avenue subway line, a phantom subway to nowhere, real only in the minds of those who were extracting money from it.

But the excavation sites themselves were real enough. The one at the intersection of St. Mark's Place, for example, near where I lived, was undeniable—huge holes dug under Second Avenue up to Ninth Street, sections of paving and sidewalks gone, buildings swaying and foundations cracking. When work stopped at five o'clock, steel plates and wooden planks were laid across the gaps. But as funds for the project blew away in a crosswind of accusations between the city and the state, plans for the line were scrapped.

So even after the crews and machinery disappeared from the neighborhood never to return, a dangerous cavern remained, imperfectly sealed off from the streets above. Walking through the area at night meant negotiating the unknown—especially for me, because at about that time I had so much on my mind I forgot to look where I was going. Even during daylight hours, life on the streets of the East Village had taken on a problematic air. In 1976, the neighborhood wasn't in the least desirable. Poverty-stricken Puerto Ricans and paranoid Ukrainians, dazed hippies resentfully aging, venomous bikers and junkies, desperado Vietnam veterans with shaved heads and cancelled eyes—these were the residents of the area.

And above all, the homeless, many of them demented. Ragged, ill, hallucinating, they'd been saturated with Thorazine and released into the streets as part of a new "community care" program to clear out the state's mental institutions. Outbursts of cryptic graffiti covered walls and sidewalks. It was impossible to tell whether they were the secret messages of psychopaths, advertisements for obscure rock groups, or anonymous works of art:

MISSING   SUCKER FOR FATE

OFF THE BLUE KICK TORSO

REVOLUTIONARY SCHIZOPHRENIA   BRAILLE TEETH

WHAT'S THE SOUNDTRACK FOR PEOPLE TALKING?

CROCODILES DON'T DREAM   WIPE OUT DEATH

One thing I knew for sure, though, my own life was at a crossroads. Dana and I were coming apart at the seams, no matter how often either of us denied the fact. For no reason at all we'd start arguing, hurling accusations back and forth, turning ourselves inside out in a matter of seconds. As if that weren't enough, I'd also completely lost interest in the string of journalistic assignments with which I pieced together a living.

I was going nowhere, attending the same music business parties and writing dozens of breezy record reviews, as well as the occasional book review in which I tried to sound intellectual. I was covering all sorts of lame acts for no pay, simply to keep up with the scene, and attending rock concerts which seemed to grow bigger and more glitzy by the week. All for possible articles in downtown papers like *SoHo Weekly News* and *The New Jag*, which paid next to nothing anyway.

It took a long time for me to wake up to the reality of my situation in New York, but by then I was burned out. I didn't care anymore. Too much of the same kind of time had gone by. I'd seen it all before. Watching bloated acts at Madison Square Garden, with top-heavy production numbers and half-hour-long guitar solos, I realized I was no more than a glorified publicist, another cog in the entertainment machine.

Even after a whole new scene emerged downtown at CBGB's, I felt like everything was taking place behind a pane of glass. And something else surfaced as well, a resentment I'd never felt before. I wanted to be onstage myself. I wanted to perform. Seeing unknown bands with names like the Dead Boys and the Raving Treetops, the Talking Heads, the Ramones, and Worship/Destroy, I was envious. Half these fucking people couldn't even play their instruments. It got so I couldn't walk into a club without putting everyone down, though, and I hated that. *So change your life then, fuckhead.* Give up writing about your precious, sacred rock and roll music. Nobody'll miss you. When you step outside of your niche you disappear, don't you know enough to understand that? Don't you, little baby, little curly-headed one?

But there was another reason the underground music scene lost its glow for me. Bobby Addison was my oldest friend, we'd known each other since the early Sixties when we'd gone to Antioch College together. We'd become close there because of our mutual immersion in Chicago blues, which we listened to day and night. Each new record by Howlin' Wolf, Elmore James, and Muddy Waters was a revelation. Unlike me, however, Bobby only pretended to be a student. He spent all of his time playing guitar.

After graduating from college I came to New York. I dreamed of writing poetry and I did that. I even published a few books, but they were mimeographed books which 30 people read, and meanwhile holes were appearing in the soles of my shoes and I was always broke. By 1970 I resolved to survive as a writer for pay, a professional. It was time for me to get real, act the same as everybody else. "It is not doing what we like, but liking what we have to do, that makes life complete." I found that gem in a fortune cookie in 1970 and—I'll never forget it—reading it was like being poleaxed. So that's what was required of me? Well, I'd learned my lesson. I was up for making my life complete.

Meanwhile, in '67 Bobby quit school and moved to San Francisco. He fit right into the Summer of Love, living a supersonic, disordered life. He played with lots of groups out there and even had his own blues band for a while. But by the last time I visited him, in '71, Haight-Ashbury was dead, the Jefferson Airplane lived in a mansion by the sea, and Bobby's band had disintegrated for lack of work. Bobby came to meet me at the airport, grinning and happy to see me, but by the time we got back to his place I knew he was doing heroin. Suddenly we had nothing to talk about anymore.

Imagine my surprise, then, when he turned up in New York in the fall of '73, off heroin and newly married. Penniless and wary, but determined to make it this time, he took a job driving a taxi and found his way into the New York scene, doing studio work and assembling a new band. He and his wife, Faye, moved into an apartment on Avenue A and soon Faye gave birth to a boy named Kevin.

The new underground music on the Bowery included Bobby Addison from the very start, and in the spring of '75 he finally emerged with the Frozen Donuts, an entirely different sound from anything he'd had in California. Ironic and assaultive, it had nothing to do with the blues he'd been playing for years, but instead eerily descended from the simple hooks and refrains of early Sixties white rock and roll.

He looked different now, too. Gone was Wild Bill Hickok, the flowing locks, the buckskin jacket and cowboy boots. Watching him as he waited with his band to go on at CBGB's, I could hardly believe this was the same person. He looked like an uptight, sexually repressed high school science major from 1959. A throwback with flattop haircut, torn chinos, and klutzy high-top sneakers. When he sang he was doing you a favor, garbling and twisting his own sardonic lyrics to melodies which everybody in the room remembered from the far reaches of their adolescence. Gone was the air of music as gift, as celebration.

I'll never forget my amazement when I first saw the Frozen Donuts play. It was spooky because of how much Bobby himself had changed. It wasn't only an act. His determination to succeed this time around was so intense he'd become steely and unsympathetic. Then Bobby discovered cocaine, which made him aggressive and judgmental. And its high cost threw him into a rage. He longed to be able to splurge, to put his taxi-driving days behind him and buy Faye some beautiful clothes, blow money on a vacation. So far he had released only one 45 and played in just a few clubs. But Patti Smith already had signed with Arista, and rumors that the Ramones and Blondie were soon to follow suit with other major labels fired him with uncontrollable impatience. He didn't take it kindly when I teased him about his newfound ambition.

"You just happen to be dead wrong, ole buddy," he drawled in his east Tennessee accent. "This here's serious, it's my *career* we're talkin' about." He eyed me dubiously. "And from what I can make out, you could use a shot of initiative yourself. You believe I plan on playing for the rest of my life in these *holes* in the fucking wall? No way, brother, no way . . . Listen, Roy, let me clue you in on something. The scene down here started on a real friendly note, remember? We all went to each other's shows and hung out together. But things are different now. Since Patti signed with Arista she don't come around much anymore," he sniffed disdainfully.

"I ain't gonna be left behind this time like I was in Haight-Ashbury. I'm two years older than you, man, I'm thirty-four already, this is *it* . . . You just wait, a year from now, the Frozen Donuts will be a household name," he announced portentously, but in spite of himself he paused to look me in the eye, and we broke up laughing.

The next time I saw Bobby was on a freezing cold afternoon in January, 1976. We ran into each other on Second Avenue and went into the little Ukrainian bar on Seventh Street to have a beer. We hadn't been seeing much of each other lately. For one thing, Bobby had taken up with a string of girlfriends with whom he was spending all his time. Talking to Faye on the phone, pretending I didn't know about all that, left a bad taste in my mouth.

Bobby filled me in on what he'd been doing lately. While he talked I noticed his eyes, glittering and bloodshot. For the first time since he'd come to the city I was reminded of the person I'd left in S.F. six years before.

"I'm tellin' you, brother, instead of being a slum landlord on the Lower East Side, I've become a big ole slum *tenant*. It's clean outta sight. I got me two apartments now, and thinking 'bout a third one, too. Don't nobody know about this either, Roy, so I'd appreciate you keepin' it to yourself. See, Faye and Kevin are still on Avenue A, and the Donuts still practice in the loft up on 28th Street. But I discovered a person can rent these places over in the jungle—Avenue D—and nobody knows you're there. I got mine in October, 38 bucks a month and it's even got heat sometimes, which is a miracle considering it's only about three people in the whole building paying rent . . . I go there to get away, you understand? No furniture, no wailing infant, no telephone. I fixed the place up a bit, covered the walls and ceiling with silver mylar, it's like bein' inside a spaceship. Colored lights, some pillows, that's it. I pull down the shades, plug in my Stratocaster, and play that fucker as loud as I want, all night long. Nobody knows I exist, most of them buildings are deserted anyway, it's great! It's only junkies around there and they don't care none about the noise. I'm telling you, brother, it's paradise!"

Bobby insisted on taking me over there one night real soon, we'd get stoned and listen to Muddy Waters, just like old times. Three days later—January 26, 1976—he was dead, shot in the side of the head in the hallway outside his Avenue D hideaway, the door to his place open, his guitar and amps gone.

The strangest thing was my disabling grief after the phone rang that day and Faye's voice came on the line telling me Bobby was dead. Strange because really it had been years since we'd been close, and yet from the moment I set down the receiver I was numb. Suddenly I felt a searing pain in my side. Later that week, going to the funeral, I had difficulty walking down the street. Dressed in a shiny black suit two sizes too large which Dana had bought for me at the Salvation Army, I kept thinking I was on acid. I felt an unbearable creepiness under my skin and was full of rage that every day I would wake up and have to confront the same fact, that Bobby was gone. As his oldest friend I was supposed to deliver the eulogy at the church, but I just stood there behind the pulpit, my hands and feet numb, my jaws clenched tight, my heart racing, certain that at any moment I was going to pitch over onto the floor.

"Who the fuck's in control here?" I finally shouted. "Where's the doctor?"

After Bobby Addison died I let the music reviews go for good. I couldn't walk into a club without feeling numb again. Dana was upset. She kept asking me what would happen to Faye and Kevin now, as if I knew the answer. In the weeks after Bobby's death Dana started changing, thinking of herself more, of ways to revive her stalled art career. She talked of moving away from St. Mark's Place to some- where safer, Brooklyn maybe. She stopped smoking grass then, too, and gave me a hard time when I persisted.

I wanted to concentrate on doing interviews, the one form of jour- nalism which challenged me, but instead, for survival purposes, I was writing snappy articles on the New York social whirl, one mini-event after another—parties and openings, art performances, little scandals and trends. I'd head uptown along with a staff photographer and find myself standing in the corner of the Terrace Room at the Plaza Hotel, waiting for Tina Turner to appear, or at opening night in the garden of the Museum of Modern Art, staring into the silver foxes covering the shoulders of semi-embalmed matrons and feeling a million miles away.

Without connections I couldn't line up the interviews I wanted to do. Those celebrities whose conversations *Playboy* or *Rolling Stone* might publish had no time to waste on me. But in April of '76 my first break came, or so it seemed. I interviewed Truman Capote for a fea- ture on literary celebrity in *The Village Voice*.

Our meeting took place a little over a year after the notorious "La Côte Basque" section of his roman à clef, *Answered Prayers*, had ap- peared in *Esquire*. This consisted of conversations which supposedly had taken place ten years before between Gloria Vanderbilt Cooper, Mrs. Walter Matthau, and two fictitious characters. They discussed a socialite friend of theirs acquitted after possibly murdering her husband with a shotgun, and a week before *Esquire* hit the stands, the real-life Ann Woodward committed suicide, swallowing cyanide. Subsequently, Capote was accused of opportunism and dropped by dozens of his high-class friends. I badly wanted to interview him, but although I tried, I couldn't even get a message through. Then, out of the blue, Dana's old roommate at Barnard, Cissy Wyatt, dropped by St. Mark's Place. When I mentioned Capote, Cissy claimed that nothing would be easier to arrange, her mother was a pal of Truman's. And sure enough, before going off to Italy, and as a favor to Caroline Wyatt, he consented to meet me in her Park Avenue apartment.

Cissy's father, Arthur Dean Wyatt, a Wall Street investment banker, had died the year before, and her mother lived in a large, opulently furnished apartment filled with antique Chinese figurines, several inches high, on every available surface—exotic birds and dragons, spitting dogs, and Buddhas doing handstands. This collection jarred with the big abstract paintings on the walls by the likes of Barnett Newman, Helen Frankenthaler, and Mark Rothko. I realized that the paintings must have been her father's contribution to the household, while the figurines were her mother's. The two personal statements didn't mesh at all, yet somewhere along the line they had produced Cissy, a tall, ungainly, withdrawn person who always wore dark glasses, indoors and out.

Cissy and Dana had been close at Barnard, but Dana said she'd been glad when they no longer were roommates. For one thing, Cissy would corner Dana for hours at a stretch and talk obsessively about her parents. For another, Dana had been into men in a big way back then. For the first time in her life she wasn't living at home and could do as she pleased. Yet Cissy was so uncomfortable around the guys Dana brought back to their room that Dana somehow would end up feeling guilty, as if she were fooling herself, and the men no longer looked so enticing.

Five or six years had passed since then. According to Dana, since her father died Cissy was unable to finish anything. Unsure of what she wanted to do with her life, she was more guilty than ever about all the money she had.

Cissy was twenty-eight years old. Recently she'd been travelling a lot and, when she was in town, staying with her mother on Park Avenue. I found out later that Caroline Wyatt had thought journalism might be a good thing for her daughter to get involved in. That was why she'd arranged the interview. Cissy was to sit in on it. The fact that I hardly knew Cissy in those days, and had never before met her mother, didn't seem to bother Caroline Wyatt in the least. A vivacious blond in her fifties with a sleek, gilded look to her, she swept out of the apartment in yards of cherry red silk soon after introducing me to Capote.

"I'll return for you in an hour, Truman," she announced in a vibrant, conspiratorial voice, "so please be here! You *know* where we're going at five o'clock!"

A short, puffy-faced man with a head which seemed too big for his body, Truman Capote sat in the living room on a cream-colored sofa, eating candy from a silver dish and smoking a cigarette. He wore a yellow linen suit and a polka dot bow tie. I was taken aback by the air of authority he projected. Somehow I'd expected him to be elfin or droll, like a sprite. Instead, he had an intense, formidable gaze, his eyes full of mischief yet also penetrating. He quickly sized me up. No one had ever scrutinized me with such thoroughness before. Splayed on the sofa with a regal expansiveness, he beckoned to me with a sweep of his arm, simpering in an exaggeratedly falsetto voice, "Sit down *here*, my boy . . . Caroline's told me *so much* about you, which is to say nothing at all, but you look too young—or is the word *dweamy?*—to be a reporter. There must be some terrible mistake!"

He giggled and then coughed, a mighty hacking cough which momenarily shook the light out of his eyes. I felt abashed in his presence. Capote was a star, a bona fide culture hero, and I was used to interviewing monosyllabic rock and rollers. Acutely uncomfortable, I mumbled a few words in response, at which his high-pitched laugh burst across the room.

"Let's talk about you and Cissy here instead of about little ole me, I'm sure it'll be lots more interesting. How do you two know each other? Do you fuck, or just *hang out?*"

He giggled again and lit another cigarette. I turned and gave Cissy a look of puzzled inquiry, but—inscrutable as ever behind her shades— she merely raised her eyebrows and shrugged.

When he saw my tape recorder on the coffee table between us his mood immediately changed. He groaned, eyeing the machine with aversion, and I remembered he prided himself on his gift for total recall, disdaining to record the numerous conversations he'd had while putting together *In Cold Blood*. From that point on he adopted a tight, suspicious manner. After half an hour during which we mostly discussed how he'd written *In Cold Blood* ("I felt perfectly free to make things up, what those boys said to each other, because I had done my homework. I knew them *down to their bones* . . ."), I finally couldn't contain myself and broached the topic of the *Esquire* story.

Unsure of how to approach the subject, I disregarded the coldness which crept into his eyes and found myself attempting to flatter him.

"Weren't you appalled when your society friends turned on you after 'Côte Basque' was published? I mean, you should have been the one to feel betrayed—betrayed by their stupidity. After all, you're a writer, what did they expect you to do with the stories they told you?"

Squirming on the sofa, his lips narrowing, he replied petulantly, "I don't care to discuss it."

The room was silent. We stared at each other for a moment. I should have steered the interview onto another topic, I certainly had plenty of other questions, but instead I persisted.

"Why not?" I asked, with more of a challenge than I'd intended.

His face blanched.

"*Why not?*" he echoed in an offended, grating whine which set my teeth on edge. "Do you suppose I owe you any explanations? Who are you, anyway? I only discuss such things with people I know, people who amount to something, that is. Clearly you're not one of *those*. It was *so* obvious what you wanted from me, it was hanging out of your pants the minute you walked into the room. And I must say, you have lots to learn about interviewing someone. You simply stumble along without charm or grace and expect me to hand over the goods. Well, it won't work. You have to romance me, sucker, don't you even know that? I'm afraid you'd better try another line of work—carpentry, perhaps. Something relatively undemanding. But you're in over your head here."

I gaped at him, hot with embarrassment.

Turning to Cissy he added acidly, "Really, my dear, I'm disappointed in you. I assumed you were more discerning. Where did you pick *this* one up, at the laundromat?"

Addressing me he said, a look of fatigue on his face, "Why don't you just leave. You're boring me." He made a dismissive gesture with his left hand, waving stubby fingers toward the door.

Before I knew what I was doing I was on my feet, my voice cracking as I shouted, "From what I've read in *Esquire* you don't have anything to be snotty about. How repellent, slandering people who you know won't fight back. You must have been desperate to get something into print. Don't you at least feel any remorse at Ann Woodward's death?"

I stood over him, mesmerized by his eyes which glittered now, hard and bright as diamonds.

"How dare you try to insult me," he hissed. "You're nothing but a pathetic little ass-licker, depending on your connections with Cissy here to—"

But I lost my cool then. I grabbed at him, pulling at his bow tie until it came off in my hand. He let out a terrified squeal and shot sideways along the sofa, his arms raised protectively, taking swipes at me with his claws. I felt like strangling him, I don't even know why, maybe because as I threw down the tie and gathered my things to leave, he kept smiling at me like a gargoyle. I went rigid.

Cissy was horrified as she steered me away. Her lips next to my ear, she whispered, "Will you get *out* of here, for gosh sakes!" When we reached the door and were out of sight of Capote, she snickered, her eyes unreadable behind the shades. "God," she said, "you really screwed up, didn't you?"

So here I was, ten years after I'd first come to New York, broke and obsessing over a new project I had in mind: *Angels of the Me*

Generation, a coffee table book about rock stars, with full-page color photos. I planned to sell the book as a sort of combined celebration/exposé, a fresh, irreverent look at the stars. It'll have more pictures than text, I thought, and what text there is will be zippy and airy, full of gossip and assorted up-to-the-minute revelations—drug life and sexual preferences, what the guys think about their home towns, their opinions on current affairs, how long their hair is (there'll be a chart at the end comparing the length of their respective locks)...

And suddenly I realized what was wrong. The entire project turned my stomach. How could I seriously be considering such a book? It meant nothing to me. I was no more than a toady and a hack. Soon I'd be thirty-three years old, to be followed by thirty-four and thirty-five. And why not forty, while we're at it? And if death were to come looking for me one day, what would it find me doing? Riding up and down elevators, flogging a book I didn't believe in? There must be some other way for me to survive in this city, I said to myself. Maybe now was the time to find out.

TWO

In order to clear my head, I decided to drop *Angels of the Me Generation* for a while. I wanted to try one more interview, even though my chances of landing it were slim. It was July now, the city suffocatingly hot and jammed with Bicentennial tourists come to see the tall ships sail up the Hudson River. On TV, wagon trains converged on Valley Forge and time capsules were buried in back yards. At Yankee Stadium, the Reverend Sun Myung Moon held a huge rally of the patriotic faithful. But if Oliver Hartwell, the novelist, would agree to an interview, I'd be able to sell it for more than usual to Margo Kopperman at *The New Jag*, and Dana and I could take a vacation.

Hartwell's masterpiece, *A Time of Walls*, had been published the previous winter to worshipful reviews, and at sixty-nine years of age he had reached the summit of his career. *A Time of Walls* chronicled, in unrelenting detail, the hapless psychodrama of upper middle-class WASP family life, and suburbanites were snapping up copies in record numbers.

In May, Hartwell had come within a hair's breadth of beating out Saul Bellow for the Pulitzer Prize. *A Time of Walls* quickly outsold all his previous efforts—some ten novels written over several decades—and his publishers wanted to capitalize on the sudden rush of publicity. Oliver Hartwell was hot. But in the five years since his second wife had divorced him and he'd returned to Manhattan from their remodeled Connecticut carriage house, he had become something of an urban recluse. Vague rumors of psychological peculiarities had surfaced which could be explained only partly by professional jealousy. And although in the Forties and Fifties Hartwell had been a kind of workhorse for the literary establishment, cranking out essays and criticism in addition to a new novel every few years, he now had a reputation for being cantankerous and unreasonably zealous in defense of his privacy.

As I discovered later, it was only because reporters from two national news magazines unexpectedly failed to keep their appointments with him that I got to see Hartwell at all. The small weekly paper I worked for meant nothing to him, and when I talked to him on the phone he sounded cold and impatient, interrupting to ask how I'd gotten his number. He was extremely busy now, he said. He was leaving town soon, and so he regretted that he couldn't see me. The following day would be the last on which he granted interviews and he was booked solid. When, without warning, both news magazines cancelled on him the next morning and attempted to reschedule, he turned them down flat. I called that morning, too, hoping he would reconsider. He was fuming mad, and consequently in the mood for the vernacular.

"Those flaming assholes," he barked, "they thought I was joking when I said today was the last day I could see them. In one ear and out the other, they don't even hear it. Advertising revenue's all they pay attention to, everything else is expendable. But, by God, you mark my words—in the end, everything *but* their sacred bottom line will finish by doing them in!"

As I puzzled over that last remark, he concluded by giving me his address. He'd let me have the interview after all.

"Come over right away!" he shouted so loudly I had to hold the receiver away from my ear.

Oliver Hartwell lived on Central Park West in a massive pre-war building a few blocks below the Museum of Natural History. The doorman buzzed his apartment and I heard that same imperious, excitable voice on the intercom, ordering him to send me up. When I knocked at his door it swung open and a voice called out, "Come on in!"

"Shut the door behind you!" he bellowed.

I wandered through the living room and kitchen of the large old apartment and finally found him in a bright, spacious study filled with books and plants which overlooked the park. Gymnastic equipment had been installed at one end of the room and copies of *Runner's World* lay on the floor. The distinguished novelist, wearing only gym shorts and strapped into strange metal boots, hung upside down from some sort of contraption which looked like the frame of a child's swing set. His face was beet-red and he was perspiring profusely. With a start, I noticed the unmistakable sign of an erection pushing at his shorts.

"Sit down over there," he ordered, jerking his head toward a desk by the window, "I'll be finished in a minute."

He swung back and forth a few times then hung perfectly still, his body fully extended, eyes closed, breathing deeply. Lifting his upper body until he could reach the boots, he tugged at them, and when they opened he did a neat backflip onto the floor. Amazed by his agility, I couldn't help noticing with envy his flat stomach and hard legs. At sixty-nine he seemed to be in better shape than me. He stood there examining me with a frankly challenging stare which made me more and more uncomfortable, then said he'd be back after changing into his clothes. We still hadn't introduced ourselves, yet from the next room he was already advising me to get more exercise.

"You young people act as if you've got all the time in the world, which is pathetic. Don't you understand? Pathetic! Gravity's insidious effects are eating away at you all the time. If you won't neutralize them by means of a regimen of constant exercise, then what do you expect but to deteriorate like a piece of fruit? Especially at your age! I can tell you've turned thirty, you're no spring chicken any longer. You disregard what I'm telling you at your peril!"

Returning to the study he eyed me superciliously and continued in that peremptory manner of his, "It was obvious to me right away that you don't breathe deeply enough, either. Breath is the life force. It's the key to energy, to well being, to *everything*," he stated categorically. "Come on—try it!"

He started breathing exaggeratedly, almost hyperventilating, forcing me to join in until I felt dizzy, then raising his hand abruptly like a traffic cop.

"You'll get the hang of it—if you persevere," he said in a patronizing voice which I resented. Who did this old geezer think he was? Before the interview had even begun he was involving me in a skirmish of egos. Perhaps he acted this way with everyone. No wonder his wife had left him.

Hartwell had grown up in a well-to-do family on the North Shore of Long Island, and had gone to Yale. Until the late 1930s he'd been a Connecticut lawyer. But then, at the cost of much personal sacrifice, he abruptly changed careers. Divorcing his first wife and losing his home in Hartford, he had moved to New York toward the end of the Depression, determined to be a writer. Too old for active service during World War II, he worked for the OSS in Washington, decoding foreign documents. After the war he immersed himself in New York's literary life, slowly building a solid reputation.

Now the grizzled old warhorse, he had a combative air of robust self-confidence about him. Occasionally his eyebrows moved up and down as he talked, reminding me of Senator Ervin during the Watergate hearings. But Hartwell, unlike Sam Ervin, appeared to be in surprisingly good health. Strength and energy fairly radiated from his body, even though certain telltale signs of age were undeniable in spite of his demanding physical regimen. I noticed the thin grey hair, the rheumy eyes which grew tired behind his wire-rimmed glasses as he talked, and the hands which trembled now and then.

From the vague stories circulating about him I was expecting an anti-social crank who would resist my attempts to draw him out, but as we talked he turned out to be an enthusiastic conversationalist. Apparently he had decided to be obliging with me. Possessed of a repertoire of anecdotes about famous writers of his day, he trotted out one after another—getting drunk with a delphically deranged Jane Bowles in a Manhattan hotel room in 1943, coming to blows with Delmore Schwartz in the offices of the *Partisan Review*, playing poker with James Jones in Paris in the Fifties. After we'd been talking for a while I realized the interview was going really well, and I even regretted having to give it to *The New Jag*, convinced I could get more money for it elsewhere.

However, an animosity toward me, not evident at first, surfaced midway through our talk when, out of the blue, he started calling me "Sprout." Nobody had ever done that to me before. This sudden gambit of his irritated me, but he continued to use it even after I corrected him.

"My name is Roy," I said in no uncertain terms, but he pretended he hadn't heard me, an infuriating little smile playing at the corners of his mouth.

After more than an hour had gone by I went to use his bathroom. On the floor under the sink was a small refrigerator. My curiosity got the better of me and I looked inside. There, staring me in the face, were several syringes and, behind them, rows of ampules whose labels, neatly typed in French, read:

Sanitorium Forestier
St. Genêt, Suisse
M. Oliver Hartwell
Une fois par semaine
Cellules de fetus de mouton

Lamb fetus injections—what were *they* for? Afraid of being discovered, certain Hartwell would become suspicious if I remained in the bathroom any longer, I rejoined him in his studio. I tried to get him to talk about himself, hoping to learn something about those ampules by focusing on the present, on his plans and opinions, but I found it hard to know what to believe. By turns sarcastic and sincere, he spoke with increasing emotion, but at the same time he seemed suspicious of being drawn into the open. An awkward tension soon filled the room.

The last question I had for him was obligatory; still, I often wonder what direction my life would have taken if I'd never asked it.

"Are you working on a new novel now?"

He grimaced, peering at me from behind his wire-rimmed glasses with the misanthropic air of a hermit, drumming his fingers impatiently on his desk.

"You journalists are all alike, always asking the same brilliant questions. Yes," he drawled facetiously, "of course I'm working on a new novel—isn't that what novelists are for? It's about a mouse who suffers from delusions of grandeur."

"You mean, he keeps thinking he's a rat?"

Hartwell laughed, snorting into his cupped left hand, with which he periodically covered his mouth. Another habit of his was to bite the inside of his thumb before replying. I noticed the skin there was red and raw.

"Right," he said, "you could put it that way. But personally I prefer thinking of it in ontological terms. The fact that my protagonist is a mouse then becomes the central issue, which is the all-important one of personal change, of breaking free from the stranglehold of habit. Without thinking why, we insist that the hero of a novel be more than some lowly rodent. What dull predictability! Well, I refuse to give in to it any longer. Why not call a spade a spade? In our lives dominated by fear and a paralyzing concern for security, how are we so very different from mice? I'm only being true to life!"

His eyebrows were dancing again.

"You're putting me on," I said.

"That's what *you* think," he replied contemptuously. "I wouldn't be so sure if I were you. Don't be so complacent, Sprout. You're only alive once. Why accept without question the guff everyone feeds you?"

We stared at each other.

"I'm at a great turning point in my life," he intoned, his eyes flashing. "I feel expansive and invulnerable all at once. I'm at the age when conventional wisdom dictates that I should be running out of gas and getting feeble. There's only one problem, though—I've never felt better!" He thrust out his chin pugnaciously, daring me to contradict him.

"I sense a limitless energy inside me," he said in a clear, exalted voice, "ready to spray out in every direction like a form of light. And guess what? For the first time in my life, with *A Time of Walls* selling so well, I'm free to do whatever I want. How utterly marvellous!"

Were the rumors true that I'd heard about Hartwell? He certainly looked strange, his face flushed as he leaned forward in his seat.

Now he was mimicking himself savagely.

" 'Yes, of course I'm working on a new novel.' " Quickly he added, "Are you joking? On the contrary, I'm finished writing, at least for now. Who knows, I may never type another word. It's high time I quit this game and did something real, before it's too late."

"I'm not sure I follow you," I said. "Do you mean you're going to put off work on your new book?"

"Obviously you don't follow me," he snapped, "so I'll spell it out for you. I no longer care about my career. I don't give a hoot in hell. I feel that, with the publication of this final volume of my exploration of upper-middle-class suffering, I've earned a lost weekend, as it were. After all, I've written eleven novels, for Pete's sake! Screenplays, collections of essays, even two books of poetry. What more do you want? . . . You know, the thought struck me recently that it's all become symbolic: 'So-and-so publishes new novel.' Big deal, my boy, except for the fact that, according to how it is received, the author moves up or down a notch in esteem. How many novels published five years ago can you remember? Simply the titles, that is, forget about whether they had any impact on your life. It's a charade! The movies, the plays, the media personalities, they flare up and then vanish. It's all an exercise in fashion. And I should sit here adding to the warts on my ass? My eyesight's starting to go bad on me, too, from pecking away at the machine. Maybe I've lost interest in writing fiction. *More life* is what I need today."

"God," I said, "it's so uncanny what you're telling me because recently I've been feeling—"

"I'm not interested in your feelings, fella, can't you tell?" he growled, his manner growing peevish. "I'm not thirty years old anymore, like you. I don't have the luxury of floundering around as you do. You've barely got the faintest idea what it's all about, anyway."

"Now wait a minute," I protested. "What gives you the right to say that to me? You don't even know me."

He became very agitated, gnawing at the inside of his left thumb.

"I'll tell you what gives me the right! My God, soon I'll be seventy years old! When I think of all the years I've spent maneuvering for the highest spot on the literary totem pole, I could burst. I see things in an entirely new light now. For example, not winning the Pulitzer. I was disappointed at the time, even furious. I admit it. But now I see that episode in my life as a blessing in disguise. If I'd won, with all the accompanying hoopla, it would be much more difficult for me to do what I have to do. So I'm grateful to those numbskulls for passing me up. Because, you see, I still have my books, I've written some very good ones, no one can take *A Time of Walls* away from me . . . You know, Nietzsche says somewhere that, alone among people, the artist—because of all the work he's produced—can feel an almost malicious joy when he sees his body and spirit destroyed by time. It's as if he were in a corner, watching a thief break into his safe, all the while knowing that it's empty, that all his treasures have been rescued. Now that's pretty good, but ultimately I'm afraid I don't have Nietzsche's faith in the endurance of culture . . . I've come to the end of all that . . . A sea change . . . I can no longer sit like a mollusk on the ocean floor, secreting page after page of faultless prose."

Hartwell turned away and faced the brilliant late morning sunlight pouring in through his picture window. I found myself staring at his hands, which looked hard and capable. He closed his eyes and breathed deeply, and when he began talking again his voice was calmer. He hardly seemed aware of my presence. He paid no attention as I changed cassettes in the machine sitting on the desk between us.

"The world's changed so drastically, that's the problem. Places I loved thirty, forty years ago have been transformed, they're as far away from me now as the moon. The worst thing is, you lose people with whom you can connect. Even the ones who do survive become caricatures of themselves. Eventually there's no one left, and that's when the problems start. Then you're simply floating . . ."

"But that's horrible," I said. "That can't be true at all. Otherwise, nothing would get handed down through the generations, there'd be no real interaction."

He sighed impatiently. "Listen, Sprout, you fail to understand. Ultimately it's a question of demographics, you see. Control the world population glut by getting rid of the elderly. Out of sight, out of mind . . . Programmed senescence . . . It's quite extraordinary the way one generation is programmed to supplant another."

"Programmed?" I echoed incredulously, but he didn't seem to hear me.

". . . A change of scenery, all of a sudden you're obsolete, what's happening no longer applies to you. It's time for you to move along, here's your hat and coat . . . Life simply is taken away from you; like a relay racer in a dream, the baton is lifted right out of your hands. The question is, though, programmed by what? By whom? After all, you can hardly blame the sprouts, now, can you, even if they do act with the blissfully ignorant arrogance of anyone who's got center stage. Are we talking about God, then? Give me a break! Or entropy, the second law of thermodynamics? But how typically faint-hearted, to lay the blame for our growing old on an abstraction. I'm afraid it just won't do. DNA and RNA and all the rest of it, the six-mile-long strands inside every cell nucleus gradually getting balled up, garbling their messages with increasing frequency as we grow older? Big deal! That sounds like a rationalization to me, it's begging the question, nothing more. The only reason we have strands of such infinitesimal magnitude inside us in the first place is because we've invented the hardware with which to look at them. After all, you'd better be made aware of *something* with an electron microscope, don't you think, otherwise why bother going to the great expense of constructing one? Anyone acquainted with quantum physics knows that all those particles are mental constructs anyway. No, the answer's somewhere else, under some godforsaken rock or other. And we'll find it, too, as long as we've got the time to look for it. That's the key—time . . . If there's a way to beat death, it must be on its own terms, it must be tied to breaking the habit. Because death *is* a habit, like cigarette smoking or alcohol, like life itself. A habit taking place on the cellular level, you might say, and therefore that much harder to break, but a habit nonetheless . . ."

He paused, suddenly becoming aware of me, looking at me with ill-concealed distaste.

"I'll be frank with you, Sprout," he said. "For most of my life old people—I mean the really old ones, the ones in the walkers, the doddering, drooling ones, the ones crippled by strokes—seemed grotesque to me. I avoided them. Their infirmities appalled me. And why? Because they were as good as pointing at me and saying, 'Take a good look, you pathetic boob, you're next!' But now that I've become one of them myself, I can't stand the shameless way we're all being brought to heel. Have you any idea what life in 1976 is like here in New York City for senior citizens, as we're called now? Thousands of the elderly are being abandoned. People who can't cope, the disabled and mentally ill. They're simply put out on the street. How do you like them apples?"

He was almost frantic now, twisting his hands together in his lap. He shook his head in dismay.

"So, as I said before, one must ask why. Why and by whom? Why are old people put in this position? Is it the result of conscious policy? . . . Lebensraum, indeed! . . . You don't think it's just possible, for example, that something like this Legionnaire's disease business that's been popping up isn't the result of gene splicing research gone awry— or worse? Are you trying to tell me new diseases simply appear out of nowhere?"

What was this crazy old guy telling me, anyway, that death's a trick? I was on the verge of making some wisecrack to dispel the tension when I saw he had more to say. Beads of sweat dripped down his face in spite of the air conditioning in his apartment.

"So much still remains to be discovered about all this. I want to see life from the underside up. This world's rotten, it's going down the drain," he said, and cackled. "Out on the streets, at least, I'll have the opportunity to make other contacts," he added cryptically, then paused. He looked down at the tape recorder as if noticing it for the first time.

I felt the color rise in my face. "But yesterday over the phone you told me you were leaving town. You said you were going away on vacation. What do you mean by *other contacts*? I'm afraid I don't quite—"

"I'm not leaving town, you idiot, I'm going to try something new," he exploded. "I'm not going to answer the phone or read the mail. I'll stop seeing my friends, there aren't many of them left anyway. I'll just fade out . . . Stop being Oliver Hartwell for a while. In fact, you're probably the last person who'll see me for quite a long time. But that doesn't mean I won't be here. You'll pass me on the street without knowing it's me . . . And Goddamn it to hell, I've already told you a lot more than I intended!"

He glared at me hatefully, but suddenly I didn't care about that. I had visions of a very valuable interview if he did, indeed, drop out of sight.

"Are you really going to disappear from view? Tell me your plans, please, Mr. Hartwell," I implored. I reached over and turned off the machine, lifting out the second cassette and pocketing it as nonchalantly as possible. "I promise I won't include this in the interview, if that's what you're worried about. It just sounds so amazing and I want—"

"Listen, you fucking Brussels sprout, I'm not interested in what you want. Not a word of this interview gets published—and I have the lawyers to make you sorry you'd ever try—unless you solemnly promise to forget what I just told you, understand? If you do, you're free to print the whole first part of it—you know, the gossip about Baldwin and Roth and Bellow, the poker games with James Jones, all of that . . . My writing habits, how many drafts I usually do, how long it took me to write *A Time of Walls*. It'll make a damn good interview and that's what you came for, isn't it?"

He stared out the window at the light coming in from Central Park. His apartment was on the tenth floor, and the trees below, dense and richly green, swirled in the summer haze. He tugged thoughtfully at the grey stubble on his chin, and bit the inside of his thumb again.

"If you do me that favor—if you oblige me by keeping perfectly quiet about this—I'll reward you someday. You have my promise you'll be the first person I contact when I reappear. It may be a month from now and it may be three years, but when I do, I'll grant you the exclusive interview of your life. On the other hand, if you try to publish everything prematurely, you'll never hear from me again. It would sound so vague you'd only be making a fool of yourself. The story would be seen as mere sensationalism and end up damaging your reputation, whatever *that's* worth. But just think of it!" he bellowed enthusiastically. "When I return from the dead the world will want to hear about it. Talk about a seller's market! No more of these half-assed downtown weeklies, you'll be able to dictate terms to any magazine in the country. All it takes from you now is some patience."

I had to respond. I knew he was perfectly capable of forcing me to hand over the two cassettes. At the same time, I regretted not having baited him more during our talk. The messianic fervor of his mission to aid the elderly, the sense he seemed to have of himself as being invulnerable to time, a sort of superman—what a laugh! But I knew he was right. I couldn't publish his boasts if he was gone. Nobody would believe me.

"OK," I said, "I'll do what you want. I promise."

I transcribed the tape exactly as he wished and Margo Kopperman was pleased with the results. She gave me three hundred dollars, twice what she usually paid for such pieces, and Dana and I went up to Cape Cod for ten days, staying in a little cabin by the sea.

Being isolated only made matters worse, however. We slept in the same bed without touching each other. In between bouts of arguing we stalked off in opposite directions and roamed the beaches for hours on end, until, on the last night of our stay, the situation erupted into a tearful reconciliation.

THREE

Four months later, in the middle of November, about two weeks after Jimmy Carter was elected President, I happened to be sitting at the window table in a little restaurant called Chiquita's on Christopher Street in the Village, brooding over my imminent break-up with Dana and ordering frog's legs Valenciana from a bald, muscular guy wearing a sleeveless T-shirt and a necklace of tiger's teeth separated by lumps of amber on a leather string. I noticed an old man loitering in front of the newsstand across the street.

As I sat under the Carmen Miranda posters and ate my solitary dinner I looked out on Christopher Street, watching people walk along through the evening. It was Sunday, and a stream of single young men with bold, searching eyes, wearing lumberjack shirts and skin-tight Levis, cruised the sidewalk. Meanwhile, the old man wandered from the newsstand to the corner and back, holding some sort of forked stick in his hands. It was only gradually and without thinking that I singled him out from the other pedestrians. Something made me pay attention, made me study closely that grizzled, unshaven face with the restless, wire-rimmed eyes under a soiled Yankee baseball cap. Then it hit me.

Like Halley's Comet, Oliver Hartwell had burst into my life again. I couldn't get over it. He was dressed as a derelict in an ancient, torn double-breasted suit coat and shapeless, stained grey pants, and kept weaving around the sidewalk like a drunk, now and then extending the stick toward the ground as if dowsing for water. But it was a cold, misty evening and few people scurrying past seemed to notice. Those who did paused momentarily and smiled, however, since when the stick dipped downward he did a little dance, hopping from one foot to the other. He confronted whoever stopped before him, mimicking their indulgent smiles and waving the stick up and down. Occasionally he held out his cap for spare change.

My table in Chiquita's gave me a clear view of this scene. After the initial shock of recognition I settled back in my chair to watch him. He wandered back and forth holding the dowsing rod before him. It never entered my mind he might walk away, and with a broad smile I sat there drinking glass after glass of Muscadet. What heaven, to be the only person in all of New York City who knew what had happened to him!

And then he was gone.

I jumped up, grabbed my coat, and ran out into the street. Hitting the wet, windy air made me realize how drunk I was, and arbitrarily I stumbled several blocks south, peering down darkening side streets.

Upset at losing him so quickly, I returned along Bleecker and was crossing the corner of Christopher Street again when, happening to look west, I spotted the back of a faded suit coat retreating down the opposite side of the street more than a block away. I ran past the gay bars on the south side of Christopher as fast as I could, trying to keep him in view. I was determined to find out if this really was Oliver Hartwell after all. He had abandoned his apartment in July and disappeared, just like he said he would. The police, his publishers, his ex-wife—nobody had a clue to his whereabouts.

When I had thought about him during the intervening months the interview would come back to me and I'd see his face again. He had seemed so sure of himself then, enthusiastic and full of plans. As time went by my initial impression of him changed. I no longer thought of him as a crazy old man. To the contrary, I saw that Hartwell had been sending me a message when we'd talked, a message I'd been too self-involved to hear: if you believed in yourself, if you staked your life on that belief, then anything was possible. When comparing myself to him I felt only half-alive. I was filled with questions I wanted to ask him.

I ran until I was ahead of the figure weaving along, then crossed the street near the corner of Hudson and watched him approach. For a drunk he seemed very aware of his surroundings. He noticed that I was staring at him, although he didn't appear to recognize me. Passing within ten feet of me, he eyed me with quick, searching darts from under the brim of his cap.

I stepped alongside and tapped him on the shoulder. He whirled around, his eyes growing large as he realized I was about to speak. His face was different than the one I remembered, thinner, more elongated, with narrow featureless eyebrows. Yet the glasses looked the same, he seemed to be about the same height.

"Mr. Hartwell? Is that you?"

He began growling.

"Mr. Hartwell?" I paid close attention to his eyebrows, waiting for them to move in the way I remembered, but they didn't. Were those his lips? His eyes? "It's me," I said excitedly, "the interviewer from *The New Jag* at your apartment last summer? I was eating dinner just now and saw you from the window. I had to make sure it was you."

"Mighty clouds of death," he hissed, rolling his eyes.

But I wouldn't be put off. "Please tell me what you're doing now. You look exactly like a derelict, it's a wonderful disguise! Are you really living incognito?"

"Get out of my life!" he wailed, and before I knew what was happening he had lunged at me, placing one foot behind me and stiff-arming me in the chest. I fell back over his leg onto the pavement. I had no chance to sidestep him; his strength and agility were astonishing. In a moment he was gone, sprinting around the corner.

Hartwell had knocked the breath out of me. I got up as quickly as I could, ran to the corner and continued running up Hudson Street until I spotted something on the sidewalk. Crumpled but unmistakable in the light from a streetlamp lay a navy blue Yankee cap. When I picked it up I felt the sweatband, still moist. More excited than ever, I put the hat in my coat pocket and started running again, looking up and down the side streets, but he was nowhere to be seen. Soaked and shivering from the light rain that was now falling, I squandered the last of the cash I had with me and took a taxi home.

Hartwell's disappearance in July had been in the news for quite a while. The daily papers ran front-page articles about it. FAMOUS NOV-ELIST VANISHES, the *Post* proclaimed. Speculation about his fate ran rampant. The police came to question me—luckily I had the presence of mind to claim I'd lost the tape from which the interview had been transcribed—and for a few weeks I was a sort of celebrity myself, since apparently I had been the last person to see him. Even his ex-wife called from Connecticut, demanding to know everything he'd told me. The issue of *The New Jag* containing our conversation sold out immediately. I guess I should have taken better advantage of the contacts I made at the time. As it was, I managed to set up an interview with Calvin Creesus, the easy-listening pop star, which appeared in *Rolling Stone*. But then I discovered, quite by accident, that Dana was sleeping with Richard Pinkus, and this distracted me to the point where I no longer cared about interviewing Mr. So-and-So or Ms. Whatsis.

Now that Hartwell had resurfaced in my life, however, I was determined to find him. By the time the taxi pulled up in front of my building on St. Mark's Place I decided to return to the area where I'd lost him, but realizing I had no money left I climbed the stairs to the apartment, hoping Dana would be home.

Dana's involvement with Richard Pinkus, a bartender and sometime performance artist, hurt precisely because she hadn't told me about it. The fact that Pinkus was a grinning twit, as far as I was concerned, did nothing to lessen the pain. Previously we had shared details of our occasional affairs, thereby neutralizing their effect and even bringing us closer together. But this time she denied, with a variety of maddeningly ambiguous responses, that anything was taking place. She accused me of being paranoid, of trying to shift the blame for our deteriorating relationship onto some fantasy.

But I knew for a fact she was seeing Pinkus, and I couldn't understand why she would lie. Or rather, why she pretended to lie, why she was play-acting. Dana had never been devious before—hot-headed and stubborn, yes, but not devious—and the fact that she refused to level with me now seemed perverse. I didn't know how to react. Confronting her with what I knew would be as good as admitting we were through, because it would demonstrate there was no trust left. I was in the middle of a no-win situation. It had gotten so I avoided going home unless I knew she wouldn't be there, even though I wanted more than ever to be with her.

Meanwhile, Dana had her own problems. At twenty-eight, she was still going to art school, for one thing. In 1970 she had dropped out of Barnard and, after several jobs as waitress and proofreader, she started attending the School of Visual Arts. Her parents gave her an allowance which paid for tuition and art supplies, but nothing else. She even had her own one-person show at a small SoHo gallery. Although nothing sold, I had been very proud of her. But as far as I was concerned, the show's effect had been vitiated by the contrast between the strength of her earlier paintings and her later constructions, which were composed of words, images, and objects fixed directly to the walls of the gallery, and which I found forced and self-consciously clever. That show had taken place a year before and now she was back at Visual Arts again, enrolling, for the third time, in a course with the same successful older artist who had originally encouraged her to "open up" and change her style.

Lately, I think, she'd also been feeling guilty about taking money from her parents, even though going back to waitressing was out of the question. This dilemma had resulted in her sudden pronouncement, one day last summer, that *I* wasn't being realistic about life. The Sixties were over, in case I hadn't noticed, she said. If journalism couldn't support me, I should show my commitment to her by finding some kind of work which would. With the sort of art she was making now, the apartment had become too small—and even in 1976, loft space didn't come cheap. Either we should get serious about each other, or we should break up. The brittle, humorless tone with which she delivered this ultimatum would have been impossible six months before. Since my own sources of income were so undependable, we had always been chronically short of money. As a result, we'd lived on St. Mark's Place in grittily authentic fashion, especially during the winter of '73–'74, when the landlord had refused to fix the boiler and we had no heat for two months. One week it got so cold the water froze in the toilet bowl, yet we had laughed it off and had retaliated by not paying the rent until that June. We had always lived lightly and in the moment, improvising the game of survival so as to have the freedom to do what we wanted. Now everything had changed. The wavelength we'd shared was gone. I felt a suffocating weight on my chest whenever I saw her, my heart heavy with all the things I couldn't say.

I opened the door and there she sat at the kitchen table, wrapped in a large red Turkish towel. She was drying her hair with a smaller towel. The *Post* lay open before her.

"Hi, baby," she said pleasantly.

"Hi."

She resumed turning the pages of the *Post*.

"Listen, Dana, have you got any cash on you? You won't believe this, but I was in the Village just now and saw Oliver Hartwell on the street. He appeared out of nowhere, dressed like a wino. It was amazing! He gave me the slip, but I just have to go back and look for him."

She glanced up from the paper and smiled indulgently.

"Oh, come on, Roy, you're seeing things. It's dark out already, how can you be sure it was him? He's probably in the Bahamas or someplace like that, lying on a beach in the sun. It's so ridiculous."

Dana was the only person I'd told about Hartwell's request, but from the first she had belittled it. I'm sure if the interview had occurred the year before, she would have loved the idea of his wandering the streets in disguise. We would have gotten stoned and played the tape over and over, laughing like crazy. But in July, when he disappeared, she merely declared that either he'd been mugged and killed, or he had played his little joke on the media and gone off for an extended vacation. In any case, my willingness to believe he was on some secret mission, living a life of voluntary indigence, she viewed as the most gullible sort of romanticism.

"Look," I said, my voice rising, "I'm just asking you for ten dollars 'til tomorrow. I'm not interested in your analysis of the situation."

"But I thought we were going dancing tonight! I came home early and washed my hair. I could've stayed out, you know."

This insinuation exasperated me, especially since we had made no such plans. We'd hardly spoken to each other in the past week.

"What do I care?" I said. "Stay out all night if you want. You've been doing enough of that lately, anyway."

By now I was glaring at her.

She stood up slowly, letting the towel unwind from her body and slip to the floor. Her large, dark nipples were erect, the flesh around them prickled with goosebumps. Her long jet black hair, still wet, glistened in the light from the lamp on the kitchen table. I'd always loved the contrast between her pale skin and that long, full head of glossy black hair, black as tar.

"What's the matter, honey, don't you like me?" she asked in a sarcastic vaudevillian imitation of a teasing femme fatale. Her tongue flicked out from between her teeth as she advanced toward me, laughing. "Don't you think I'm sexy? Can't you see the animal in me, Roy, can't you live in the moment?"

"For Christ's sake, Dana, this isn't a time for games. Hartwell told me he was going incognito, he as much as spelled out for me how he was going to change his life. God knows what he's really up to. Thousands of people would love to know. Everybody thinks he's dead. Don't you understand? I have to find him."

She took another couple of steps toward me and stopped in the middle of the floor, her smile replaced by a frown.

"No, I don't understand."

"Look," I practically shouted, pulling the soiled baseball cap out of my coat pocket. "This belongs to Hartwell, I swear to God. I found it on the sidewalk when I was chasing him. The sweatband's still wet! What do you think of that!"

Her green eyes widened. "You're really serious, aren't you? . . . Oh listen, man, I've had enough of this. I'm going dancing tonight, I don't care what you do."

She started to turn away and then added, "And I don't have any money. None to spare, that is. If I'm going to Spiro's I'll need at least fifteen bucks, unless you want some guy to pick up my tab."

"Spiro's—that rathole?" We both knew that Richard Pinkus was a bartender at Spiro's part of the week and usually could be found there in attendance on other nights. It was her way of telling me she was going with Richard tonight.

"Listen to me, Dana, I'll be back in an hour or two, we can go dancing then. I just have to satisfy my curiosity. I'll be back by eleven at the latest. I promise. Please wait."

She looked at me without speaking.

"I'm asking you to say home tonight, Dana. Please . . ."

She stooped to the floor, retrieving the towel and winding it around her again. At first she didn't answer, then she said softly, "Maybe I'll see you tomorrow." She paused. "All right?"

To my horror, I found myself crying. I rushed into the bedroom and went through my desk until I found a few dollars.

"To hell with this, who needs it?" I said, my voice breaking, as I pushed past her and opened the door to the hall. "I hope you dislocate your frame," I gasped, and ran down the stairs into the street.

The weather had changed for the worse while I'd been upstairs. A cold steady rain slanted through the headlights of the taxi taking me across town. The Sunday night sidewalks quickly became deserted and I had to laugh out loud at my predicament. The driver—a worried-looking Greek with three days' growth, his ashtray overflowing with dead butts—eyed me uncertainly in his mirror. I had been so distracted by Dana I forgot to take an umbrella or raincoat, and I visualized the shape my dyed fur car coat would be in after tramping around in the rain looking for somebody who possibly was no longer alive and wouldn't want to see me if he were. As the Greek and I rode through the rain I remembered the *Rolling Stone* interview with Calvin Creesus I had conducted in his suite at the Hotel Pierre right after Dana and I returned from Cape Cod in September.

Creesus, an unctuous, gangling man in his later thirties, with fault-lessly coiffed shoulder-length blond hair and a swashbuckler's mous-tache, was a star of the first magnitude in that gray area between rock and roll and kitsch which seemed to be expanding every day. He crooned slickly sentimental ballads backed by syrupy horn charts, and his audiences, comprised for the most part of ex-bobby-soxer house-wives, ate him up. But the fascinating thing about Creesus was that before launching his new career as a singer, he had been one of Madison Avenue's most successful ad writers. Since I hated his music I decided on a confrontational strategy for the interview. I wanted to focus on his motives for getting into the entertainment business. Otherwise I knew he'd simply deliver a smokescreen of self-promotion.

No matter what I asked him, though, Creesus responded by restricting himself to amiable p.r. copy. He'd always loved to sing, he said. His songs fulfilled a need for authenticity of feeling which he found sadly lacking not only in the advertising business but in most pop music as well. He felt humbled by the response his music had received and he only hoped he could live up to the expectations of his fans.

"Roy, I've learned that if you want something badly enough it'll be yours. But you have to really want it, you have to keep working at it, not give up, and have faith in yourself. I know it's not fashionable to say this in the pages of *Rolling Stone* these days, but I'm grateful for the virtually unlimited opportunities to be a success in this country. I'm proud to be an American. If you really want to make it you can. All it takes is work, work, work . . ."

And then he winked at me, signalling that he and I were sharing this little joke to the exclusion of the tape recorder and the poor, gullible public. For him, the interview was nothing more than propaganda.

"That's all well and good," I replied pointedly, and he looked at me, his pale blue eyes blinking, "but still it leaves me wondering. After all, you went about developing your career in such a big way. It's no secret that your promotional budget, from the very first song you released, was unprecedented. You inundated the media with your name and face. And you never let up, you never stopped priming that image for one minute. That took a lot of cash, and not only yours—you had investors. I suppose you just didn't want to leave anything to chance, right?"

He was staring at me now. His moist smile was gone. At least I'd captured his attention.

"And the songs you released were saccharine—empty calories, hot air. But each one sold more than the last and you kept pouring in the cash. And then finally your fourth album was a hit, and that impressed people. It impressed people in the industry, important record people who until then hadn't been impressed by you; they'd been embarrassed. But you were tough, you hung in. And when *Cherry Pits* finally exploded on the charts you were on your way, the weight was off your shoulders . . ."

Creesus sat on a sky-blue satin couch edged in gold trim in the elegant sitting room of his suite at the Pierre. He wore a deep burgundy suede smoking jacket over tight white leather pants, and he looked irritated. He was holding his jaw in his hands and scowling, bent over like an old man in the soft light coming through the windows from Fifth Avenue.

"So you simply continue grinding it out. Now you're going to star in a movie opposite Samandra Johns about nineteenth-century Kenya. Love and death on a coffee plantation. You've just completed a string of concerts, sellout successes coast to coast. Your next LP is gold even before you press it. You keep a finger in TV, too. In fact, you're working on a pilot for a series of Calvin Creesus specials next year. You're burning it up at a tremendous rate but it's just you, you, nothing but you . . ."

My head was reeling, I'd never talked to anybody like this before and I couldn't stop.

"It's unlimited ego and not even interesting, there's no integrity in your life . . . Surely you've got enough money already. And your recent concerts have betrayed the fact that you're bored with what you're doing, you're going through the motions. What's the point of it all?"

He sat there quivering, his face a mask of barely suppressed rage. Nobody talked to him this way. Obviously *Rolling Stone* had made a mistake, they'd sent the wrong guy. But instead of blowing up, he did something I'll never forget. Slowly a wide, false smile completely obscured the eyes on his lean, suntanned face and he drawled in a fake Wild West accent, "Ah lahk it, cowboy, ah lahk it just fine . . . She's nice an' salty . . . You print 'er up the way she is, you heah?"

And, still smiling, he took me by the elbow and guided me swiftly to the door. The next thing I knew I was standing in the hallway outside his suite.

I couldn't believe he would allow *Rolling Stone* to print the interview, but he did, and the editors there loved it. It seemed to make no difference what I said to him, everything could be used to his advantage. The fact that he'd rigged his career didn't matter, as long as people bought his records. The only thing which did matter was what he thought of himself, and obviously there were no problems in that regard.

By the time we arrived in the Village I owed the driver three dollars and I couldn't give him a tip. I figured I'd be going into places to keep dry and I needed what little cash I had left. He cursed me sourly in Athenian and drove off.

The rain was coming down steadily now. I walked around for a while but my quest suddenly seemed futile. Probably Oliver Hartwell had a cozy little hideaway somewhere in the city. In fact, since July several things had come to light which he'd neglected to mention during our talk. For one, his agent already had sold, for an undisclosed six-figure sum, the paperback rights and movie option for *A Time of Walls*. For another, before disappearing he had withdrawn most of his money from the bank, although when the police searched his Central Park West apartment they found nothing missing. It was foolish for me to continue looking for him in this neighborhood simply because I'd seen him here earlier.

I walked home through the rain. When I finally got upstairs the phone was ringing but I didn't answer it. Dana was gone. I downed a Valium with a shot glass of vodka and filled the bathtub with hot water. After my bath I sat down on the bed, smoked some grass and turned out the lights. From down on St. Mark's, a distraught voice in the night cried out, "Nina gone to Florida? Nina gone to stay?"

I woke up early Monday morning with a splitting headache. As I made coffee I decided I had to forget about Oliver Hartwell for a while. I wanted to see Dana. She'd certainly be home by nightfall and I had plenty of work to do. Book reviews were piling up, Margo Kopperman phoned every other day asking if they were in the mail, and if I wanted to interview Lynn Redgrave I had to call her agent right away to set up an appointment.

It was a clear day, crisp and bright, the sun pouring onto the living room floor. I walked into the light and lay down on the sofa. The light hurt my eyes, however. The ancient, stained sofa sagged under the weight of my body, protruding springs and lumps sabotaging my every turn. Sometimes Dana and I couldn't figure out why we didn't throw it out on the street where we'd found it years before. I got up and walked back through the bedroom of our long and narrow railroad apartment into the kitchen, poured a shot glass of vodka and sipped it. Soon, in spite of my intentions, I was sitting at the kitchen table slowly downing one shot after another, because I knew that Dana wasn't coming home today either. I could sense it.

I switched off the overhead light and closed the door leading to the front of the apartment. The single window behind me, which looked down into a little courtyard, was covered by a heavy velvet curtain tacked to the frame. It was so dark in the kitchen now I had to feel my way back to the table. From behind the door the phone rang in the living room but I made no move to answer it. A change of plans. I watched two slits of light at right angles to each other on the floor, one coming from under the door leading to the bedroom, the other to my left seeping in from the hall outside. Dana was with Richard Pinkus now. And when she finally returned, then what? Something was signalling to me, my life was changing, maybe I'd be alone now.

I'm not going to answer the phone or read the mail, Hartwell had said.

I turned on the light, made a pot of espresso, and got dressed. To hell with Lynn Redgrave anyway. I knew that outside it was a bright, sunny fall day and I felt like going uptown and walking around in it, dissolving into the midtown crowd of faces. At the last moment I thought of Hartwell and filled my knapsack with a camera and tape recorder, just in case I ran across him with dowsing rod in hand somewhere in the haystack of New York City.

Then I walked to Broadway and withdrew twenty dollars from the bank. I asked the teller to check the balance. A total of fifteen dollars and sixteen cents remained in our account . . . $15.16 . . . How was that possible? I'd gotten a thousand dollars from *Rolling Stone* for the

Creesus interview in September and I knew we hadn't spent it all. Hadn't there been several hundred bucks the last time I'd checked? I couldn't remember, really. Dana was the one who kept track of money, I'd never been able to deal with it. Had she withdrawn something recently without mentioning it to me? Was this her way of telling me to shape up and get a regular job? But the bank had no record of recent large withdrawals. Had she been taking out twenty or thirty bucks at a time? Or had we simply been living off what was there, as usual, paying no attention to the situation until things got tight?

I took the Broadway local uptown. Struggling to keep a straight face in the impromptu psychiatrist's waiting room of the subway car, I studied the ads, the walls covered with graffiti, and finally the fat, pimply schoolgirl carrying her battered black clarinet case, who sat across from me. She must have been about twelve years old. Her facial expression shuttled from lassitude to fear and back again. I tried to imagine what she was thinking, but nothing came through. Maybe she wasn't thinking, in the strict sense of the word, but simply reacting to her surroundings, to the implied threat of anybody who approached her, to her glandular and digestive processes. She looked unhappy, but then most people riding the subway looked emotionally distraught, as if something about being underground made them unable to suppress entirely what was going on inside them. It came surging up to their faces and out of their eyes, unless they chose, like initiates in a protective ritual, to bury their noses in newspapers or books. I kept staring at her until, with an involuntary jerk of her chin in my direction, she became aware of me. Her eyes widened and when I smiled she began perspiring, wringing her hands and squirming in her seat. Then I looked away.

I emerged into the sunlight on 57th Street and walked north to the park, then along Central Park South to Fifth Avenue. Sitting down on the stone steps of the fountain in front of the Plaza Hotel, I smoked a cigarette and watched people hurry by. Mounting the curb, stepping into the sun, their shadows weaved and joined behind them, their faces and gestures making them as distinct and variegated—as isolated from one another—as separate species. Their faces were evocative, yet detached and momentary, swept away by the current seconds after they appeared.

Soon my attention was drawn to a heavy black woman of indeterminate age, dressed like a gypsy in a long red velvet gown. Unlike everybody around her, she moved at a slow and stately pace, self-possessed and serene. Her gown was torn and patched with bits of rag, trinkets, and tiny ornamental mirrors. Dozens of cheap rings covered the fingers on both her hands. She wore a baggy old gray crewneck sweater over the red gown, and two or three scarves around her neck. She pulled a wire laundry cart, inside of which were shopping bags stuffed with an assortment of soiled clothes, old shoes, and other detritus including a broken umbrella and what appeared to be an empty gallon mayonnaise jar. She hummed and talked to herself as she proceeded up the sidewalk. When she shuffled past me, moving slowly in spite of the cold, I heard several phrases in a Caribbean accent, each phrase preceded by what sounded like "oily tambarina."

"Oily tambarina go solid blue mighty, yes, and file down baseball guns. Baseball guns gone run backyard soon, cold old amaretta . . ."

"Oily tambarina, solid mighty, headlines Jew black coffee table . . . Coffee table chew black stew . . ." She chuckled and began humming again.

"Jew black coffee table, lunch too . . ."

Approaching a trash basket she bent over to examine its contents. The sleeves of her sweater rose to her elbows and I saw several wristwatches, one after the other like bracelets, on her left arm. She reached into the bottom of the basket and extracted a book and a length of red string, which she buried in one of the shopping bags in her cart. Then she moved on, crossing the street slowly, looking out for speeding cars.

After a while my ass began to ache from the cold steps and I got up, walking north across 59th Street about a block behind the tambarina lady. The crowd of shoppers thinned out here alongside the park and I could see her clearly, the mirrors and trinkets on her gown glittering in the sun as she moved from one trash basket to the next. Working girls in short fur jackets and troops of children leaving the zoo swept past. Nobody paid any attention to her.

At the corner of 63rd Street, a boy of about ten on a heavy, old-fashioned bike came hurtling west across Fifth Avenue against the light and smacked into the black woman and her cart, knocking her off her feet. The bike flipped over and the boy hit the pavement, his head striking the curb. He began wailing, holding the side of his face. Several people including me rushed to the corner. The tambarina lady was bleeding on the arm and neck. She shivered as I helped her to her feet, her eyes glazed and frightened. She smelled wonderful—like a musty old shed in a summer garden.

The others helped the boy to his feet, and then they all looked at the tambarina lady, seeing her for the first time. Her cart was intact but its contents lay strewn across the sidewalk, and as she clutched my arm and moaned, everybody else took a collective step backward. The boy was whimpering and wiping at his eyes with the sleeve of his torn blazer. The side of his face was bleeding and the knuckles of one hand had been badly scraped. Somebody offered him a handkerchief.

Then the black lady let go of me, began humming to herself, and released a wide, dazzling smile. But as she moved off the curb, the boy backed away. With severely cut hair and pale skin, he wore private school colors, a blue blazer and grey wool pants. Staring wide-eyed at her, he dropped the handkerchief and ran to his bike, jumping on it and riding down the lane into Central Park as quickly as he could, without looking back.

The other people beside me also moved away. One woman, after walking half a block, glanced back over her shoulder and laughed. The tambarina lady bent down to her shopping bags, slowly filling them with kerchiefs, flattened aluminum cans, bundles of newspapers, jackets and sweaters. I stood beside her, uncertain whether to lend a hand.

"Are you OK?" I asked. "You got quite a bump on your arm."

She stood up. "Just fine, thank you," she said, and did a little curtsy, bending at her knees and lifting the folds of her voluminous, ratty gown.

"Much obliged to you, kind sir, then I say just fine, thanks."

She bent down again and wedged another bag into her cart.

"Yessirree, gingerfolks broken tooth today . . . It hurt too . . . Ha ha . . . No sir, it don't hurt, thanks . . . Ginger broke slowpokes . . ."

Suddenly I felt cold. We stood in the shade, now, although the Hotel Pierre across the avenue, where I'd interviewed Calvin Creesus months before, still sparkled in the sunlight. In front of the hotel a man in a business suit stood at the curb watching us, his arms stiffly at his sides. The wind picked up. It was only November but winter already was in the air. I realized the tambarina lady lived her life utterly alone, in spite of her disposition, and this made me feel nervous and empty.

I left her and walked further up Fifth Avenue. The striped awnings of apartment houses across the avenue caught the wind, rippling slightly. Except for two limousines double-parked with chauffeurs asleep at the wheel, no sign of life came from the homes of the rich. The traffic thickened along the avenue. It must have been three-thirty or so.

I thought about Oliver Hartwell. I knew I'd seen him in the Village. Sooner or later I'd run across him again if I had any luck. The key to publishing his story was documentary evidence. If I had a few clear photos of him I could write something, even if he refused to talk. One thing was certain, though. If I found him again I was going to write that story, I was going to tell all. I needed the money.

I felt uneasy as I walked along. I took a Valium—then two—out of my pocket and swallowed them dry, while I was walking. Inside my knapsack I found Hartwell's old Yankee cap and put it on my head.

FOUR

The city, my real wilderness, virgin forest full of unknown beings . . .
Sometimes, as I sat looking out of one of the front windows of the
apartment, I remembered this line from a poem I'd written years before. One flight up from sidewalks and street, these windows gave me
an unparalleled view of the streams of people going by in both directions. I would sit there at any hour of the day or night, stoned or
straight, looking out onto St. Mark's Place between Second and Third
Avenues, completely absorbed by the ceaseless procession below.

Not more than twenty feet from the pedestrians passing along the
sidewalk in front of my window, I was close enough to see the expressions on their faces, their heads and shoulders in view for a few seconds
only. Soon after Dana and I rented the apartment in 1971 I got over my
embarrassment when somebody happened to look up and noticed me
sitting there. It also stopped bothering me that the place was so noisy,
or that fumes from the crosstown buses and the big trucks cutting over
to Second Avenue drifted into the living room. And if some smart
aleck noticed me and was in the mood to make something of it—if he
stopped and stared or pointed up at me—I glared back at him, matching his stare with mine, refusing to acknowledge his sarcasm or gestic-
ulations, until my dimly lit face behind the grimy window grew too
eerie for him and he wandered away spooked. I loved that moment
when his attempt to make fun of me gave way to discomfort. I loved
seeing uncertainty appear in his eyes.

The angle at which people came and went along the sidewalk on my
side of the street allowed me to see eight or ten faces and torsos at any
one time. But if I looked up at the line of stores across the street—from

the plumber's office and ancient kosher butcher shop with Hebrew-lettered window next to Gem's Spa on my left, past the seedy all-night fried chicken take-out place and the East Side Bookstore with a poster of Jimi Hendrix in the window, then along the stoops of the two brownstones on my right, and finally the entranceways of two newer apartment buildings with their storefronts selling saris and sheep-skins—then an unending panorama revealed itself to me.

On that far sidewalk I watched an inexhaustible flow of people as they came into view and disappeared: winos wandering on swollen feet; hippie survivors in bellbottoms and decal T-shirts (*Grand Funk Railroad Forever!*) and long billowing hair; pot-bellied and swaggering Hell's Angels; hard black men down from Harlem no longer wearing the dashikis of the Black Power era but dressed now in quilted over-coats and tight skullcaps; disco habitués straggling home at all hours; exuberantly happy gay couples wrapped in each other's arms; nervous single women at night walking doberman pinschers and great danes which strained at the leash, barely under control.

And always the solitary psychos picking their way along, running their fingers along walls or tree trunks . . .

There's the pale thin woman with stringy white hair who writes madly in the air with her stiffly extended forefinger, tracing word after word as quickly as possible. Her other arm is thrust deep inside her dress. As she writes, her face runs through a series of expressions: interruption, uncertainty, sorrow, irritation. By turns she looks vi-cious, withdrawn, supercilious.

And the man with long blond hair and wounded blue eyes, he can't be older than twenty-five. Dressed in a pair of filthy pants with the legs torn off at the knees and covered with bruises and scabs. Looking rigidly up into the sky, repeating to himself as he passes below my window, "A break to the left, a light to the left."

And the woman in her thirties wearing a knit cap who rummages in trash cans. Her misshapen mouth, her mad eyes looking for trouble as she walks her pack of six or eight dogs on leashes like a deranged Artemis, ancient huntress lost among the traffic lights.

And Walt Whitman, his beautiful glowing dome surrounded by

wisps of pale hair and a flowing, dirty white beard which reaches down to his heart. Delicate and unobtrusive, he drifts along the sidewalk, a blanket filled with his possessions slung over one arm.

And the Chinese man wearing a latex bathing cap with the cerebral cortex painted on it, and pulling, right up the middle of the street, oblivious to the traffic, a wire laundry cart containing two black metal boxes . . .

But even in the borderline slum which the so-called East Village was back then—a semi-abandoned neighborhood with the Fillmore East closed and the Five Spot gone, with few restaurants or stores—some of the people passing by were respectable citizens, modular-looking young whites in suits with briefcases in hand. Often these law-abiding, responsible ones were more mysterious than the misfits and crazies among whom they made their way, because they alone seemed unaware of their strangeness.

Sooner or later the endlessness outside my window unnerved me, undercutting my desire to remain there forever, waiting for the next face to appear. So I'd pull back from what I was seeing. I'd close the curtains and walk away, only to find myself a day or two later sitting again on a folding chair a few feet from the window sill, lights off in the living room behind me, my eyes glued to the parade outside of my urban day lilies, my primroses, my thistles, my columbines. Life stories gone in an instant, fugitive and insubstantial, already like memories. I longed to cling to them, merge with them. I loved running my eyes over people's features, their noses and cheeks, their bodies, the expressions on their faces.

And now I'm looking at a tall, gangling white guy in his twenties, stubbly beard and tattered sneakers, loping quickly along shouting at the top of his lungs, "Manson case! Manson case!" People stare at the pavement, embarrassed, and as he walks he's glancing back over his shoulder out of lonely eyes, loony and hopeless, to see if anybody's listening, if anybody dares make eye contact after he's exposed himself by shouting in a voice so loud it leaves a wake of momentary silence up and down the block. "Manson case! Manson case!" That painful, challenging glance back over his shoulder and he's gone, but in spite of myself a chill sails along my spine and I'm bent over staring at the living room floor hoping he hasn't noticed me, ashamed of my failure of nerve, while at the same time I'm seized by a paroxysm of coughing, marijuana smoke scalding my throat and stinging my eyes, the vanishing roach burning my fingertips. After I stub it out on the floor I bring my hand up to my nose to smell the weed stained into the skin, the smell making me salivate, causing my stomach to rumble, and then, stoned out of my gourd once again, I'm staring at a long, frisky cockroach which has come to a halt beside my feet, and from between whose wavering antennae rises the petulant, antagonistic voice I hear, loud and clear, saying "Whaddya think I am, asshole, your little errand boy?"

I lift my head just in time to see two teenagers arguing with each other, shoving back and forth without breaking stride as they hurry along toward Third Avenue. It's four-thirty or so in the afternoon, the grainy November light already starting to fade, and I realize with a start that I've been sitting here at the window since early in the morning and haven't eaten a thing all day. Dizzy, disoriented, I close the curtain and rush out of the apartment for a bowl of soup at the B & H, where the aging Jewish countermen, veterans from the heyday of Second Avenue's Yiddish theaters, aim splenetic barbs between the eyes of the customers.

"He's a self-starter, all right," one says sarcastically to the other, jabbing a finger in my direction and repeating in an exaggeratedly solicitous voice, as if to an idiot, what I hadn't heard the first time: "Cabbage or split pea, boychick, what'll it be? Or should I just call for the men in the white coats to come and pick you up?"

And once I start laughing it's as if I'm never going to stop.

I bought a copy of Friday's *Post* at Gem's Spa and glanced at the headlines as I returned to the apartment, gingerly stepping over the shuddering steel plates laid down across the corner of Second Avenue and St. Mark's . . . DATA MISSING IN DAY CARE PROBE . . . MOONIES HEAVILY INTO TUNA FISHING.

Sitting down at the kitchen table I cleaned more grass, and while espresso coffee gurgled on the stove I smoked another number and

turned the pages of the paper . . . SEEK TO TIE SHOOTING TO RUB-
OUT . . . TRY TO FIT PIECES IN KILLING . . . JETS OBJECT TO "LOS-
ERS" LABEL, REPORTER ATTACKED IN LOCKER ROOM.

Then I read FREED YOUTH HELD IN ARSON:

> A 17-year-old Queens youth, freed after allegedly robbing and as-
> saulting an 80-year-old woman in her Flushing home, was
> charged today with returning to the house and setting it on fire.
> The new allegations, part of a growing pattern of younger crimi-
> nals victimizing elderly persons, came as police continued their
> hunt for Edwin Russell, 20, the Bronx suspect who was released in
> the robbery-beating of an 82-year-old woman.
>
> Russell, whose juvenile record included the murder of a 92-year-
> old man in 1971, disappeared after failing to appear for a court
> hearing last week. The case has triggered widespread calls for re-
> peal of laws that keep juvenile records out of the hands of criminal
> court judges.

I finished the joint and took my cup of coffee into the living room,
wondering what it would be like to give in to an emotion like that, to
set fire to somebody's house. Or kill a defenseless person. Would I
automatically be insane to consider something like that, much less to
carry it out?

As the failing light drained away the features of the people parading
along the far sidewalk, I fell into a reverie by the window, smoking pot
and sipping slowly at my coffee—and waiting, as I had for days, to see
Dana's face appear among the others, even though I knew it wouldn't;
even though I knew that evening would turn into night and I'd close
the curtains and watch TV, go to bed and wake up the next morning
without her.

The cold weather of a few days before had given way to an unsea-
sonably warm, overcast, muggy atmosphere with temperatures in the
sixties, and all afternoon some people had been walking around with as
little on as possible, pretending it was summer again, while others
refused to acknowledge the change, remaining wrapped in overcoats
and sweaters. Now, as I looked down at the near sidewalk under my
window, a young guy strolled by, shorts cut so high they showed his

bare cheeks. He wore big rubber galoshes and clumped along awkwardly. Somebody approaching from the opposite direction pointed at him and shrieked, "Ooh, Manny, I can see your balls!"

Behind Manny came a Hindu woman and her teenage daughter, the woman in sari and overcoat, the girl in jeans and spiked heels. There was tension in the air because the day had been so muggy. I kept noticing the stinging smoke from lit cigarettes in drawn, contorted faces. The unnerving paleness of predominantly white skin, all of these white faces, had just begun to irritate me when suddenly my attention was captured by the appearance of a gorgeous, statuesque black girl of eighteen or so who stopped on the sidewalk and was looking into the window of the dress shop directly below the apartment next to mine. At least five-nine and as powerfully imposing as a figure in a Renaissance fresco, with her copper-colored skin glowing almost red in the harsh light from the shop, she looked so tough and unapproachably beautiful that I gasped. She had a blunted pug nose set in a large, strong, clear face and wore a fancy brown leather jacket, quilted at the top and covered with pins and buttons. The silver scarf around her neck, the red patent leather boots, the arrogant pose she struck as she stood there without moving . . . Oh baby, I whispered.

I opened my belt and unzipped my pants, and while she stood there pouting, staring fixedly into the shop as if it contained the key to her future rather than simply another sweater or scarf, I began to masturbate in the darkness of the living room, slowly and luxuriantly, taking my time, certain that I'd connected with her in some subliminal way so that she wouldn't walk away. We continued like that for several minutes, this black girl and I, the slight breeze from the open window ruffling the curtains beside me, until finally I came, barely able to keep myself from moaning aloud, from kicking over the chair in my ecstasy—even, I thought, from crashing headlong through the window and falling into her arms. Finally she snapped out of her trance, and with an angry smile she turned away from the storefront. Her eyes caught mine momentarily. Majestically she walked off toward Third Avenue, tall and svelte, somebody used to living well—a model, perhaps, or the girlfriend of a rock star—her pug nose and strong cheekbones in profile as she passed making me sigh. I fell to the floor and lay there, curled up in the dark, the contents of the overturned espresso cup soaking into my shirt and leaving the most wonderful smell—musty and acrid, more like mud or earth than coffee. Eventually I stumbled back through the apartment and took a long bath, my mind a blank. I felt relaxed for the first time in weeks.

Half an hour later, though, sitting in the living room watching "Candid Camera" on TV with the sound turned down, I got the jitters. I pulled a record at random from the long, disordered stacks of them on the floor and played a cut—"Sunshine of Your Love" by Cream—but it sounded pointless, dragging around the ghost of Chicago blues it didn't know what to do with, and after vengefully jacking up the volume to earsplitting level until the room shook with sound, I turned it off.

In the suddenly intense silence I thought I heard Dana's step in the hall outside the apartment. She'd been gone for a week now. I had stopped shaving and didn't answer the phone. I went outside only to get something to eat and spent the rest of the time laying in bed or looking out the window, smoking grass. Luckily, I had bought an ounce the previous week, so there was plenty to smoke, and I rationed the remaining Valiums in the house, allowing myself no more than one each night before bed.

"Suck my pussy!" a drunken male voice outside proclaimed, followed by raucous laughter.

It was nearly eight o'clock. They were probably going out to dinner at this very moment. I became furious thinking about what Dana was putting me through. Was I supposed to wait like a puppy in a corner until she ran out of clean clothes and decided to show up?

I looked around the living room walls. They were monopolized by her latest art works—collections of everyday objects sunk into sheets of resin, like lumpy shards of peanut brittle, and accompanied by arch, ironic little printed texts from driver instruction manuals and foreign language lessons, with the sense coyly altered. Many of the nouns had been replaced by her name. ("Dana's judgment of speed and distances is distorted. She has difficulty judging her vehicle's true speed and how close it is to other vehicles and objects.") I much preferred her earlier paintings, some of which still hung in the bedroom, but according to her they were naive and one-dimensional.

The phone was ringing now, vibrating in my hands, but I didn't answer it. Instead I placed it carefully under the sofa. "Stay there and be quiet, like a good doggy," I said. I walked into the kitchen, sat down at the table and methodically cleaned more grass. The pile of stems and seeds in the ashtray grew until it overflowed onto the floor, and soon I had finished my task: a row of thirteen joints sat before me on the table. Before I knew it I was arranging them into the letters of her name, and they fit exactly.

"How fucked," I said aloud and started laughing. "How grotesque!"

From the floor below my feet came the sounds of the gypsy family that lived in the storefront underneath us: muffled shouts, melodramatic threats, and jokes in a kind of pidgin English interspersed with what must have been Romany, all emerging from an uninterrupted sea of noise made up of the television and record player on at the same time. The front door of their storefront led into a highly decorated little cubicle in which one of the women would read your palm for a dollar. But the rest of the space was living-eating-sleeping-and-partying quarters, and the real source of income instead had to do with stolen cars: late-model Cadillacs, Buicks, and Oldsmobiles pulled up at the curb, always with Jersey plates. A gypsy I'd never seen before would jump out and disappear into the back room. Animated discussions then took place below our kitchen floor, often degenerating into shouting matches, and soon one of the resident gypsies would emerge and drive off with a squeal of tires and a vibrant laugh. Dana and I had given up trying to shame them into lowering the noise level. They never turned off the TV until one-thirty in the morning, and never stopped talking until an hour or two after that. But "Man is boss here, woman not!" or "Frankie, you stop shit now, stop shit!" might drift up at any time of the day or night. Every month or two, when a gathering of the clans took place with fancy cars parked out front and forty people dancing and drinking downstairs, it was like living over a land of no tomorrows.

* * *

I lit a joint and picked up a paper from the pile of that week's *Post*s which lay on the floor. In the news, Gary Gilmore was about to be sent to the electric chair in Utah, while in New York the Bernard Bergman nursing home scandal had erupted. I glanced at the headlines from Tuesday's paper—or was it Wednesday's? . . . KOREA CIA USED MOONIES TO HELP NIXON . . . BEAME CONDEMNS JDL ATTACK ON SOVIET VIOLINIST . . . Earl Wilson's column revealed that young Americans were giving up torn jeans and getting serious . . . Then I read GANG BEATS DECOY COP:

> A decoy police officer dressed as a shabby old man was beaten and robbed by a gang of about fifteen youths on a Queens street this morning before his backup team could move in. Two juveniles were grabbed, but not before youths disfigured Police Officer Donald O'Brien's ear and took his wallet. The pair will be charged with juvenile delinquency.

The idea of *fake* old people being robbed . . . Before I could stop myself I was laughing, wondering what Oliver Hartwell would say to that—he had been so outraged by the victimization of the elderly—when out of nowhere his voice full of quiet contempt said to me, "You think that's funny, Sprout? You're a pig. But if so, I'm sure you'll also get a kick out of this!" And I felt my head being jerked downward until my eyes fell on the following article, TWO BOYS HELD IN FATAL MUGGING:

> Two 15-year-old boys were charged with juvenile delinquency today in the fatal mugging of an 88-year-old man in the Flatbush section of Brooklyn. Lorenzo Vergoni was mugged at 8 P.M. last October 10th as he entered the apartment house where he lived. The aged man was injured when his head struck the hallway floor. He was taken to Kings County Hospital where he died on November 16th.

I spun around in my seat. Nobody was there, but by that time I was shivering, my teeth were chattering. I jumped up and raced around turning on all the lights, looking in the closets and under the bed. But then I switched off the lights and felt my way in the dark back to the kitchen table where I sat down.

"Please," I pleaded, my hands finding another joint on the table and lighting it, "please talk to me, Mr. Hartwell. I won't betray your trust. I won't tell anybody about what you're doing, I promise."

I sat there in the dark, listening.

"He'll never talk to you again because he knows you're lying," a voice whispered, and a limitless rage ran through me. I stood up roaring, "Fuck you, Hartwell!" at the top of my lungs and flipped the kitchen table over onto one of the bentwood chairs around it. It was a heavy oak table and the chair splintered with a shriek. I ran into the bedroom and fell onto the bed.

I must have fallen asleep that way, because the next thing I knew the phone was ringing again and I lay there pasted to the sheets. How could it be so fucking hot in November? I walked into the living room and stared at the sofa. The phone underneath it wouldn't stop ringing. It had to be Dana.

"Bitch," I said. I pulled at the extension cord, lay down on the floor and picked up the receiver.

"Roy, is that you? What do you think this is, some kind of *game*? It's ten-thirty already! Where have you been? You were supposed to meet Jerry Rubin for drinks at the Plaza Oak Room at *seven-thirty* and interview him for our special issue . . ."

The New Jag was doing a special anniversary issue on the decade *Sixties into Seventies: Day and Night*. It had completely slipped my mind. Margo Kopperman's nasal Bronx whine rose to hysterical proportions as she continued, leaning hard on almost every other word.

"Jerry was so *pissed* he refused to reschedule. He told me this was *no way* to run a ship, that he remembered me from the old days in the movement as having been a real *professional*, that if I hadn't been with him during the Chicago Seven trial he never would've even *considered* this interview! Can you imagine that? The little momser's sure got some *nerve*, boy. But the fact is, we're stuck. We need him for this issue. Eldridge Cleaver's schedule changed so he's not coming to preach at Madison Square Garden 'til next *May*, something about court dates out in California. There's no way we can get to him before the deadline so Jerry was going to be the *lead article*—are you *listening* to me?"

I was holding the receiver away from my ear. Margo's voice had given me a splitting headache and I suddenly felt ravenous. I knew I would faint unless I ate something immediately.

"*Now* what am I going to do?" she was wailing. "I'll *tell* you what I'm going to do, I'm going to give you Jerry's unlisted number and if you *ever* want to write for the *Jag* again you're going to call him and *apologize* and try to set this thing up again. Do you have a pencil? The number's 431—"

"Shut up, Margo," I said evenly. "Just please be quiet."

There was a long pause.

"What did you say?" she whispered. I looked across the living room at the silent TV screen. Two women dressed in police uniforms chased a dark figure down an alley, firing their guns and shouting soundlessly. The headlights of a car sprang up at the other end and rushed toward them.

"I can't help it," I said. "I just forgot. I'm sorry, but some things in my life now . . . I can't explain."

"But why didn't you *call* me? We set this up *weeks* ago. I could have gotten someone else."

Silence.

"Roy?"

"I have to get something to eat, Margo," I said, and hung up the phone. Day and night, indeed.

Five days before, I had withdrawn twenty dollars from the bank. Now, after a prolonged search, all I could find was two. I went outside. The entrance to my building was several steps below the sidewalk, and a clean-shaven, prosperous looking businessman in his thirties, sweating profusely in suit and tie, sat on the upper step facing me, an overcoat draped across his knees and an attaché case beside him. He seemed out of place here, quite uptown and professional, and I noticed his unhappy, red-rimmed eyes.

"I've been waiting for you all night," he said in a hostile voice, looking me in the eye. He was very drunk. "Have you seen the movie *Death Wish*? I dreamed it up all by myself. You wanna know why?" His hand came out from beneath the overcoat and there was a bottle in it, which he drained with a flourish.

"I know you wanna know why," he said, pointing the bottle at me, waving it.

I stepped past him and crossed the street to the all-night fried chicken restaurant, the only place open late on St. Mark's in those days. Two dollars got me a series of deep fried chicken parts in a paper basket, some french fries, and white bread with margarine. Curled up in their greasy basket, the pieces of chicken looked like little drowned birds. I hurried back across the street and, not without trepidation, brushed past the businessman, who sat with his head slumped between his knees.

As I ate my dinner I watched him from the living room window. I didn't see how this person could possibly know me, but I was paranoid enough to wonder about it until he got to his feet and staggered off, leaving his attaché case behind. In a flash I was downstairs and brought it back inside. With some difficulty I managed to stand the kitchen table on its legs. I found the table lamp and turned it on. The attaché case was locked, but I opened it with a hammer and screwdriver and found myself looking at a copy of the *Wall Street Journal* on which lay some color photos, a pair of socks, and a gun. The gun was black and very small. It fit snugly into the palm of my hand. I ran to the front of the apartment and looked outside, and waited there for fifteen minutes, but he didn't return.

"Out of sight, Roy boy," I said. "An automatic . . ." I didn't know much about pistols, but this one had no barrel. On the handle was a button and when I pressed it a clip fell out of the bottom. Inside the clip were seven little brass cartridges, with the bullet tips. I reloaded the clip and put it back into the handle. On one side of the stock was engraved *Made Baretta USA Corp, AKK, MD. On the other, Mod. 950-.25 cal. Made in U.S.A.*

"Twenty-five caliber," I said to myself. The gun felt fantastic in my hand, it was light and fit perfectly, and when I closed my fingers around it only the tip of its snub nose was visible. I deliberately put the gun aside and forced myself to study the contents of the attaché case.

Underneath the newspaper I found several bills and circulars, all addressed to Mr. Robert Archer, 26 Deer Trail Rd., Port Jefferson, New York.

The photos were 4 x 6 color enlargements of a woman and a small boy, taken outside in the sunshine, trees and clouds behind them. They were holding hands, and certainly looked like mother and son . . . And Daddy makes three . . . She was smiling, wearing a red sweater and slacks, and was quite attractive in a placid way, with well-groomed honey-colored hair. About thirty-five; calm, confident eyes. She looked secure. A gold chain around her neck, a pretty bracelet. The boy was about five, smiling too, so much so, in fact, that I couldn't make out his eyes, maybe because of the sun behind the camera.

Soon I had invented a grievous scenario involving man and wife in which he rode the train home to the North Shore, crept up the darkened yard to the kitchen window of their rambling old brick house, and shot her in the back while she was bending over to feed the cat. The photos were so big and shiny sitting in the attaché case, how could they not be there for a reason? He had looked so very unhappy. In spite of her calm, satisfied air they must be going through hell. Or was the gun for self-defense, and he'd simply had a bad day at work? But then what about *Death Wish*? Maybe his wife and child had been murdered by some punks and he was out for vengeance. I stared at the pictures but I couldn't find anything more in her face besides that smile.

I just couldn't see walking around outside with this stuff, even if only to throw it in a garbage can somewhere. It made me too nervous. So I hid the gun in the cabinet under the kitchen sink behind the roach traps and Mr. Clean, and threw the attaché case into a corner. Pot seeds were strewn all over the floor and it took me a while, crawling around on hands and knees, until I had located all the joints. The chair was a total loss. There were broken plates and cups. I saw the letters addressed to Robert Archer on the table and tore them into little pieces before flushing them down the toilet. At first I was shocked I'd done this, but then it made sense. What was I to do instead? Call Port Jefferson and when she answers, say "You don't know me, Mrs. Archer, but I found your husband's attaché case and, uh . . ." Or wait until he gets home, and say what? "Where shall I send it?" Now that I'd destroyed the letters I could hardly contact the police. What proof was there the gun belonged to Robert Archer or anybody else?

Boy, you can no more fucking help these total strangers than you can yourself . . . Dana's never coming home and that's that . . . I got angrier and angrier until I was pulling her clothes out of the chest of drawers by the front door and stepping on them, tearing them and kicking them around the room. I piled everything in the middle of the kitchen. On the wall facing our bed was a self-portrait I liked, which she had done years before, with her long black hair spilling over her shoulders. I got out her oil paints and started squeezing the tubes onto her face, smearing the paint around and crying, until I'd had enough.

I searched the place for more money, found none, and rushed out the door, walking as quickly as I could to SoHo. Richard Pinkus lived in a loft on Mercer Street, and soon I was standing in front of his building, pressing the buzzer. There was no response but when I tried the door it opened and I took the freight elevator up to the fifth floor. I pounded on his door, yelling "Richard, open up! Open up!" and finally there he stood with a knife in his hand. He looked frightened until he recognized me, then his face turned pale and he started screaming.

"What the fuck do you think you're doing?"

"I just want to talk to Dana," I said, my voice shaking. "Let me *in*, will you?" I pushed past him into the loft and looked around but there was no sign of her.

"I don't know what you're talking about," he said.

"Come on, Richard, what are you trying to give me? I have to see her!"

"But Dana isn't here, man. Don't you understand? I haven't seen her in days. She was supposed to come over last weekend and never showed up . . . I just figured you two were working something out," he concluded mockingly.

I stood there not really hearing him, certain he was giving me some sort of runaround, but soon hiply distant Richard Pinkus looked very worried and I knew he was telling the truth. We decided to call the police—or rather, Richard decided I should call the police since I was the one who'd seen her last.

"I can't believe you haven't notified them before this," he was unable to refrain from adding.

"Kiss my ass," I replied, and went home in a daze.

I couldn't face calling the police or anybody else until the next day. I took two Valiums and went to bed, then I got up and took one more.

FIVE

The place was a mess. My body felt like somebody had been walking all over it, and I couldn't clear my head. I stood in the middle of the kitchen staring at the joints lined up on the table and debating whether to get stoned again—at eleven in the morning—or call the police, or crawl back into bed. I couldn't believe I had painted all over Dana's self-portrait, but fiddling with the hardened bursts of color just made things worse. "Oh, baby," I moaned, "what if you've been in trouble, trying to call me for the last few days and I've been too wrapped up in my feelings to pick up the phone? Jesus!"

I called several of her friends including Cissy Wyatt, casually inquiring if they'd seen her lately, but they had nothing to tell me. Then I called Faye Addison.

"What do you mean you haven't seen Dana?" she said, instantly getting the point, her voice sober with concern. I realized I shouldn't have called her, she had more than enough to worry about already, broke in the city with her squalling kid and her memories of Bobby. I refused to let her know how long Dana had been missing. It would only alarm her needlessly.

"Don't worry, it's nothing," I said. "Maybe she stayed over somewhere." Faye knew about Richard Pinkus and I was sure she wouldn't want to discuss it with me, she'd been at the wrong end of the same sort of situation herself and we'd never talked about it. In fact, I hadn't seen Faye for several months.

"Listen," Faye replied, "you call me right away if anything's wrong, OK? This is New York, Roy, anything can happen, you know that."

"Give me a chance to figure things out, Faye. I'll call you soon."

I walked into the living room and sat down on the sofa. It was raining, and the weather was still so warm that I had no clothes on. I knew I should call her parents out in Scarsdale, I knew I should call the police, but I couldn't stop thinking about Dana. I remembered a night six months before when everything had changed between us.

We had been making love in the dark. It must have been about three in the morning because I remember how quiet it was, how every now and then when we paused, no traffic could be heard out on the street and no noise came from anywhere in the building—the gypsies below and the woman painter upstairs, the old lady next door and the guy with the radio on the third floor, all were silent. But I heard the faint sound of the city itself, that unending, distant hum, and in the middle of the night listening to this sound was as breathtaking as floating among the stars in the sky.

We were fucking and then all of a sudden we weren't, we were talking instead. I was trying to explain that sexual attraction, for me as well as for most men I knew, wasn't always synonymous with love, and couldn't be. This seemed pretty straightforward and harmless but no sooner were the words out of my mouth than they became momentous, because actually I was talking about something else. We had always told each other the truth, we'd been proud of not hiding anything, and in an onrush of desired intimacy I now was bringing up a fact we'd both scrupulously avoided mentioning, namely that we no longer satisfied each other. The thrill was gone. I felt Dana tense up and move away from me.

"You sure know how to romance a girl, don't you?" she said, and reached for a cigarette.

"Did you come tonight, Dana? Was it good?" I asked tenderly. I knew she had, but she jabbed the cigarette into an ashtray and turned away from me, facing the wall. I put my arms around her and felt her body shaking. She was crying.

"I'm scared, Roy, I feel so far away from you. It was so mechanical this time. I feel lonely when we make love now, sometimes my chest tightens up and I have trouble breathing, and meanwhile you're moving on top of me, plunging away, trying so hard to please me and it isn't working. We rarely have a good time together anymore."

"What do you mean?" I was stunned. Sitting up in bed, I switched on the light. I pulled at her to roll over and face me but she resisted, hooking her arm under the mattress.

"Leave me alone," she whispered.

"Dana, what is this, why can't we talk?"

She turned to face me, tears rolling down her cheeks. "What do you want to talk about, Roy? You want to tell me again how love and sex aren't synonymous? Please spare me . . ."

We sat there staring at each other. My heart raced as I said, "But damn it, Dana, that's not it! Can't we discuss what's happening, instead of pretending it doesn't exist?"

"Pretending it doesn't exist?" She was sitting up now, her back against the wall, looking at me as if she'd never seen me before. "Is that what I've been doing the past year and a half, pretending it doesn't exist? You've got to be joking. I've tried to make you see what's going on, Roy, I've dropped hints and made allusions but it was like you didn't hear me, like you were in another world. Maybe it's all that pot you smoke, or something else, who knows what, but I'm tired . . . I'm tired of trying to make you see things you just won't admit to until ages later, when you suddenly start delivering these half-baked explanations of human sexuality."

"But, Dana, wait a minute! What do you mean, year and a half? *Year and a half?* Jesus, this is just so crazy. Because it's been really good together until recently, hasn't it? Hasn't it?"

I was tugging at her arm, I couldn't believe what she had said. "I don't remember you bringing this up before, certainly not in any direct way."

"Let go of me, Roy . . ." Suddenly her face contorted and she was screaming, "Who cares how long it's been! That's why we can't talk about it, you always derail things into some examination of sequence or detail, like some awful goddamned notary *public*!"

"Please, Dana, calm down. I've got to get this straight. Do you really mean you've brought up the problem we've had making it before now? If so, when? I'm not doubting you, I just—"

"See, there you go again." She lit another cigarette and glared at me. "It's no use. I can't take this anymore. You're so obtuse and stubborn . . . Isn't there anything to drink in this house?"

I found a bottle of cognac and filled two glasses. We sat there in the silence, drinking and smoking cigarettes. Then, from the apartment above us came the unmistakable strains of Frank Sinatra singing "I Only Have Eyes For You," and I knew we had awakened Doris Lepske, the uncommunicative hermit painter in her mid-forties who lived upstairs. It had been months since she'd acquired the habit of playing that one song, over and over, presumably while she worked.

In spite of everything Dana and I couldn't help smiling at each other. "Oh, dear," she said, "another masterpiece being gestated . . ." Once we had come upon a stack of Doris' paintings in the hall—uniformly dark and turgid renderings of craggy landscapes—and had collapsed in hysterics.

"Dana," I said eventually, misled by a sense that the air had cleared, "we've got to figure this out. You mean too much to me just to let it slide by. We've always been straight with each other—let me try and explain what I mean about love and sex, OK?"

"Oh, God, Roy, please I—"

"No, really," I said. "Listen. I don't know if it's the same for women—please tell me—but I can guarantee that for most men, after sleeping with a woman for a while, no matter how much they care for her they start thinking about new ones. While making love they begin to have fantasies of other women, anonymous girls they saw on the street that day, somebody they glimpsed once months before, it doesn't matter who and it doesn't have anything to do with whether they love the one they're with. Some men accept this situation while for others it's a big problem, they feel terribly guilty and resentful, but one way or the other it's a fact that most lovemaking going on has at least one partner secretly far away. Now wouldn't it be great if there were no guilt, if we were able to accept fantasizing at the same time as caring for the other person? Because the two aren't even related!"

I saw I was losing her and, panicking, added, "But you look like you think what I'm saying is awful. It's not awful, how can it be if so many people are experiencing it? Take me for example. I love you, Dana, you know that, and yet I have this need to—to—track the beautiful stranger, how else can I put it?"

"To *what*?"

"Please, baby, let me continue . . . I'm just thinking this through myself . . . It's like, I think it's tied to the hunt, you know? Something really primitive. Our animal natures, maybe. Male and female as expressions of elemental physical forces. For men, at least, the excitement of sex is tied up with distance, with the mystery of the stranger pursued and captured. The hunt," I said, "you know, partner as prey, as object, as unknown . . ."

"Partner as *object*! What are you, some kind of cave man? What about love?"

"Well, there's love too, like I said, but it's different in nature from sexual attraction."

She was staring at me open-mouthed.

"But what you're telling me is so cut and dried, Roy. For a woman, sexual involvement isn't the mechanical thing it can be for a man. Aren't you aware of what's going on in the world at all? Don't you know anything about history? Prostitution was created by male culture in order to satisfy a craving for mechanical sex. It's got nothing to do with love. Men divorce sex from emotion. They're afraid of real emotion; that's why they play around so much."

I saw we were getting nowhere. I wasn't talking about victimization, I was no more in favor of that than she was.

"I'm talking about biology, damn it, not sociology or politics. It's bigger than politics, don't you see? The gap between love and sex is a dilemma!"

"Stop shouting at me, Roy. The fact is you *are* talking about politics whether you admit it or not. How people treat each other is politics. If someone's simply being used as an erotic object, well then—"

"Wait a minute. Let's be fair about this, Dana. Haven't you ever had fantasies of other men when we made love?"

We looked at each other.

"That's not the point," she said sadly.

"But what *is* the point? What is love anyway? Let's get the dictionary." And before she could say anything more I was out of bed and standing in front of my desk in the next room.

"Look, baby, it's right here in Webster's, I can't believe it. Listen to this: 'love, noun. 1. An intense sexual desire for another person. 2. An intense affectionate concern for another person.'" I slammed the dictionary shut. "See, even they can't decide. And you want to know why? Because it's both, Dana, both and neither!"

I ran back into the bedroom, excited that I'd finally uncovered something crucial, but she was in the kitchen quickly getting dressed and throwing a coat over her shoulders.

"What are you doing? Can't we discuss this like two reasonable people?"

"I'm going for a walk," she replied in a brittle, distant voice, "I can't take it anymore. Don't wait up for me," she added as she opened the door and stepped out into the hall. "If you have trouble sleeping, why don't you just revert to your animal state and fantasize yourself out on a *hunt*," she said sarcastically. "I'm sure you won't even notice that I'm gone." The door slammed and I was alone, sounds of Sinatra wafting down from overhead. *Maybe millions of people go by, but they all disappear from view . . .*

I got up to look at Dana's art work again. One section of object-imbedded resin had a typed strip of paper glued along the top. *Wearing the dress your husband likes, you come slowly down the stairs*, it said. It was from an early edition of Emily Post, advice for young homemakers of the 1920s, and I remembered Dana reading aloud from it once, how fantastically antiquated it had sounded. Now I knew what it meant. Instead of simply painting portraits, she insisted on taking the risk in her new work of trying to figure out who she was. Whether or not these works were "aesthetically engaging" became superfluous. I couldn't understand why I hadn't seen this before. I wanted to tell her so but she wasn't there.

Wandering around the living room talking to myself I came upon Hartwell's Yankee cap. It was the old-fashioned cloth kind—no adjustable plastic strap—well-worn and shiny with grease. Marvelling that the thing fit me I put it on my head and, otherwise naked, sat down on the sofa. Slowly stroking myself I saw Dana's ivory skin, those shoulders I loved to touch, her black hair and green eyes—she'd always looked more Irish than Jewish to me. Then the doorbell rang. I went to the window, opening the curtain just enough to see outside.

People flashed by, visible for a second in the narrow shaft of light, but nobody was waiting for me. As I was about to turn away I glanced at the opposite sidewalk and there—peering straight at me, one hand raised above his face to shade his eyes—stood Oliver Hartwell.

It all happened so quickly, one moment he was there and when I looked again he had vanished. I raised the window and leaned out, bare-chested, looking up and down St. Mark's Place, but he was gone. I stood in the middle of the room, overcome with the most unreasonable fear.

"This is absurd," I said aloud, "you're being completely irrational. Hartwell's probably no longer even alive. Why don't you get out of the apartment, go for a walk?" While I was finding something to wear the phone rang.

Sibyl Miller's bored, superior, sarcastic voice came over the line. "Hello, dear, it's so nice you're finally answering one of our calls. We're profoundly grateful..."

Sibyl Miller often was condescending to me, which infuriated me because I had no respect for her and yet somehow never could get this across without sounding heavy-handed. I never was able to score points with either of Dana's parents. I disliked them too much to remain cool. They had long ago concluded I represented their daughter's biggest mistake so far in life. They considered me a failure who wouldn't go out and get a steady job, a person with no future. Occasionally they intimated I was living off their daughter, which of course made me apoplectic.

"I know Dana doesn't like for her mother to call her," she was saying, "but even though she's a woman now Dana is still my daughter. I have the right to talk to her once in a while, don't you agree?"

I was stupefied. I had heard these exact same words so many times already. Even if she and Dana had talked the day before, Mrs. Miller was apt to come up with this litany again.

"Jesus Christ," I said, my voice sounding hoarse, "don't you ever get tired of using that line, Mrs. M.?" When we'd first met she had insisted I call her Sibyl, "just like my friends do," but I had never been able to.

There was a silence while she shifted the phone from one hand to the other. I could hear what sounded like her teeth crunching on something. She sighed. There were sucking noises.

"Roy, don't make a production with me. I *am* Dana's mother, in case you've forgotten." God, how had she managed to work that in again? More sucking noises followed.

Finally she said, "Listen, my dear, I have better things to do than get involved in this *mishegas* with you. Stop playing games with me. I've been trying to reach Dana since Wednesday. Today is Saturday. Where have you two been?"

"Nowhere."

"Will you kindly put her on?"

"No," I said. This conversation was going to be awful, I thought. I only hoped I could get out of it without talking to Lou Miller.

But sure enough, she turned away from the receiver and said, "Lou, this boy is giving me such aggravation. What do I need it for? Will you please talk to him?"

I drew a deep breath and interrupted her. "Look, Mrs. Miller, you're not going to like this, but . . ." Without mentioning Richard Pinkus or our mysteriously low bank account I explained what had happened as clearly as possible, adding that I had been about to inform the police when she called.

"My God, I'm dying," she wailed. "He says Dana is gone and he hasn't called the police. My baby, my only child!"

There followed an epithet-filled exchange between Dr. Miller and me during which he threatened to have me "skewered like a lamb," and insisted he would deal with the police himself.

"You obviously can't even tie your shoes. You have no sense of responsibility. My daughter's welfare means nothing to you," he boomed.

I told him as quietly as I could to go fuck himself and hung up. I remembered—it was the only time my parents and Dana's had met—a frightful dinner we'd all had in 1973 at a fancy French restaurant in the Village. Even though neither Dana nor I had sisters or brothers, my parents couldn't have been more different than hers. Humble, deeply religious storekeepers who emigrated before World War II from a village in Galicia, in the foothills of the Carpathian Mountains, they now were isolated in a small town in Ohio, gun-shy and obsequious from decades of selling dry goods to the surrounding redneck *goyim*. They reacted with intimidated dismay at the spectacle of this flashy, arrogant, hard-drinking allergist and his wife from Scarsdale, with plenty of money and pretensions to culture, who lost no time in making disparaging remarks about the old country.

"Galicia in the springtime must have been *truly* glorious," Sibyl Miller simpered after nearly a bottle of wine, patting my mother's hand, and I slammed a water glass down so hard on the table that it shattered, slicing open my palm. As blood dripped onto the tablecloth I bundled my speechless parents into their coats and rushed them out the door. Since she had met them only once, Dana adored my father and mother. She saw them as simple, unspoiled people working away like selfless angels in their dry goods store in the middle of nowhere. After they returned to Plainview, she telephoned and apologized for her parents' behavior. She even wired flowers.

Visions of Lou Miller sometimes materialized before my eyes at the oddest moments. But the rings on several fingers, the gold chains, the country club membership and Cadillac, the not-so-secret flings with Las Vegas showgirls, the name change while in medical school from Myrowitz to Miller, all paled beside his politics. Lou Miller was a hardcore conservative—even, in his little jokes about the mating and working habits of blacks and Puerto Ricans, a racist. I vowed not to let him take charge of the search for Dana and freeze me out in the process.

As far as I was concerned, by pardoning Richard Nixon in 1974, Jerry Ford had demonstrated that America was no longer a democracy, because a citizen supposedly equal among others had been absolved of responsibility for his crimes. For me, during the '76 elections, Carter and Ford were no more than inch-high figures on the TV screen who represented competing strains of the ruling oligarchy. The institution of the presidency was a red herring, it conjured up a father figure with whom to hypnotize the public. Except perhaps on a local level, the democratic process was pro forma, done with mirrors, a sham. When Lou Miller heard what I had to say on the coming elections—this had been in August at a Chinese restaurant uptown, the last time Dana and I had dinner with her parents—he turned purple, sputtering that I was a Communist, an anarchist like Patty Hearst, and that he was going to take legal action to pry his daughter out of my hands. Dana and I had looked at each other and laughed ruefully, since by then we were hardly together anyway.

"Whatever happens between us, Roy," she had said later, squeezing my arm as we left the restaurant, "I'll always be grateful you weren't anything like my father. It's so much easier for me to deal with him when you take all the flak."

"I told you already, we won't accept anything from you."

"But, Detective, what do you mean? She's been missing for six days already, all I want to do is file a missing persons report."

"Look, I'll run through this again. First off, Police Department policy, we only take reports from immediate family. That lets you out, because you tell me you're not married. Second, she's over eighteen and hasn't broken any laws. How do we know she didn't decide to go on a vacation, or live somewhere else, or whatever? We have no right to pick her up, we don't have the authority to do that. If we took reports like yours, all we'd be doing is running around New York City looking for people who don't want to be found. We'd be searching for half the fucking city. It's a free country, she can do what she wants. You follow me?"

"But this is absurd. I've contacted her friends and her parents and—"

"Fella, we're going around in circles. If she's an adult she can do what she pleases. She's twenty-eight years old, right? Let's be realistic. If you were some old guy telling me your wife is gone, that would be one thing. But we're in the East Village, we're talking lifestyle. You tell me she was on her way to meet this other fella and go dancing . . . See, I mean no offense, but maybe she told the same thing to *him*, understand? Another week or two goes by, her parents want to get in touch with us, fine. Then we file a report with Missing Persons downtown. They send out a description to the hospitals, the morgue. They take it from there. But we can't do anything now, and we're *never* gonna act on the basis of your request, anyhow. It's gotta be immediate family, OK?"

What else could I do? There were more friends to call, but that seemed pointless. She had left to meet Pinkus at Spiro's bar, all dressed up with fifteen dollars in her pocket. She had never arrived. Everything she owned was still here. It freaked me out to think of the psychopaths loose on the streets. I had explained all this to the detective but it hadn't fazed him. I was amazed that from a legal point of view she had just blithely wandered off.

I tried to figure out where she might have gone and thought of visiting Dana's grandmother in her nursing home in the Bronx, but I didn't feel up to it that day. The home was too depressing. Dana tried to see Grandma Bessie, who was in her mid-seventies, at least once a month. They'd have tea together and talk. Bessie told stories of the Ukraine before the Russian Revolution, and of her life as a young immigrant wife in New York. At certain moments, Dana said, it was like two girls confiding in each other, because the stories always pertained to when Bessie had been young.

The previous April, not long after Bessie had been committed by the Millers, I went with Dana to the Sunset Towers Home. Sibyl rarely visited her mother, claiming it was too painful.

"Please, dear, don't try to make me feel guilty," she once told Dana over the phone. "The anguish we went through before finally deciding on a nursing home . . . It's not like we put your grandmother in one of those Bernard Bergman pigsties. We're doing all we can for Bubba, the best doctors, everything. Don't forget, she's not on Medicaid. You have no idea how much these places cost."

As for Lou, forget it. He was always too busy. "Besides," he once confided in me, "Bessie's had a long full life. Seeing someone as healthy as I am would only upset her now."

But the fact was, Bessie *was* on Medicaid. Before being admitted she'd had to relinquish control of her estate to the Millers and plead poverty in order to cover most of the exorbitant rates charged by Sunset Towers. And she'd been sent to the nursing home only because she had trouble with her hip and couldn't get around without a walker. After three x-ray sessions the doctors still were unable to tell if the hip was really broken. The time I'd gone up there with Dana, Bessie had been disagreeable and testy. She couldn't see very well but there was no sign of serious illness. "I shouldn't be here," she kept repeating in an anguished voice, "who does Sibyl think she is?"

Sunset Towers was filled with people in much worse shape than Grandma Bessie. I remembered walking through the rec room. Five or six of them sat in front of a big TV, staring into space. Their faces showed resignation, apathy, anger. Not one of them was watching television. And the woman Bessie had shared a room with was incontinent and seemed paralyzed. The entire time we were there she had lain with open mouth looking up at the ceiling from within the confines of her railing bed.

One really strange thing was that Christmas carols had been playing softly on the p.a. system, even though it was April and Sunset Towers was a kosher home filled with members of the faith. I remembered children's toys in a corner of the rec room, and one old woman who sat on the floor dressed in a cotton nightie, with little satin bows in her hair. I was in no hurry to return to Sunset Towers but I knew that Bessie virtually hated her daughter and if Dana recently had visited her she certainly would withhold that information from Sibyl.

As it was, though, I didn't even have enough change to get on the subway. Thirty-five cents was all I could find in the house and unless I wanted to borrow the money from somebody I'd have to wait until the bank opened on Monday to get at the $15.16. I was in no mood to ask my friends for a loan—I didn't feel like talking to anybody—and in any case, who were my friends? Bobby was gone now; aside from him there were fellow journalists, for the most part, who had started treating me condescendingly the moment they discovered I wasn't keeping it together anymore. Friends like Peter Arney, who recently had published a book about famous record company executives and was now working on a rock musical for Broadway. Five years before, I had gotten obsequious little Peter his first job writing record reviews for *The Village Voice*.

$15.16 . . . The checks Dana had been getting from her parents for tuition, modest though they were, had tided us over the rough spots and wouldn't be arriving in the mail anymore. And after my conversation with Margo Kopperman I wouldn't be writing for *The New Jag* even if I wanted to. Where was December's rent going to come from? What was I supposed to do, wash dishes? The last project I'd been working on, *Angels of the Me Generation*, seemed faraway and unreal now, like a piece of junk out on the ocean.

I thought of calling my parents and asking them for a loan but I knew what their response would be. They had been used to living a life of unremitting thrift for so long, scrupulously adding a few dollars each month to their savings account, that the idea of suddenly withdrawing a sizable amount and sending it out in the world to their mysteriously unsettled son would be akin to dropping it in the river.

I had to get out of the house, I had to stop thinking about $15.16. In the refrigerator I found some cheese and two old carrots and ate. I hammered a nail in the kitchen wall and hung Dana's ruined self-portrait on it, then went into the bathroom and looked into the mirror. Unshaven face, red-rimmed eyes that wouldn't return my glance, Hartwell's navy blue baseball cap. I forced myself to look into my eyes, widening them until they didn't seem afraid anymore and were big and round and empty.

"If you think that plants don't talk to each other, you're crazy, Bill," a girl dressed in baggy jeans and Birkenstocks was saying earnestly to her companion. "They carry on conversations the same way we do. They even know when they're about to be mistreated because they can read our thoughts. They pick up on intentions. Plants are very sensitive—they just can't run away, is all."

"Far out," Bill replied dubiously, craning his neck past her to look up the street.

I brushed past them and walked west toward the Village, past the St. Mark's Baths and the rundown transient hotel filled with prostitutes and junkies on the corner of Third Avenue. On Waverly Place I saw an elaborate graffiti, SUCKER FOR FATE, surrounded by stencilled hearts and daggers. I wandered the Village for a while until, circling back late in the afternoon, I came to Washington Square Park.

Under the Arch, near the hot dog stands, a guy with a beard and long, very clean hair sat behind a table with macrame god's eyes hanging from the corners. The table was covered with an amazing assortment of Sixties paraphernalia: old Avalon Ballroom posters, banners in paisley patterns showing marijuana leaves, Op Art decals, peace insignia, and pictures of the Grateful Dead, Jefferson Airplane, and Janis Joplin. From a little speaker on the ground next to him came the strains of "This is the age of Aquarius . . ." When I paused to look more closely he got up and handed me a flyer for something called

THE SUB-LUNARIAN FESTIVAL

OF MUSIC & LIFE

Tomorrow—Sunday—In the Park

Rain or Shine

Washington Square Park is Ours!!

"Remember the Be-In, man?" he asked me. "We can do it again. All it takes is believing. We're getting together tomorrow, and it's gonna be outta sight. Buckminster Fuller's gonna speak, a delegation from Starwind Commune is coming from Colorado to show us how to grow our own, and all the great bands are gonna play for free . . . Power to the people!"

His rap was expansive on the face of it, but in fact the enthusiasm of his words was neutralized by his strangely disinterested manner, as if he'd been hired for the occasion. He didn't seem to be taking money or selling anything. I couldn't figure it out. When he finished what he had to say he looked expressionlessly into my eyes and sat down. I felt a chill move along my back. It was as if he and I were in a plastic bubble isolated from everything else. Nobody had stopped at his table, nobody seemed to notice him but me. For a moment it became dead quiet, except that in the distance I faintly heard an airplane droning. Fearful, I quickly walked away.

The park was jammed with people. Kids in T-shirts tossed Frisbees, mothers pushed perambulators through packs of ice-cream slurping tourists, and old people sat in rows on the benches, soaking up the freakish November sun.

I sat for a while on a bench next to two old ladies ("So? You been in the house all day?") but my eye kept being drawn to the outsiders, the abandoned ones, the crazies . . . Jamaicans in dreadlocks selling pot; two semi-naked, drunken bikers punching each other out; teenage runaways sucking on cigarettes, staring around in a Nembutal haze. One man stood alone against a tree, oblivious to all else, banging his head against the trunk and then smacking his forehead, over and over, with the palm of his hand. The sound of his head hitting wood carried to where I sat and made me wince.

I drifted toward the southeast corner of the park, deep in the shade of the big trees where the crazies congregated. A middle-aged black man with a kerchief on his head sat on one of the curving benches near the exit. He was punching the air around him and talking. His smell was so ripe in the warm air that I nearly gagged. In his hands he held a deck of playing cards which he periodically shuffled and then slapped against his knee, turning it over to look at the bottom card whereupon he would lay the deck in his lap and punch the air again. He talked continually, jerking his head violently to the right to address somebody who wasn't there. Then he turned to face me. "Dogshit! Ratshit!" he shouted, and distorted his mouth into a frozen smile. He turned over a nine of clubs and showed it to me, grinning until his face became an empty mask.

I moved away from him, lighting a cigarette, my last one. It was getting late, the light from the park fading as a cold wind started to blow in from the north and the temperature dropped. Hungry and disoriented, I left the park and walked east. I had thirty-five cents in my pocket, not even enough for a slice of pizza. Without thinking I turned to face the people leaving the park and stuck out my hand.

"Anybody got a dime?" I croaked meekly. Noses lifted in the air, faces looked aside.

"What is this, white boy, some kind of joke? Only niggers allowed to beg, don't you know that? Go on home to momma." I felt something cold and hard dig into my back and took off running until I reached Broadway.

I walked in Great Jones Street past grimy, deserted loft buildings, the walls covered with graffiti, layers and bursts of it . . . FREE PATTY

HEARST, GRUESOME GRANNIES, I LOVE LINOLEUM . . . And, painstakingly lettered,

COCKROACH ARE REAL PEOPLE
BUT CRIMINALS ARE ALL ALIKE

Drifting along the Bowery toward home I felt light as air. In the gathering dusk I began to catch glimpses of vanished friends and acquaintances in the faces of people on the street. I felt apprehensive as I approached St. Mark's Place. It was strange knowing Dana wouldn't be there when I got home. Something made me feel like I was returning to an uninhabited place—uninhabited even after I got there.

PART TWO

SIX

Sunday morning dawned raw and rainy, and I was awake to see it. Up
on the third floor the mystery man of our building, James Yankton,
had left his radio on again, full blast, all night long. The ritual procession up the stairs at three A.M., the pounding on his door, the
threats—all took place as before, to no avail. I had lived in the building
since 1971 and in those five years I'd seen Yankton not more than ten
times: a tall, angular, sour-looking recluse in his fifties, he wouldn't
speak to you even if addressed directly, he'd walk right by. Some said
he worked uptown for the YMCA. Dana claimed she'd heard he was a
night clerk in a midtown hotel. The radio was always tuned to AM Top
40. Calls to the landlord, the police, the city, all had resulted in no
change. The police, we discovered, were not allowed to break into an
apartment if nobody responded to their knock. Luckily for us, in his
inscrutable way Yankton only chose to do this several times a month.
Our only solace came in thinking what it would have been like every
night.

Anyway, this time I didn't mind the noise, or rather, for long
stretches of time I wasn't aware of it. Because the evening before I'd
come home and found that most of Dana's clothes were gone, as well
as several of her art works, her paints and supplies and various other
personal possessions. But her self-portrait still hung on the wall, and
on the kitchen table I found a note: *Roy, don't wait up for me anymore. I
don't want to hurt you ... And I like the way the painting looks now. I think
you've got real talent. Please keep it. Dana.*

I liked Sunday morning very early, nobody around, no traffic. Looking out the window in the purple-gray dawn, I ran my eyes over the

two beautiful stone caryatids supporting the entrance to the brownstone across the street. *I don't want to hurt you.* Thanks a lot. Fuck you too. What about me worrying whether you were dead or alive? You think that was fun, not being told anything, being treated like the enemy? And who are you to be the only one capable of inflicting hurt?

At eight A.M. Yankton's radio stopped and I drifted off to sleep, waking with a start at two in the afternoon. All I could find to eat was a jar of peanut butter. No crackers or bread, no milk, no juice. I settled down in front of the TV to watch some football, washing down spoonfuls of peanut butter with cup after cup of coffee and smoking my first joint of the day. Joe Namath led the Jets in a heavy snowstorm in Buffalo against the Bills and O.J. Simpson. Double images caused by the recently completed World Trade Center combined with the snow to create a picture in which the players on the field looked insubstantial, their figures coming in and out of focus. At times the sidelines and the crowds in the stands showed through the players' bodies, turning them into raging ghosts. I couldn't bear to eat another spoonful of peanut butter and yet I was weak, undernourished. Then Doris Lepske decided to do her thing upstairs and the lyrics from "I Only Have Eyes For You" dropped around me like a shroud.

At that moment, a mouse ran along the baseboard behind the TV in that hesitant, herky-jerky way mice have, as if possessed, and the hair stood up on my head. Every year when the cold weather came, no matter what traps or poison we used, a colony of mice took up residence in the apartment until the following spring. This never failed to freak me out. They were like miniature soul remnants. In this case, upon seeing the mouse disappear behind a bookcase, I thought of the old Czech woman who had lived in the apartment in the 1950s. Sister to the senile old woman who still lived next door to us, the woman supposedly had died here long before I ever moved in. Generations of tenants separated us, we had never met, and yet simply having heard about her was enough to bring her back on the premises when the time was right. Then I remembered Oliver Hartwell, and his sarcastic rejoinder during our interview about how the main character of his next novel was going to be a mouse. A mouse suffering from delusions of grandeur.

The moon may be high but I can't see a thing in the sky, 'Cause I only have eyes . . . I couldn't stand it in the apartment another instant and ran down the stairs into the street. The rain had let up but it was still misting and cold. Shivering, faint from hunger, I stumbled around for a while until I found myself approaching Washington Square Park again. In contrast to the day before, the place was nearly deserted. The benches were wet and covered with leaves and, aside from a few derelicts, only the hardiest citizens were in evidence, huddled here and there in raincoats. I walked through the park from corner to corner searching for some sign of the Sub-Lunarian Festival of Music & Life, but there was none.

"Naturally!" I exclaimed in a caustic voice, a wave of self-revulsion passing through me. "Of course it's not here. How could it be, since *you're* the one looking for it, butthole?"

Slapping myself on the side of the head, trying to regain control, eventually I approached a man sitting alone in the middle of the park and asked for a cigarette. He was rosy-cheeked and heavyset, in his sixties, with a halo of snowy white hair.

"I don't smoke," he said reprovingly. "You shouldn't either." This unsolicited advice enraged me. I was just about to tell him what to do with it when he smiled and said, "I've got a little something to drink though. I'll give you a nip from my flask if you'd like."

The bourbon tasted wonderful. I relaxed and was about to engage him in conversation when a young, fit-looking black guy pulling a laundry cart full of shopping bags approached and sat down on the other side of the man.

"How's Emma?" he asked the older man brusquely. "I don't see her around." He didn't acknowledge me at all.

"Oh, she's fine," the rosy-cheeked man replied. "She just don't like the rain, she'll never come out with me in weather like this no matter what."

"She's got brains," the black guy said, whereupon they both fell silent.

After some time went by I began to feel the two men were keeping silent because of my presence, and I was about to leave when the black guy started talking and the older man joined in. They traded cynical complaints about the powers that be—the mayor, the governor, unnamed honchos on Wall Street, the president of the taxi drivers' union—and I marvelled at how unlike the usual derelict this young black man seemed. He sounded resentful and hard-nosed but completely sane. I admired him: here was somebody living the life he wanted to live, somebody who was on the street by choice. But then I heard him say, "Sure they control the weather."

The other man said nothing.

"You don't think they control the weather? I've seen 'em control the wind, man. Once I needed it to go my way and instead it went the other way . . . I hate the wind, it blows all kinds of junk around, not only dust and like that but diseases, microbes . . . You don't think they can control the weather, with all those satellites they got up there?"

He pointed up through the trees.

"Darn right, Edward," the rosy-cheeked man finally replied, perhaps out of politeness.

"Edward? Who's Edward?" the black buy said pointedly and they both paused, glancing at me until I got up to leave. I wanted to stay and talk to them but obviously Edward, in particular, had no need of my presence.

"Thanks for the drink," I said to the older guy.

"Oh, sure," he replied, smiling.

I looked at Edward. "And good luck to you, man," I blurted out, but he just snorted and looked away.

I was at the western edge of the park about to go onto MacDougal Street when I noticed an old man with a cane sitting alone on one of the benches. I went over to him and asked if he could spare some change. He looked straight ahead without responding, and I had passed the deserted chess tables on my way out of the park when I heard a commotion behind me. Six or eight teenagers had surrounded the old man and were taunting him.

"So what's it like being old?" I heard one of them ask. His friends roared with laughter.

"Is it as much of a drag as they say? Huh?"

He leaned over the old man, breathing in his face, baiting him, until, trembling with fear, the old man shouted, "Get away from me!" and swung his cane at his tormentor. In a flash they all were on him, wrestling the cane from his grip and shoving him. Then the old man spat in the face of the one who had been baiting him and the kid grabbed the cane and beat him over the head with it, leaving him slumped on the bench, bleeding. They ran past me out of the park, laughing and shouting, swinging the cane through the air.

I ran over to the old man and asked if he was all right, but he was moaning, holding his head. He refused to respond. I went back into the park in search of a police car I'd seen some time before, near the Arch. In the middle of the park I looked back and noticed a squad car parked on MacDougal, and two cops climbing the railing toward the old man. I continued east toward NYU when I looked to my left and saw, sitting near the children's swings—when I saw . . .

His back was turned to me. He had his arm around somebody and was talking earnestly, soothingly, in a voice full of commiseration. It has to be him, I thought excitedly, he's not getting away from me this time. Going into a crouch, I crept up to a bench facing in the opposite direction—virtually back to back with them—and sat there as unobtrusively as possible. Sneaking a glance out of the corner of my eye I could see wire-rimmed spectacles. Neither of the men noticed me, they were deep in conversation. Or rather, it was Hartwell who did most of the talking.

"Come on, *you can do it,* I know you can," he was saying intensely. "I have faith in you, see, and that makes all the difference."

The other man mumbled something in response which I couldn't hear.

Hartwell then replied in an encouraging voice which had the slightest flinty, impatient edge to it.

"I know what you're up against, Mike, believe me. I used to think it was hopeless, too, but then I learned what being alive is all about. I had faith in myself, I refused to give up. I fought back, Mike. I learned how to turn fate around, and you can do it too. Don't try to tell me you can't! You're no older than me. But you have to get serious, see, there's not much time left. You must *will* your life to change. Habit is the enemy! Don't you see, Mike? It's the same when you use certain muscles habitually and neglect others. Habit shapes your personality, too, limiting your disposition to try anything new. But exactly in the way you might change the exercises you do, you can change the way you are in the world, the way you see the world. Do you understand what I'm telling you, Mike? I'm sure you do, I have confidence in you. Break the spell cast by habit and you'll be free, mentally as well as physically. But it's hard, it takes work. The forces of evil are still out there trying to suck us back into their diminishing world."

His words floating through the cold, misty air electrified me. I wanted so much to talk to him, to find out what he was doing and ask his advice.

"I discovered I'm condemned to extinction when I play the game on society's terms," Hartwell went on, his arm still around the other man's shoulders. "Only when I act from the deepest part of my being do I stand a chance of realizing my potential. Otherwise I waste my life tilting at phantoms while my deathbed's being prepared for me. So it's absolutely necessary to begin by ignoring everything society says you should do. This applies not only to politics and your job but also to your family, which unconsciously is busy hastening you along to your demise with sweet words, reinforcing images of senility and decay. In order to win out you must have the strength to turn your back on society . . . Mike, when you do that, with the loving support of others in the same boat as you—your true *compañeros de la vida*—amazing things will happen! Yes! By listening down into the biology of your own being you'll grow stronger, younger. And you'll realize that *old age is a con*, Mike, a shuck that's been forced on us. You don't have to die, at least not in the manner you've been told," he said softly, continuing to whisper words of encouragement which I couldn't make out, hugging the other man close to him. Then he turned and saw me. In spite of myself I was facing them, listening eagerly.

Frowning he jumped to his feet, leaped the bench separating us in one easy motion, and approached me.

"What are you doing eavesdropping?" he asked testily. "Huh? What gives you the right to eavesdrop?" Looking around the park briefly, he grabbed me by the lapels of my jacket and yanked me up off the bench. He stared at me with cold, piercing eyes.

"But Mr. Hartwell, all I want to do is talk to you."

"Hartwell? Who's Hartwell, kid, huh?" He shook me a few times then slapped me across the face—once, twice. "Make tracks, you understand me? This doesn't concern you."

"Damn it," I said, my face stinging, "what is this? Can't we just talk for Christ's sake?"

He glanced around the park again then pulled the baseball cap down over my eyes, took hold of my jacket and jerked me toward him, kneeing me in the groin. I rolled over onto the wet, muddy path, writhing and gasping for breath. He stepped on my right hand, grinding it into the path until I cried aloud, then leaped back over the bench. "Come on, Mike," he said. "Let's get out of here."

The two of them strode quickly away.

"You see that old guy?" somebody said, and I heard people laughing. I struggled to my feet, still doubled over in pain, and began shouting at the receding figures.

"Fuck you, Hartwell, you hear me? I'm gonna publish the rest of our interview after all, what do you think of that? Then maybe you'll talk to me!"

He stopped and turned around, staring at me blankly. From fifty feet away his hair appeared dark, not grey. His hands, held loosely at his sides, didn't tremble in the slightest. Even while I shouted at him I debated with myself whether this was, in fact, the same man I'd interviewed—but that voice, those eyes . . .

"Yeah," I went on in a humiliated rage, "you know what I'm talking about. A lot of good it's doing me now, but I know plenty of places that would love to publish it. I'm sick of waiting!"

He shrugged and, pointing at his forehead and rotating his finger as if I'd lost my marbles, he walked nonchalantly away, holding the other man's arm.

"Drop dead, Grandpa!" I shouted so loudly my voice cracked, to the amusement of the little band of bystanders. I spied one man grinning as he stood there in jogging outfit and running shoes and said to him, "What're you looking at, shithead?" He gulped and took off quickly down the sidewalk, his shoes slap-slap-slapping on the wet pavement. The others soon dispersed and in spite of the burning pain in my balls I dragged myself home. I'd been so angry at Hartwell I hadn't known what I was saying and I regretted it. Because I *was* going to publish the rest of that interview. I had no alternative, I needed the money. And now I'd gone and told him all about it.

The New York offices of *Rolling Stone* were on the twenty-second floor of a fancy office building on 57th Street, and I found myself sitting in Jeffrey Allen's reception room, chain-smoking cigarettes I cadged from his secretary and waiting while he read my complete, unexpurgated version of the Oliver Hartwell story. The city streamed away below me in the afternoon sunshine while off in the distance, barely visible, were the big factories in New Jersey . . . Hoboken . . . Just this year, people had started moving over there from the city, renting cheap, spacious apartments. Maybe that's where Dana was, beginning a new life as what, and with whom . . . Rising early every morning and making art all day, cooking great meals for him at night. After coffee and cognac he'd tell her about the incredible things he'd done that day, she'd show him a few of her new works, then they'd jump in bed and fuck each other silly. Or maybe they were beyond sex, they simply retired to their panoramic bay window and stared contentedly into the void.

The night before, I'd stayed up drinking cup after cup of espresso and forcing myself, in spite of the pain in my right hand, to transcribe the second cassette of our interview. I then added an account of what I'd overheard in the park. As I listened to the tape again after more than four months had gone by I couldn't get over some of the things Hartwell said. They cut right through the usual hogwash people fed each other. In spite of how angry I was with him for what he'd done to me, like a star-struck kid I couldn't help wondering what he was doing at that very moment. What sort of people was he getting involved with?

I'd fallen asleep at dawn on Monday, awakened at eleven, with-drawn the fifteen bucks left at the bank, and then taken the train up-town. And now, for an hour and a half already, I'd been cooling my heels, looking back and forth between New Jersey and a lime-green upholstered wall on which hung rows of old *Rolling Stone* covers in metal frames. It's true, I'd come in unannounced, cut right into Jeffrey Allen's day, and Jeffrey was one of the world's busiest people, as he put it.

His door finally opened and Jeffrey emerged, looking dapper and thoughtful and motioning me inside.

"Terrific, Roy," he said in that hurriedly ingratiating way of his. "This is really terrific. We like it a lot. But, Jesus, he says some really weird things, like he flipped his lid or something. Although on the other hand he's certainly lucid and in control of himself . . . I just don't know . . ." He frowned, then smiled, while his restless eyes darted around the room from telephone console to window to baby pictures to ceiling, never resting on me directly.

"But one question we have to ask ourselves here at the magazine is why are we suddenly publishing this? For that matter, why'd you de-cide to come out of the woodwork with it now?"

I started to reply but he held up his hand.

"Please . . . So I called old Margo the K to hear what she had to say. I mean, maybe we publish everything at once, reprint the first part too. I'm just thinking out loud, you understand. And, like—"

He paused and looked me in the eye ever so briefly, then noticed my bandaged hand.

"—We have to hear the tape first, before we even consider making a decision on this."

"You *what?*" I hadn't spoken in so long my voice croaked.

"Roy, where's the original interview? We need to listen to the whole thing, especially since there's no record of your conversation with him in the park. We have no evidence this guy is really Hartwell—no pho-tos, nothing but your word."

"But, Jeffrey, do you think I made all this up? Don't you trust me?"

"Of course I trust you," he answered impatiently. "Just bring me the tape, will you? I can't go to bat for you on this until I hear it. I've got problems enough already. At first glance this piece is sensational but I don't even know if it's right for the magazine and before I think about that I have to hear exactly where it came from. You must have the cassettes at home, right? I mean, what is this, Roy? Do you need cab fare or something?"

"As a matter of fact, I do," I said, my ears burning. "But what really pisses me off is I don't know if I should feel insulted or what. Here I've offered you the exclusive story on Oliver Hartwell's disappearance and you're giving me some static about how maybe your readership won't go for it. Then you get an earful of God knows what from Margo Kopperman and suddenly maybe I've made it all up. That's bullshit, Jeffrey, and you know it. I don't need this kind of treatment. Hartwell's a nationally known figure, I can take the article to any number of other places. But I came to you. I thought I was doing you a favor."

He sighed. "Roy, please don't make my life difficult. Of course we're interested or I wouldn't be sitting here talking to you. But there are legal things to consider. It's a question of following standard procedure. We have to cover ourselves. We require a copy of the tape so we won't have to worry about getting sued by Hartwell—or his wife or his publisher. Do you understand? Now, come on, you live downtown, right? Get back here with it, and I'll take you to lunch." He smiled. "Fontana di Trevi, how's that sound? I'll wait right here."

Then he looked down at my hand again, which I had bandaged with a strip of kitchen towel and some adhesive tape the night before. There hadn't been any Bandaids. "What did you do to it?" he inquired solicitously.

"Nothing. Cut it on some ice."

"Ice?" His eyes met mine for a second, then looked away. "In November? Ice?"

"Things are a lot colder down on the street, Jeffrey," I said peevishly. "You should check it out sometime." And I walked out to the elevators.

* * *

He hadn't given me the cab fare after all, so I took the Lexington Avenue local downtown. Thanksgiving was coming soon and several people lurched through the subway car collecting donations for the needy.

"Help give the homeless a nice turkey dinner with all the trimmings, folks; help Catholic charities," a big, wild-looking guy in cowboy boots sang out, shaking a can under people's noses. "What's the matter, lost the holiday spirit?" he said threateningly to one old couple who cowered against their seats. Everybody else in the sparsely populated car turned to stone, but then the guy disappeared into the next car.

Across from me sat a man biting his nails to the raw nubs. He mumbled to himself now and then but always chewed—chewed incessantly, remorselessly, savaging his fingers. He was a middle-aged albino, with black horn-rimmed glasses and blotches of darker colored skin against the pale pink. No doubt a dozen Thanksgivings had come and gone with him still devouring himself. I felt queasy and when the train pulled into the 51st Street station I considered leaving to get some air, but decided that nailing down the article as soon as possible was more important.

At 51st Street several people got on, including a sleek, tanned, wealthy-looking man dressed in a beautiful double-breasted flannel suit and spotless raincoat, accompanied by another man who walked with a limp and acted deferentially toward him. As the train jerked to a start they paused in the middle of the car, grabbing for the straps right over my head and continuing a heated conversation about stress convection curves. Suddenly, a minute or two into the tunnel, the train came to a dead halt and a garbled, incomprehensible voice screeched over the p.a. system.

"Vonnh gu tram maxxit sabit CAM," it said twice.

The two men glanced at each other, then the sleek one looked down at me and asked, "Excuse me, but does this mean the train is disabled?"

I shrugged, while a scruffy young white guy sitting next to me tittered and said, "Whadd*you* think?"

We all waited silently, then the sleek one turned to his major-domo and hissed in an urgent undertone, "Frank, damn it, I *told* you we should have taken a taxi. The last time that limo broke down Potamkin sent us another one, remember? We could've called them. But no, the subway's faster, you said. Now what?"

Frank looked down at the floor, his face reddening. Suddenly the guy sitting next to me started breathing heavily. Cheaply dressed, with ratty hair and filthy hands, he became progressively more excited until, his eyes widening, unable to contain himself, he pointed a finger in the sleek man's face and said, "I know you! You're Jerry Ballantine, the big real estate developer! I saw your picture in the *Daily News!*"

In the most astonishing, seemingly coordinated way, the two immediately retreated to the center of the car, spread their legs and swung their arms loosely at their sides, bracing for an attack. Had they learned this move in some corporate karate class? But instead of rushing them, the guy next to me opened his mouth and in a fiery voice made eloquent by pent-up emotion, exclaimed, "Always! Always in my life I've wanted to talk face-to-face with somebody like you, and now here you are! I can't believe it!"

The two men said nothing, staring past their interlocutor toward the end of the car.

"Why have you got millions and me nothing?" the guy asked with magnificent directness, standing up but not approaching them.

"Can you answer that? Can you tell me why you're born with a silver spoon in your mouth and go to the best schools and make connections there for life with your important friends? Why you come into this world set up with a bankroll and all the right contacts, so you can make more money buying out blocks of houses where poor people live and tossing them out on the street? While I have to drive a fucking truck fifty hours a week and pay off the unions if I want to keep working? Why is this country filled with such bullshit?" he said, turning to me for confirmation, since he was getting no response.

I had something else on my mind, however: we had been sitting in the tunnel for ten minutes now and the albino across from me was getting more and more upset. Rocking back and forth, chewing madly on his nails, he was beginning to roll his eyes and spittle leaked from his mouth. I wondered if this signalled the onset of an epileptic fit. Should I try to help or would that only precipitate a crisis?

"It sucks, this country," the guy went on, addressing the two men again. "There's two classes of people, rich and poor, and the rich have about as much compassion for the poor as I do for a fucking hamburger. They just eat them up, they eat them for lunch and the system says no problem. No problem!" he shouted grandly, taking a step toward them in his frustration.

"No problem, my ass! It's all by chance that I'm me and you're you!"

They tensed, readying themselves for combat, while the other passengers froze. But then the albino self-eater jumped up, ran to one of the doors and began pounding on it, shouting. "Fire sale! Fire sale! Damaged merchandise!" A minute later the car filled with fumes and acrid black smoke. There was panic then, and just as everybody began desperately trying to pry open the doors and escape, yelling for help and coughing, a squawking voice came over the p.a. and the train sprang forward, throwing people to the floor.

By the time I got to St. Mark's Place—after arriving at Grand Central, we were all fed oxygen from masks by members of the transit crew and given two tokens each—it was nearly three o'clock.

. . . That sickening feeling you get in New York City, coming up the stairs to your apartment and seeing the door ajar, knowing you had locked it before you left . . . As I pushed open the door there was a voice behind me in the hall.

"Sticks and stones will break your bones," it said, and I was clubbed in the back of the head and lost consciousness. When I awoke I found myself trussed and lying in the bathtub in the darkened bathroom, a rag stuffed in my mouth. I could breathe through my nose but in spite of that I felt I was choking to death. To keep from panicking I concentrated on working free from the extension cords which I later found had been binding my hands. That took about half an hour. There was an ache at the base of my skull which intensified when I finally opened the door to the kitchen and saw that the apartment had been ransacked. Somebody had trashed every room. My tapes and files were gone, my typewriter and tape recorder too, as were Dana's antique rocking chair—the best piece of furniture in the house—and some

Indian pottery. But they hadn't taken the records or the record player, they hadn't taken the TV or my camera. Then on the kitchen wall I found spray-painted in red letters OPW . . . OPW? What the fuck . . . And looking down I saw two large turds on the floor. I could hardly believe my eyes and involuntarily bent down to get a better view . . . OPW . . .

Thunderstruck, I kept repeating to myself, "Hartwell did this, Hartwell did this." I couldn't stop shaking. I tried breathing deeply, regularly, in order to calm down, but surges of alarm kept flooding my system. I sat down at the kitchen table and tried to think about what had taken place. Had Hartwell or somebody sent by him been here, clubbing me over the head and shitting on my floor? Or had I simply been ripped off by just anybody, as had happened four times already since moving to the city? But why didn't they take the TV, the record player, the camera? Was it because I'd interrupted them? Or, on the contrary, because they hadn't come for those things in the first place? . . . Come on, butthole, all your tapes and files are missing, all of them. All the interviews you've ever done, all the articles you've written. The cassettes containing your interview with Hartwell are gone, and you still think it wasn't him? So what if Dana's chair is gone, and her Zuni pottery and kachina doll? Wouldn't Hartwell take those things in order to mislead me?

The back of my head ached, echoing pain across my temples to my forehead. My wrists were black and blue and my infected palm throbbed with each beat of my heart. I couldn't tell if my fear of Hartwell was irrational. I needed another person's advice, and that had to be Dana's. I had to find her, I didn't know anybody else well enough with whom to discuss this.

I should have called Jeffrey to explain why I hadn't showed up, but what was the point? Obviously *Rolling Stone* wouldn't publish my article without solid documentation, and no doubt that held true for the other big magazines as well. It looked like I wasn't going to have the chance to betray Hartwell after all. This article should have gotten me a couple thousand dollars, but without the evidence it was worth nothing. Besides, I was scared. Maybe losing the tapes was the best thing that could have happened, because now I knew how serious Hartwell was. He would do anything to prevent me from publishing that article. But he had the cassettes now. Hopefully it would occur to him that my credibility was gone along with the tapes, that he needn't concern himself with me any longer. He's got what he came for, I kept telling myself, maybe now he'll leave me alone. He'd been so violent with me the day before in the park. And taking the tapes was one thing, but jamming a rag down my throat so that I almost suffocated . . .

That voice behind me in the hallway, it certainly hadn't been Hartwell's, but something about it sounded familiar nonetheless. And what about those letters, OPW? . . . At that moment I remembered the pistol I'd found in the drunken guy's attaché case the week before. Had Hartwell taken that too? Down on my knees under the kitchen sink, pulling away rags and bottles, I found the little black gun. I pulled it out, blowing dead roaches off of it. Then I looked for the attaché case but it was gone.

"Suck on this, big boy," I cackled gleefully, brandishing the Baretta in the air. "Now we'll see who beats up on whom!"

Making certain the safety catch was on, I wrapped the gun in a towel and put it inside my knapsack. That's when I realized, God knows what I'd do with it if he ever jumped me again. Hartwell moved so quickly everything would be over before I had the chance to unwrap it. Laughing ruefully I decided to leave the gun at home after all . . . Probably end up shooting myself in the foot . . . Walking around the apartment I found myself in front of the bathroom mirror and saw a soot-blackened face with deepening frown lines between the eyes. I swallowed two Valiums.

I had to talk to Dana. I decided to visit her grandmother at her nursing home up in the Bronx. Visiting hours, as I remembered, were until six P.M. on weekdays and it wasn't yet four. There was a chance Dana had been to see her since leaving me. Grandma Bessie hated Sibyl and Lou, but I was sure she didn't think much of me one way or the other; I'd only been there once. If they hadn't turned her against me and she knew where Dana was, maybe I could convince her to tell me. It certainly was worth the trip up there. I felt like, with my two free tokens and all, I didn't have anything to lose.

SEVEN

Sunset Towers was on Bainbridge Avenue above Gun Hill Road in a neighborhood of monolithic apartment houses a few blocks from Woodlawn Cemetery. They certainly picked a convenient location. Not far to travel when it comes time for the final journey. I wondered if that was a discreet element of the sales pitch to families of prospective patients.

Dana had mentioned how important it was to bring a gift when you visited somebody in a nursing home, so I stopped at a florist and bought Grandma Bessie a large bunch of daffodils. That left me with ten dollars and eighty-five cents. At the front door an old lady in a wheelchair sat staring into the street. Beside her a sign announced, "We reserve the right to inspect all packages entering or leaving the building." Silver and blue Stars of David hung from the ceiling, twirling slowly. A security guard poked around in the flowers and told me to sign in at the front desk.

Bessie didn't recognize me when I walked into her room.

"You're a little late with the bouquet, young man," she said, gesturing to the empty bed next to hers. "Mrs. Hershon passed away last week, God rest her soul."

"No, these are for you, Bessie."

"Who said for you to call me Bessie, you little *kocher*?" she spat out irritably. "What do you think I am, the maid?"

"But don't you remember me? I'm Dana's boyfriend."

"Dana . . ." she whispered, looking at me blankly. But then her eyes lit up.

"You're Marshall," she said, and lifted an arm off the bed. "So now

it's Dana's husband, not even my own flesh and blood anymore. Forget about my daughter, you think she visits me? Once a month Sibyl
comes for five minutes and when she does she brings me candy, even
though she knows I can't eat it." She sighed. "Sit down, Marshall, and
let me smell those wonderful flowers."

She inhaled deeply a few times, then looked out her window at the
apartment house wall across the street. Her room smelled of disinfec-
tant. It was painted bright yellow, just like the daffodils, with construction paper Thanksgiving decorations—pumpkins, pilgrims, and
a rosy-wattled turkey—here and there on the walls. Both beds had low
railings around them.

"A perfect stranger," she said dreamily. Her hands shook faintly on
the bedcovers. Bessie looked noticeably frailer than six months before.
Her hair, which in her youth had been black and glossy like Dana's,
now was entirely white. Her face seemed to have grown insubstantial.
As we sat there in silence I began to feel uncomfortable. The Valiums
I'd swallowed on an empty stomach had taken effect and I struggled to
keep awake. Not having any idea what she might consider an interesting topic of conversation, I finally asked how she felt today.

"Much better than you think, judging from the way you're staring at
me," she replied, the color flaring back into her cheeks. "I shouldn't be
here, really," she said with conviction. She pointed to the walker in the
corner of the room. It looked like a TV cart with handles. "They think
I'll be tied to that thing for the rest of my life, but I wouldn't need it if
only someone took the trouble to help me learn to walk again. But the
therapy they provide here is a travesty, they refuse to listen to a word I
say. And after all why should they? As Ed Reed says, they're getting
paid to be permanently hard of hearing."

"Who is Ed Reed?"

"And what business is that of yours?" she shot back.

"I—I'm sorry, I thought maybe I knew him."

She laughed. "How could you know Ed? You're just a boy!"

We sat there in silence once more, then she added softly, ". . . to be
professionally hard of hearing, that's what he said. And he's right, too,
even if he is a crazy *goyim*."

Suddenly conspiratorial, she turned to face me and whispered, "The people who run this place are awful, Marshall. You wouldn't believe half the things that go on here. They steal checks and jewelry from the more helpless ones. And if any of us breaks the rules we're all made to suffer. We're forced to watch television with the sound off. How do you like that? . . . *Gadles ligt oyfn mist* . . . And they call us by our first names, as if we were children, while we must address them as Mr. or Mrs. This is why I snapped at you when you came out of nowhere calling me Bessie. I'm Mrs. Goldman, Mrs. Avram Goldman, do you understand?"

She fell silent again. Nurses and orderlies walked by in the hallway, peering into the room at Grandma Bessie. The late afternoon sun was leaving the cornices of the building across the street. Their detailed scrollwork flared briefly reddish-gold and then went out like a light. After another five minutes had gone by she began to hum softly, staring into a corner of the room as if I weren't there. I was just about to leave when she said matter-of-factly, "I know you're not Dana's husband, you're not big and strong enough. My Dana wouldn't marry someone like you, you don't even look Jewish."

She glared at me and added, "*Fun loyter hofenung ver ikh nokh meshuge* . . . What does that mean? Translate it! You don't know, do you? How can you be Jewish? Well, I'll tell you what it means: Overfeed on hope and you'll sicken with madness."

Turning away and looking at the wall she added in a flat, dull voice, "Did Avram send you to spy on me?"

A shiver ran down my back. Avram, Bessie's husband, had been dead for at least ten years.

"He's such a tyrant, you know. 'Only the best for you, my Bessele,' he says, 'only the best.' And this is what I have to show for it, this is what I get for listening to him all those years, for raising that snake of a daughter, for waiting and waiting like a prisoner until finally I *am* a prisoner."

"I'm sorry," I said helplessly and then added, "But you're wrong, Mrs. Goldman. I love Dana. That's why I came here to see you. I have to find her."

She gave me a searching look. The light in the room had grown quite dim.

"My marriage was an entirely different affair than yours. Avram Goldman ... He was such a beautiful boy when we were young—open and considerate, not like the crude Mister he became later on here in New York, I can assure you. But a man is what he is, not what he used to be ... Do you know how we came to be married, Marshall? Avram used to love the woods, especially the great park fifteen miles south of Kiev, Pushcha-Voditsa, it was called. An ancient park, it used to be a hunting preserve for the nobles. We were sitting under a tree in the forest, we were as innocent as children, this is 1916 I'm talking about, I was seventeen years old. We weren't thinking of marriage, believe me! Avram Goldman had barely kissed me even once and I had my eye on another boy. And in the middle of the afternoon, in that wonderful forest under the trees, it was May and so lovely, do you know what happened?"

She turned to face me and repeated forcefully, "Have you any conception of what took place then?" Her face hardened. "Well, my fine young friend, we heard a distant sound of horses, many horses, and soon the militia appeared, twenty men with rifles and swords, and they surrounded us. The *komandant* got down off his horse and said—in Ukrainian, of course, it sounds so much more brutal in Ukrainian but you wouldn't understand—he said, 'What are two filthy Jews like you doing here in the forest? You're revolutionaries hiding guns out here, no?' He turned to Avram and said, 'Maybe we should kill you now, without spending all day looking for the weapons. What do you say, men?' They all laughed. You see, not long before many Jews had been killed in the village at the western edge of the forest, and the survivors had rounded up a few miserable firearms to protect themselves. Naturally they were murdered, as soon as the weapons were discovered. And poor Avram, with wonderful presence of mind considering that he was afraid they would slit his throat and do with me God knows what, said, 'No, your excellency, this is my fiancée, we're to be married soon, I've just proposed to her.' Because I would have been a tramp in their eyes if he had told them anything else. And, of course, in Russia in those days military officers were empowered in certain cases to conduct marriage ceremonies. So, even though we were Jews, what do you think? In order to prove to this anti-Semite thug that we weren't revolutionaries, we consented to be married by him that day right then and there in the forest . . ."

"God almighty," I exclaimed. She had tears in her eyes.

"And that's not the end of it," she said. "My daughter was conceived that day, Marshall, under the eyes of all those men with their guns and their knives. While they sat on their horses and watched. We were forced to do it. We had no choice. So, you see, when you tell me in your anxious voice that you are looking for Dana, all I can say is that you live in a different world. You're like spoiled infants who can't make up your minds. I never even had the opportunity to choose . . ."

A nurse stepped into the room holding a blue glass vase and said, "How are we today, Bessie?" Getting no reply she picked up the daffodils. "What pretty flowers! How lucky you are to have such a thoughtful visitor. We'll put them in some water right away." She filled the vase at the sink and arranged the flowers in it, setting them on the dresser. "Twenty minutes more," she said to me and left.

We sat there silently for some time, then Bessie began humming softly.

"Have you ever been to the Cafe Royale, Marshall, on Second Avenue? You really ought to go, it's close to all the Yiddish theaters and not far from where you and Dana live . . . Such a grand place, the Cafe Royale, so many smartly dressed people. The foremost artists and intellectuals of our day, arguing and laughing until late. All the great actors, lionized like royalty . . . Stella Adler was such a conceited girl, you can't imagine. Her long hair in the mirror at the entrance, combing it out while all the men watched. Their voices quavered when they talked to her. 'Is she a bitch or a goddess?' Morris Lipansky used to ask sarcastically, but even Morris was in love with her. Not to mention my Avram, of course. As devoted as a lapdog. 'Hurry,' he would say, 'we have to close the shop now and go eat, I want to be at the Cafe Royale no later than ten; she will be there.' . . . *She* . . . Avram can be such a *schnorer* sometimes. And then sometimes so cruel, so thoughtless, you'd think he had been brought up among the Cossacks . . ."

"Among the butchers," she added in a voice hollow with hate, then turned and looked at me with a puzzled, exasperated expression. "What do you want from me? Dana's a good girl. She comes to see me when she can."

I didn't know what to say except goodbye. I rose to leave and was on my way out the door when my path was blocked by a sturdy-looking, nearly bald little man dressed in pajamas and holding a cane. His mischievous eyes were a deep marine blue and his nose looked as if it had been broken more than once.

"Is this punk making trouble for you, Bessie?" he asked, peering around me. "Is he on the way in or on the way out?" Planting the handle of his cane in my chest he pushed me back into the room. "Do you make a habit of standing in doorways like a cigar store Indian? If so, in the name of our Saviour, please back off!"

Bessie giggled, "It's Dana's husband, Ed. Leave him alone. He thinks she's hiding under my bed, just like you did. Remember?"

He frowned at her. "No state secrets, now, my dear. How do we know he isn't from the Mafia?"

They both laughed uproariously. The change that came over Bessie when Ed Reed appeared was remarkable.

"He thinks I'm joking, don't he?" Ed remarked. "The fact is, son, if you had half the sense of your grandmother here, you'd accept the testimony of those who have already begun to listen and to look." He stuck his face in mine, raising his eyebrows dramatically. Ed Reed was of Irish stock, he told me later, but even then I was wondering how he could be a patient in a Jewish nursing home. "Yes," he said, "the thing called *Our Thing* is no further away from you than your nose. We have a fancy place here, you understand, no roaches, no mice, but the home for invalid Yids is merely a cover-up, a front. It's really more like a country club, isn't it, Bessie? At least on the upper floors. A life of splendor for the few. And I, in my innocence, thought that within the priestly confines of my glorious diocese of St. Hilary's I had seen everything in the way of lost illusions. But I was wrong. I've lived a sheltered life!"

"Do you mean the staff here?" I asked.

"No, no, no! The poor boys and girls in white may be our jailers, but they're decent folk for the most part who get on the bus after work and go home to their little rooms like all other working stiffs. No, sonny, I'm referring to the single man with the funny dago name who's on the payroll of this institution without doing any work and who lives in the penthouse upstairs," he said, gesturing at the ceiling.

Bessie gave him a warning look and, suddenly deflated, he sighed and hobbled across the room to sit down on the other bed. He looked tired now, and vulnerable. I didn't know if he'd been joking or not, and to change the subject I asked about the Christmas carols I'd heard on the p.a. system when I'd visited the previous spring with Dana.

Bessie moaned. "They do that occasionally to test us. Those who don't complain vociferously like good Jews, lose their exercise privileges on the theory that they are no longer aware of their surroundings and would only do themselves harm. It saves them money on towels and things."

Ed said, "Oh, come now, Bessie. You know the music is for poor Mrs. McGonnigle and me, lost here among the Hebrews. They simply were a few months late with it, is all."

I was surprised that so thoroughly Jewish a person as Bessie Goldman had made friends with this man. Earlier, when he'd uttered the words *invalid Yids* I'd expected Bessie to explode but instead she had smiled.

We introduced ourselves and I found out he was a widower from Manhattan, with two sons who lived in California and never visited him, and a daughter in the Bronx. For many years he had been a high school gym coach in Inwood. More recently, he had lived with his daughter and son-in-law in Riverdale, but in April he somehow hurt his leg and had trouble walking. Sometimes he couldn't move around at all, other times he felt fine. They helped him pay for doctors and physical therapy for a while, but when he failed to improve they insisted he go to a home. Just as the Millers had done with Bessie, they had forced him to transfer his remaining assets to them, whereupon he became formally indigent and the Government subsidized the cost of his stay at Sunset Towers through Medicaid. Even though he had paid into social security for years, Medicare itself only covered acute episodes, not the chronic illnesses of old age. To qualify for long-term coverage you had to be destitute.

"I am incarcerated in this place," he said matter-of-factly, "due to the underhanded shenanigans of the man my daughter married. He wanted what little money remained in the old flannel sock, and in the bargain have me out of the way. My splendid Catholic family put me in with a bunch of dying Jews because it's conveniently located, you see. Just a ten minute ride from Riverdale, don't you know. As Mrs. Hagenheimer said to me this morning at breakfast," and here his voice shot up into a high falsetto, "'For forty-five years my Herman and I denied ourselves for the children, we worked hard preparing ourselves for retirement, and this is the thanks we get!'"

He shook his head mournfully and looked down at his hands. "Now old people are having to sue their own children to keep from being dropped in the compost heap. Have you heard about that, Bessie? Some guy down in Jersey, it was on the news last night.'"

A nurse appeared and said, "I'm afraid visiting hours are up, young man." I asked Bessie if I could see her again and was saying goodbye when, behind me, I heard an indignant snort. We all looked up to see Sibyl Miller standing in the doorway, dressed in a fur coat and holding a box of chocolates. Her frosted beige hair glistened in the harsh hallway light. She was apoplectic.

"What are *you* doing here?" she hissed at me. "Who do you think you are? You haven't made this family suffer enough without imposing yourself on my poor defenseless mother? Ruining one member of my family wasn't good enough for you?"

She took a step toward me. "Or have you heard from Dana and not told us?"

"What's wrong with Dana?" Bessie asked.

"We hoped we could keep this from you, Bubba, but my poor Dana is gone." She began whimpering. Bessie eyed her skeptically. Sibyl collapsed into a chair next to me. Then she asked her mother, "What does this pathetic creature want from you? What's he doing here—

spreading lies about Lou and me? I suppose *we're* the reason our daughter has vanished from the face of the earth."

Bessie sat up in bed and took a deep breath. Her features seemed to fill out. "I don't know what you're talking about, Sibyl. All I know is that this sympathetic young man is Dana's husband. He has spent more time in my company in one visit than you do in ten, and you're the daughter I raised from nothing."

There was a hushed silence. Ed Reed studied the wall beside him. Sibyl stood up and, narrowing her eyes, said icily, "How can you compare me to this—this *freeloader*?" She began shivering, dancing around the room with little, mincing steps, barely under control. "So he's passing himself off as Dana's husband, now, is he? And you, who have trouble remembering your own name half the time, you have decided that he's better company than your own flesh and blood."

Bessie and Ed looked at me. "I don't know where Dana is," I said, "and I never claimed to be her husband, Mrs. Goldman."

I turned on my heel and left Bessie's room. As I walked down the hall I heard a voice from one of the other rooms repeat tonelessly, "A blue moon is a new moon, no moon at all . . ."

Riding in the first car of the IRT train headed back to Manhattan, I found myself at the window at the very front, watching the Bronx rush by. At each elevated platform dozens of people waited to get on the train, but the first car remained nearly empty. Just before we went underground, a beautiful Puerto Rican girl got on. Dressed in army surplus battle gear, she couldn't have been more than fifteen. A rhinestone skull and crossbones, with ruby-red eye sockets, was pinned to her chest. As the train zoomed underground she got up from her seat and joined me at the window. At a loss for words, I simply turned toward the void rushing up at us and we both watched, transfixed, as the bulb-lit track sheathed in its dark tunnel jerked from right to left or flattened out, shivering, straight ahead. As the train pulled out of the larger stations a variety of tunnels would present themselves, holes angling off to nowhere. But the train never hesitated, immediately picking one and hurtling down it into the darkness.

* * *

Tuesday morning, as soon as I woke up, I made a pot of espresso and stood in the middle of the kitchen looking at the big red letters spray-painted on the wall . . . OPW . . . Were they the initials of somebody's name? Did they stand for a motto of some kind? I couldn't shake the suspicion Hartwell was still after me and before long I was sitting at the window, watching the street. It was noticeably colder today and the few passersby hurried through the raw west wind. The brownstone caryatids across the street stared straight ahead as usual, gently enigmatic. Two flights up, a man framed by white gauze curtains sat motionlessly. Above his head a pale yellow window shade, and behind him, in the depths of the apartment, barely visible, stood an old woman. She faced him, bent over and motionless. Was the man looking at me? Why, after five minutes, had neither of them moved?

Dinner the night before had cost three dollars. Soon the seven I had left would be down to zero. Then what? I went back into the kitchen and began poking in the peanut butter jar. Out in the hall I heard a conversation in Czech between the old woman who lived next door—occasionally she sat at her window, too, shouting denunciations and hexes at the passersby—and her husband, a muscular man in his sixties, usually monosyllabic, who owned the building but didn't live here. He camped out permanently with another woman in Queens, I'd been told. Only some problem with the tenants or his wife's periodic spells of madness brought him into Manhattan. They were arguing about something, and their voices sounded heavy and ornate, like medieval weapons. Hers rose several notches, becoming shrill as they entered her apartment and the door closed behind them.

The phone rang. It was Richard Pinkus, asking about Dana. He sounded upset. "Man, I've been trying to reach you for days. Where is she?"

I laughed. That's exactly what I'd demanded of him at his loft. "I don't know, Richard," I replied. "The police won't look for her unless her parents initiate the process. You've never had the pleasure of meeting them, but they know she's missing. There's nothing more I can do."

He growled at me and hung up.

A vivid image of Lou Miller's diamond pinkie ring flashed before my eyes. His voice sounded in my ear—the talk of *shicksas* and *shvartsas*, of going in with a consortium of doctors on a race horse in Florida. And then those whispered asides, strictly man to man, winking broadly, of how great the floor shows in Vegas are. And in the next breath bragging about their season tickets to the New York City Ballet—"Sibyl insists on going to watch those pansies dance," he says, rolling his eyes in mock discomfort . . . For a moment I thought Lou Miller might have been behind the break-in at the apartment. It certainly fit with his brutally forthright style. Maybe he'd hired somebody to take a look around . . . I moaned and rubbed my eyes, forcing him out of my mind.

From the floor below came more voices. Howls of laughter, hyper shrieks and recriminations, imitations of dogs barking and sirens wailing, sarcastic mimicry of children crying. Then the phone rang again. This time it was my mother's imperturbable, heavily accented voice.

"How are you, my lovely son? Well, I hope? And how is Dana? Are you having friends come for Thanksgiving, or are you going out? Your father and I plan to stay in, God willing. Maybe the Bermans will drive up from Cincinnati, that would be nice, but Leo Berman works so hard, you know. They'll probably just stay home. In any case, they're supposed to call back soon to let me know, so I can't talk for very long. I just wanted to see how you were and to wish you two a happy birdy day." She chuckled softly. In spite of the fact that my parents had been living in this country since the beginning of World War II, they still looked on American customs and holidays as if they were quaintly arbitrary.

At a loss to reply, I sat there holding the receiver until she said, a note of concern in her voice, "Roy? Is everything all right? Is there something wrong with the connection? The telephone company really has some nerve charging what they do for the service they provide, but that's monopoly capitalism for you." She chuckled again, "I was just talking about it the other day to Sadie Cohen . . . You remember the Cohens, don't you? Sadie and Barney? You were hardly more than a child when they left Plainview for California, but now Barney has a

new job in Chicago so we'll get to see them for Chanukah, I'm sure . . .
A real *mitzvah* for us . . . I'm just sorry they didn't return before the
High Holy Days, but as your father says, we can't have everything.
They're such nice people, such *gutn mentshen*, the Cohens. I was so
upset when they left Plainview, do you remember? After they moved,
we were the only ones left in the entire county. It made me want to
leave too, of course, but what could we do? We had the store and
everything, and as your father says, it's a living . . . Roy, are you there?"

I cleared my throat. "Yes, mother, I'm here. I've just had a few problems lately, that's all . . ." Now why did I go and say that? My parents
hadn't the slightest idea what my life was like. Whenever they called,
no matter what was happening, I conveyed the same message—everything was fine, I was busy writing articles. Dana was painting, the
weather was great. And how about the weather out there? Has it
snowed yet? Is it too hot for words?

"What did you say, dear? Is something wrong? What problems?"

Turning away from the receiver, she mumbled something to my
father who, as I knew, was sitting nearby. My mother always was the
one to call me, while Pop listened from the background, "too busy to
come to the phone." Actually, after all the years first in England and
then in America, his English was still quite poor.

"Your father wants to know what you mean by problems."

I took a deep breath. "Look, Mother, I know you don't have anything to spare, really, but do you think you and Pop could lend me
some money for a while? Not much, of course, three hundred dollars
would be plenty . . . I just have a few problems," I repeated idiotically.

There was a long pause during which she put her hand over the
receiver while discussing my momentous request with my father.

"You know, dear," she offered tentatively, "if you're ever truly in
need . . ." I waited, but that was it.

"But I *am* in need!"

"What do you mean, darling? The last time we talked, after the
High Holy Days, you said everything was all right. Aren't you still
working for that magazine, whatever it's called? You'll have to forgive
me but I can never remember the name, we're so busy here . . . Anyway, your father says we really don't have the money now. Of course, if

you really needed it I'm sure we would be able to send you something, but we must prepare well in advance for such a thing, darling. I needn't remind you that we're hardly well-to-do, like Dana's parents. Have you asked them for anything? They're such, well, unusual people, but I'm sure they would come to their daughter's aid. As for us, dear boy, there's an old Yiddish saying, *Yidishe ashires iz vi shney in merts . . .*"

She paused and sighed. "But you wouldn't know the meaning."

It had always been a special sadness for them that I refused to learn Yiddish even though it was spoken every day in the home. Early in my childhood I developed a block against remembering more than a few words. They were devastated that their only child in an alien land had given in so completely to the scourge of assimilation, embracing American culture with a vengeance. When I was twelve years old we used to have titanic fights over rock and roll, with my parents breaking my Little Richard 45s, my Elvis and Jerry Lee Lewis. I had consented to be bar-mitzvaed only after they agreed to let me listen to whatever music I wanted.

"It means, Jewish wealth is like snow in March," she said, and then continued in an innocent tone of voice, "and now that I think of it, Dana herself doesn't have a job, is that correct? It hurts sometimes, I know, but one has to be realistic in this world. People such as us don't have the luxury to live in a land of make-believe. Now, your father says that, as soon as the bank opens on Friday morning, after Thanksgiving, he'll arrange to have twenty-five dollars sent to you . . ." She lowered her voice. "He went into the store just now to take care of a customer, so I'm telling you that I'll try to convince him to send fifty, but . . . well, here he is again, I guess they didn't want to buy anything. I'm telling you, Roy, you'd think the Great Depression was upon us again. You wouldn't believe the number of people who come into the store nowadays simply to finger the merchandise, like diabetics in a candy store . . ." She chuckled again.

It was hopeless, I'd known that before I asked, but they had called me, after all. Twenty-five bucks!

"Roy, we must get off the line, I don't want to inconvenience the Bermans who are probably trying to reach us at this very moment. We love you, my wonderful boy, you know that. If anything really, truly is the matter you'll let us know far enough ahead of time so we can help you to the best of our ability. Please give my love to Dana, and Happy Thanksgiving to you both. Don't eat too much! Oh, wait a moment, wait a moment . . . One more thing. Do you have a *plan*, your father wants to know. If you have a *problem*, he says, then you must have a *plan* in order to solve it."

A plan! Of course, that's what was missing from my life. Why hadn't I thought of it before? Everybody in America had a plan, it's what made the country great. They had plans and I didn't.

"*Keyn mazl*," my mother said softly before hanging up, "good luck."

During most of my childhood we had been the only Jewish family in Plainview, a town of 3,500 in the middle of south central Ohio. For my parents, who had ended up there operating a dry goods store after uncertain peregrinations along the East Coast, Plainview presented a delicate situation which they dealt with by being as unobtrusive as possible. They had been forced to flee Polish Galicia soon after their marriage in 1939 and had moved first to England and then, during the war, to the United States. In Galicia my father had been a railroad station master, but he refused to learn English well enough to find similar work here, so they became tradespeople. They had absorbed a certain diffidence during their years in England which, coupled with their innate sense of discretion, resulted in a self-effacing presence in Plainview.

Although some kids in the town gave me a hard time occasionally, the only serious incident of anti-Semitism took place one Christmas Day after my parents had blithely kept the store open on that holiday for several years. A brick was thrown through the window and the phrase JEWS KILLED JESUS was scrawled across the door. My parents reacted by becoming even more discreet than before, as if, among the townsfolk, their Jewishness was a thing best not called attention to. I felt they were still living—in their heads—in the hostile environment of the old country, but they refused to buy that argument.

"You have no idea what you're talking about," my father would say.

"You're a Jew, Roy, whether you admit it or not. Sooner or later the *goyim* make you well aware of that! As long as we're outnumbered here it's best to stay out of their way. The other races will always look on you with suspicion, ready at any time to flare into hatred. Never forget what I'm telling you." My parents never abandoned the belief that around the next corner it could all happen again, the pogroms, the fascists, the murders.

Meanwhile, at home they compensated for their neutral public image with a cloying, intense Jewishness which pervaded all aspects of our private world and, by the time I was a teenager, made me long to escape. This daily immersion in religious waters included elaborate preparations for and celebrations of all holidays. During important events like Rosh Hashana, Yom Kippur, and Passover, we would journey to Cincinnati or Columbus to join in the services there. But in Plainview their isolation took the form of a curious kind of gloating over their purity. My parents would laugh at the predicament of two ritually clean beings such as themselves stranded in a jungle of pork-eating barbarians. Sometimes it seemed as if the smell of frying bacon and the evangelical rallying cry "Praise the Lord!" were everywhere around us. Occasionally, in front of a customer, they would make jokes in Yiddish about the possibility of his reverting right then and there to his savage, unclean state, sprouting cloven hoofs and a tail.

In the small town mid-America of the Fifties that I knew, the Jews isolated in little places thanked God for each new member of the faith they discovered. For this reason, if no other, I was a profound disappointment to my parents. By the time I finished college they had become more or less resigned to my religious indifference, but still, the approach of the High Holy Days in September always spelled trouble. The long distance phone calls would start, full of exhortations to come home for the services or at least attend *shul* in New York. "There are so many of them in New York," my mother would say despairingly, "you're so lucky." Out of patience, she added once, "Why wasn't I able to have more than one child? It's a curse sent from heaven!"

My father appeared to be shy and retiring, but he had one great passion. After we'd been living in Plainview for some years he installed in the basement of our house a beautiful antique train set. It ran on rails through an elaborate toy landscape he had constructed himself of the towns, lakes, and forests of his native Galicia. He recreated the Carpathian hills of his youth out of balsa wood and plaster and chicken wire, making station masters from bits of cloth and buttons, and cows out of old shoe leather. In the evenings he used to disappear downstairs, running the trains through fields and meadows, their lights flashing and whistles sounding, while in the background, on a portable record player, famous cantors from another age sang their hearts out on scratched old 78s. Only at such times might my father become unruly and obstreperous, locking himself down there with the trains and a bottle of schnapps for hours on end, ignoring my mother's shouted pleas to come upstairs. He'd tell her to go to hell, then, while the whistles rang over the melancholy, high-pitched keening of Yossele Rosenblatt singing *"Hallelu Es Shaym Hashem"* or "Omar Rabbi Elozar." And upstairs in my room, I'd put on "Long Tall Sally" as loud as the volume on my little machine would go.

EIGHT

I went across the street and bought the *Post* and a chocolate egg cream. On the way back I ran into Alvin Garrett, who had played rhythm guitar in Bobby's band, the Frozen Donuts, and was now with a group called Less Work for Mother which was appearing, that night, with the Ramones at CBGB's. He asked me to come see them and said he'd put my name on the list. And also there was this new band everybody'd been talking about that he thought I should catch.

CBGB's was an insane crush of jittery kids. I had two beers and smoked a joint. Alvin's band, eight guys from New Jersey including saxophones and horn, tried to take a lush studio sound someplace new. The crowd hated it. Try again, Alvin, I thought. The place was packed to the rafters and went wild when the Ramones came on doing "Judy Is a Punk," "Loudmouth," and "I Don't Care," songs delivered like bullets, each lasting just a minute and a half. It was a great compacted cartoon of early Sixties music. Sixteen-year-old girls were up on the tables, their asses in my face, going nuts for Joey Ramone, while a line of zonked out people along the wall gyrated like puppets. In spite of how sensational it was to be laminated into the middle of all this pulsating humanity, only rarely did I see people I knew. Everybody was eight or ten years younger, a new crop of faces. My ex-protégé, Peter Arney, came up to me and started a conversation, but the look in my eyes made him stop short and move away. I didn't have anything to say to him and he knew it.

Then the lights came up on the cramped stage at the back of the room and a group called The Final Solution appeared, four middle-class Jewish boys from Queens dressed in yarmulkes and prayer shawls over magenta and chartreuse body sheaths, and black engineer boots. They wore mascara and delicate black lace gloves. Phylacteries dripped like seaweed from their arms as they launched into a series of blatantly provocative anti-Semitic songs. The audience didn't know what to make of them, suddenly everybody was real quiet, intently checking them out. Word had gotten around about this band. A few people even gasped, which in this ultra-hip crowd almost never occurred. "Jew Me Down" detailed the group's difficulties in selling their songs to a record company executive; "Semites Fucking" declared that the only way out of the bloodbath in the Middle East was for Israelis to drop their fanatical purism and mate with the Palestinians, "those pretty Arab girls with the dark, sexy eyes . . ." The lead singer, a skinny, handsome kid with a sardonic grimace on his sensual Mick Jagger mouth, made the whole thing work. He sang with absolute conviction, managing at the same time to strut around the stage in a way that was turning everybody on.

"This next one's called 'The Facochta Duck,' " the singer said, and they kicked into a hard rocking number during which he did the "duck shuffle," a duck walk, rolling step copped from Chuck Berry, while he sang: "Do the facochta duck—that kosher duck, Momma . . . All them Hasids, grooving in a line/ Having theyselves a real cool time/ Musta been somethin' in the food that they ate/ Cause 'em to toss they prayer books away/ Tossing they yarmulkes up in the air/ Suddenly these boychiks don't have a care/ Grab they Yiddishe mommas with they wig-hat hair/ And do that duck—that facochta duck . . . That kosher duck, Momma . . ."

By now everybody was rolling on the floor when from the back of the room near the entrance on the Bowery came an angry shriek and dull, popping noises. We all turned around to see a cloud of smoke drift over us. Then we began coughing and crying. My eyes stung like they were on fire. The tear gas created a situation of instant chaos, and in the midst of it three or four men with ski masks over their faces leaped onto the stage crying out, "Never again!" and savagely beat the members of The Final Solution. Producing leaded canes from under their raincoats, they caved in heads and broke shins. The place at that point was in a mad uproar, as people climbed all over one another to somehow get outside to the fresh air. Meanwhile, the men in raincoats disappeared down the hallway which led to CBGB's dressing room and the rear alley door, waving guns and threatening to kill anybody who tried to stop them. I climbed onto the stage and stood there trying to breathe, not knowing how to get outside. Two boys still dressed in yarmulkes and talliths writhed on the stage beside me. One of them, the lead singer, was curled into a fetal position, moaning and holding the back of his head. I bent down and touched his wound, brought the blood on my fingers up to my nose, and sniffed. Then I lost consciousness.

The next thing I knew I lay spread-eagled and naked on my living room floor, staring up at the ceiling with no memory of how I'd gotten home. The daylight pouring in through the windows stung my eyes and I felt a disabling tension in the pit of my stomach. I lay there without moving, as if I'd entered some blank, larval state. Finally I rolled over onto my side and saw the prescription bottle for Valium. It was empty. Then I saw that, all around me like a green snowstorm, were many tiny pieces of dollar bills. I got to my feet, staggered into the kitchen, and found my wallet on the table. All the money was gone. Had I gotten my wallet sometime during the night and torn the seven dollars to bits? Was this insane sabotage the result of my own two hands? I looked around the apartment but nothing else seemed to be missing. Then I tried to tape the pieces together into bills but there were too many of them, they were like confetti, and I gave up. I threw the pile of shredded paper into the trash.

My right hand, from when Hartwell had stepped on it, felt swollen and throbbed with pain. Stiff all over from a king-size hangover I made my way to the bathroom and unwrapped the dirty bandages, holding up my hand to the mirror. Oddly enough, it looked OK—not even any pus or infection, just a little bruised.

I thought, sure, that makes perfect sense, my hand's all right because *this isn't my hand I'm seeing*. It belongs to somebody else. . . . I wandered around the apartment naked and stunned, blanking out, until I found myself staring at my body in the full-length mirror on the bedroom door. I looked at my receding hairline, at the beginnings of a double chin, at my spreading midsection. I'd been aging fast recently. I stood there looking down at my limp cock and stroking it but nothing happened.

"Fucking bastard," I said. With tears in my eyes I ran to the kitchen and unwrapped the little black automatic. Returning to the mirror I waved the gun around, pointing it at the ceiling, pointing it at my feet, sticking it into my mouth and rolling my eyes. I pulled back the hammer and released the safety catch. From far away I watched myself grimacing and bouncing up and down. Then I aimed at my face and pulled the trigger. My hand jerked back and with a terrific crash the mirror exploded, sending glass everywhere. A moment later the buzzer for the door sounded. Once, twice, again.

Throwing the gun under the bed I pulled on my pants and pressed the button on the intercom. Faye Addison's voice floated into the kitchen. "It's Faye, Roy. Can I come up?"

I couldn't believe I'd actually answered the buzzer, I was fighting for self-control, but as soon as I saw her open, concerned face I melted. I let out a deep breath and embraced her. I hadn't seen Faye Addison in months.

She had dropped Kevin off at his pre-school and was alone. "Sorry I haven't been over to see you," I said. Ten months had gone by since Bobby's death and during that time Faye had withdrawn from the rock and roll scene and from most of their friends. But she had remained close to Dana. Faye had delicate features and soft, light brown hair. She had seemed wonderful for Bobby, somebody with whom he could build a real life. She had grown up as part of a large family on a farm in Washington State. Her sisters and brothers still lived in the Spokane area, but Faye was determined not to go back, even though she'd be able to survive there much more easily than in New York. Meeting Bobby and going away with him had changed her life for good. Faye intended to stay in the city.

She looked around the apartment.

"What a mess," she said. "What's been going on here?"

When she saw Dana's spattered self-portrait on the kitchen wall she turned to me and winced. I felt the blood rush to my face.

"I—I've been . . ."

She held me. "It's OK, Roy . . . You don't have to explain."

We picked our way over the broken glass and sat down in the living room.

"Do you want anything to drink?" I asked, but I was unable to move, so Faye made coffee in the kitchen while I sat on the sofa, staring straight ahead, gritting my teeth. I made faces, telling myself that my rage and fear had no basis in reality. I had to pull myself together. When she returned with the coffee I forced myself to talk about something, I told her about Dana's clandestine visit and the note she had left. Faye couldn't understand why Dana hadn't contacted her.

"I'm so worried," she said. "This isn't like Dana at all. My God, we used to talk on the phone practically every day. You know, I called her parents but they were totally frosty and suspicious. And one thing's for sure, they don't like you much!"

She laughed in that engaging, easy-going Western way of hers. Apparently she'd managed to retain her equanimity after all that had happened to her. I'd always loved the sound of her voice. Faye had seemed a strong person to me even before Bobby died, solid in her commitment to him but not taking any shit from him either. A month before he was shot, she had started sleeping with a guy in one of the other bands. Bobby had freaked when he found out, angry as hell at her but also instantly forgetting about the girls he'd been fucking, realizing in a flash how much Faye meant to him.

"Yeah," I said, "the Millers actually hold me responsible for her disappearance, isn't that too much? I think I'll let them keep looking for her. I'm certainly not going to tell them that Dana's been back here. That's her business, not mine."

We sat there sipping cups of hot, bitter Bustelo. I touched her hand. "You got any cigarettes, Faye?"

"Roy, you know I don't smoke. What's wrong, anyway? Please don't tell me if you don't want to, I'm not prying, but you look so out of it, like you fell down a flight of stairs or something."

"Wow, I don't know, I'm spaced out. It's too complicated to explain. I'm completely broke, though. And I hate to ask, but do you have five bucks I can borrow? Just 'til next week. I'm expecting a check in the mail."

"But I can't, Roy, I spent practically my last cent yesterday buying a turkey for Thanksgiving. You have no idea how difficult it is trying to survive with Kevin to take care of. Single parents in this city, boy, forget it."

Faye was turning thirty and her forehead creased with lines as she talked about her problems with Kevin, his crying jags, his temper, his little illnesses, the clothes she couldn't afford to buy him, the attention he constantly demanded.

"Kevin misses his daddy, he insists on sleeping with me in my bed and snuggling up to me. And you know, I'm not sure if it's the right thing but I let him, his little body feels so warm against my back . . . Being alone like this is a killer. I haven't had much luck finding a boyfriend. I haven't got any time to myself and, besides, who wants to get involved with a single mother?"

She laughed ironically. "But I didn't come over here to complain . . . I came to find out if you've heard from Dana and to invite you to Thanksgiving dinner tomorrow at my place. It'll just be Kevin and me and a few friends—you remember Barbara and Jimmy Cassidy, don't you? Can you come?"

Barbara and Jimmy were theater people living in her building, actors or something, whom I'd met a couple of times.

"That's sweet of you, Faye," I said, but I knew I wasn't going. A turkey dinner in that dreary, cramped apartment with Kevin squalling and Bobby gone wasn't my idea of a holiday. It would bring back the wrong kind of memories.

"I wouldn't be good company now, I better say no. I've got too much on my mind."

Her clear grey eyes were attentive. "On your mind? What do you mean? Are you talking about Dana?"

I grimaced. "See, the problem is I can't write for magazines any-more. I know it sounds crazy but it's the truth. I feel like a baby saying it, but I don't believe in the music anymore. I can't stand working in somebody else's hit factory. Do you understand what I'm saying? I don't want to do *anything*."

"Oh, Roy," she said tenderly. I put my hand on her cheek. It slid down her neck, slowly, to her breast. I pulled her close and we kissed.

"It's all right, Faye," I whispered, stroking her hair, kissing her neck softly. I put my hands around her head and tilted her face up until I could stare into her eyes. "Will you sleep with me?"

Faye and I had been family, she was like a sister to me. Faye trusted me. I'd never wanted her before, it had never entered my mind. I placed her hand on my cock, feeling her resistance.

"Will you?"

"Oh, Jesus," she replied exasperatedly, looking away but rubbing my cock with her hand.

We undressed and moved onto the bed, her thin slight body under mine. I kissed her waist and hips, licked her nipples. I dug my fingers into her pussy. Finally I got hard and entered her. She moaned, gripping my ass, arching her hips into mine. I began to sweat. "Bobby," she whispered.

I drew back, momentarily frozen. Then I slapped her across the face. I hit her hard, my open palm slamming into the side of her head, and suddenly I was rock solid inside her. She was wet, her body rigid from the blow. I forced my hand into her mouth until she gagged. I heard her say yes. I pulled my hand from between her teeth and hit her again. I heard her gasp and saw tears on her cheek. My cock collapsed inside her.

"Faye, I'm sorry."

I rolled off her body and lay staring at the ceiling.

"Faye . . ."

She wouldn't answer.

"Listen, Faye, please believe me, I don't know why I hit you. But I heard you say yes. I thought you wanted me to."

She whispered in a tense, angry voice, "Let's get one thing clear. I didn't say anything. I mean, I *thought* yes, for one moment, at the very beginning, but then I changed my mind. But I never said one word. I *couldn't* say anything. I was afraid to open my mouth, you were hurting me. I never said yes, Roy . . . That's all in your head."

I was incredulous. "What do you mean? You didn't say yes to me? You didn't call out Bobby's name?"

She blushed. "What are you talking about? I could never do that."

She stood up and hurriedly got dressed.

"Don't go!" I shouted. I tried to take hold of her arm but she pulled away. "Leave me alone, Roy. I mean it."

"But this is grotesque, Faye, I'd never keep you from leaving. I only want to apologize. There must have been some misunderstanding. I'm not into hitting . . ."

I felt confused and couldn't finish what I was saying.

"What time is it?" she asked coolly.

Glancing at the clock by the bed I replied, "Five o'clock," and she immediately said, "I have to leave now, please don't stop me. I have to pick up Kevin at pre-school."

She left without looking at me.

"I'm not trying to stop you!" I screamed at her back as she went down the stairs.

Five o'clock, fifteen o'clock, twenty-five o'clock, what the fuck difference did it make? I paced back and forth in the dark, thinking about Bobby, wondering if somehow he was aware of what had just happened.

"I don't know what got into me," I kept repeating, until I realized he couldn't possibly know about Faye and me. He would never know anything past the moment he died. Nothing either Faye or I did would ever bring him back. Tears in my eyes, I went directly to my dwindling stash and rolled a couple of joints. Then I closed the curtains, turned on all the lights, and began going through my hundreds of record albums. Down on my knees tunneling through time, past David Bowie and Led Zeppelin and Crosby, Stills & Nash, back to the source, my treasured blues originals on Chess and Kent and Sun, Specialty and Vee Jay, back to the music Bobby and I listened to in the early Sixties. I waded through endless promo copies of Chicago and

Grand Funk Railroad, back to the music I hadn't heard in too long: early Stones, early Dylan, Tim Harden, Jimi Hendrix, the Velvet Underground, not to mention Buddy Holly and Slim Harpo and Carl Perkins.

I flew into a rage because I couldn't find this or that album and soon I was tossing aside everything I didn't want to hear—the fallout of the last decade's rock explosion—throwing albums against the wall and into the lampshade, calling out their names one after the other as I bent them in two with a snap or tore the covers, going faster and faster until I couldn't stop myself, trashing the Bee Gees, Wings, Herb Alpert, Peter Frampton, Rod Stewart, Spooky Tooth, Elton John, Suzi Quatro, Tiny Tim, Cream, Traffic, Pink Floyd, Moody Blues, Black Sabbath, Jethro Tull, ELO, Santana, the Hollies, the Faces, Three Dog Night, Steppenwolf, the Fifth Dimension, Deep Purple, America, Aerosmith, Rush, the Osmonds, Al Kooper, Fleetwood Mac . . . None of this could touch somebody like Elmore James. Elmore James, my God.

I put "The Sun Is Shinin'" on the record player and listened, entranced: "I had a dream one rainy night/ I was lookin' for my baby/ And you know the sun was shinin' bright . . ."

I played one blues after another, followed by Jerry Lee Lewis and Bo Diddley and early Elvis, and then, finally, "Not Fade Away" by Buddy Holly, which made the hair on the back of my neck stand up, it was so perfect. My head flooding with memories I played that song over and over again, floating back and forth between 1956 and 1976—the distance between them greater than between the earth and the sky.

I ran into the kitchen, opening the big closet which contained— hidden behind coats and jackets, behind the broken slide projector and the once-used cross country skis—cardboard boxes full of letters, photographs, postcards, journals. I found a pair of cracked and fractured old boots—favorites of mine—which I'd never been able to throw away. Hand-made black Spanish boots with strange red leather designs on them, beautifully constructed. I remembered how I couldn't find anything to replace them when they'd finally worn out. That must have been about 1968 or so . . . San Francisco . . . Now here they were staring up at me again, warped and stiff like something from an old hoofer's trunk. I took them out of the closet and put them on. They looked great, although my feet hurt with every step I took. My eyes burning from the weed I was smoking, I continued to sort through everything, reading letters mailed to me by vanished friends, looking through dust-covered boxes of old notebooks. And the photos . . . Here's one of me standing in a forest of towering redwoods, a long-haired, smiling, bell-bottomed dwarf. I couldn't remember who took that picture, not to mention a whole series of blurry shots of me and Bobby in the front seat of a car somewhere in California, stoned and hollow-eyed, grinning like Halloween skulls.

Then I came upon a shoebox full of photos and souvenirs from the trip Dana and I had taken to New Mexico in the summer of '73 to visit friends who had moved out there the previous year from the city. We drove out in an old rusted blue Ford I bought from somebody on Second Avenue for 75 dollars.

Dabney and Frank and Eddie and eight other people were living then in a rambling old adobe farmhouse on a mesa in the San Juan Mountains sixty miles north of Santa Fe. The purple mesa's vistas were intoxicating, especially at night, when numberless stars emitting a clear diamond light crowded the sky, and the summer air smelled of desert plants. Dana and I slept outside in spite of Frank's warning that there were rattlesnakes everywhere around us. Dabney became furious with Dana. She felt we were ignoring her because we wanted to be alone together. Dabney felt isolated out there in New Mexico, only one other woman in the group to talk to and they didn't get along. She'd been looking forward to Dana's visit, counting on Dana for aid and comfort. But Dana and I were close then, we only wanted to be alone together in this magical place. Visiting pueblos during the day, coming back at night to help out with dinner and then retiring to our little fire a quarter mile off in the sagebrush and juniper. We built a sleeping platform because of the snakes, not knowing what else to do, and left cups of water at each corner for them to drink.

I carried the shoebox to the kitchen table and opened it. Inside were envelopes of color photos—snapshots of pueblos, of Dabney and

Eddie and Frank looking disconcertingly sober, and half a dozen of Dana and me. Grinning naked on large rocks, peeking out of our sleeping bags, holding a rattlesnake skin, smiling into the camera with our arms around each other. Under the jumble of yellow Kodak envelopes, matchbooks, and postcards, there lay a bulging white envelope. I tore it open and out fell an embroidered maroon silk pouch with a black ribbon around it. And inside the pouch were the mushrooms.

I emptied the psilocybin on the table, dry mottled pieces of pale yellow streaked with unearthly blue and crumbling into dust. I bent down to examine them, sniffing their faint but gut-wrenching aroma. All at once I sneezed, and inhaled sharply to keep from sneezing again. The dust coated my throat and I began coughing, and the nearly weightless mushroom pieces flew up into my face, settling onto the table again. I got up and drank some water and then brought the half-filled glass to the table and sat down. I coated my finger with the mushroom dust and licked it, then picked up the biggest piece and ate it. Then I ate the rest. And then it all came back to me.

A few nights before we left New Mexico, Dana and I had taken psilocybin together, out on the mesa long after everybody in the house had gone to bed. The night sky was cloudless, as it had been since we arrived, and we lay in our sleeping bags under the stars. The coals of a small fire glowed in a pit in the ground beside us. The series of tremendous inner adventures brought on by taking the mushrooms had just subsided and for the first time in what seemed like hours we were aware again of the fire and the night. When we looked at each other something happened which brought us together making passionate, shaky love. Overwhelmed with tenderness and abandon, we were in sync as never before. But our epic lovemaking eventually gave way to a spooky emptiness, something unlooked-for in the mushrooms suddenly reasserting itself when we tried to talk.

"Where should we go from here? . . . Should we have children?"

I don't know who's asking them, Dana or me, but the questions sound absurd, monstrous, pathetic, like words pronounced by overanxious puppets, and the wonderful, unasked-for identification with each other of a moment ago is gone. We're two people again now, two defensive bundles with separate names, with watchful eyes and different trains of thought, peering out at each other from the other end of the universe inside our skins. And now we're crying, of course—how else can these visions end except to come back into focus as two people weeping for the lonely void in everything while we gaze from behind our separate windows, trying to give each other courage? Swallowing our fear now, we observe each other: is this the same person as before, who's seen in the meantime everything I've seen? Is she a phantom to herself as well, or only to me?

Tremendously upset now, I got up from the kitchen table and began prowling through the apartment, unable to keep still. Thoughts and images came in uncontrollable waves until I felt my head swell and then explode, and, moaning and clutching my ears, I ran through the apartment turning off all the lights and then dove head-first in the dark onto my bed. A wild smell—prehistoric and insatiable—came up through the floor, and a distant, crooning sound like humming. Was it somebody bereaved, mourning over a gypsy corpse laid out on a table? Then I thought I heard Frank Sinatra sing, but I realized it was me, and I wasn't singing. I was opening my mouth and a siren-like wail was coming out. I knew it was deafening, I expected somebody to break down the door at any moment and silence me forever. In the darkened apartment, knobbly, irregular pockets of dull light on the walls soon gave way to a fantastic, lush, purple-black velvet sensorium, in the center of which I hung like a lemur, swaying with the wind and sweating profusely. Rain fell everywhere, it was suffocatingly hot, and in the distance, around the corner of the old shed in which I now lived, I could hear Oliver Hartwell issuing commands to his natives, whose shrieks of joy soon turned into the pitiful squeals of wild animals about to be slain. They came galloping around the corner and charged right into me. The smell of fear on their bodies terrified and paralyzed me. So intent were they on escaping that they never paused to sink their slavering teeth into me. They ran over me and around me, and then, slowly but implacably, came Oliver Hartwell, a very old man now, nearly blind, his beard and moustache white as chalk. He held a cane in one hand which glowed and vibrated like some futuristic toy, and when he pointed it at me his head swelled and began to shine. He smiled and said, "They ought to run a wire from ear to ear."

"They ought to run a wire from ear to ear . . ." He repeated this over and over in a variety of intonations, now sounding contemptuous, now compassionate, now threatening, at times seeming to refer to me, then to himself, then to others. The more he repeated the words the less sense they made, until he was just a frightening old man babbling in front of me, blocking my way, cutting me off from my life. I swung at him with my fist, but it was as if we were underwater, his body dipped backward to avoid me. He pointed the cane at me and this time his head became transformed, his hair dark and sleek. He looked forty years younger, wily and capable and strong. "Your eyes look as if they've been here before," he said, "but you won't admit it. The time to look forward has arrived. You can push the clock back but you can't move it forward, can you? But I . . . I can *push* you forward," and he lunged toward me. I began to scream, to yell in terror, my voice ricocheting off the walls like a rubber ball of fear, bouncing faster and faster, out of control. It came sailing across the room in the dark, a phosphorescent blur, and entered my mouth, choking me. I crawled across the kitchen floor and stood at the sink drinking water in the dark, then I was in the bathroom pulling at the light switch, looking at myself in the mirror, my head a cantaloupe filled with crazy little seeds, thousands of them, they were my thoughts and they jiggled around as I shook my head up and down. This ceased, instantly, as soon as I became aware I was looking in the mirror and seeing myself beside myself. The me in light—and the other me, the hidden one, shadow one. The dark one underneath, shadow man peeking out, showing himself in order to communicate with me. But I wasn't ready to talk. I shook my cantaloupe back and forth. I joined my hands and raised them, spreading the fingers so that when I held them up to the mirror there was only one hand, until I moved the fingers of my right hand and the past—the other hand, shadow hand—sprang up behind it.

Staring at myself looking at myself in the mirror I heard a voice, Hartwell's again, although it sounded low and intense now: "Listen carefully, Sprout, I'll only be saying this once . . . Your present life, seemingly so sharp and real and new, is actually already someone else's past filled with memories. You are living out someone else's future memories, you exist in that mind sometime in the future, and only when and how he or she thinks of you. Do you follow me? The life you're living now is being recollected by someone in the future . . . So if you don't like your life now you must change it, and the only way to do that is by doing what I did, which was to go out and find that person and destroy him. And do you know who that guy in the future is, Sprout? Guess who he is."

I stared into the mirror, dumbfounded. He waited for a reply and when he got none, continued talking, his voice harder now, running out of patience. "*He's you, Sprout.* That's why the gun has come into your possession, don't you understand? You think these things come about by chance? You're mistaken. This is your destiny we're talking about, your fate. Either you destroy that future person or you accept his control over you. But in either case you won't belong to yourself until you stop whining and act. Because now you are nobody. Nothing. You don't exist . . ."

His voice stopped. It had been going on while I made faces in the mirror and now suddenly it was gone. A red rash spread over my face, I was sweating, my head was on fire, and I knew I must be very sick. I saw a death's head in the mirror, a skull which emerged from my head and then sank back into it. I was dying, little time remained before I'd be dead, already the skin on my cheeks had suppurated and turned gray and chalky yellow. My face became rigid and my eyes rolled up into my head. I collapsed onto the floor, striking my skull against the side of the bathtub with a hollow vibrating ring like that of a bell. As if summoned by the sound, dogs with fiercely working jaws came and stripped my flesh, eating my stomach, my liver, my heart. I had to hold onto the side of the tub to keep from being pulled away by their jaws clamped into me and tugging. My tears had long ago dried for the very last time on my cheeks—long ago, on the cheeks of a little boy, five years old. I lay there petrified, unable to move. The wind rushed by overhead, the sub-zero polar wind that sweeps over the high ridges surrounding the mountain where I lay, twelve thousand feet above sea level, staring up at the hard stars in the sky, starving, freezing to death. I must have fallen while hiking, fallen down a precipice to this ledge, sprawled out on the stones unable to move. The insects, tentative at first, soon were working away at me with abandon, like fever blisters all over my back and the bottom of my legs, as if I were tied down to a flaming hot griddle, the contrast between the intense cold on top of me and the searing heat below driving me wild with pain, driving me insane. Little specks of light plunged by overhead, flying saucers or satellites miles away in the frozen night. Nearby—much closer, in fact—I heard a sound of branches being snapped, of something heavy moving toward me, a heady overwhelming smell and then the bear came into view, enormous next to my prone, bleeding body, its fur glistening in the starlight. Nudging me with its cold black nose, rolling me over with its paws and digging into my back, ripping out my kidneys, licking up my spine. The pain was excruciating. But when I couldn't stand it anymore suddenly my spine came alive, I could feel it incandesce as he licked it, slowly and carefully. It lit up, energy surging along a crystal latticework, along the vertebra one by one, an ungovernable energy crackling upward past my neck, into my brain, until I felt utterly alive, pumped up and invulnerable. I began softly chanting, over and over, "You can't burn my bones . . ." while I got to my feet and moved forward. Fantastic shadows were being thrown from the bathroom light into the kitchen. The wall beside me opened up. Slowly I descended, along a slippery, cobbled passageway which led under the streets. Looking up I saw the traffic going by above and heard people's voices in the distance.

Eventually I came to a huge underground cavern like the boarded-up Second Avenue subway excavation site. I stood at the rim of a long, irregular space lit here and there by bare bulbs, its further recesses shading off into gloom. I saw exposed pipes and building equipment, rolls of steel cable and cyclone fence. Clean, well-lighted tunnels, some of them quite large, snaked off in various directions. I looked down at the floor of the cavern and saw myself, naked and whole again, spread out on the ground. A man whose features I couldn't make out approached and poured liquid from a five-gallon can onto my body. He tossed a match and I ignited, going up in a wall of flames, my long hair rising off my head and sparkling as it burned. Nothing was left but my bones. I watched the man fade off into the darkness, and when I looked at my skeleton again it glowed like crystal.

I picked my way down to the cavern floor along a rough path cut out of crumbling bricks and earth, and walked over to my skeleton. I bent down to touch it and sprang back, electrified. "You can't burn my bones," I sang. I felt fabulous, vibrant and full of strength, impatient to get outside again, out into the world. I had my knapsack on my back and was wearing Hartwell's Yankee cap. Choosing one of the tunnels I started walking, but it seemed to go on forever and soon I broke into a steady loping trot, cruising along for what seemed like miles, past occasional mesh-covered light bulbs, and numbers stencilled on the white enamelled brick walls. Finally I came to a metal ladder and, looking up, saw a manhole cover slightly askew, and a crack of daylight. I climbed onto the street and replaced the cover. Looking around, I saw that I was on Mott or Grand or Elizabeth Street— somewhere in Little Italy—and that it was early morning, the streets deserted . . . My cold morning sunshine! My blessed air!

NINE

"Happy Thanksgiving!" I shouted, my voice ricocheting around the frosty streets, bouncing off the buildings, flying into the sky. "Happy Thanksgiving!" What a rush! I began slowly trotting south, heading down Broadway toward the bottom of the island. To the occasional passerby I must have been taken for a jogger out on his morning run, except that anybody paying attention would have noticed my eyes—that stare fixed on the middle distance—would have seen the big grin on my face and the peculiar way I was moving, a sort of shuffling lope, more like a buoyant rolling walk than a trot. I felt no exhaustion as I skimmed along the sidewalks, block after block, past Canal and Chambers and Fulton. Lower Broadway was completely deserted so I moved out into the middle of the street, trotting down the slot between the buildings, past the pale gravestones in the yard of Trinity Church, past the tuning fork of the World Trade Center, past the Customs Building at Bowling Green and into Battery Park. Finally I stood looking out over the water toward the Statue of Liberty, inhaling the salt air and grinning from ear to ear. I had a new name too, a secret name I had acquired in the cavern and which nobody else knew, or would ever know, if I had anything to say about it.

"If I have anything to say about it," I announced in a loud voice. My family name and my past meant nothing to me now. They were arbitrary, accidental, like the slave names the blacks used to talk about. "Blacks used to talk about!" I exclaimed. "From now on call me X, fella, though that's not my name either . . . And if you don't like X then call me Y, I'm not particular . . ." I looked around the park, nobody within forty yards. "I´M NOT PARTICULAR," I shouted at the top of my lungs. I felt invincible. I couldn't get over how bracing the air was down here at the water's edge. To go on like this forever I only had to keep breathing. How fantastic.

"You can't burn my bones," I sang out, my head bobbing up and down as I grinned at the waves glittering in the sunshine. I really felt it then. I'm in control, in control of my life. I'm the only one responsible for what happens. I can change my life. Otherwise I wouldn't be standing here right now in Batter Park. Rigid and impregnable. You'll never find me in my perfect place.

After a while the ferry from Staten Island appeared, sounding its horn, sliding out of view behind the terminal building where it eventually docked. Strangely bundled figures glowing like iridescent mummies spilled out of the terminal and spread across Battery Park, some running, others walking. Two policemen appeared nearby. They were playing with their nightsticks, surreptitiously clicking them together as they walked. When they passed in front of me an unmistakably sensual, yeasty odor wafted through the air. Two burly Irish cops in their navy blue sheaths: were they not-so-secret lovers who had arranged to walk the same beat?

Giggling, I trotted back across the park to the bottom of Broadway. At the end of the park I veered over to a well fed, proper-looking guy in overcoat and spectacles who sat reading the *Times*. "I'm hungry," I announced imperiously. He looked up with a start, the color draining from his cheeks, and pulled some change from his pocket. "This is all I have," he said nervously, "and I don't smoke, either."

Approaching people and laughing—I couldn't stop laughing—by the time I'd returned to the vicinity of Little Italy I had three dollars in change, and I ate two bowls of wonderfully rich lentil soup with escarole at a tiny espresso bar. But I felt awkward indoors. An attempt to make conversation with the proprietors—a rail-thin man, and his pear-shaped wife—fell flat after I remarked on how good the soup tasted. "What else do you expect?" the man replied in a bored voice as he taped a sign to the window: WE CLOSE TODAY AT FOUR P.M.

The old man and his wife were only half-there. Their spirits had vanished while their bodies remained. I felt emanating from these two a terrible, carefully hidden resentment—a force that, if suddenly released, would be powerful enough to bring down the walls of the building around us. They were lost in interiorized corridors of habit, rather than giving themselves to the world around them: the sunlight, the effervescent air, the remarkable beings who drifted by outside their windows. I hurried to finish my soup before the ceiling caved in, and skipped through the doors into the cold sunshine.

Gradually working back into my trot I headed uptown, loping along sidewalks and across intersections, threading my way through knots of people, my eyes straight ahead, my mouth open. Now and then I slowed to a walk, examining shop windows and the faces of pedestrians. People took on the gossamer-light form of apparitions, casting their corporeality before them like shadows on snow. I leaned toward them with an expression of wonderment I couldn't conceal. Somewhere in Chelsea this got me into trouble. A young guy out walking with his girlfriend stared back at me wound tight as a toy, his features hard. "What you lookin' at?" he snarled, and threw a punch which I just managed to avoid. "Your mistake, not mine," I said and then had to hot-foot it up the street with him in pursuit, cursing in Spanish. At the last second his girlfriend called him back.

"*Dejele, es loco,*" she yelled, and abruptly he stopped.

As I trotted up Broadway toward Macy's and Herald Square, I noticed the working stiffs out with their families for a holiday stroll, peering at merchandise in the camera and appliance stores. Everything seemed so arbitrary to me. Take the forty-hour work week. If it were cut in half—if everybody worked twenty hours a week and the system readjusted itself to a new rhythm and volume of output—happier, saner, less compulsive people would result. Therefore, laboring nine to five, fifty weeks a year, amounted to submission to a kind of mass trance. Why was such a trance in place?

Preoccupied by this question I came to a halt on the sidewalk, realizing why I'd always hated holidays. It was on holidays that the prisoners were allowed outside the grounds of their prison. A wave of sadness swept over me. I suddenly became aware of what lay behind the plate glass window I had been gazing at: the store was closed for Thanksgiving but lights inside remained on and I saw square, newspaper-covered cages filled with sleeping puppies of all kinds, piled on top of one another. In the distance a much taller, larger cage contained hundreds of parakeets which skipped back and forth along their perches, opening and closing their beaks. I put my ear to the window but heard nothing.

I walked to Greeley Square. There stood a middle-aged man with the penetrating look of a self-appointed prophet. He had matted blond hair and a full beard and was dressed in a long white robe, his chest covered with strands of prayer beads. Cigarette stains in the beard around his mouth had turned it an intense orange. A cloud of incense rose from a small bucket at his feet. Beside him on the pavement stood a lank-haired, sallow woman who looked like a displaced hippie and thumped listlessly on a tall Conga drum. Behind them was a platform at about shoulder height on which was propped, like a hunting trophy, an immense stuffed buffalo head mounted on a wooden plaque. Bright green cylindrical plugs were stuck in its ears. These, I learned as the man caught my eye and went into his rap, signified the animal's refusal to listen.

"Have you ever meditated?" he asked me, fixing me with a glance full of significance. "Well, even if you haven't, you can still see that the Old American buffalo here is in deep trouble. This poor beast represents our animal nature imprisoned inside us. Men dressed in their fancy Fifth Avenue three-piece suits won't admit there's a wild animal inside them, and so that energy gets distorted and they do horrible things to themselves and the environment. The future of the world is at stake."

His prayer beads were three dollars a strand and he was giving a talk that night in a loft on 14th Street to which everybody was invited. "The truth is better than roast turkey," he announced, "with or without the stuffing."

I stood there open-mouthed. What I'd been thinking about minutes before had been twisted into this New Age duo with their drum and buffalo head, somehow materialized into a form to which I hadn't given the least assent. I turned away and began running at full speed, block after block, until, exhausted and dizzy, I came to a halt in Times Square.

As much to keep warm as anything else—in the shadow of the big buildings it was getting colder by the minute—I went down into the subway. Underground, in the rambling station where four train lines converged, Thanksgiving had brought out every last psycho in New York City. They paced back and forth, mournfully eyeing the clocks mounted throughout the station, each of which told a different time. Bored young cops nudged the homeless alcoholics and druggies slumped over behind trash barrels and against railings, the insensate ones holding smudged turkey drumsticks donated by some charitable organization. Eyes lidded over. Dead to the world.

Those who had it together enough to panhandle were making out better than usual beside the donut stand and flower shop. Occasionally, trembling wide-eyed fourteen-year-old boys would appear from 42nd Street, shadowed at a discreet distance by vicious-looking older men. Fights broke out, knives were pulled. And through it all solitary musicians played, their open instrument cases beside them. On the BMT platform it was Haydn. By the shuttle, "Blowin' in the Wind."

Returning to the open area near the Spanish record shop I saw—ten yards ahead of me, her dark brown arms covered with wrist watches, her body swathed in a long red gown—the tambarina lady I had encountered on Fifth Avenue two weeks before. She ambled along, pulling the laundry cart loaded with possessions. It seemed like months had passed since I'd last seen her.

As I came up behind her I heard a soft, beautiful humming. I followed as she shuffled down an empty passageway. Turning a corner and mounting a flight of steps we came to a busier corridor, and halfway down that stood the most extraordinary figure. The tambarina lady walked past this man and bent over—I could see her talking to another man who sat on the floor a few yards further along—but I was mesmerized by him and stopped in my tracks.

A tall, thin man in his sixties with coal-black skin, he stood against the wall like a sentinel, rigid, cool, and superior, wearing a dark blue

African robe and white beaded skullcap. He looked about grandly with a fixed expression, his eyes wide and protuberant, not reacting in any way to the people rushing past . . . His searing gaze, his face frozen into a mask . . . As I looked closer I saw that he was shivering. Beads of sweat rolled down his face. I stood gaping at him. At one moment he seemed proud and formidable, suffused with the mystic coolness of a god. Then he was mad, schizo, out of control. Finally, feeling abashed and confused, not knowing what else to do, I moved past him to where the tambarina lady had joined his companion on the floor. They were chatting quietly.

"Hello," I said to her, "do you remember me? I helped you when that kid ran over you with his bicycle up in Central Park."

She giggled, and the man sitting beside her motioned me closer. He was young, about thirty, wafer-thin and small with a little trimmed beard. Wrapped in a checked blanket, he was wearing shades. He grinned at me and said, "Say, mon . . . Dey some bery nice boots you got on dere. Bery nice . . . My master," he continued, gesturing at the other man who meanwhile hadn't said a word, "he tell me he like dem bery much. Dem boots hab power, mon, dey warrior boots. He say you must be messenger. You know what I mean by messenger? You do don't you? I can tell, just don't you worry none about it . . . I know where you coming from."

His voice had a sardonic edge which aroused my anxiety. I wanted to inform him how invulnerable I felt, how I'd been destroyed and made whole again with a new name. "You can call me X," I wanted to shout. I wanted to laugh aloud and say, "Of course these are the boots of a warrior!" But something was bothering me. The word *boots*, for one thing. I looked down at my feet and saw my old, cracked red and black high-heeled Spanish boots. The left one was split clear down the side and my sock showed through. I couldn't believe it. Had I actually been wearing these things all the time I'd been running? Running through the city for miles and miles? I stared around, disoriented. The man on the floor roared with laughter.

"Sometimes, you know," the tambarina lady said in a soothing voice, "de peoples need to sleep. Dey need to lay down and take dere rest . . ."

She looked up at me and her eyes, friendly at first, turned into pinwheels which locked into mine, drawing me closer, sucking me in.

I had the horrors for real now and tore myself away from them, their mocking laughter echoing in my ears as I ran down the corridor. Shaken by this experience, I wandered around the station and then was heading toward the BMT platform to go home when I came upon a man squatting on his haunches, his elbows over his knees, the knuckles of his hands brushing the floor. A piece of cardboard covered with writing, about three inches square, lay on the cement in front of him. There were a few coins scattered around it although he wasn't begging. White, in his mid-thirties, with an unshaven, bruised face and torn clothes, he stared stonily straight ahead into space. Overcome with curiosity I dropped a quarter on the floor. The crudely printed ball-point letters were indecipherable until I leaned closer:

BE QUIET

I DON'T WANT

TO TALK AT ALL //

DON'T BOTHER ME

ASK ANOTHER

STRANGER

He reached out with a stiffly open hand and shovelled the piece of cardboard over, slapping it on the floor. I bent down until I was almost on my knees and, squinting in the dim light, read:

KEEP TEN YARDS

DISTANCE FROM

ME SCUM OF

LIFE // FUCK

IN YOUR MOTHER'S

SAVAGE SKULL

He stared straight ahead, rigid as a pole. Devastated, I was about to say something to him when his head ducked abruptly two or three times and, without warning, he lunged forward and sank his teeth into my leg. I cried out in pain. Several people around us stopped momentarily, whereupon this guy unhooked his mouth from my calf, rolled up in a ball, and faced the grimy tiles behind him.

Looking down at my pants I saw a row of bloodstained holes which grew brighter and larger as I watched. I went berserk, kicking the son of a bitch over and over until a middle-aged black woman stopped right beside me, gave me an angry shove and screamed that I was no better than an animal, hurting a poor defenseless man like that. I hobbled off down the stairs to my train, numb and obsessing over the prospect of infection, of coming down with rabies, tetanus, gangrene.

Everybody else waiting for the downtown local moved away from me. Standing there, I tried to think about what had happened to me that day. The time spent on the street and at Battery Park had been luminous and exalted, but as soon as other people entered the picture, things had gone sour . . . Ask another stranger . . .

I took the train downtown and limped up into the cold evening at Broadway and Eighth Street. Walking home along St. Mark's Place in the gathering dusk I felt encased in myself to the point that I could hardly make out the people around me. My feet ached, the wounds on my leg burned. Then I saw lights ahead of me, yellow bulbs swinging back and forth like Japanese lanterns, casting shadows with delicately scalloped edges. Entranced, I stepped forward. My foot slid over loose gravel and before I had a chance to take hold of anything I slipped and was tumbling into emptiness. I lay in the dark next to an enormous concrete culvert. A resounding crash penetrated my heart each time a bus or car or truck rolled over the steel plates in the street above my head. I wondered how far away I was . . . Far away from what, though, that was the question.

Far away from what? The question nagged at me, it wouldn't let go. I lay there for a long time until a moment came when I understood, when I knew it would be all right for me to get up, that nobody was going to hurt me anymore. Because it didn't matter how far away I was—everyone was far away, as far away from one another as stars in the sky. That's just the way it was. And I did get up.

PART THREE

PART THREE

TEN

Three months later, by the end of February, 1977, without leaving New York and without grandiose schemes or dramatic dislocations, I had changed my life. Since the first of December I had been working—washing dishes at a fancy Chinese "natural" restaurant in SoHo called Bamboo Mountain. From six in the evening until one A.M., six nights a week, I cleaned and loaded one tray after another of dirty dishes, glasses, and silver into the big stainless steel Hobart washer. I was happier than I'd been in years. Within the dimensions of my little realm I was in control. I liked the late night hours and the anonymity, the fact that usually, unless I also had to play busboy out on the floor because they were short-handed, nobody bothered me. At home, during the day, I exercised and read. I kept to myself and I liked it.

I'd put on the rubber gloves, flip the switch to the hot water booster, and disappear into a cloud of steam for seven hours. At one A.M., when the restaurant closed, I'd spend a final hour cleaning Hobart, taking the garbage out to the street, and helping the Chinese kitchen staff scrub down the kitchen. Only one tray went into the machine at a time and each cycle lasted about a minute. Forty-five seconds wash, five seconds off, fifteen seconds dry. So all evening I was constantly in motion, scraping leftover food into big garbage barrels and then loading and unloading the trays, stacking the plates, collecting tubs of dirty dishes, and beginning again. Bamboo Mountain was a large restaurant—135 capacity, 42 tables, and ten waiters—and eight or nine barrels a night filled with food from the prep tables and from people's plates. I shoveled many virtually untouched dinners into the garbage, especially late at night, when the clientele were often too wrecked to eat. Plate after plate of Oriental brown rice, of mushrooms and snow peas, barbecued jumbo prawns, whole sea bass in black bean sauce, sliced pork with cashews. It was enough to make me permanently lose my appetite, but on the other hand I loved being responsible for disposing of the detritus everybody left behind—endlessly making clean, endlessly renewing. Tray after tray of gleaming crockery emerged from Hobart's cloudy maw.

Each night I left work exhilarated and went home determined to clear out the rest of my life as well. I discovered how little I actually needed in order to survive. Survival was what mattered. I didn't need journalism, didn't need interviews and book reviews and record reviews. I was paying the rent. That was enough. And rather than being a burden, living alone was a great stroke of luck. It furnished me with the quiet time I needed in order to turn my life around.

The day after Thanksgiving I'd spent in bed, recuperating from the mushrooms and wondering about what had happened to me. I remembered the glorious invincibility that had been mine while standing and looking out over the bay. I didn't need anybody else. Now I'd have to find some work and I didn't care what sort it would be.

The following night, misty and cold, I happened to be out late walking through the city. Finding myself in SoHo, I stopped for a moment near the corner of Broome and West Broadway, absorbed in the patterns the streetlights were making on the moist cobblestones, when suddenly an unmarked metal door flew open in the wall nearby and a thin, slight guy in his early twenties stumbled out, weeping to himself, bent over as if he'd been punched in the stomach. The door slammed shut and for a while he stood there sobbing, oblivious to my presence, his long silken hair swinging in the glow of the streetlights.

"Those bastards," he finally whimpered. He sounded wounded and resentful, and seemed to be trying to pluck up his courage with this phrase, which he repeated several times until, looking up and seeing me, he fell silent. I was about to ask if I could be of help when the door swung open again and a Chinese man in his thirties with a hard handsome face leaned out and shouted, "Get back inside, Andy. Now! Do you hear me?"

The young guy shuddered and moved closer to me, turning his face away and refusing to respond.

"Do you hear me?" The Chinese man's voice rose to a peremptory shriek. Then he noticed me and made an effort to control himself, saying quietly and sarcastically, "I suppose you think this is just a game, Andy. You can cut out like that, with the place full of people, no warning, nothing, like a baby who has to have his way or else. Now what do you suppose is going to happen? Do you expect me to wash those dishes myself?"

"Leave me alone, Matsu," Andy finally replied, standing so close to me I could feel his body shivering in the cold air. He was wearing just a T-shirt and bell bottoms. "Go find somebody else. I'm through with you and your brother. I quit, I told you that already."

Then his tone softened, he became almost apologetic as he said, "I'm sorry, Matsu. I just can't handle it. It's too much for me. I don't trust you anymore."

They glared at each other. The Chinese man started to say something further but instead his voice got caught in his throat and he gulped. That's when I realized he too was terribly distraught. He'd been shouting at the younger guy in order to hide his feelings.

"Please," he implored in a whisper. "I need you. Don't do this to me . . ." When there was no response he began breathing rapidly and his face became cold and remote. "How dare you?" he hissed. "Who do you think you are? You're finished, Andy. Get out of my sight." The door shut once more and Andy turned to face me, tears in his eyes.

"What are you looking at, turkey?" he growled.

"Take it easy, man," I said. "Calm down. Everything's gonna be all right."

"Are you kidding me?" he responded incredulously. "What do you know? Are you some kind of prophet? Everything's *not* gonna be all right. *Nothing's* gonna be all right. That Chinese fucker's gonna keep coming after me and I don't want him to, but when he stops it'll be even worse." He looked at me antagonistically. "Whaddyou think of that, Mr. Happy Face? How's that grab you?"

He wiped the tears from his eyes and ran his fingers through his hair. When he lifted his face to the light I saw he had beautiful high cheekbones. Now he seemed no more than fifteen or sixteen years old. He touched me on the arm. "You have any change? Can you spare a few dollars?"

I grimaced and turned my pockets inside out. Suddenly he kissed me lightly on the cheek. "There's a job in there waiting for you if you want it. You ever washed dishes before?"

We both laughed.

"Good luck," he whispered, his lips next to mine. Breathing on me, kissing me again, making my face flush. "'Cause you're gonna need it."

Bamboo Mountain was an elegant two-story place with a balcony overlooking a spacious open ground floor area. In the center of this room, surrounded by tables, was a grotto with a dozen or more bamboo trees whose towering stalks reached to eye level of the diners above. Water trickled over rocks to a pool of goldfish. Lots of money had been spent on interior design, on sea-green rock walls and gold leaf wallpaper, red terrazzo floors and a long, elaborately carved bar. With its skylight roof and floor-to-ceiling windows giving onto West Broadway, during the day Bamboo Mountain glowed with opalescent, diffuse light. However, I almost never saw the restaurant while the sun was up. I worked the lunch shift only once, when the day dishwasher, a Filipino boy named Clang, called in sick. By the time I came to work the place was illuminated by dramatic track lighting with spots thrown here and there into the nodding tufts of bamboo.

The Chinese kitchen staff was comprised of three cooks and two apprentices, none of whom spoke English; and Bobby Chin, the "pulling horse" as he was called, who did speak English. His job was to take the orders from the waiters—all of whom, conforming to the image developed for the restaurant, were young, good-looking white males —and translate them into Chinese. At the same time, he assembled the ingredients for each order on a plate and handed it to one of the cooks, thereby streamlining the operation and giving an organization to it which was never compromised, even on the busiest nights. On those occasions when the pressure mounted and waiters screwed up the orders, interrupting the flow by returning with plates the customers hadn't asked for, the cooks would curse at them in Cantonese. In the interest of peace Bobby Chin refused to translate these verbal assaults. I got to know Bobby a bit; he was thirty years old, serious and likable, methodically saving his money to open a restaurant of his own. The cooks treated me with a polite reserve, in a manner circumscribed by the position I held. I washed dishes, I was the latest in a string of Latin and teenage white boys, whereas they were professionals. The three cooks had been working, first in China and then in the U.S., for forty years, and they were possessed of an imperturbable authority.

Eating at Bamboo Mountain was expensive. In fact, it had been one of the very first upscale, trendy new restaurants in SoHo when it opened the previous year. But since late '75, the entire neighborhood had crossed the threshold from artists' haven to fashionable playground and lofts were suddenly selling for ninety thousand dollars, five times what they went for in 1970. Contrary to the laws still in effect which reserved the area for practising artists, the new generation of loft dwellers were uptown professionals and wealthy Europeans. Elitist and chic, they in turn attracted clusters of boutiques, bars, and restaurants to an area where, six years before, raw loft space had been rented illegally to artists for almost nothing. But nowadays, renters were being booted out of where they lived because tenants in industrial areas had no statutory rights. SoHo, originally a desolate collection of warehouses and sweat shops, was still zoned industrial by the city.

An atmosphere of rampant speculation prevailed, and nobody profiting from loft renovation was interested in looking back to an earlier era. Landlords, some of whom were artists themselves, paid off the city in order to sell to people not remotely connected to the arts. Instead of serving violations and shutting off fuel, Buildings Department inspectors took bribes. Now, however, this seller's market had given way to an unstable situation in which many investors, convinced the market finally had become saturated, were trying to unload their property. Deals were becoming parts of other, bigger deals having nothing to do with SoHo or even with real estate. The scene was turning sour.

I found out about all this because Quemoy and Matsu Sheridan, the

Chinese twin brothers who owned Bamboo Mountain, were also involved in an ongoing process of buying buildings in the area, renovating them with their own Chinese work crews, arranging co-op associations with a token artist or two, and then selling the finished lofts for some serious profits, at least when everything went as planned. But Quemoy and Matsu, once I'd gotten to know them, complained about unpredictable variables that, without warning, could sabotage their operations. They had to worry about paying off not only the city but also a shifting cast of characters from the Mob, people who controlled various aspects of the construction industry. The brothers did this not only for protection but also so they could use their own non-union workers on the job.

Quemoy and Matsu lived in the fast lane in those days and even when no real estate deals were in the air they kept late hours, rarely returning to their matching, sparely opulent lofts on Greene Street before dawn. They spent a good deal of time away from the restaurant, and Bamboo Mountain was left in the hands of the manager and maître d', Jimmy Wu, a skinny, avuncular Cantonese in his fifties with graying hair and a bemused, skeptical smile. The twins trusted Jimmy Wu. They depended on him to visit the food markets every morning, order supplies, and keep the place running, although the menu and the hiring and firing of personnel remained the brothers' turf.

But I only gradually came to know about them, because at first I had my hands full learning the ropes. Aside from a few cracks about "the guy with the college degree working for wetback wages," once Quemoy and Matsu saw I could handle the job they seemed to forget about me, which suited me fine. This lasted into the beginning of January when, little by little, they included me in conversations. Quemoy, especially, began to treat me as a familiar, intrigued by the anomaly of a white guy in his thirties willing to wash dishes. And I, in turn, was equally curious about these English-speaking identical twins from Taiwan.

And identical twins they indeed were. Sometimes you couldn't tell them apart. Not for long, of course, but even two minutes of not knowing who you're talking to can be unsettling. Both were swarthy—

Jimmy Wu used to joke that they weren't really Chinese at all, but Korean. Muscular and capable-looking with glossy black hair and black eyes, they had a permanently impatient air about them as if they didn't have a minute to lose. Matsu was a harsher person and his features somewhat harder than Quemoy's. If you didn't know to whom you were talking you had to listen and look carefully, remembering that Matsu didn't like people much. He tended to be taciturn, whereas Quemoy was convivial. Quemoy liked to make jokes and tell stories, he enjoyed eating and having other people around. But at bottom they were both serious businessmen. Quemoy was more sympathetic, that's all. Not as quick to fly off the handle. And Matsu had a scar on the back of his neck which he covered up with hair. He didn't like for anybody to see it.

Energetic and intense, the twins were interesting to be around because they took chances, they were entrepreneurs. They loved to start something where nothing had been going on before and this made them charismatic. And they were hungry. The twins liked money. They always wanted more. One night after work in February, after I'd gotten to know them a bit, Quemoy and I were talking and drinking cognac in the kitchen when I asked him how he and his brother came to be in New York. He never answered that question. Instead he launched into a story which began with why they hated their father.

"Foster father," Quemoy corrected himself quickly and spat into the corner of the kitchen. "Colonel Mathew Brinkley Sheridan, U.S. Marines . . ." He looked at me with an exasperated expression and shrugged. "It's not my fault," he said.

The twins were born in mainland China and orphaned when they were infants. They ended up as refugees on Taiwan. Quemoy and Matsu were found by Colonel Sheridan in a relocation camp in the mountains.

"He appeared out of nowhere one day," Quemoy said, "and plucked us out of that chaos and took us back to Meijun Jidi, the big base outside of Taipei where he was stationed. Talk about night and day. Suddenly we were learning English and playing with all these defensive, anxiety-ridden blue-eyed brats, white boys whose folks were from places like Iowa and Nebraska, beautiful blond kids . . ." He laughed mournfully. "Real fucked up. Afraid to show their feelings. Always trying to beat up on Matsu and me, and then crying and ganging up against us when they got busted in the face. And this guy, Colonel Sheridan! Insisting we call him *Dad*. Real nervous, trying to treat us as his sons, trying to put us at ease, but by fiat, like an order from HQ that we were supposed to immediately fall in step with. He had this stiff, uptight concern for our well-being that just freaked us out because we'd never really been with white people before. Everything about them was different, they even smelled different . . . *Hua na* . . . ghosts," he said and giggled. "We didn't know what to make of this guy, we couldn't see where he was coming from. The weird thing was, when we were kids, for a year after he got us, he used to teach us English at home by telling us about his childhood. It was real nice. He was a different person then, loose and relaxed. It was the only time he laughed . . . A farm somewhere in Minnesota, he grew up on a farm in the Twenties, he liked to tell us about that . . . He meant well at first but soon it was like being in a relocation camp again only worse, because he knew so much more than we did. And he had that fucking authoritarian style, that makes you want to go against it, you know what I mean? So Matsu and me, we learned. That's what we wanted more than anything, to know more than he did. We realized *that* would be our only way to get out from under him, realized it when we were eleven, twelve years old, which is something, when you think about it . . . All our lives, Matsu and me have only had each other . . . So meanwhile we learned English and we dug being at Meijun Jidi, it was like being right inside the skull of the empire. Five years go by like that and then one day, lo and behold, the whole equation changes because he gets ordered back to the States, and that blows him away. It just kills him . . ."

Colonel Sheridan spoke only Mandarin, so the twins talked to each other in Taiwanese, which made him furious. He felt they wouldn't allow themselves to trust him and as time went by he became more and more suspicious of them. A widower with no children of his own, he had fought the Chinese in Korea. In 1953, when the Korean War ended, he was sent to Taiwan. He had been there before, in the late Forties during the defense of the island against Mao Tse-tung. A rabid anti-Communist, Colonel Sheridan legally changed the boys' names to honor the Nationalist defense of Quemoy and Matsu, two little islands only five miles from mainland China which were still in the control of Chiang Kai-chek.

Colonel Sheridan was on the scene in 1949 when the Communists attempted a landing on Quemoy and were driven back with heavy losses. "I saw those gutsy freedom lovers defend their turf from the red menace," he told the boys more than once, in spite of the fact that the Nationalists themselves were looked upon as an occupying army on Taiwan and were resented by the islanders for expropriating property.

Quemoy and Matsu were shelled regularly from the mainland but when the bombardment intensified in 1958, the United States declared itself in favor of reducing Nationalist forces there if the Communists would stop bombardment, and made it clear that America had no commitment to help the Nationalists return to the mainland. And it was then that Colonel Sheridan got angry. He saw nothing but a betrayal of the memory of the fighting men he had seen lose their lives on Okinawa in '45, a betrayal of the cause of freedom, a betrayal not only of the Chinese but of America itself. He complained to his superiors, he wrote letters to the Pentagon, he called John Foster Dulles a traitor on Armed Forces Radio, and within a month was relieved of his duties and reassigned to the States. Enraged and dispirited at being stuck in Camp Pendleton in California, he joined the fledgling John Birch Society and became even more intransigent.

"He hated being back in America," Quemoy said. "He hadn't really lived here since '43 and he thought it had completely changed for the worse. Can you imagine, Roy? This is more than fifteen years later, his family's gone and everything, this is 1959, 1960. He *hated* Southern Cal, all these phony degenerates and lazy Mexicans. He wanted to go back to Taiwan but the Pentagon wouldn't let him. By that time we were in high school out there and loving it. You see, suddenly we knew more than the old man did, *way* more. We fit in and he didn't. We became ABC Chinese, we forgot about writing it though we still spoke it, of course. They put us back a grade, so high school was easy. We had a ball, Matsu and me. We cut classes and went to Santa Monica all the time, to the beach, and meanwhile he's stewing out there at Camp Pendleton in the desert, getting older and more isolated. Stuck teaching security force trainees from all over Southeast Asia, sent to America to learn from the experts. And then—our senior year in high school—he discovers that my brother and me are gay, we're homosexuals, and that absolutely blows him away. It sends him over the top, they have to sedate the guy to keep him from damaging himself, not to mention us. And the next day, what do you think? Matsu and I left home for good. We told him we were freedom lovers, too, just like Chiang Kai-shek. He didn't appreciate that at all," Quemoy said with a brittle grin. Then he threw back his head and laughed that big, infectious laugh of his.

The apartment on St. Mark's was my refuge all winter. The place was a shambles and soon after I got the job at Bamboo Mountain I cleaned it out. Piling possessions from closets and drawers and cabinets onto the floor, it came to me that the only way to proceed would be to get rid of everything. Once I started I couldn't stop. I threw away old clothes and busted appliances, generations of books and magazines, and then, in an onrush of elation and sadness, I got rid of everything in the big kitchen closet: photo albums, boxes of letters, old notebooks, Dana's portfolios of art school drawings, my own student papers from a dozen years before. They were nothing more than remnants. The people who'd made it all come to life were gone now, including me, I thought. What better way to make that fact crystal clear than to have absolutely empty closets and drawers? I had to restrains myself from disposing of every last article of clothing and implement in sight, realizing that if I did, I'd be stark naked and eating off the floor. At the end, I collected all of Dana's things too, all the art works she'd left behind, including her self-portrait, and threw them away.

Somebody—and although I had no memory of it, who could it have been but me?—had scrawled I HATE OLIVER HARTWELL on the kitchen wall over the red spray-painted letters that said OPW. And, in the living room, above the sofa—applied with such force the plaster was gouged out of the wall—dozens of little stick figures of men and animals had been drawn in heavy pencil, one on top of the other, like paleolithic cave drawings. I decided to paint the apartment, which hadn't been done in years, and while I was at it I got rid of all the furniture in the living room, including the television, the record player, and that hopeless old sofa. I pulled the rancid curtains down from the windows and replaced them with Venetian blinds. In December I bought a full-length mirror and installed it on the wall where the sofa had been. The front room was virtually bare now. Besides the mirror it contained a trunk, painted white like the walls, and a few pillows.

I vowed to stop taking drugs and tossed out my entire arsenal. I gave up cigarettes as well. Looking in the mirror I was appalled at how out of shape I'd become, soft and flabby like an aging bus driver. I improvised a series of exercises that I did every afternoon in front of the mirror before going to work. Eventually I was able to run through longer and longer sequences of them until I slipped into a sort of reverie. By the middle of January my body was trim and hard.

All in all I'd never felt better. I'd eased into a routine, an equilibrium within the bounds of which I was content to stay indefinitely. It felt good to have my feet on the ground, to know where I was going to be the next day. Whenever I had a desire to get stoned I'd remember the paralyzing indecision of the previous months. It was such a relief to see things clearly for a change. I swore I'd keep a clear head from then on.

The telephone rarely rang that December but when it did, invariably one of Dana's friends came on the line inquiring after her. Cissy Wyatt called regularly, peppering me with questions. Had I heard anything? Was I still looking for her? Then, on my way to work one day I was stopped in my tracks by a flyer taped to a lamp post at the corner of Third Avenue and St. Mark's:

REWARD $500

HAS ANYONE SEEN THIS PERSON?

29 YEARS OLD, FEMALE

5' 6" 120 LBS.

BLACK HAIR, GREEN EYES

LAST SEEN IN VICINITY OF EAST VILLAGE

CONTACT DET. GUTTNER, NINTH PCT.

477-7811

ALL CALLS KEPT CONFIDENTIAL

And there at the bottom was Dana's face, pale and wide-eyed, looking at me with a startled expression, as if she'd just been tapped on the shoulder.

Immediately I remembered my conversation with the police soon after she'd vanished. Obviously Lou and Sibyl were taking matters into their own hands. I saw three or four more of the flyers as I walked to SoHo and by the time I got to Bamboo Mountain I was on the verge of calling the Millers to tell them Dana had come to the apartment and taken some of her things, but I didn't. They'd only start their hostile spiel again, blaming me for what had happened. And living each day without thinking of Dana was one of the tasks I'd set for myself.

But I couldn't forget that face, wrapped around a lamp post in the freezing gloom of a winter's dusk. She looked far from happy, like somebody perfectly capable of running away. I had to fight the impulse to take down one of the flyers and study it further, get drawn into the whole thing again. But I insisted to myself that wasn't going to happen. I'd had enough of chasing after phantoms.

As the weeks went by, one by one the flyers disappeared, torn down, papered over with other announcements. The last one I saw, over by NYU in the middle of a raging snowstorm, was covered over the next day by a fancy four-color poster of Peter Frampton lounging in an open silk housecoat and tight satin pants, advertising his upcoming concert at Radio City Music Hall.

The last week in December an invitation addressed to Dana and me came in the mail for a New Year's Eve party given by James Rosenquist in his new loft on the Bowery. "Come celebrate Jim's new digs!" it said in jagged day-glo lettering. I had never met Rosenquist but I decided to drop by there anyway after work. I hadn't been to a big party like that in ages.

When I arrived at two A.M., Rosenquist's cavernous loft was packed, and immediately I felt that rush you get surrounded by an ocean of strangers, drinking and doping it up, dancing and shrieking. Off in the corners, knots of self-possessed art world cognoscenti talked business. Even on New Year's Eve they radiated that exclusivity which had always turned me off in the past when I'd gone with Dana to smaller versions of a party like this. Tight little circles, breaking only to turn and give you the supercilious once over. But this scene was too overwhelming for such vibes to make more than a small dent. Music thundered from huge speakers, an open bar was dispensing thousands of dollars of liquor, and in the middle of it all stood Jim Rosenquist—a puckish, orange-haired presence in a Hawaiian shirt—sweating profusely, his eyes starting out of his head from the sheer energy being released all around him. He looked several notches beyond exhilarated, as if at any moment he was going to take off and join his monumental *F-111* somewhere in the stratosphere. For the heck of it I fought my way over to him and shook his hand, saying thanks for the invite. He swivelled in my direction, looked me in the eye and bellowed, "Great! Great to see you! I always knew you'd show up!" We both laughed uproariously and the next second his back was turned.

Dozens of celebrities were there, faces I hadn't seen since my days at *The New Jag*. Beautiful young models were surrounded by elegantly fashionable men with deep tans, slicked-back hair, and fake toughguy demeanors. I didn't see anybody I knew besides Cissy Wyatt, and we just waved to each other from across the room. She wasn't wearing her shades for once and, in fact, I wondered what she was doing here. It didn't seem like her crowd. Although, come to think of it, I had no idea what Cissy's crowd might be. She was the sort of person you always were surprised to see again if you hadn't seen her for a while, because there seemed to be nothing holding her down to the ground. You kind of expected to hear one day that she'd simply floated away.

I had a few beers and danced with a teenager named Argyle, whose hair was dyed a fantastic patchwork of rust red and bright yellow. I'd never seen anybody like her before. She had safety pins in her ears and rings of charcoal under her eyes for that ravaged look. She wore black lipstick and high-topped paratrooper boots. At one point she grabbed me by the elbows and announced in an affected, high-pitched voice, "This is *nowhere*, Bill. Yesterday's papers. Wait'll you see the Sex Pistols. You'll never be the same again!"

"The who?" I asked, but it was impossible to carry on a conversation. A second later she was gone. I decided to leave and began fighting my way toward the door.

And that's when I saw her, not more than thirty feet away, wedged in the middle of a crowd of people right at the door. Like a riot scene in a movie, the crowd swayed back and forth and then she turned, her black hair glistening in the light from the hallway beyond, and saw me. Her mouth opened and for a second our eyes locked. The crowd surged out the door and I followed. A minute later we stood face to face in the hallway surrounded by people coming and going. Beside her stood a shorter woman, blond and slight of build, who in the next moment moved between us as if to protect her. I stood there, awestruck.

"Dana."

"I knew we shouldn't have come," she said to her friend. "I just knew it."

I felt an onrush of emotion, above all relief at seeing her alive and well.

"This makes me so happy," I said, moving forward to embrace her. "Everybody's been so worried about you, you have no idea."

She took a deep breath and in a tense voice said, "Just stay away from me, Roy. Leave me alone. I don't want to talk to you. We don't have anything to say to each other."

"But, Jesus, Dana, I'm not asking for anything. It just makes me feel so good to know you're OK."

"Roy, I'm not interested in your feelings. Can't you understand that? I want you to pretend you haven't seen me tonight. Just forget I exist. And above all, I'd appreciate it if you'd do me one favor. Please don't mention this to my parents. I'll tell them in good time, when I'm ready to and not before."

"It's all right, baby," the woman next to her said reassuringly, holding her by the arm and trying to guide her away. "It had to happen sooner or later. Everything's going to be fine. Trust me."

"Listen, Dana," I said. "I'm not threatening you, whatever you're doing is ok by me. I mean that. And of course I won't tell your parents, although I'm sure they're as worried as I've been. All sorts of people have been calling, even Richard Pinkus."

She snorted. "Richard Pinkus! Wow, Roy, I don't want to listen to this. I don't care how worried you've been, *or* Richard." She threw back her head, her nostrils flaring, and said defiantly, "Why do I have to consider either of you before I do what I want? You think you two guys are my only options? What a laugh! What a stinking male-chauvinist idea! You think it was heaven, being obliged to fuck that deadbeat? Yes, *obliged*, I was obliged to fulfill his boring little erotic fantasies. Being with Richard was like being with a perpetually born-again adolescent, constantly trying to prove himself with women. And as for you, Roy..."

She paused, a faint smile playing nervously across her lips. "As for you—slow death funnies!"

She gave a raw laugh that sent shivers down my back. In spite of the noise and crush of people, the tone of Dana's voice had attracted a small group of onlookers which now was tittering gleefully.

"So keep away from me, I mean it. I can get along perfectly well without you, believe me."

"But damn it, Dana, you're not listening to what I'm saying."

I wanted to let her know that my life was changing too, that everything was different now, it was ok she had left me. And then I realized that the woman beside her was Dana's lover. I was glad for her. Finally coming face to face with Dana made me understand that everything between us was over. We both had new lives to lead. I wanted to be her friend now, not her antagonist. I tried to catch her eye.

She stood there uncertainly. The woman beside her leaned over and whispered something and Dana's face changed. She sighed, and a resigned smile appeared on her face, a smile of almost condescending compassion.

"I'm sorry I've caused you so much pain," she said, calmly now, in control of herself once more. "But there's no way in the world I'll ever come back to you. I'll straighten all this out soon with my parents. It's the final thing I have to do and it won't be easy. I've been waiting until my life feels really solid before I deal with them."

She turned and smiled at her friend. "It does now."

Then she said, "I may as well tell you. Barbara and I are lovers. We're living together in Brooklyn, I'm working on my art again and I'm really happy. But please don't try and follow me. Don't bug me, Roy . . . I'll never come back to you in a million years."

I blinked. I had the crazy sensation of being locked in a funhouse. Whatever I said was warped by her refusal to listen to me. She didn't want to hear what I had to say, didn't trust me, didn't see me. Instead she saw the guy from before.

"You've got it all wrong," I said.

"Please, let's not keep going over the same old ground. I'll come by soon and get the rest of my stuff. I'm sorry about the last time but it's just as well you weren't home then. We can arrange to come get the rest of my things when you're not there, if you'd like."

I paused, then blurted out, "There's nothing left to get."

"What do you mean?"

I took a deep breath. "Look, Dana, a lot's happened since you split. It's not like I've been hanging on a hook in the closet all this time. I've got a job now, I painted the place too, and . . . it's hard to explain, but I cleaned out the entire apartment, it was an important thing for me to do. I threw away the old furniture and all that junk in the kitchen closet. It was liberating for me and I guess I got carried away. I mean, all the clothes you didn't take—your summer clothes—all your stuff, all *my* stuff—it's gone. I needed to start over . . . I kept going until I felt I was *there*, you know?"

"You can't be serious," she said evenly.

They looked at each other. "All my old paintings are gone? The ones you liked so much?"

I nodded.

"Everything went down the tubes. It was sensational, a force of nature. No boxes of letters left, no photo albums, no records, no Indian blankets, no magic mushrooms . . . I even threw away the TV." I tried to laugh but she glared at me and whispered, "What a control trip."

"Control trip!" I shouted, losing my temper. "Who's been controlling whom, Dana? Where've you been all this time? Why didn't you at least tell me you were all right? I don't give a fuck about your precious new relationship, I really don't care. But I didn't even know whether you were dead or alive, for God's sake. And as for me, I felt like I was buried alive in the past, I had to get out. Suddenly the past became synonymous with those belongings, with all that *property*, and I had to get rid of everything. Can't you understand? I had no choice."

I tried to catch her eye again but she wouldn't look at me and I became exasperated.

"Why didn't you take all your stuff the first time if it meant so much to you? Why didn't you come back sooner? Six weeks have gone by. Some big changes have taken place in my life."

"Your life? What about my life? That was my property. You had no right to get rid of it."

"Look," I said, "you're right, I had no business doing what I did but I did it. I'm sorry. I've tried to explain. I wasn't being selective. It had nothing to do with you personally."

"Are you kidding? If all this isn't some fantastic bullshit *lie*, I don't believe for a second you didn't do it to hurt me. But you can't hurt me."

She looked at me intently. Then, taking her friend's hand to leave, she said as sarcastically as possible, "Thanks for being so considerate. I always knew you had my best interests at heart. At least that much hasn't changed about you."

And they turned and walked down the stairs to the Bowery at four in the morning on New Year's Day, their bulky winter coats side by side—one black and the other, shorter one, red.

ELEVEN

I felt like I fit right in with the news that January. A NEW PRESIDENT, A NEW BEGINNING, the papers announced, lingering on the symbolic importance of the fact that, after his inauguration, Jimmy Carter walked to the White House with his family beside him: we now had a President who would mingle with the people. American democracy still worked, it hadn't been short-circuited by Richard Nixon after all. Carter's campaign pledges had played to the desire for moral purging of the body politic after the dark excesses of Vietnam and Watergate, and the day after being inaugurated Carter announced a blanket pardon for all draft evaders and resistors. Even though this didn't apply to deserters the right wing became incensed, with Barry Goldwater calling it "the most disgraceful thing a president has ever done," and the VFW predicting it would turn the United States into a nation with no men willing to fight its wars. Several weeks later, Carter followed with the announcement that U.S. ground forces in Korea would be withdrawn within five years, and soon after that he ended travel restrictions to Cuba, Vietnam, North Korea, and Cambodia.

Meanwhile, GILMORE EXECUTED *Last Words: "Let's Do It"* the *Post* proclaimed as Gary Gilmore, the convicted killer who repeatedly requested that his death sentence be carried out, was shot by a firing squad in Utah. It was the first execution in the U.S. in ten years. And in New York, winter finally came on strong. After the middle of January when the first big cold snap hit and temperatures plunged below zero, the Brownian movement of the headlines—NEW EVIDENCE IN JFK KILLING, SWINE FLU FIASCO, MOB WAR SHAPES UP OVER DRUGS, AMIN DETAINS 240 AMERICANS, SWIPE 25 LBS. WEAPONS-

GRADE URANIUM, COPS SAY FEWER CALL THEM BRUTAL—gave way to recurring stories like 95, SHE FREEZES TO DEATH and PAIR FROZEN IN BKLN. Throughout that winter I came upon lines such as "'We've been without heat for months,' said Hettie Smith of 636 E. 5th Street," and "The body of Miss Shotter, 80 years old, barefoot and garbed in dress and sweater, was found in five inches of ice on the kitchen floor."

It was hard to believe things in the city could get any worse. With shells of burned out buildings staring into icy streets, the Lower East Side began to look like the end of the world. Venturing east of First Avenue meant taking your life into your hands, with squads of desperate junkies holding down Tompkins Square Park. But the climate of imminent peril was by no means restricted to the slums alone. My favorite headline that winter was hardly reassuring, whether or not you chose to believe it: TRANSIT AUTHORITY SAYS SUBWAY SAFER THAN CITY.

The city's financial crisis wasn't the only source of problems, though. THUGS HURL WOMAN, 77, INTO CAR'S PATH . . . The elderly were getting hit harder and harder. Kids under sixteen couldn't be prosecuted as criminals and were handed over to the custody of a Family Court which they considered to be little more than a joke. They confessed to preferring elderly victims—"crib jobs"—because such people represented low-risk crime, like taking candy from a baby. Arrested youths told police they believed all older people had money hidden in their homes. The newspapers began to feature these incidents more prominently.

COPS GRAB SLEEPING PAROLEE

A 19-year-old parolee with a record of assaults on elderly women was roused from his bed early this morning by police and charged with the rape-murder of a 73-year-old Staten Island woman. The accused man, Rulon Jennings, was sleeping in the apartment of a girlfriend who lived directly across the hall from the dead woman. The murdered woman was found naked and tied to the bed, lying face up with her hands and feet bound. Her throat had been slashed and she had been stabbed in the breast and stomach. An autopsy revealed she had been raped.

As a result of public outcry, the police instituted a Senior Citizens Robbery Squad which consisted of decoys—lady cops, for the most part, disguised as elderly women carrying shopping bags who slumped in doorways while their backup teams waited nearby. This program hardly scratched the surface, though, and political action groups encouraged old people to defend themselves by carrying whistles and cans of Mace. A debate sprang up about whether resistance would only backfire and lead to increased fatalities, but many elderly welcomed an alternative to feeling like sitting ducks.

Winter, too, saw an outbreak of the darkest violence of all. Sometime in January an anonymous-looking, short white guy in his thirties, wearing a ski cap, began attacking only blacks and Puerto Ricans near the midtown subway stations, usually around dusk. He carried a large knife under his coat which he would thrust through layers of winter clothing and then twist, all the while silently grinning from ear to ear. In the space of two months, "The Slasher" killed six people, injured four more, and became the object of a city-wide manhunt. People began to wear bullet-proof vests, especially while riding the subway at night. And in my neighborhood, in coffee shops and little stores, these incidents were all anybody seemed to talk about, with some of the more trigger-happy Ukrainians encouraging the formation of vigilante groups.

Around the end of February I thought of Bessie Goldman, Dana's grandmother, up there in her nursing home in the Bronx. Had she recovered from her hip injury sufficiently to go for walks outside? Did she worry about getting mugged? My parents and I had several conversations that winter, which always ended with the advice that I should leave New York, get an apartment in Cincinnati or Columbus, somewhere near home, and find work with a local newspaper . . . And look for a nice Jewish girl to marry, and drive out to visit them on weekends . . . My mother knew it was all make-believe, but once she started she found it difficult to stop. Listening to her voice over the phone, it was almost like being back in the store with them on drowsy afternoons when business was slow and the dreams and fantasies started flowing like sweet kosher wine.

* * *

Motionless and withered, her hands lay on the neatly made bed. I sat on a chair in the corner. Beside me a small portable TV, with the sound off, showed pictures of a daytime soap opera. The other bed was occupied now by a shrunken old woman who seemed to be sleeping, but Grandma Bessie went on talking as if neither her roommate nor I was there. I was sure she'd recognized me when I came into the room but there had been no response to my greeting. She'd been talking as I walked in and she continued talking. Her words filled the room, quietly insistent and lucid except that they weren't directed at anybody. The dim afternoon winter light filtered through unwashed windows. I felt as if the three of us were suspended in some state between life and death. I sat there, the bunch of gladiolas I'd brought still in my lap.

". . . Avram changed so slowly at first, it wasn't as if one day I woke up and there was this stranger next to me, not at all. Life went on today the same as yesterday, Sibyl would eat her breakfast and go to school, and an hour after Avram left for the shop I would follow him . . . It was more like tree rings . . . Tree rings . . . You can't really tell: one year's growth is slightly more or less than the year before but the difference is imperceptible, it's nothing, and you don't know what year it is anyway, which ring applies to what year, it's all so gradual you can't put your finger on it except that time is passing and passing, distant and vaguely sensed, like the sound of traffic blocks away. And suddenly one day you wake up and the tree is enormous, it's grown up between the two of you without your noticing it until you can't see the other person anymore. He's blocked by all these lies and half-lies and insinuations. This voice you've been listening to for years without admitting that you don't understand it anymore, you don't trust it, don't believe it, you haven't believed it in a long time but you won't admit that to yourself because what would that mean? What would you do then? Where would you go? To Wyoming? . . ."

She chuckled.

"We used to joke, Avram and I, about selling everything, selling the business and moving to Wyoming, out west with the cowboys, can you imagine? Two Jews from the Ukraine out west with the cowboys? 'Where seldom is heard/ A discouraging word/ And the skies are not cloudy all day . . .' We'd been no further than Philadelphia since the day we stepped off the boat. There was no time. No money and no time. Just the shop. Except that as the years went by Avram became— I would say desperate, yes desperate, because above all he wanted finery, he wanted *gelt*, and he felt trapped in his middle age. He was incredibly vain, Avram, he forgot the old saying that whoever would avoid old age must hang himself in youth. He thought he was losing his looks, that it was simply a matter of time before the ladies wouldn't notice him anymore, and then what would he do? The finest toupee in the world wouldn't save him then. Because poor Avram was a terrible flirt, he loved to pretend he had *assignations in the night . . .*"

She laughed disparagingly.

"I could take any of it, his absurd carryings-on, his sarcasm, any of it but the cruelty. Because he started to beat me, and that was the limit. Who had ever heard of a Jewish wife-beater, it was completely *meshuggah* . . . His heart wasn't in it. He was hardly a truck driver, Avram, so he never really hurt me, just some black and blue, but it was awful all the same. He was appalled at what he was doing, he was abusing me instead of himself, we both knew that, we weren't fools. It was simply that, as time went on, we shared less and less. Avram with his pretensions to the fashionable life, *dying* when he couldn't afford tickets to the opera or the best seats at the theater, and the meals afterward, and the clothes . . . And me . . . Because after the Depression came I lost whatever interest I had in that world. In the Thirties all I could think about was the oppression of the worker, the rising threat of fascism, the urgency for some sort of response. And Avram refused to discuss all that, not that he didn't know what was going on but he hated politics. To him it was poison. It was all *realpolitik* under the surface, with one side out to liquidate the other by any means possible. It was a game of power to him, not like the opera, whose transports of joy were so real . . . Ever since the days in the Ukraine when we watched people betray their own in order to be allowed to have a little farm, some chickens, a pond . . . Ever since then Avram refused to have anything to do with politics. And when I joined the Party, well. For seven years until I quit in '39 we hardly spoke to each other, and many were the nights he didn't come home, especially after it was discovered I could no longer bear children. That was the final indignity. He grew coarser, drinking in a way he'd never done before, philandering in some desperate fashion, full of foul language and abuse. In the end he became an enigma, a cipher. I didn't know this man I had lived with my entire adult life. I didn't know him at all . . . *Es geyt mir vi a tsadik oyf der velt.*"

She broke off and lay there, staring out the window. I was about to say something when the door opened and Ed Reed walked in looking preoccupied. He was holding his cane in one hand and a shuffleboard stick in the other. He propped the stick against the wall and then, noticing me, raised his eyebrows in surprise. He motioned me to follow him out into the hall.

Closing the door behind us he eyed me intently. I was upset and told him so, explaining that Bessie had been going on about her husband without relating to me in any way. He nodded and said in a low, agitated voice, "I don't know why you're here, Marshall, but since you are you might as well understand a thing or two. Your grandmother isn't well and—"

"Look, Mr. Reed, she's Dana's grandmother, not mine. Dana and I used to live together but we don't anymore. I'm sorry to interrupt you but we should at least get straight who I am. My name's Roy—not Marshall. And Dana and I were never married. I hope all that doesn't matter as far as my coming up here is concerned."

"Are you finished," he snapped impatiently, "or should I get a chair to sit on while you continue yammering? They've had me on my feet all afternoon playing that game with the sticks and the pellets, like we were hamsters in a cage. If they post a list and your name's on it, don't ask, brother, you better play or they get the idea you're an invalid, see, you're fading fast, and then they restrict you to your bed and start dosing you with those pills. Horse capsules of Valium, and that's just for starters. Because maybe then they decide you're depressed. So they take a left turn and give you Lithium. Or if it's a heavier case, you can't take it anymore but you haven't started gnawing at the furniture yet, why then they'll slip you Positril . . . You ever had Positril, Roy? It elevates you. You're up. Just *up*, you follow me? You're enthusiastic about *everything*, you wander around giving pep talks and bumping into walls like a wind-up toy, see, a cheerful word for all, and soon they can't turn you off. And meanwhile maybe you've hurt yourself, reinjured that old knee, you know, in your enthusiasm, and that means you can't take care of yourself, you're a walking hazard, see, you're so up. So then they bring you down, they administer the Thorazine. If that doesn't work, why, they trot out the hypos with the heavy stuff, the bottles in the back of the doc's Frigidaire. And then you settle down, *way* down. You turn into a blimp with a cotton mouth and a mind like a willow tree. Now that hasn't happened yet to Bessie but they're moving in for the kill at this very moment. Do you understand? Do you detect the note of urgency in my voice? I haven't got time to listen to your mouthwash about you and your wife, or your cousin, or whoever she is . . . Bessie's been hearing voices for the past month or so, that confounded cloth-cutter she was married to. One day he started talking to her, criticizing her, telling her this and that 'til she couldn't stand it, and that's when the staff made its entry with their little cart full of pills and encouragement . . . Oh, believe me, it's not restricted just to chemicals, they'll also talk your ear off if you let them. And you can talk to them too, you're encouraged to talk to them endlessly, like I'm talking to you now, see? It's contagious, the talking here goes on all the time even if you can't hear it, people murmuring. And offstage voices too. It's a regular menagerie which our visitors aren't aware of. The dear relatives, they show up and see us here and we're passive and silent, or we speak up to tell them how grateful we are they've come, don't you know, but all the while we're gurgling, see, we're talking to beat the band, talking to ourselves and each other and the doctors and nurses and our dead wives and husbands and little children all grown up into strangers now, even talking to the cop who gave us a ticket twenty years ago. And then these people start talking back, of course, it's only natural. So you see there's quite a chorus here. And as far as I remember everybody's like that, sonny. Every Irishman I've ever known talked to himself 'til he was blue in the face, and after a few drinks he'd include you in the conversation too, and maybe punch you right in the kisser for something you never even said, because you were too busy talking to yourself, you follow me? Only when you get older you can't keep it hidden so well, the guff you got fed by so and so, the acres of malarkey you had to swallow, it all starts bubbling up to the surface because you have so much less to do in a place like Sunset Towers. The whole joint is set up for you to do nothing but brood. Even all the activity and such, the games and projects, they're only a way of keeping track of you. Well, some people have trouble dealing with that. It kinda gets their goat, don't ya know . . ."

Ed Reed had delivered most of this in an urgent undertone inches from my ear for fear of being overheard, and now he stood there sighing. Sweat covered his face and he looked weak. He talked as if all the patients at Sunset Towers had somehow been tricked into their present condition, which obviously couldn't be the case. Yet I was worried about Bessie. I asked what I could do, how could I help them.

"What can you do? Nothing . . . I don't know . . . She's got to stop dwelling on the past. I tell her that but it doesn't do any good. And how do you *make* someone not dwell on the past? Those pills they're feeding her sure won't help. I keep telling Bessie to pretend to swallow them and toss them out but she won't listen to me. She's usually so sharp, she's got pluck, that woman, but something's changed recently, it's got me upset . . . Most people are such godawful sheep, my boy. They're afraid of their own shadows."

I got excited. I wanted to tell Bessie that I understood what she was going through. I wanted to tell her she had to jettison the past, all of it, and start over. But then I realized I'd only be pressuring her, a strange person she hadn't seen in months. After all, Ed Reed seemed to have the right attitude. What could *I* do, give her magic mushrooms? I laughed aloud at the thought and Ed looked at me sourly.

"I didn't realize I was being funny, Roy . . . Clue me in, would ya . . ."

"No," I said, "it's just that I've been changing a lot recently myself and I can really identify with what Bessie's going through."

He grimaced. "Yeah? Well, you look the same to me . . . You can identify with her, eh? Go soak your head, Roy. You have no more problems than a dog in a park, trying to decide where to pee. But Bessie's in *trouble*. I've got to find a way to pull her out of it."

His ears got red.

"Because I love that lady in there. I admit it's hard to believe at my age, but it's true. I'd do anything to keep Bessie from disappearing alone down the big road. I mean it. Anything."

A nurse approached, asking what was the matter. Ed mumbled, "Visitor for Mrs. Goldman," and pushed me into Bessie's room, closing the door behind us.

He said, "How's tricks, Bessie? You remember this scamp? Dana's live-in? He can't seem to get enough of the old folks at home. Brought you some flowers, or so he says, though I don't see any."

They still lay on the chair and I picked them up and gave them to her. She smiled.

"Of course I remember Marshall!" Her face was drained and pale, but then she blushed. "Oh, God, Ed, I can't stand it. It's so embarrassing. I remember everything now. Dana's husband was here before, I knew who he was and wanted to talk to him but all that came out was Avram and more Avram. I can't control it, it's . . ."

She fell silent.

"But Bessie," Ed said, "you mustn't give in to your fear. That's what they're counting on, because if you don't face your fear and overcome it you'll have to keep taking those pills and you'll get worse."

She shifted uncomfortably in bed and looked out the window again. Her roommate, I noticed, had awakened and was now staring blankly in my direction, looking directly into my eyes. It was like the empty gaze of a dead person. Bessie started crying, very softly.

Ed turned to me.

"Look, Roy, I'm glad you came to see Bessie and I know she is too. You're welcome to visit again soon but I think you should leave now."

Out in the hall once more, his blue eyes flashing and a grainy note of determination in his voice, he said, "The next time we see you she'll be better, I guarantee it."

"It'll be a dramatic improvement, then," I said, "because I plan on coming back sometime next week."

But February turned into March, weeks went by, and in spite of wanting to, I didn't visit them. Something else had come up.

* * *

I loved Hobart, and usually he reciprocated by giving me a minimum of trouble, although keeping on top of everything called for constant vigilance. If I didn't clean out the various screens then the tank wouldn't function properly and might cut out in mid-cycle. I'd have to scramble to unload the machine, clean and check the parts, and load it again. This was no big deal early in the evening, but it was a different story if Hobart cut out on me when the place was jammed. Immediately running short of dishes wasn't the problem so much as continually falling behind from then on, which might reach crisis proportions if anything else went wrong.

Tempers grew short at Bamboo Mountain when the place was full and everybody's attention span was extended to the limit. But no matter how frantic things got, the cooks remained insulated from all that and proceeded at the same measured pace no matter what, rapidly but calmly turning out dish after dish with marvelous economy of movement. I loved to watch them in action: the woks, the big containers of vegetables, the cauldrons of steaming broth and water, Bobby Chin's quick hatchet taking apart a duck or reducing a slab of beef to cubes in seconds. And at the end of the evening, with everybody else run ragged, the three cooks would have a beer and head off to Chinatown, bags of leftovers under their arms.

I got along fine with the waiters since we hardly came into contact. But it was a different story as far as the busboy was concerned. He'd jump on me whenever the supply of dishes was insufficient. About nineteen years old, Eddie Saint, as he called himself, always dressed in what was fast becoming the punk uniform of the Lower East Side— torn T-shirts, chains around the neck, and safety pins in the ear. From my first day of work when he saw that I was not only white but over thirty, Eddie began to ride me. He couldn't believe I was working back there at the end of the kitchen next to the delivery door.

"I'm gonna report you to the city, man, you're taking away some Mexican's job," he joked, and soon he started calling me Grandpa. Eddie's nasty, self-satisfied laugh was even worse than his sense of humor. A pasty-faced, pimply ectomorph with prematurely thinning brown hair, he treated me as the person with the least rank at the restaurant because I'd been there the shortest amount of time and had the most menial job. He wanted the "big money" that came with being a waiter and pestered the twins about it, but he was too crude and unappealing for the job. Bamboo Mountain had a polished ambience which would be ill served by Eddie Saint in white shirt and chains, sneering at the customers. Whereas, Quemoy pointed out to me, as a busboy Eddie was perfect, a periodic disreputable presence in the dining room to offset the uniformly spiffy, good-looking young waiters.

Around the beginning of March, Quemoy offered me a waiter's job that had come open and when I turned it down, Eddie lit into me with a vengeance. He was infuriated by what he took to be my snobbery, whereas I simply wanted to continue doing my work and going home. But Eddie, in some crazy way, took it personally when I refused the job, as if it were a negative comment on his having wanted it.

"What's the matter," he hissed at me, "you're too good for this place? Or did old Kee-Moy ask you to do somethin' dirty, suck a little Chinese dick maybe, like that kid they had working here before you, and you just couldn't deal with it." He delivered this in a livid whisper, then threw back his head and laughed, loudly and raucously. Everybody else in the kitchen froze. "And so you made up this bullshit about not wanting it when that's really what you meant—you didn't *want it*." He winked at me and then, giving me a significant leer, took off into the dining room.

But later that night, Quemoy said something to me which wasn't very different. He, too, couldn't understand why I had turned down a chance to make over fifty dollars a night. He was nonplussed by a supposedly intelligent, able white guy like me not only washing dishes but liking it. Up to that point he had never really asked me about myself but when I refused his offer he had looked me up and down and said, "Let's discuss this later."

After everybody else had gone home he said, a note of irritation in his voice, "I can't believe it, you know? I mean, it's none of my business, I got lots more to think about than you, but, like, just last night Matsu and me were talking about you, figuring out whether or not to offer you the job, and we realized you're the same age as us!"

I hadn't thought about this before but it was true.

"Yet I could be your father, almost, you seem like such a kid. Matsu and me've been through ten times the experiences that you have, I can tell by looking at your face and comparing it to mine. I mean, I take good care of myself, I go to the health club and all, flush the poisons out of my system, but talk about wrinkles, man, talk about worry lines. I got the market cornered, Matsu too. We been *around*, man. But you . . . In fact, come to think of it, you look even younger now than when you first showed up—you're in lots better shape, anyway—so I guess washing dishes agrees with you, right? It's all you want out of life?"

"I like what I'm doing, Quemoy, it's as simple as that." I didn't volunteer any further information and he didn't ask.

Instead, he gave me a long, judgmental look but couldn't help giggling when he said in a tone of mock rebuke, "What's wrong, fella, you lack ambition? Don't you believe in the American dream?" Becoming serious again he added, "Look what it's done for two chink orphans like my brother and me. Sure, you have to want to, there's no way around that, but damn it you can *score* in this society. The whole shot's wide open, Roy. You just have to want it bad enough."

"You mean I have to want to take shit from those assholes out there on the floor for eight hours at a stretch? Then I'd be living the American dream?"

We glared at each other and he started to laugh, but didn't. "No, I guess you got a point there, Roy. I have to tell that one to Matsu. He'd appreciate it. He likes that kind of perverse humor."

But I *was* content washing dishes, perfectly content, especially after an incident a few weeks before when Eddie called in sick and I had to bus tables in between my sessions with Hobart. Because suddenly, as I straightened up holding a tub piled high with dirty dishes, I found myself looking directly into my ex-colleague Peter Arney's face.

He was sitting at a big round table with a party of record industry types, everybody dressed to the hilt and gaily chugging down glasses of champagne. Our eyes met and he blanched, becoming so embarrassed that he turned away and stared off into the bamboo fronds in the middle of the restaurant. But in order to do so he had broken off the conversation he was having in mid-sentence, and several other guys at the table, all of whom looked vaguely like Rod Stewart, gave me stagey, antagonistic stares. The fact that Arney tried to pretend he didn't know me wasn't as upsetting as his embarrassment, which resulted from assuming I was humiliated because, in my place, that's how he would feel. Actually, I wasn't in the least humiliated appearing as a busboy before this table of music business shills, but the definition of the situation was out of my hands. His version would be accepted by anybody to whom he mentioned it.

"Guess who I saw busing tables at this Chinese restaurant in SoHo, man," he would say. "Go ahead, just guess! I'm telling you, it was downright *awkward*."

This encounter only reinforced my desire to stay off the floor. I didn't need the contact. My relationship with Hobart was good enough for me.

However, apparently there were a few wrinkles in the American dream even for Quemoy and Matsu, because early in March they began appearing at the restaurant less often, and when they did they had an uncharacteristically preoccupied air about them. They seemed nervous and distracted and were doing more and more lines of coke in the kitchen. Quemoy's jokes and pranks had vanished and Matsu, sullen as ever, began showing up in the company of his big, mean-looking German Shepherd named Sally. The sight of this dog stationed in a vigilant crouch near the entrance upset more than one prospective diner, but Matsu didn't seem to care. He also started carrying a briefcase with him, never letting it out of his grip, as if it contained his protection. I had never seen anybody who looked more like he meant business. There were times when he spent the entire evening sitting at the bar facing the entrance, the briefcase on his knee, drinking club soda and chain-smoking cigarettes. It wasn't long before everybody at the restaurant got nervous and made jokes about Mafia hitmen busting through the door.

There had been rumors at Bamboo Mountain for a while now that the twins were dealing coke as well as using it. But I couldn't see that.

I couldn't imagine them getting involved in something as dangerous and chaotic as drug dealing. They'd always talked about how important it was to be in control, to call the shots in whatever they did.

Meanwhile, the twins were also having trouble of a different sort. For weeks now, one after another of the big trees in the bamboo grove in the middle of the room had been wilting, the leaves gradually being covered with a sooty black mold and sticking together. Lately, the graceful, thirty-foot-high stalks had begun dipping perilously close to the diners' plates. The twins were very upset because this extravagant, sumptuously green island of bamboo was the restaurant's namesake and centerpiece, and had been expensive to install. Apparently the only domestic source was a stretch of South Carolina coastline where they were bulldozed out of the ground on order and trucked north. But Quemoy and Matsu refused to consider replacing them with an assortment of other tropical plants.

"I don't want Bamboo Mountain looking like a doctor's office," Quemoy sniffed. "I hate all those dumb rubber plants and stuff. They're so banal. Whereas our bamboo trees, they were beautiful, they made this room soar . . ."

He complained about the people out on Long Island from whom he had bought the grove. "Now suddenly these guys are telling me how tricky it is to keep real bamboo in the city winter. They're telling me we shouldn't even try unless we have greenhouse conditions. But last year, when we opened, those same bastards said it was fine, the skylight gave enough light, we have good heat, no problem. I mentioned that to them this afternoon," he told me incredulously as we sat in the kitchen after work, "and they refuse to admit they ever said it. *Now* the story is that everybody in the business knows how difficult bamboo is, that they never actually recommended it, they were just giving us what we wanted. So I guess Matsu and me were dreaming, right, when we were designing this place and asked them about it. When they sold us that bamboo for three grand, three thousand fucking dollars!"

Then, one Saturday at the end of March an extraordinary thing happened. Jimmy Wu opened up in the morning to find all the trees keeled over dead and the place full of thousands of tiny yellow aphids.

Virtually invisible, apparently they had attacked the underside of the leaf blades, feeding on the plants and excreting sugar-water on which the mold had developed. Spraying them with insecticide only resulted in a poisonous golden layer of dead insects over everything, so the twins closed the restaurant before lunch while they figured out what to do. I showed up for work as usual that evening to find a crowd of waiters standing around looking at the bamboo. The sight of those long brown stalks collapsed across one another was unsettling, but the tension in the air clearly resulted from something more than dead bamboo. Matsu was gone and Quemoy paced back and forth wearing an incongruously flamboyant yellow nylon jumpsuit. He took large sips of cognac from a water glass and looked distracted. He kept shaking his head. Around his neck I noticed the gold razor blade he sometimes wore. It was past five o'clock but he looked like he'd just gotten out of bed. "Alex Haley was here last week with all these people from *Roots*," he moaned, "we're finally getting hot, we're getting mentioned in the press, and now this has to happen. I can't open the place looking like this—just cart these fucking trees off and leave a gaping hole there with that fountain sticking out like at a store or something. It would be like eating on the floor at Sears . . . Forget it."

He eyed the trees resentfully.

"I've had it," he said. "Everybody gets a couple of days off. We reopen Tuesday for dinner, unless those crackers wreck their truck on the way up here. I think we could all use a vacation anyway. That scene with the swordfish last night was too much."

The night before, several customers had complained the swordfish tasted of gasoline, and Matsu had lost his temper with the last one, a man who turned out to be somebody in Mayor Beame's administration and threatened to throw his weight around. "I can close this place down overnight, you don't realize who I am!" he had intoned, a little drunk. And Matsu had shot back in that surly, cold way he had, "Neither does your poor mother, fathead," whereupon they almost came to blows. The entire outburst hadn't looked good to the other diners, either, that was for sure.

As I was about to leave, Quemoy turned to me and said abruptly, "I need you tonight, Roy . . . Will you come with me?"

The plaintive, deliberate way he said it stunned me. For a moment I thought he was coming on to me.

He took me into the kitchen and said intently, "Look, Roy, I don't know why but I sort of trust you. You won't tell me anything about yourself and that's never a good sign, is it? On the other hand—what can I say?—you look like a nice Jewish boy who isn't gonna steal the family silver." He laughed. "So I'll level with you."

He was examining me with bright, nervous eyes, watching for my reaction.

"And the way it is," he continued, "Matsu isn't here, I don't know where he went. He may or may not be in trouble but I can't think about that until I go someplace *right now*, see, and talk to a guy. And I need somebody else along. I need a witness, somebody who can back up what I'm hearing from this person, do you understand? Because he's kinda strange . . . Very jumpy . . ."

Drops of sweat were forming on his forehead. When he stopped talking he looked at me, waiting for an answer with an impatience which didn't mask how upset he was. But his vagueness irritated me and my first impulse was to say no.

"What do you mean, Quemoy? What kind of guy are you talking about? I don't want to get hurt."

He found this remark very funny and let out that infectious laugh of his, his face suddenly warm and sympathetic, his black eyes glowing.

"Holy cow, Roy, do you think I'd let you come to any harm? This is just talk, no danger, no drugs. George Adolphus wouldn't hurt a fly, it's just—I don't want to go into the details, you don't want to hear about my life, believe me. I'm asking you to do me a favor, that's all. I need somebody to corroborate whatever he says to me . . . *Seriously* . . . I haven't got time to go scouting around for somebody else to bring along. And if I took a tape recorder Adolphus would flip out, he wouldn't talk to me. He's paranoid, just the sight of it would freak him out. So you're working for me, understand? You're part of our construction crew."

I stared at him, trying to figure out what was going on. He got anxious and impatient again.

"Look, you don't *have* to do it. It's not part of your job. That's why I explained it to you. But I gotta go see him right now, I can't wait for Matsu anymore. I need you. Will you come?"

He held out his hand, touched me lightly on the arm, smiled again.

"Yes," I said.

TWELVE

Before we left the restaurant, Quemoy did a few lines of coke, shaking his head in disbelief when he offered me some and I refused. Now, as we walked through SoHo he was in a talkative mood and began breathlessly confiding in me. I'd never seen him so wired.

"My brother and I got into this real estate thing late, you know," he said, "and sometimes I have the feeling we're in over our heads. You wouldn't believe the kind of guys we have to deal with. Matsu and me know enough about construction now to do the job right, but the process is more complicated than that. Getting a line on available buildings at this stage of the game means doing favors for people, and scraping together the money to buy them—boy, has that been weird. See, we can't go to the bank for this. Starting the restaurant was another story, the bank loved that, but to go through them for these buildings is too time-consuming. There's all these bullshit restrictions that everybody ignores—we know that and the bank knows it—but it makes them skittish as hell, and we're mortgaged up to our eyes already. Also, we're in a hurry. We can't afford to play around. This scene downtown is changing by the minute—just in the last year, prices all along the line have been going haywire. You can get more for finished conversions that six months ago, but the buildings cost more too—a lot more—and some of these people with the money do funny things, like upping the interest rate on a loan they made to you, or even deciding they want more principle than you agreed upon . . . If they can get away with it, they just do it. It's a fucking jungle . . ."

He sighed and, looking around, began pointing out various loft buildings, telling me what they'd sold for originally and what they were worth now.

"Take that one," he said, gesturing toward a cast-iron facade on Greene Street. "Ninety-seven five in 1971, the entire building, right? Two hundred grand a year later, six hundred and fifty thousand now. Can you believe it? The place is totally raw loft space—they used to make cardboard cartons in there or something, with sweatshops on the upper floors, dinky little operations with rows of Vietnamese refugees hunched over their sewing machines. So the total outlay of cash—buying the building, renovating it—is enormous. It's driving everybody out but the big guys. The guys with enough clout in this city to change the laws so they can sell to whoever they want. It's a fever zone down here, and Matsu and me are moving to make what we can before the market becomes saturated. We're taking a big gamble. Most people think this scene's gone as far as it can go, but we feel otherwise. Still, lately things have been getting too hairy. And when the people you're depending on start acting erratic—well, take it from me, it's tight . . ."

According to Quemoy, George Adolphus was a legendary figure in SoHo. A lot of artists hated him now because he had burned them in various ways, installing faulty plumbing or wiring, not taking care of paper work, charging them for things he never did. But, on the other hand, if it hadn't been for George Adolphus there very likely wouldn't even be a SoHo. In the late Sixties when the area's rundown commercial lofts were being abandoned, he was the first to come up with the then completely illegal idea of putting artists into them. Single-handedly he developed ways of getting around outmoded residential laws. He encouraged penniless artists he knew to move in. Landlords were willing to take almost anything for these spaces. In the early days that meant living behind blacked-out windows, never answering the door because it might be the Fire Department, and tapping into Con Ed's power lines so no record existed of their presence.

In 1968 he was a pioneer. The artists he helped were his friends, and he opened building after building to them out of a real commitment to their work. But by the mid-Seventies SoHo had caught on and suddenly he was making a fortune. Soon the artists to whom he sold space were strangers. In order to finance what had originally been a kind of charitable crusade, he became involved with borrowing from questionable sources. After several potentially violent run-ins with these people over the previous two years he became more and more cautious, until lately—what with many of his old friends refusing to speak to him because of the money he was making, and the neighborhood full of slick Europeans he didn't know—Adolphus had become a virtual recluse. He was in his late fifties already, and lived with his aged mother ("She's this shrunken old peasant woman in a black kerchief who never goes out at all," Quemoy said) in a custom-built, window-less bunker at subway level, a kind of fortress sub-basement of a build-ing he owned on Mercer Street. It was almost impossible to see him anymore. Recently, in fact, he had bought a yacht and claimed he was going to live on the ocean where nobody could get at him.

Quemoy said, "The whole situation has turned inside out on him and he feels like a guru under siege, or something. It's really strange. I'll tell you, Roy, I don't like stereotypes—if you're Chinese in the States you get fed that shit all the time—but I can't help feeling that most people in this city are basically paranoid. Everybody you meet is touchy and secretive. You rarely come across anyone who'll level with you, and everybody's so grimly determined to make it. Sometimes I wonder why Matsu and me ever left California. At least there, people smile while they're trying to fuck you over, and if things get to be too much, you can grab your board and take off for the beach, ride those waves all afternoon . . . But there's no escape valve here, you just go up and down these cold streets trying to stay one step ahead. And the winters, man—I still haven't gotten used to them. Every year about this time, February or March, I start having these visions of Taiwan— the colors, the heat, the countryside—and I'll wake up one morning and really can't figure out why I'm here . . . It's a problem, because the kicker is, I *love* New York, I really do. I wouldn't trade my life here for anything. It just gets so crazy sometimes . . ."

We stopped at an elevator entrance on Mercer Street and Quemoy rang one of the buzzers three times, then once, then three times again. "More games," he said in exasperation. We stood there waiting and after five minutes the door suddenly buzzed and we pushed through into a big freight elevator with a television camera in the ceiling. Then we went down. The steel door slid open and we stood face-to-face with a stooped, gray-haired, exhausted-looking man with dark pouches under his eyes and a forlorn, distrustful expression in them, as if at the first wrong move from us he might flap his wings and fly away. He had an olive complexion and prominent birthmarks on his face, a bushy moustache that in contrast to his hair was completely black, and a twitch that jerked across his cheek when he talked. He spoke with a lilting Eastern European accent, although the vocabulary was pure street American.

"Who's this?" he croaked, pointing at me. "Where's your brother?"

I looked around the long room with its dark old-fashioned furniture and didn't see anybody else. The place was in disarray, with half-filled boxes and cartons everywhere.

Quemoy frowned. "This is Roy, George. He's from our work crew. We're finishing up a job on Grand Street, that carriage house that used to have the live poultry butcher on the ground floor. God, what a mess that place was! And I don't know where Matsu is, he was supposed to meet us at the restaurant but never showed up. If I had time to worry about it I would, but I gotta clear something up with you right away, George. We're running out of time. My brother and me are getting leaned on by that bastard Angelo and I don't understand why."

"Angelo's OK," Adolphus responded in a flat, disinterested voice.

"No, he's not, damn it," Quemoy said urgently. "You been telling us that from day one, but meanwhile he won't take the bucks. He won't take the money, George, understand? We can't afford any more than what we owe, not one dime. We're stretched to the limit. I don't even really know who Angelo *is*, for Christ's sake. We never would've got involved with that guy if it hadn't been for your assurance that—"

"My assurance? What am I, the king of SoHo? I never promised you anything, Quemoy, and you know it. I don't owe you zip. I simply came up with the name of a man who was straight with me in the past, and that's more than I can say about most of the fellas I've dealt with. What he's saying to you now is for you to figure out. I have other things to think about. Besides, what makes you and your brother so special? You're like everybody else down here, trying to score as fast as possible off the neighborhood. But that's not the point. The point is that not only is this none of my business, but you're bullshitting me."

He paused. The three of us still were standing right by the elevator.

"Bullshitting," Quemoy said, "what are you talking about?"

"What I'm talking about is that you make a big production about how Angelo's threatening you, insisting you have to see me right away in person, the phone's no good, and what you're really trying to do is pump me for information about him. But I know for a fact that you're not paying him on time. You and Matsu are overextended. You've been late with the payments more than once . . . And another thing, while I'm thinking about it, since your brother's not here I can tell you that he's a liability, Quemoy. He's too hot-headed. You can't act that way with somebody who's got you by the balls and expect to get away with it. Matsu is crazy."

Quemoy took a deep breath and, grimacing, shifted his weight from one foot to the other. He smiled and said, "Jesus, George, aren't you even gonna invite us to sit down? I been working hard all day and—"

"Working, Quemoy? In that absurd monkey suit you've got on? That's more baloney. It's like an epidemic with you. You're not even telling me the truth about this fella you brought with you," he said, gesturing in my direction. "He's a lie, too."

"What do you mean?"

"Look at his hands, Quemoy. How much construction work you think he's ever done?"

They eyed each other warily. The buzzer to the door upstairs rang, but Adolphus didn't answer it. Then Quemoy suddenly became panicky and said in a despairing voice, "OK, George, I'll level with you. Matsu's made a few mistakes, but that's not the real problem. It's true, we *are* overdue, and you're also right about me coming here to find out whatever I can about Angelo, because we're up against it. We don't have the money."

I had never seen Quemoy upset like this before.

"What are we gonna do, George?" he pleaded. "I'm scared, and I don't like it. He won't give us any leeway. It's put up or suffer the consequences. But I didn't come here to ask you for cash, I know you won't give it to me anyway. I just need your advice. What kind of compensation will satisfy this guy? He's already making noises about taking part of the restaurant, but we won't do that, George. We worked too damn hard on that place to let someone else gobble it up."

Sweat poured down his face now, in spite of the fact that the basement was as cool as a food locker.

"I know you don't owe us anything. But I need your help . . . And Matsu and me *are* different, no matter what you think. We're not ripping off the artists like everybody else down here. We buy their paintings. Check out the walls in my loft if you don't believe me. We make sure they're not getting in over their heads before we let them get involved with us. We really *do* care about art."

This sounded so preposterous that in spite of the tension in the air they both laughed. Quemoy looked at the old man ruefully and added, "I don't know who else to turn to, George, I mean it. We've never been in a situation like this before."

Adolphus started humming to himself, half-closing his puffed eyes. The buzzer sounded again—three times, then once, then three times. Quemoy smiled weakly. "That must be Matsu," he said, but Adolphus made no move to answer it. He was thinking something over. A slight smile creased his face.

"Listen," he said eventually, "you haven't been straight with me since you walked in here, but at least your timing is right. This last month has been hell for me, and as soon as Mother returns from the hospital we're pulling out of here for good. The middle of next week at the latest. I'm packed up already. A couple of fellas are out there who make Angelo look like Santa Claus. I was *shot at* last week, my friend, right out there on Houston Street in the middle of the afternoon, like this is Palermo, Sicily. I've had it with this city. I'm *tired*, I'm sick, Mother's sick. I just want to get on that boat and disappear. I've been working day and night tying up loose ends, and everything's set except for this one structure on Greene, down by Canal. I can't unload it, nobody wants to buy it, and I'm not hanging around to fix it up, that's for sure. So if you want it, it's yours. Get me? It's not very large, 3500 square feet on each floor, only four floors. Used to be a doll factory, so there's a lot of work to do. All this machinery and junk's still in there, doll parts ankle-deep on every floor—the eyes on one floor, the heads on another, legs and arms on a third . . . Ankle deep," he said dreamily, "like some kind of toy store Auschwitz . . . I don't even know what condition the foundation's in, I've completely lost interest. But I'll give it to you. Maybe you can work something out using that as collateral, I don't know. Sign it over to Angelo. It's better than winding up in the trunk of a car at JFK. I'll have my lawyer prepare transfer of ownership papers right away, you call him tomorrow afternoon—you know my lawyer, don't you? Lawrence Kramer, on Broadway. His number's in the book. Lawrence E . . ."

Quemoy stood there dazed, his mouth open. Finally he said in an agonized voice, "*Doll factory!* I know that building . . . But I don't get it, George. Is this some kind of joke? Why would you do something like that for me? How do I know you're not just jerking me off to get me out of here? Goddamnit, George, I'm *serious*, we need help, we only got a couple more days. How can I trust you?"

Adolphus' eyes widened and his face twitched. "How can you trust me? I've already told you, I can't stand it here one more day! I'm not just blowing hot air. I don't want to be killed, can you understand that? This isn't a game. They're after me. Why do you think Mother's in the hospital? She knows what's happening to me . . . Terry Ackerman, Denise Simmons, Margaret Bailey, Joe Fuss, Eddie Lee Ellis—I helped them for years, I found them places to live, bought their paintings when they were starving, introduced them to gallery owners—now they won't talk to me, they accuse me of selling out. It's a nightmare. I start out in the early Sixties knowing people like John Cage and Jonas Mekas and Charlie Mingus, involved in a whole new life with them, and now I'm ending up with you. A queer chink speculator! I don't care anymore, can't you hear what I'm saying? I have to get out. I'm sick of these buildings, of the people I see on the street, these ex-friends of mine with their smug, superior smiles, their lists of complaints, their petitions to the city. Take the building! Make more money! Take it!"

Shaking with rage, tears in his eyes, he turned and ran back into the depths of the bunker. The phone rang, over and over. We let ourselves into the elevator and rode up to the street. Outside, Matsu was squatting on the sidewalk, his back against the wall, waiting. He jumped to his feet and ran over to us, dressed in a black leather motorcycle jacket and jeans, gold chains around his neck.

Quemoy was stunned, torn between elation and doubt. He turned to me and, tugging at my arm said incredulously, "Did that really happen? Come on, Roy, tell me. You were there. Am I dreaming or what? Do you think he's crazy? Do you think his lawyer's gonna have those papers? *I have to know.*"

He grabbed me by the shoulders, shaking me until I yelled at him to stop. Matsu stood there perplexed. His brother finally noticed him and started jabbering in Chinese, but Matsu still appeared confused. He asked me what had happened and I related everything I could remember.

"How should I know whether it's the truth or not," I concluded. "But why would he make such a promise otherwise? Why not simply tell Quemoy straight out that he wasn't going to help him?"

Slowly Matsu's face softened and he smiled. "Wow," he said. "What a day this has been. Maybe we're off the hook after all." They both became excited, laughing hysterically, fighting off the edge of uncertainty that kept closing in on them.

"This is unbearable," Quemoy shouted, "I feel so high, like I'm going into orbit!" His eyes shining he embraced me, squeezing me in a bear hug that left me breathless, and said, "I'm so glad you came along, Roy. God knows where I'd be at if all that had gone down and I'd been alone. I'd be going nuts . . . Because I think it's gonna happen, I can feel it. Just like you said, why wouldn't he tell me to get lost? What favors should I expect from George Adolphus?"

Doubt clouded his eyes again and he moaned, gritting his teeth. "God, I can't stand this," he said. Then he seemed to have made up his mind for good and turned to his brother with a big grin. "Hey Matsu," he said. "Party time—let's celebrate! That scene up by the Whitney. They said to come early, remember? Let's go!"

Matsu looked at me then said, "I think it's a little *too* early. It's only eight-thirty now."

"Yeah, so what? You know that doesn't matter," Quemoy replied impatiently.

The brothers exchanged glances. I felt like Matsu was questioning my presence there. "Listen, Quemoy," I said, "I'm splitting. I hope it all works out for you."

But he wouldn't have any of that. Giggling, throwing his arm around me, he insisted I come to the party with them. Addressing Matsu, he said, "Roy's absolutely cool, can't you tell? Cool like a rock. I brought him along 'cause God knows where *you* were and I had to have another set of ears with me. And I was right!"

Then he said to me, "You must party *once* in a while, no? I guarantee you won't be bored where we're going . . ." He paused then grinning mischievously, added, "Uptown, man, you know? We travel in the best circles. Plenty of pretty women for you. Who knows, you might meet the love of your life, she'll turn out to be the daughter of Prudential Insurance. You won't have to keep washing dishes then, right? Although I'll miss ya, kid . . ." He was giddy now, cackling and making faces at Matsu, who scowled at him and said reprovingly, "Watch your step."

But then Matsu smiled, which seemed to make Quemoy ecstatic. "Where's the van parked, oh most esteemed twin brother? Let us decamp from this dreadful place." As we approached a shiny black customized van, Quemoy turned to me and said, "You know, the Chinese language is very precise. Very accurate. The theory of relativity in a nutshell, and five thousand years old, too . . . For instance, there's no word for brother in my native language. Instead, we have separate words for younger brother—*didi*—and older brother—*gege*. It all depends on your relation to the person in question. That determines who he is, you see what I mean? But Matsu and me, we're not like that. We're special. Identical twins. *Shiang shin.* The same term for both of us. Although I must have come out of the gate first, I just know it. 'Cause—haven't you noticed?—Matsu's always the one who's trailing behind!"

* * *

The van had two bucket seats up front—roomy and plush like first-class airplane seats—and was shag-carpeted in the rear, with a bunk running along one side on which I sat, hunched forward to look out the windshield. Matsu drove, and as soon as we hit a red light Quemoy pulled out a vial of cocaine and began cutting some on a wooden board he took out of the glove compartment. The light changed to green and Matsu gunned it with Quemoy laughing and cursing, shaking coke all over the floor. "Goddamnit, pull off the road into the bushes for a second, will ya?" he said, and Matsu parked in the east twenties some-where, engine running, while Quemoy made neat little lines. I turned down their offer of a hit and they both snorted away, rubbing their noses and coughing, chiding me about my abstention. "What are you, in training?" Matsu asked sarcastically. "Is it part of your religion?"

"I'm just not interested. It's a long story."

"I'll bet it *is*, mystery man," Quemoy said, "and wouldn't we love to hear it!"

We parked on 74th Street east of Madison, around the corner from the Whitney Museum, and were let into a small, elegant townhouse on the south side of the street by a young man in a dark suit and tie, who asked us what we'd like to drink and then disappeared. The build-ing was narrow. A black and white tiled entranceway gave onto a stair-case running up the right side of the house, while to the left there was a long living room with a kitchen area at the back.

"It's beautiful, isn't it?" Quemoy said. "The house has three stories, each one's different. You should wander around and check it out."

Matsu was already gone, and as somebody materialized at my side with a glass of wine, Quemoy drifted off toward the kitchen. The lovely antique furniture and wood panelling, the Persian rug on the floor, the Renaissance prints on the walls, and the fire going in a stone fireplace with andirons in the shape of two kneeling deer—all radiated a self-assured refinement. The living room was filled with all kinds of people—sober, fastidious men wearing three-piece suits and specta-cles; strapping models or actors dressed to kill in the latest European styles; dudes with staring, searching eyes in leather jeans and nylon shirts open to the belly; deeply tanned individuals with the svelte, cossetted look of the very rich—all kinds of people, except that every last one of them was male.

As I glanced around the room, sipping my wine, it was the eyes I noticed. Arrogant or inquiring or brazen, they met me at every turn fairly bursting with an incipient sexuality, until soon I felt distracted and abashed. Everybody mingled, looking at one another, drifting out the door and going upstairs, wandering back down for a drink. I didn't know what to do. I walked up to the fireplace and found myself staring down at the deer, on whose backs a pyramid of split logs was burning. Their mouths were open, a small tongue visible in each one. I suddenly remembered the bear licking my bones clean that night on psilocybin four months earlier, and I stood there, looking down into the flames and whispering the phrase, "You can't burn my bones," wondering what I was doing at this party. I decided that bringing me to the house had been another of Quemoy's little pranks, and I was about to leave when a group of men standing nearby sort of re-formed around me. They were very friendly. Each introduced himself with a first name. Harvey, hairy and tanned and muscular, had silver wisps of hair on an almost completely bald head, and looked to be in his late forties; Jeff, at least half his age, blond and faultlessly handsome, with wonderfully arrogant, full lips; Aaron, intense and sweaty, dressed in suit and tie, who looked like a strap-hanger without a briefcase; and Armando, Latin, in his twenties, dark and supercilious, who reminded me immediately of Matsu. Matsu had that same kind of proud, "dare me" expression in his eyes sometimes.

"*I am Cuban,*" Armando added significantly after introducing himself, as if that explained everything. The others chuckled at this. There was a lot of joking and whispered asides going on among them. They made cracks about a distinguished-looking man at the other end of the room who sat in an easy chair, alone except for the enormous brown Great Dane wearing a silver collar which lay at his feet. This person seemed quite aloof, puffing at a pipe, dressed in a forest-green velour smoking jacket. He had a becalmed, remote expression, like a matinee idol from the Thirties. Aaron said to Harvey, "He's clearly earmarked for opium, don't you think?" and the others broke up. "Oh, I think that would be a waste," Harvey replied. "He wouldn't even notice it." They all laughed again.

"Who is he?" I asked.

Armando arched an eyebrow and replied impatiently, "How should we know? We thought maybe you come with him. He's—you know—your father or something."

This brought on more subdued chuckling.

"Well," Armando continued, "if you're not with that—that *institution* over there, then who are you? Besides Roy, I mean. What do you *do*?"

There was a pause. Out of the blue I replied, "I'm a consultant."

More chuckling. In this conversation, it didn't seem to matter what you said as long as somebody found it amusing, and I liked that.

"Well, please," Armando said, "you will allow me to be the next in line for one of your consultations. I have *so* much to ask you. Or maybe this isn't the time and place . . . You have regular office hours, you don't mix business and pleasure, I can tell. A very good idea—unless you're like me, and business and pleasure are the same thing. That can lead to so many problems. Only the mentally tough need apply . . ."

More snickering, this time with a bored sound to it, as if one had heard quite enough from Armando for the time being.

Looking restless, Jeff kept pouting and giving the eye to another boy across the room. Soon everybody in our little group was aware of this, and instantly Harvey became uncomfortable.

"Please, Jeff. We just got here," he said in an urgent undertone which Jeff pretended not to hear.

"I'll just be a minute," Jeff said. "Guy I know."

He walked off. We watched the two of them greet each other and leave the room.

"Oh, God," Harvey moaned, "here we go again. I can't take it anymore."

"It comes with the territory," Armando said listlessly.

Aaron chucked Harvey under the chin and drawled, "Well, old man, it's not as if no one warned you. You made your bed, now lie in it . . . Or is it *lay*?"

"Thanks loads," Harvey said. "Now I know just where to turn when I need sympathy and understanding."

Aaron and Armando laughed and walked off toward the kitchen.

"Well, Roy," Harvey said, "maybe you won't desert me . . ." Clearly upset, he stood staring at the doorway through which Jeff had disappeared.

"It can't be as bad as that, can it?" I found myself saying.

He sighed. "Oh, can't it." Then he turned to face me, giving me a look of such plaintive longing that I flinched.

"You don't understand anything about it, do you?" he said. "You have no idea what it's like being my age and falling for somebody like him, and I do mean falling, with a capital c-r-a-s-h. You make a fool of yourself. Everything you do out of desperation simply drives him further away. I'm forty-eight years old, Roy, and he's nineteen, or so he says. When we're together it's heaven. But I'm so afraid he's going to leave me and he just plays into that, of course. Showing him how much I care is the stupidest thing I could do, but I can't help it. The desire I have for that boy is endless. And the irony is that deep inside I'm the same person I was when I was in my twenties. The same! The desire, the longing, never leave you. Do you understand? Obviously not. How could you? But just wait fifteen years. You'll see . . . Will you ever . . ."

He paused and then added in a resigned voice, "You know, they say that secretly everyone wants to be turned down, everyone wants to be rejected. But I just can't handle the pain. I really mean it."

He looked at me with that penetrating hopelessness again and I didn't know what to say.

"Listen, Harvey, it'll work out. I'm going to walk around for a while. It was nice meeting you."

"Oh, sure thing," he replied coolly.

On the second floor were two rooms: a dining room overlooking a garden in the back and a library. I walked into the library, a claustrophobic space, richly decorated, with a ceiling of tufted blue silk, shelves lined with leather-bound books, and a sort of banquette, covered with rugs and pillows, which extended along the walls. In the center on a table stood a large filigreed brass lantern, which threw very dim golden light into the room. Arabic music played softly in the background and on the banquette sat various couples making out and talking. I stood there for a few minutes and then picked out a book I could barely see and leafed through vellum pages of *Robinson Crusoe*. Nearby an intense conversation was taking place.

"Are you ready for this?" one person was saying. "Herbert has a pet rat, a gray rat he bought from some scientific laboratory and keeps here in the house, lets it run loose. He likes to frighten the guests. I just thought I'd warn you."

"Surely you're joking," a deep, sonorous voice replied.

"I wish I were . . . You know, Donald, I really wonder sometimes where it's all leading. Herbert just gets battier and battier. All he can talk about now is that horrid latex molecule scam. He's been taken in hook, line, and sinker. He thinks that simply because he went to Harvard with Bunny Gordon thirty years ago he can trust the man. But Bunny Gordon is positively insane, my dear. I mean, *latex molecules*, for heaven's sake. It's another of these wonder drug mirages where desperate wealthy people are taken advantage of. So much money's being made off those who are afraid of growing old. It's unbelievable. Injecting themselves with BHA preservatives—you know, the kind they use on *vegetables*; or enduring thirty days of microsurgery and seaweed diets. And now this: wonder-working protection against all diseases, no less, including cancer. Positive insulation from all toxins, which, once perfected, will allow the lucky recipient unchecked self-indulgence and dissipation. Endless cigarette smoking, endless bottles of champagne, endless drugs. Because, you see, the protein coating in natural latex molecules contains a substance which, when grafted onto some virus or other and injected into the human bloodstream, results in almost unlimited reinforcement of the body's immune system. Not only that, it somehow cuts down on the wear and tear of cell systems in general, resulting in indefinitely extended vigor and vitality."

"My God," the deep voice interjected.

"I'm telling you," said the other, "I sat there listening to all of this, paying close attention, mind you, determined to take it seriously. After all, Herbert's been one of my closest friends for years, and to listen to him go on and on like a *child* . . . Well, you've no idea."

Donald replied, "It's just like what that fellow—"

"Who?"

"I'm trying to remember the name. We met him up at Scott's once . . . Cleveland, or something?"

"Oh, God yes, Allan Cleveland. Why didn't I think of him before? Oh Lord, absolutely! . . . The clinic in Switzerland, the Swiss rejuvenation process. For a hundred and fifty thousand dollars you're wrapped in a mummy-like material that burns off your old skin. Meanwhile, you also undergo a program of injections of raw lamb fetus. Of course, you are fed gourmet meals during your ordeal, which lasts altogether one month. You emerge at the end with a new skin, pink and soft as a baby's. And you should see these people! Allan Cleveland looks so young—alarmingly young—not a wrinkle on his face and you know he's sixty years old. He looks waxen, like an alien from outer space. You haven't seen the man since he came back, but I'm telling you, Donald, it's frightening."

The deeper voice responded, "Well, the only real problem I can see for those who undertake such a program is that they will find themselves with a senile brain lodged in an adolescent's body."

They both laughed mournfully.

"Like poor Somerset Maugham . . ."

"Indeed."

"Or Mrs. What's-her-name up in Newport."

"*Really* . . ."

Then they noticed I was eavesdropping. They looked up to see me not ten feet away, rooted to the spot, unable to believe what I was hearing. Suddenly, for the first time in months, Oliver Hartwell was on my mind. I had the strangest feeling that he stood somewhere nearby, watching and listening. I remembered squatting in front of the little refrigerator in his bathroom and reading the labels on the ampules. I remembered him saying to me, "Maybe death's a habit, like cigarette smoking or alcohol."

One of the men on the banquette cleared his throat and started to speak to me, but I replaced the book on the shelf and almost ran out of the room.

By the time I climbed the stairs to the third floor, however, Oliver Hartwell had been forgotten. It was pitch dark and I had to grope my way along the hall and into a long, rectangular room bare of furniture except for two small sofas, and lit only by street light coming in through curtainless windows. Loud disco music—a song popular then called "Hard Feelings"—ricocheted harshly around the room. On the floor in the silvery dimness lay six or eight couples, or groups, of naked bodies, while more men embraced on the sofas or stood against the walls. Sounds of arousal and abandon temporarily drowned out the music. Directly in front of me on the floor, one man with an enormous rigid cock lay by himself, moaning in ecstasy, arms and legs writhing. After a minute or two he quieted down, whereupon another man swiftly knelt beside him, drew his legs up, and shoved a fist into his rectum, rotating it while the man on the floor began to moan uncontrollably again. He rolled over and faced me. His eyes were wide open, locked into an unseeing stare, and foam flecked his lips and dribbled down his chin. The smell of sweat and marijuana smoke mingled in the room. Spent capsules of amyl nitrate lay on the floor like shell casings.

There was nothing for me here. I turned to go when Quemoy, fully dressed, appeared beside me, his eyes glistening. "Let's get out of here," he said, taking me by the elbow and pulling me into the hall. "Things are getting out of hand in there. Someone ought to call the police. It's outrageous." He giggled.

As we walked downstairs I said nothing, and when we got outside he remarked, "I can see you're in a bad mood, Roy—no girls at the party and all. It was a practical joke on my part, done in the name of fun. I hope you won't hold it against me."

"Don't worry, Quemoy," I said. "It just freaked me out. Those people on the third floor were on another planet."

"No," he said, suddenly contentious, "they *weren't*. This is happening on earth, right here and now. My friends and I are *not* freaks; to the contrary, we're at the forefront of history on this crazy planet—and high time, too, if you ask me."

"But someone must be getting hurt," I insisted.

"Getting hurt?" he replied crossly, "Who are you to say what they're doing? Isn't that being holier than thou? I mean, where've you been, Roy? . . . What do you think the last decade in this country's been all about? Blacks, women, gays, finally being given a chance to figure out who they are underneath the shit laid on them by centuries of compulsive bigotry . . . "

I became incensed. "Quemoy," I said, "For your information, while you were off somewhere in Southern California making money, I was going through one experience after another right in the middle of the counterculture. For years. And one thing I learned was, nobody had a lock on the truth, although almost everybody claimed to. I saw a lot of people burn themselves out, destroy themselves, because they had no idea what they were getting into."

He immediately replied, "You don't have to try and pull rank with me over where each of us was during the Sixties. You have no idea what Matsu and me were doing then. But I can guarantee you one thing—we weren't running any Chinese restaurant. That's hardly my idea of fun, Roy, and I can tell already that you and I have radically different ideas about fun. You probably think it's a dirty word. You don't realize that fun can be sublime. In any case, that's what my brother and me were doing back then, as best we could. We had us *very* much fun . . ." His swarthy face creased into a wonderful smile, unguarded and wistful.

We wandered around for a few blocks, slowly coming back down to the median of New York sidewalk reality. A hard wind was blowing, it had been raining, and suddenly the air seemed as cold as in February.

"I'm fucking freezing," Quemoy said. "Matsu stayed at the party and he's got the keys to the van. Let's catch a taxi. Come back to my place and have a drink and we can talk. I have a few things I'd like to tell you." He noticed the look in my eyes and laughed. "Hey, Roy, take it easy, will ya. I was just pulling your leg, bringing you to that party. I'd do anything to get a rise out of Matsu. I know that's kind of silly, but I can't resist. I love to try and make him smile. But, like, no harm done, right? I knew you could take it. You're secure in your heterosexuality, my dear, that's obvious. You're tough enough, as anyone can see."

His voice sounded faintly mocking.

"I know you're not gay," he went on. "I'm not about to try and seduce you, believe me. I have more lovers than I know what to do with. I just need to go home and talk, I'm kind of wired from the party and I can't stop thinking about George Adolphus. If he doesn't come through for us, we're gonna be in deep trouble. I doubt if I'll get much sleep before Monday, that's for sure . . . You know, it's nice having someone besides Matsu to confide in, Roy, I really appreciate it . . . And you haven't seen my place yet, have you? I love it. It's much nicer than Matsu's, even if, on the surface, his looks the same. But that's what I mean about that brother of mine. He's always following my lead." He laughed.

Quemoy's spacious loft occupied the entire top floor of a large building on Greene Street. It had a surprisingly austere, retro look to it, with bare gray walls, sleek Forties furniture, and hidden light fixtures. The paintings which he told Adolphus he had purchased from needy painters were nowhere in sight. The overall effect was severe yet opulent. A large open space in front contained two leather sofas and looked out over lower Manhattan from a long row of high windows. In the back, behind the state-of-the-art kitchen, were several smaller rooms, into one of which Quemoy immediately disappeared to make some phone calls. "I'll be right back," he said. "The alcohol's in the cabinet above the sink. In the kitchen. Help yourself."

I wandered around and discovered that the only variation on this theme of almost futuristic austerity was one wall in an alcove next to the kitchen. The wall was covered in red silk on which hung various Chinese paintings and scrolls. A lucite shelf at waist level contained a bewildering array of expensive jewelry and precious stones, including jade necklaces and strands of pearls, which all together must have been worth tens of thousands of dollars. Quemoy found me looking at this collection in amazement.

"They're lovely, aren't they? Unfortunately, only a few of the stones are mine. The rest is business. We're selling all that stuff as quickly as possible. It'll all be gone, hopefully, by the end of the week." He sighed. "Some people from Hong Kong."

As we sat down on one of the sofas with our drinks the phone rang. Quemoy answered it and his face fell. He cupped a hand over the receiver and hissed, "It's my dear foster father, Colonel Sheridan. We keep changing our telephone numbers, making them unlisted, but it doesn't take him long to find us no matter what we do. That's the power of the armed services, son. Every few months he calls, either me or Matsu, berating us and going on about how the Commies are taking over. No, wait—actually, the Commies have already taken over . . . Why don't you listen for a while? Maybe you'll learn something."

Grimacing, he handed me the receiver, and I heard an intensely emotional voice, brimming over with righteous indignation, saying: "I was on the front line in Okinawa, Quemoy—April of '45; I saw things you wouldn't believe. An entire patrol wiped out before my eyes. April 19, 1945. Men, their faces blasted away, praying to their God. The bravery, the suffering, the heroes. What have you got to match it now? Nothing! . . . When the fire comes down and you're out there all alone with your buddies lyin' in pieces all around you . . . I was with Butch O'Hare before Wake Island back in '43. And we cleared the way for those Avengers in the Marianas, boy, that was '43 also, I remember it like yesterday, so you can't tell me I don't know what true character, true sacrifice, are all about, 'cause I do. The war was real, and life today is not. Life today is you and your brother cornholing each other while you sell Chinese food to groups of fuckin' pansies dressed in fancy clothes. Don't try to deny it, I know. I don't have to come to New York to find out about you. But what you're up to doesn't surprise me. It fits right in with the actions of that traitor we have in the White House. Can you imagine that a President of the United States would pardon the very cowards who refused to fight for their country? It's all a blatant travesty, a crime against the future . . . But I can tell you this: *some people are not going to take it lying down.* We'll see how long Mr. Jimmy Carter lasts."

I handed the phone back to Quemoy, who broke into Colonel Sheridan's tirade. "Dad, I'm too busy to listen to this. Try calling when you have something constructive to say, OK?" Without waiting for a reply he slammed down the receiver and disconnected the phone.

"Goddamn," he said, "sometimes he scares me. It's 1977 and he hasn't seen us in years, but he's still so full of rage against us I get paranoid and think he's going to hire some of the heavies he knows to come to New York and blow us away . . . Go ahead and laugh, but it's a distinct possibility. You don't know what the guy is like. If we were in the least political, it would've happened already; but we're not, of course. Thank God for little things."

He got up and paced back and forth, sipping cognac, trying to calm himself. Sometimes, when I looked at Quemoy, I noticed as if for the first time that he was Chinese. His eyes, the shape of his head, his cheekbones, his jet-black, lustrous hair and coppery skin, his slightly bowed legs—all were Asiatic features which, when I suddenly became aware of them, made his American accent and mannerisms, the loose way he walked, seem oddly out of place. But then he would simply be Quemoy once again.

"See, Roy," he said, his voice becoming fervent as he talked, "that's why your reaction to what was going on at that party bugged me so much. The stakes in all this are higher than you think. Everybody's programmed by society to react a certain way. That's why the gay movement is so important. For the first time, we can build a new world for ourselves, a world where desire isn't repressed, lied about, and distorted. Come with me to the clubs, sometime, and you'll see what I mean. The euphoria, it's breathtaking. And you ain't seen nothin' yet . . . Gay freedom has limitless possibilities—there's room for the Nellies, the quiet homebody couples faithful to each other for twenty years, just as there's also room for promiscuity and adventure . . . To be alive and have these wonderful bodies, and do whatever we want, without guilt, without restraint . . . We're *never* going back to the past, believe me. You think I plan on growing old and gray without having tasted to the full what my youth has to offer? I'm supposed to pretend my desires are aberrations? *Give me a break* . . . Sure, you have to control yourself. You can't run riot. But it's all part of a learning process, learning to let go of the tyranny of the past, figuring out how to live our lives without coercion—"

His eyes were shining as he stopped himself, clearly trying to make up his mind about something.

Impulsively he said, "Please don't be upset, Roy, I know how delicate your sensibilities are, but I gotta tell you about Matsu and me. We each have our own lovers, of course, and usually that's all there is to it, we keep it separate because we can't afford to get into any jealousy routines. Competing for the same boy would be the surest way to wreck everything we've built. But every now and then we end up in bed *together*, and it's wild. You have no idea . . . When we're really *out there*, our bodies become interchangeable. We can't tell who's fucking whom. And, being twins and all, it's great not having to worry about getting pregnant and giving birth to retarded children, right? If we were brother and sister, it would be a different story."

He looked at me expectantly, his black eyes sparkling with mischief. "I finally shocked you, right? Come on, admit it. And maybe you're a little interested, too . . ."

"Jesus," I said, "you're really like a baby sometimes. It's getting late, Quemoy, I have to go."

Pretending he didn't hear me, he reached into his pocket and spilled some pills onto the table. "Quaaludes," he said. "Want one?" For the first time that night he seemed drunk. He collapsed onto the sofa next to me and, looking soulfully into my eyes, touched me on the knee.

"I'm not gay, remember?" I said.

"You mean my big, impassioned speech didn't convert you? You won't even give it a try? How do you know what you're missing?" He groaned. "Well, *I'm* having a 'lude, even if you won't. I don't want to sit here thinking about whether or not Angelo's gonna get heavy with me next week. If I have to go to bed alone tonight, at least I want to feel relaxed about it . . . One last drink for the road, then?"

Quemoy swallowed the pill with his drink as I sipped at a second glass of cognac. By the time we got up he was distinctly woozy, and nearly fell trying to slip on his shoes. I offered to take the elevator down to the street myself, but he wouldn't hear of it.

"You're my guest, Roy," he explained without a trace of irony.

We arrived at the ground floor and he held open the door leading to the street, insisting on a goodnight kiss. "As close as I'll ever get, I suppose," he whispered, and we both laughed. I kissed him on the lips and turned to go. From out of the shadows a skinny white guy quickly approached and said, "Hey, Matsu—" Before either of us could react he stuck a gun into Quemoy's stomach and fired twice. Crying out, Quemoy fell to the sidewalk. I took off up the street at a dead run, not looking back, flinching from the impact of a bullet which never arrived.

PART FOUR

THIRTEEN

During the next few days I lay low in my apartment, trying not to panic. Whoever shot Quemoy would be coming after me next, I thought, even though at the time he'd ignored me completely. Actually, it was all over so quickly I'd seen nothing. I wouldn't recognize the guy even if he came up to me in the street and said hello.

No one telephoned from the restaurant, or from the police. In fact, no one telephoned at all. Finally, late one night, I went down to SoHo to investigate. Bamboo Mountain was padlocked, with butcher paper covering the windows and a handlettered sign on the door, CLOSED FOR RENOVATIONS.

A week later I ran into one of the waiters in Washington Square Park. I couldn't remember his name. His eyes widened when he recognized me and he said, "You're Roy, right? The dishwasher? My name's Franklin." Taking me aside he confided breathlessly, "Have you heard what happened? Quemoy was murdered! People are saying it was the Mafia. Matsu's gone, diappeared, nobody knows what became of him, nobody's been paid or anything."

I mumbled a few words in response and just turned on my heels and walked away, my eyes suddenly filled with tears. Until that moment I hadn't admitted to myself how much I cared for Quemoy. The fact that he'd been mistaken for his brother only added to my grief. But soon this grief gave way to anger, not only at the animals who killed him but also at my vulnerability. Because Quemoy died a victim of his own greed after doing his best to suck me down into his world. So I was finished doing people favors. I was finished getting involved with them and feeling hurt when they disappeared. I needed to find some way of supporting myself without becoming dependent on anyone else. I needed to call my own shots if I wanted to survive, it was the American way.

But for the time being, not having to show up for work every day was a relief. I had saved a few dollars, nothing spectacular, but at least my April rent was paid. Spring had arrived and street life was returning to St. Mark's Place. Soon I found myself sitting by the window again, hypnotized, vacant-headed. Perfect and complete.

Then one day, Dana came by. She was alone. It had been more than three months since we'd seen each other and she looked rested and healthy, her black hair shining. She said she'd come out of curiosity. She couldn't believe I'd actually thrown away all our possessions. But as soon as she walked in I knew there was something else.

"I'm glad to finally be able to come over and see you," she said. "I'm hoping we can be friends, Roy. I owe you an apology for the way I treated you on New Year's Eve. I just had so much anger in me then. I was so pissed at you. You know the way it is, when you're threatened and resentful you hurt people. But since then a whole new life has opened up for me. Living with Barbara is good, Roy, it's really the right thing for me."

She sat there on a pillow in the living room, smiling sweetly and looking around. "The apartment's so different now. I must admit, I still don't understand how you could have thrown all my things away, I was angry about that for a long time, but what can I do? It doesn't pay to hold grudges, I've learned that . . ."

She eyed me expectantly, pleased with herself for making this overture. When I said nothing in reply, the corners of her mouth turned up. There was that maddening smile again.

"Barbara's such a beautiful person, you know, so loving and affectionate, and someone who really understands the art I'm doing now. Because I'm staying home a lot now, dealing with my new situation and making my art . . ."

"'Making my art,'" I repeated mockingly. "How therapeutic, Dana."

She blinked, her mouth tightening.

Then she said, "Well, you know, the night I walked out on you to go find Richard Pinkus was the most miserable of my life. I didn't want to sleep with him and I couldn't come back to you, either. You didn't know who I was anymore. I sailed out the door with no idea where I was going. I walked up to Ninth Street and caught the crosstown bus, completely distracted, and sat there in the back staring out the window, crying, until someone sat down next to me and touched me on the shoulder, and it was Barbara."

"Oh, God, how touching," I said in a hard voice. We stared at each other.

"So you want to explain. You've got your feet on the ground now and you want to tie up loose ends here, not have any negative vibes emanating from St. Mark's Place, right? You want everything smoothed out. You want to soothe your feelings. Well, you're too late. New Year's Eve was nothing. What about how alone I felt for weeks, what about how you played with me? Yeah, and you know what? You were right to be selfish, it's a lesson I've learned. I don't care how happy you are with Barbara, I don't want to hear it, I'm not interested. The doctor told me to stay off sweets."

Her face was red as she got up to leave. "Jesus, Roy, you really *have* changed." Her eyes widened as she fumbled with her coat and I flashed a brittle, insane grin at her. "I want to go now."

"Yeah, Dana, some other time. When you and Babs are passing through on your way to your little cabin upstate, give me a call. We'll get together and hit the galleries, won't that be fun? We'll have lunch at the Museum of Modern Art."

Gary Gilmore's last words, "Let's do it," had become ubiquitous in New York during the spring of '77. *Let's Do It* T-shirts and buttons sprouted like wildflowers. But the big news was the English punk invasion. Photos of Johnny Rotten in torn T-shirt and safety-pinned ears spurred droves of imitators onto the streets. Punk people decor— wasted-looking and disagreeable—became the latest rage.

On St. Mark's this self-conscious disaffection clashed weirdly with the resident population of alcoholics and mental outcasts. Shouting matches and fistfights broke out between punks and Puerto Ricans, punks and Hell's Angels, punks and hippies. The East Village in April had the feel of a refugee camp, with disparate elements thrown together but, unlike in the Sixties, unwillingly.

In the city at large, The Slasher who had haunted the midtown area was never found. But on April 17th, a young woman was murdered in the Bronx and, according to the *News*, "a rambling and incoherent note, the product of a disturbed mind," was left by the assailant. Police refused to release this note but they said it indicated that a psychopathic killer was loose. They believed the same man was responsible for five murders and three other shootings in Queens and the Bronx since July '76, all involving young women with shoulder-length brown hair. Investigators theorized that the note was left because the killer wanted to get caught. And he signed the letter, *Son of Sam* . . .

In contrast to what was happening out on the street, in my building not much had changed. The gypsies downstairs still brokered late-model cars. The arguments and TV shows still seeped through my floor like a marsh tide, but they didn't bother me now. Frank Sinatra was gone from the record player of the woman upstairs, replaced by Barbra Streisand singing, over and over again, the song "People" from *Funny Girl* . . . "People who need people/Are the luckiest people in the world . . ." That, I admit, was considerably harder to take, but one day I got a glimpse of the artist on the stairs. Bloated and bleary-eyed, she looked so unhappy. How could I begrudge something obviously so important to her? Even James Yankton, the inscrutable sadist who periodically left his radio on full blast, all night long—him too I neutralized. I found that the noise disappeared if I willed it to. So I didn't give a fuck what Yankton did.

Jogging was big with the "me generation" singles culture which started to emerge from the woodwork in 1977, renovating apartments in Manhattan instead of living in the suburbs, joining health clubs, riding fancy racing bikes, graduating from est. Even though the blank (rather than the me) generation still held sway on St. Mark's Place, often I'd finish exercising in front of the mirror in the living room and look out the window to see a clean-shaven, with-it guy go padding by in gym shorts and running shoes, and I'd wonder. Could he possibly be seeing what I'd seen when I'd been out running the previous Thanksgiving? I remembered being on the streets after taking mushrooms. The daily routine of washing dishes and exercising had made me forget about that, but after I'd been home for a week I wanted to be out there trotting through the streets again, as I had in November.

Gradually I resumed wandering around the city. It took a while to get my wind back, but soon I was loping along the avenues feeling luminous and full of energy, my gaze focused on the middle distance, my mouth half-open. I would cover numberless blocks by sunset, return home, and collapse in a state of delirious exhaustion. Occasionally, after resting for a few hours, I'd go out again at night through the carbon-dark canyons, dreaming to myself as I ran.

As the weeks went by I began to prefer trotting after dark when there was much less traffic and fewer people on the sidewalks. It rained a lot that April but even the bad weather seemed to slacken off after nightfall. I didn't worry about getting mugged, I was in such good shape by then I easily could have outrun anybody who tried something. And besides, I felt invincible. Nobody could touch me.

I began to see odd things at night. Once just before dawn in Chinatown I almost collided with a naked woman running down Catherine Street toward the East River, her arms wide, her long hair streaming. An unearthly whine escaped from her lips as if she were imitating the siren of the ambulance coming to get her.

And, rather early one evening, at about nine P.M., I came across the so-called "panel truck robbers" I'd been reading about in the papers. On West 10th Street, right off of Fifth Avenue, a souped-up van screeched to a halt, the side panel zipped open, and a hand emerged holding, supposedly, a rag which had been soaked in chloroform. This hand clapped itself over the mouth of a prosperous-looking, portly man who was out walking his poodle. The dog yelped and ran off as the man was yanked into the van, which drove away in a cloud of exhaust. Apparently, after being stripped of money and jewelry, the still unconscious victim would be dumped on the sidewalk several blocks away. The entire sequence took just a few seconds. If I had blinked I might have missed it, and in fact the only evidence it had taken place at all came from the sight of that poodle, dragging its leash as it ran full tilt along 10th Street, barking.

Almost every evening I witnessed somebody being assaulted. I saw guns pulled on Eighth Avenue, winos rolled on the Bowery, old people mugged in Madison Square, fistfights between drug dealers, purses snatched. None of it fazed me. I was content just to watch.

But one misty night over by the Hudson River I was trotting underneath the West Side Highway, absorbed in the lights playing through the mist on the river. All of a sudden, across the cobblestones thirty or forty yards away, I became aware of an old woman slumped against one of the big girders under the highway and a slim, short white kid, no more than fourteen years old, rolling her over onto her stomach and poking her viciously with his fist, cuffing her and dragging her away from her sack of belongings. There was nobody else around. I watched, out of breath, my chest heaving, when the old woman hooked her foot behind the boy's leg and brought him down.

Getting to her knees she reached into her sack and produced a sort of cane or truncheon. The kid came up with a knife but before he had a chance to use it, she began striking him over the head, across the shoulders, along his back. He rolled into a ball, moaning in pain, and she stood up fully now and kicked him forcefully in the gut, wailing away with her cane at the same time, hacking at him. Then the cane came apart and she appeared to be stabbing the boy. I saw this imperfectly in the mist at that distance, something flashing briefly in her hand. I couldn't remember later whether I'd seen a glow, as from a flashlight, or not. Gathering her belongings, still not noticing me, she quickly pulled the boy's body into the well of the girder where she had been lying and strode off into the darkness. That was what got to me most of all, finally—she walked away self-confidently, energetically, like somebody half her age. Or somebody in disguise. But if she were a cop from the Senior Citizens Patrol dressed as a vagrant, why did she leave? Where was her backup team? I approached the boy and turned over his inert body. Still clutching the knife in one hand he was frowning, and the deep crease between his eyebrows made him look old. I thought he must be dead. He had no pulse. His mouth was open, full of blood. I was getting blood on my hands and clothes, but just before turning away I spotted something, a patch of his shirt burned away, lacerations at his neck and on his chest. And I got a whiff of charred flesh. The next moment I was running as fast as I could, trying not to wonder if anybody might be watching me, just running.

The next day I bought copies of all the papers but there was no mention of what I'd seen. However, a week later the *Post* published an account of a murky incident in a subway station on the Upper West Side, sometime after two A.M., when a "group"—nobody could say precisely how many—of homeless vagrants, after being set upon by a pack of five teenagers, beat their tormentors and left them handcuffed to benches in the station. And one kid, freed at the last moment in a state of hysteria, had been handcuffed to the tracks. All of this happened out of sight of the token seller's booth, and aside from the victims themselves there were no witnesses. Most of the kids, out of wounded pride, refused to discuss what had taken place. But the one who was rescued from the tracks, before being led away to Bellevue for observation, rambled on to a reporter in a barely coherent manner about stun guns and coordinated attacks by old people.

Meanwhile, I'd begun going out during the day as well, not trotting, usually, but just walking around, taking subways and buses, drifting, looking—for what, I didn't know. Up and down the avenues buds had opened on the trees and in Central Park everything materialized in vivid new green. Spring had finally arrived to stay and the noise level on the streets seemed to quadruple overnight. I began discovering secret meaning in things, like that beat-up old delivery truck parked at an oblique angle on Lafayette, jutting out into the street as if hastily abandoned. White but very grimy, it had a tiny unconvincing stencil on its side, *moving and storage . . .*

Barely legible, the stencil gave no name or address, no phone number. This must be some sort of decoy, I thought, some substitute for another level of activity entirely. Otherwise, why hadn't the truck been ticketed and towed away? As I stood looking at it a shrunken, withered old woman hobbled up Lafayette, layered in sweaters and garbage bag skirts and wearing old bedroom slippers. She was dragging her left foot which looked swollen and infected. When she passed she eyed me meaningfully with a sort of ironic recognition, as if we knew each other but were going to pretend we didn't. But how could I know who she was if I didn't recognize her?

Sitting in a donut shop at the corner of Seventh Avenue and 14th Street, looking out the window which afforded a clear, direct view of the pedestrians converging from every direction, I became engrossed in the endless stream of New York faces. I began to form a provisional, conditional sense of what identity meant in the city. Like messages contained within a plaintext, the deepest truths of people's lives were revealed only in the form of codes, hidden meanings folded into the textures of everyday persona. Unless, that is, like me these people were inventing who they were as they went along, in which case no code yet applied.

Then, on May 5th at about three in the afternoon, I was riding the A train uptown out of 42nd Street, standing in the first car at the front, looking out onto the tracks as the train picked up speed. And that's when I saw it. Off to the left beyond the platform, just as the train was entering the tunnel. At first it didn't register, I turned away and sat down on one of the benches, eyeing a cigarette ad. Then I broke out in a sweat and started trembling, my body jerking like a puppet's.

DEATH TO THE SPROUTS the graffiti had read, clearly legible on the stained, soot-streaked wall. *Sprout* . . . Oliver Hartwell had called me that during our interview. I remembered the passion with which he had denounced society's conspiracy against the elderly, and his increasingly contemptuous use of that word as our conversation went on.

Disoriented and shivering, I got out of the car at Columbus Circle and went back downtown, then caught the A train north again. And sure enough there it was. DEATH TO THE SPROUTS . . . In order to calm myself I looked at the other people in the car, but then I heard Hartwell's voice. I knew it was his voice even though it was indistinct and far away. With mounting anxiety I struggled to understand what he was saying but I couldn't. Perspiration poured out of me. I began swatting the air around me and then I cried out, "Get away from me, motherfucker. Leave me alone. Get away! Get away!"

I couldn't abide being cooped up one second longer and leaping to my feet I pounded on the doors. Everybody else in the car stared at the floor. At Columbus Circle I ran through the station and up the stairs, finally reaching light and air. I crossed Central Park West to the corner entrance of the park and stood there zoned out, frozen in space. I was able to think along only one line, over and over: I wasn't doing drugs. I had left Hartwell behind, changed my life, started over. And yet I was also back where I'd started. *Nothing had changed.*

Did that mean I couldn't change? The possibility drove me crazy with frustration and as I stood there I felt my eyes lock into a straight-ahead, unblinking stare, seeing nothing. My blood racing, my mouth open, I felt the air parch my throat as I breathed. And always I came back to this double bind which was pulling me in two contradictory directions. One where Hartwell wasn't a threat, and the graffiti simply a coincidence of some sort, a prank. And the other, the other direction, where—where—

Then a shock passed through me and my anxiety vanished. How wonderful, how sublime. I felt completely self-contained at last, imperturbable, rigid, perfect. I was turning into that immobile African man I'd seen in the subway station on Thanksgiving Day. Standing there so majestic and cool and untouchable, like a blue flame.

The next thing I knew, somebody—a woman—was holding my arm, shaking it. That's when I became aware of how tightly my jaws were clenched. I breathed deeply, trying to relax. The woman was staring at me, not with the fear or revulsion I expected, but with a kind of disbelieving admiration. A professional woman, stylishly dressed in a navy blue suit and white blouse, with a strand of pearls around her neck. I found myself staring at the pearls, wondering if they were real. They certainly looked it.

"Are you OK?" she asked.

"Oh, I, uh . . ."

She stepped back, regarding me attentively, a heavy-set, vital-looking woman of about thirty or so, her lank auburn hair in a smartly cut pageboy which gave her face an odd severity. Her watery brown eyes looked almost rheumy. She's younger than me. I wonder what she does for a living? I wonder how much money she makes?

"It *is* you," she exclaimed with a sigh of relief, clapping her hands together delightedly.

When I said nothing in return she added, "Roy, what's going on, anyway? Don't you recognize me? It's Cissy, for gosh sakes—Cissy Wyatt! Do I look *that* different? I couldn't believe it when I first saw you standing there. I wasn't sure it was you. Talk about being taken aback! I was afraid to approach you, you looked positively *catatonic*, like you were being electrocuted or something, so I watched you for a while. It was fascinating. Then I couldn't resist stepping up and waving my hand in front of your eyes and you didn't react at all. Boy, were you out there! That's when I got worried."

"Thanks," I said. "I think I'm all right now."

She stood directly in front of me, feet planted squarely on the sidewalk, holding a briefcase and eyeing me sympathetically but at the same time stealing glances at her wristwatch. Obviously she had more important things to do, which was fine with me. Cissy and I had never been close and I resented the embarrassment I felt. Also, I still was having trouble associating this person with Cissy Wyatt, even though when I'd seen her last, at Rosenquist's New Year's Eve party, she already had looked different. I finally recognized her voice, though, and underneath the elegant clothes there was that same ungainly body. But up close like this, Cissy appeared to have experienced a personality change as well. Gone was the awkward, brooding introvert I'd known in the past, Dana's roommate at Barnard and my entrée to Truman Capote, Cissy Wyatt of the privileged WASP background and the uncertain future. Gone were the sunglasses she'd always worn, indoors and out, night and day. I'd never really gotten a good look at Cissy's eyes before, maybe that's why I had so much trouble identifying her.

Then she did something peculiar. Stepping back at least thirty feet from the entrance to the park where I stood, she regarded me curiously, almost clinically, as if I were the new animal at the zoo. Then she approached me again, her eyes shining with enthusiasm.

She sang out excitedly, "You know, the smartest thing I've done in weeks was not walking away when I first saw you mumbling to yourself and shaking all over. People were shying away from you as if you had the plague. Instead, my own reaction—I've got to admit it—was to make a joke. I said to myself, So this is what happens to the men Dana abandons!"

"Jesus Christ, Cissy, I don't have time for—"

"No, wait! You don't understand. *Then*, after that, I observed you for a while, as I said before. I watched what you were doing, and when I put that together with who you were—this person I knew—I decided you couldn't be crazy. And you weren't having an epileptic fit, either. I figured that out, too," she said proudly.

We stood there looking at each other. She had a dopey grin on her face, like a little girl with the keys to the candy store.

"So?" I said.

She paused dramatically and then announced, in a hushed voice full of conviction, "What you were doing was making art. Performance art. And it was *very good* . . ."

"Come on, Cissy," I said, trying to control my anger. "Give me a break. I didn't ask for your help, and I certainly don't need to put up with your toying with me. What gives you the right?"

"No, really," she said, and burst out almost giddily, in a great rush of words, "just listen to me! Running into you like this is a fantastic synchronicity, because that's my life now, Roy: *Art* is my life. Everything's turned around for me. I have a gallery in SoHo now. I'm an art dealer! Isn't that fabulous? We've been in business for only three months and already I have these terrific young artists signed up. I'm just so happy, Roy. I feel like a different person since I decided to start the gallery, and I can tell you it hasn't been easy. But all that's beside the point. The fact is, you're a performance artist, whether you know it or not. What you're doing is original, nobody's ever done it before. Not that there haven't been some memorable performances, but they've either taken place in the galleries, defined by that kind of space, or when they've been out on the street usually they've resulted from some dumb conceptual *project* or arty idea, like walking back and forth for an hour on the same stretch of sidewalk. I mean, *really*. It's so old hat, so namby pamby. That's what was great about *you*. What you were doing came from the heart. The heart! I could tell immediately. It wasn't preconceived. And even better, it connected in a totally natural, honest way with the craziness, the shakiness of life on the streets nowadays. What do you think of that?"

I stared at her, irritated by this speech. As if what I or anybody else might be doing was of interest only because Cissy Wyatt decided to call it art.

"I'm serious," she said. "You think I'm pulling your leg, Roy? I haven't got time for that, I'm a working woman now. And I'm telling you that what you were doing is valid as art. It's new and risky. Why not communicate it to other people? Do you have anything against that? Because unless it's presented within a certain context, it all goes to waste. You think these jokers rushing past on the sidewalk had any idea what you were really doing?"

"But Cissy, this is preposterous. I wasn't *doing* anything. Certainly not making art."

"Right, that's exactly the point! Don't you see? It doesn't matter in the least whether you call it art or not. I'm not interested in *why* you were standing there. That's your business. What's important is the effect it had on me. The meaning of a communication is in the response it calls forth, and my response was fantastic. What you were doing sent chills up my back . . . I know art when I see it, believe me. I realized that somehow you had managed to surrender yourself totally to what was going on inside you, transforming it into clear, simple, pure gesture. It's the gesture that counts. I mean, we both know you're not a homeless psycho, my dear, let's not kid ourselves. But what you were doing had commitment, it had ten times more edge than most of the performance art going on now . . ."

She snorted indignantly, completely involved in her train of thought, dragging me along by sheer force of will. It didn't seem to matter that I'd been out of control, traumatized. She wouldn't have believed me if I'd told her about Oliver Hartwell and the sprouts, the murder of the kid under the West Side Highway, the articles in the papers. All that interested her was the effect I'd made, the image of me "catatonic" on the sidewalk. I was a simple object for her, or more exactly a presence, but in any case what I might have been going through meant nothing to her. This attitude took my breath away in its fierce, uncompromising selfishness. But I also realized Cissy wanted something from me. I was curious to find out what that might be.

"Performance art is hot now," she said. "It's the fashionable new medium, don't you know? Last year the Whitney even had a performance *festival*, for gosh sakes. Off the street and into the establishment in seconds flat! And performance artists themselves are hot. They're the new hero figures in the art world now, as Jackson Pollack and Franz Kline used to be in the Fifties. Because the art they make is fugitive, ephemeral, it's difficult to merchandize. So presumably they're beyond corruption, beyond commercialism, beyond being bought and sold—though the jury's still out on *that* score, I can assure you. But most of it is so self-referential and safe. Even if it's risky, the risk is calculated, programmatic, formalistic, all part of this arid humorless conceptualism, this *dead weight* we must abandon, my dear, don't you think, if we're ever again to see something interesting? I mean, those body art boys were the daring young men on the flying trapeze, but that was five years ago, for gosh sakes. Biting yourself all over your body or rolling around on the floor masturbating came out of the zeitgeist of the Vietnam era. All these people mutilating themselves, or simply having *ideas* and calling that art, were good for 1972, maybe, but enough's enough already. Performance is different now. We're going through a time of transition. The audiences have changed, they come to be entertained now. They're passive, sitting politely in silence as if they were at the movies and then applauding at the end whether or not they like it. And all the new young performers are responding to that, they're so theatrical. So it's a hot medium, you see, but in another way it's in danger of becoming static. Laurie Anderson's going to be big because she has big ideas, but as for the rest of them . . ."

She looked directly into my eyes and fairly shouted, "You're an artist, Roy—an artist! No matter what you think! All you need is someone behind you, documenting what you do . . . Listen, these painters I have, nobody else would touch them because they're doing all this outrageous figurative stuff, but I know they're good. Mark my words, in three years we're all going to make it big. And," she added, her lips narrowing and with a steely determination in her voice, "whether you like it or not, you're going to make it too. You're going to be my next artist, how do you like that? My first performance artist. The time is ripe. I've been looking for someone, and today I found him . . . So you'd better come along with me," she announced in a proprietary tone.

Taking my arm, she began steering me across 59th Street. "You look kind of pale, I'll bet you could use something to eat. We'll go to a coffee shop. I've got to make a phone call, I was supposed to meet someone on 57th Street half an hour ago. And we have certain things to talk about, Roy, so we may as well do it sitting down, don't you think? My feet are killing me."

Walking down Broadway to find a place to eat, Cissy pointed out an old man dressed in rags, slumped in an office tower doorway. "That's your constituency, Roy, your raw material. Nobody's paying attention to these people now. What you have to do is figure out how to present life as art in such a way that it'll be noticed. If you do it right, you may even be able to make some real money out of it, although I admit that's a long shot. There are so many performers around now, and the very nature of what they're doing makes it a headache to sell. But there are ways."

Giving me a sidelong glance she added, "And I'll bet you could use the cash. What are you doing for a living now, anyway? Still interviewing celebrities?"

Her sarcasm infuriated me.

"Damn it, Cissy, your attitude stinks. As a matter of fact, a lot has changed in *my* life, too, since the last time we really saw each other. When was the Capote interview, anyway? Over a year ago, wasn't it? Well, I've been washing dishes, for your information, and liking it. I'm finished with the entertainment world; and art doesn't seem to be much different from that, judging from how you talk about it. You make it sound like just another way to score."

"Washing dishes . . . Far out." She laughed unpleasantly. "I like it. The lower depths. Strategic withdrawal, right? A little quiet time . . . I doubt you're going to want to continue with that forever, though. In any case, if you did it would be a shame. You stopped me in my tracks back there, and I can tell you that doesn't happen too often. And—for *your* information, buster—I am *in love* with art. I live and breathe it. I dream about it at night. I don't even have a sex life anymore, I don't have time for relationships. I'm just not an artist, that's all. I know that much. I'm a facilitator, so naturally that means I'm involved in doing business. I mean, what else is new? We can't *all* be lost in our fantasies . . ."

She stopped on the sidewalk and turned to face me. "Listen to me, Roy. We'll soon find out whether we're able to work together. Maybe not. Maybe I jumped the gun on this, maybe you're not cut out for it, maybe we're incompatible. But I don't think so, and my intuition's usually pretty good. And the fact of the matter is, I have a new attitude. I know perfectly well how I come across to people now. I'm hard-nosed, I'm impatient, and it feels great. No one trespasses on my space, no one tells me what to do. And you know why? Because I insist on it. I've got all sorts of people pissed off at me—my mother, Leo Castelli, Brad Gunnert, Miriam Gould. But I'll tell you one thing: my artists like me. In gulps. Because they want to succeed. They're not ashamed of that, and they know I'm behind them. So what it really comes down to in your case is whether you want to make art, whether you *have* to. It's up to you. But if you do, I guarantee it beats washing dishes. And when no one's looking, we can both go up to the Frick and swoon in front of Rembrandt's *Polish Rider*. But meanwhile we've got work to do."

Sitting in the coffee shop, watching her ungainly pigeon-toed slouch as she ambled off in her uptown duds to make her phone call, I found myself blinking my eyes in bewilderment. Somebody familiar had been stripped away, forcibly discarded, and in her place stood revealed this brash, ambitious, single-minded, unsentimental creature. She had already won my begrudging admiration, and as I sat there eating I wondered what Dana thought of the new Cissy Wyatt.

Fifteen minutes later, when she finally returned, that was the first thing we talked about.

"Oh, God, poor Dana," she moaned, her face darkening. "I can't understand it. You know, I worked at the Castelli Gallery for nine months before I opened up my own place, and all that time Dana was supportive, even though we didn't see each other much . . . I mean, you've no idea how Leo worked me, although I loved every second of it. But I had no time for anything else . . . Then Dana disappears, and I hear nothing for a month. I'm freaked out about it, like everyone else, right? All of a sudden I get this phone call. Let's have lunch, she says. Just like that. I go, Wow, Dana, how great to hear your voice again, you're still alive! No one knew what happened to you, no one—but she cuts me off. 'Let's talk about it at lunch, all right, Cissy? I don't feel like it now . . .' "

Cissy was imitating Dana's voice—Dana's touchy, hesitant, fastidious new voice—and I flinched at her accuracy. She raised her eyebrows, giving me an exasperated look as she continued. "So, OK, that sounds kind of abrupt and weird, really, but all right. Well, we have lunch, and first she runs you into the ground. And I do mean into the *ground*, ha ha, but we won't go into that. Then she spills the beans, she's got this girlfriend—Barbara, right? I assume you know about this by *now* . . ."

"God, Cissy, you're a piece of work, aren't you? Of course I know about it."

"Ha ha . . . So, all right, I'm kind of shocked, but I'm glad to hear there's been movement of some sort on the happiness front. I've had a few flings with women myself—we won't go into that now, either— and I can sympathize. I mean, *men*—no offense intended—there ought to be a law . . . But anyway, then it's my turn, right? We get into what *I've* been doing. As soon as I say, Listen, Dana, this is the greatest thing that's ever happened to me, working for Leo, because now I know what I want to do with my life. I'm going to open my own gallery! . . . I mean, you can't imagine how desperate I was last year, Roy. At the end of my rope. Sniffing heroin, for gosh sakes. Smoking so much hash my head used to roll right off my shoulders. Taking meaningless trips to Mexico, Greece, Bombay, anywhere to get away from myself. And the therapists! The money! And the feeling guilty about it, feeling guilty about everything. So it's not like I'm talking to her about the weather, is it? I mean, this is of central importance to me, and Dana's one of my best friends, right? . . . Well, it takes all kinds, I know that, I'm not saying everyone has to go for the same things in life, but Dana's an artist, after all. It's not as if I said I wanted to sell real estate . . . So she goes, '*Well*, Cissy, working for Leo Castelli's one thing, he's a legend, but art dealers are all gold diggers. Vampires . . .' *Vampires*, yet! . . . Sucking their artists dry . . . Can you imagine? It's weird, Roy, it still upsets me when I think about it. She had this amazing judgmental thing, her voice, the look on her face. If you ask me, she's become almost dowdy since moving in with dear Barbara," she said, her voice dripping sarcasm. "*Dear Barbara*, who—have you met her? No? She's like this, I don't know, this *handler*, this trainer. So solicitous. Always kind of hovering protectively around Dana, telling her which foods are OK to eat and stuff like that . . . Make sure to put on your scarf, baby, before you go outside. It's kind of windy today . . ."

She took a deep breath and exhaled forcefully, shaking her head. "So I don't understand, I really don't. She's just not the same person since she moved to Brooklyn. What do you think, Roy? Have you seen her at all?"

"Yes, I've seen her," I replied. To find out what she'd say, I defended Dana against Cissy's onslaught. "I've seen them both, and they seem loving with each other. I have to believe her when she tells me she's happy. What's wrong with that?"

Cissy snorted. "*Chacun à son dessin*," she sniffed.

I studied her face closely and said, "Cissy, Dana's changed but so have I, so have you. Do you realize she probably sees you the same way you see her—she doesn't know who you are anymore?"

"Oh yeah? Well, too bad," Cissy replied testily. "Is that supposed to mean she's right and I'm wrong? Or that no one's right? Well, I don't buy either of those propositions. It just so happens that, ever since I took est training, I don't have to be jerked around by what other people think of me. They're simply projecting their own hopes and fears onto me, crowding me out of my space."

I could hardly believe my ears. "*est?* Jesus Christ, Cissy, you can't be involved in something like that!"

"Why not? You have to be pushed to the brink before you can really change in this world. Everyone's too connected otherwise, connected to their jobs, their lovers, their families. est forces you to see that you're alone out there . . . You have no idea what it's all about and here you go putting it down! How typical."

"But all those New Age movements, the eastern religions and everything, they're just substitute father trips. You have to work out life for yourself, Cissy, nobody else can do it for you."

She winced. "Let's not get into it. All I know is, being processed like that was exactly what I needed. I had nowhere to hide. It brought me out of my shell and showed me that whatever I wanted to do, I could do it. So it's good enough for me, my dear. If it works, use it, right? Or do you think I should still be moping around listening to Joni Mitchell records and seeing a different therapist every month?"

I had no reply to that, and I didn't feel like prolonging the issue. The last thing I wanted to do now was antagonize Cissy. Because I had pretty much decided to go along with her desire to turn me into a performance artist. I realized that Oliver Hartwell was shouldering his way back into my life, and actively seeking him out was the only way I had to control the situation instead of it controlling me. Maybe I'd have more time to look for him this way, maybe Cissy would advance me some money so I wouldn't have to look for a job right away.

As soon as I informed her of my decision she giggled like a child, and to my amazement volunteered right then to advance me three hundred dollars. "As an act of good faith," she said. "To show we both mean business. But this isn't the dole, Roy. Actually, I'm having tremendous cash flow problems at the moment, so to get more money you'll have to come up with some hot performance art. Fast."

She was teasing me, but I hardly noticed. Those three crisp hundred dollar bills sitting on the table between us seemed like a good omen. After all, how many dishes would I have to wash in order to make three hundred dollars? I had no intention of "doing performance art," but naturally I didn't tell Cissy that. On the contrary, I was prepared to tell Cissy whatever she wanted to hear. Her advance would keep me out there on the streets with enough time to watch what was going on. Because DEATH TO THE SPROUTS had been a warning, there was no doubt about it; a signal for me to start paying attention. I had seen too many unsettling things already, but trotting through the city as I'd been doing, I wasn't getting a close enough look. I had to connect with the craziness around me if I wanted to really see it.

"I'll get on it right away, Cissy," I said. I couldn't help smiling broadly. "I can't wait, actually. I've got several ideas already. The way I see it, my state of mind then *was* my performance, and there's more where that came from. Lots more."

FOURTEEN

Cissy and I spent a great deal of time together in May. I knew enough about the art world from the days when I covered the downtown scene for *The New Jag* to understand that certain very successful artists had made up their careers as they went along. Which meant that anybody could be an artist. Even me.

But just to smooth things over, since I literally had come out of nowhere, Cissy decided to establish my pedigree by furnishing me with an art school background, and appearances in a few groups shows out in the sticks.

"No one will ever check," she said, "but when catalogue material on you starts to appear, it'll be reassuring to see you've had some sort of education." The Portsmouth Academy, a small art school in New Hampshire, had burned to the ground five years before, with all its records lost. It was easy enough to say I'd taken courses in painting and art history there. "It's been done before," she insisted. "It's all for the curators and collectors, anyway. They're the ones who get nervous. Other artists, most critics, and the general public out there could care less."

She pointed out that the crucial question you had to provoke in the minds of collectors and critics was, "Is this really art?" If they asked themselves that question they'd be experiencing that indispensable *frisson* of risk which alone made them feel like artists themselves.

"The art business is an ongoing process," she said, "where every four or five years something irrefutably new must appear on the horizon. It's not so much a question of new artists as of a complete change in style—something which can be resisted and rejected at first, and then embraced. It's cyclical, my dear—Leo taught me that—just like the fashion world, except more rarefied and unpredictable. And the stakes are higher, at least in the sense that selling art involves the past as well as the future. Last year, for instance, the National Gallery paid two million dollars for Jackson Pollack's *Lavender Mist*, which had been the last Pollack owned by an individual. In 1950, that same painting was bought for fifteen hundred dollars. So you see what I mean. The right decision now might be worth a fortune later on."

It was extraordinary for me to realize that an entire, complex little world, jam-packed with frenetic activity, had been going on all around me in SoHo while I washed dishes at Bamboo Mountain, yet because of my frame of mind at that time I'd paid no attention to it.

Cissy introduced me to Carole Levy, the underpaid and overworked person who was her receptionist, assistant, and all-purpose factotum. Carole, a bright, intrepid young woman of twenty-two or so, was filled with messianic fervor where the Phalanx Gallery's artists were concerned, and every time I stepped through the door she insisted I look at the paintings of the current show "as if you've never seen them before." Large, garishly colored, disfigured faces which emerged from a welter of heavily applied paint, these works by somebody named Ed Mull left me cold, yet I never said so. Without Carole's enthusiasm, without her willingness to work long hours, the Phalanx Gallery would have ceased to function. Because, from what I could see, Cissy spent most of her time on the telephone.

"Selling art—and making careers—is mostly a question of networking, of who you know," Cissy told me. "And I know a *lot* of people, Roy. If I hadn't grown up on the Upper East Side I would never have been able to get started in this business. I've spent months pestering my mother's friends, all these ladies in state from the east sixties. And their kids, too, who are my age, with whom I went to private school and who are now up-and-coming Wall Street lawyers with money to *burn*, my dear. And with big new apartments with empty walls! . . . Although they're notoriously tight-fisted. You wouldn't believe how skittish people can get when it's a question of parting with a few thousand bucks. Most of them could care less about art, in spite of how they act. For them, it's more a question of not being made a fool of; of being able to say, I bought that guy's work when he was nobody!"

The Phalanx Gallery, up two flights of stairs in a loft building on Wooster Street, was a long narrow space. Cissy complained vigorously about the fancy stores moving into the area, which were crowding out the legitimate galleries, raising the rent for everybody and bringing along with them scores of pseudo-galleries, spaces exhibiting ersatz art to crowds of overdressed vulgarians from Forest Hills who wouldn't know the real thing if it slapped them in the face. "Already it's almost like Madison Avenue around here. I won't even tell you what I pay for rent," she said, "but if it hadn't been for a connection I made while working for Leo, I never would have found this place to begin with."

Cissy met Leo Castelli through her father, who in the years before he died had assembled a large art collection. In the Sixties he filled the family's big Park Avenue apartment with paintings by well-known abstract expressionists, expensive artists whose works were no longer fashionable. Arthur Dean Wyatt had disliked Pop Art—in fact, apparently he had loathed Andy Warhol, and used to write letters to the editor of *The New York Times* accusing Warhol of signalling the end of Western civilization. His single concession to what was new in those days was the purchase from Castelli of a Jasper Johns flag painting, for which he paid a fortune, according to Cissy, and which now, in 1977, already was worth more than the rest of his collection put together. Cissy had met Castelli as a teenager, with her father, and when she went looking for a job, Leo remembered her.

"Leo's wonderful," Cissy exclaimed. "I was so in awe of that man I used to practically have a nervous breakdown every morning before work, but that phase passed soon enough. Leo's such a world-class businessman, besides having the most uncanny sense of what's really interesting, what's worth taking a chance on. And he's so suave . . . God, it was like working with an embodiment of the only history that mattered to me. I was so grateful to be there I would've been content just to pour wine at the openings. I learned so much in nine months it isn't funny, but I couldn't see any future there beyond being one of his assistants, and the back-biting that went on was positively scarifying.

Everyone wanted to be the apple of his eye. I probably should have stayed longer than I did—every week I was meeting new people—but I couldn't wait. From the first day, I knew I wanted my own gallery . . . And, boy, was *that* a trip. My dear mother—*ma très, très chère maman*—who when I went to work for Leo had been overjoyed I was finally doing something, gave me a really hard time when it came down to opening the family coffers. I think she was jealous, actually. And since my father died, she's had so much money she doesn't know what to do with it. But she even refused to let me sell some of my father's paintings for operating capital, in spite of the fact that she hates them, and she's always spilling drinks on them and stuff. So they just *sit* there, and I have to borrow from her. She's doing it to control me, and it drives me bananas. I can't wait 'til this place takes off and I can tell her to go down to Palm Beach with her bundle of moola and shove it. Don't you agree? After all, who does she think she is? The last years of his life, my father had about as much use for her as he did for Andy Warhol. They lived in completely different worlds. In fact, since she was such big buddies with Truman, she used to spend less time with my father than she did going to parties where Warhol was the star attraction. My parents had absolutely nothing in common. I mean, you were at her apartment—do you remember her collection of antique paper weights? Her chinoiserie? She bought all that junk by the truckload, just to get my father's goat . . . And now the American Museum of Folk Art wants to borrow it for an exhibition! It's all she talks about!"

Cissy insisted that, as her new artist, I be introduced to dozens of people, and I couldn't very well refuse. So I followed her around, meeting everybody from Jasper Johns and Leo Castelli to Alvin Harriman, a desperately down-at-heels performance artist who showed up at the gallery one day, to ask Cissy for money to hire a cameraman so he could record the street piece he was going to do the following Saturday at noon on the corner of West Broadway and Spring. As soon as he materialized, Cissy said, "Oh, hi, Alvin, how nice to see you . . ." Then—I could hardly believe it—she said she'd be right back, she had to mail a letter, and she disappeared.

Alvin Harriman smiled bitterly at me as Cissy walked past us to the door. A small, intense, bowlegged man about thirty-five years old, still wiry and slim, he had a greying handlebar mustache and suspicious, doleful eyes. He said, "She won't be back until I leave . . . I don't know who you are, but my advice to you is to return to your original place of residence as quickly as possible, while you still own your self-respect . . . Cissy Wyatt is like everyone else down here now. She knows Colette and Robert Wilson both stole my idea of time, my use of mirrors. I was the first to incorporate the temporal dimension into my performances—the first performer to do so since the Renaissance! In July of 1968, on the steps of the Customs House. Way before any of those people even showed up . . . But no one will admit it, they say I'm paranoid. They think it's a case of sour grapes. I'm languishing away with no money to document what I do, and each day that goes by sees someone stealing another of my ideas and getting all the credit. I've learned that the world is filled with people who refuse to accept the possibility of another's superiority. They cut you down to size, stifle you, try to destroy you. It's no joke. And everyone in this town knows you have to either be gay or give money to the critics in order to get mentioned by the art magazines. So I don't stand a chance. I've been working on my art for years and this is the thanks I get . . . Suffocated by the creative cartel . . . Art now is just a scene. The search for truth means nothing . . ."

The hurt in his voice was so palpable that I couldn't take it, I didn't know what to say and found myself walking out the door as well, leaving him with Carole Levy, who didn't seem to mind. She got him to look at Ed Mull's paintings.

Another day, in came a young fellow named Christopher Walker, polite and well-dressed, who tried to interest Cissy in his art, which consisted of the following procedure. Wearing an elaborate costume he assembled especially for the occasion, he took color photos of himself with a timer, developed the prints, then burned them without showing them to anybody. His photos of these photos, smoldering in smoky piles on the floor of his apartment, were the objects—numbered and catalogued according to date and time of exposure—which he wanted Cissy to exhibit.

She smiled ruefully after he left. "You see what you're up against," she said. "I'd take you to some *interesting* performances but I don't have the time. I'm simply too busy to go."

That was all right with me, though. I was dying to get out into the real world again, because I sure wasn't going to run into Oliver Hartwell on West Broadway. I didn't want to spend any more time in SoHo, moving through crowds of coldly fashionable suburbanites.

Cissy did take me to one place, however, and I felt forever indebted to her as a result. She took me to meet Jack Rio.

"There's someone I think you should see," Cissy said to me one afternoon in an oddly reverential tone of voice: "Jack Rio. Although I don't know if he'll let us through the door. It depends on his mood. He's on a different wave length than the rest of us. One of the reasons for my precarious monetary situation is that I've been subsidizing him for months now, even though I know he'll never let me represent him. He despises me because I own a gallery. I'm the enemy. But since he's broke, he lets me in, at least. He's having real trouble paying his rent, and there's a rumor that he's in bad health. His liver . . . He certainly looks terrible . . ."

She sighed wistfully. "He's got these trunks full of archives, though . . . Everything important that's happened during the past two decades, he was a part of it . . . If I only could get my hands on *those*."

Cissy shivered. "Jack Rio is almost forgotten now—most of the new performance artists don't even know who he is—but he's the unacknowledged source for almost everything the little bunnies are doing. Without him, it wouldn't have been possible. Jack's very existence is a jealously guarded secret. He's a legend to a handful of friends, artists who were around in the old days. Now he's a recluse, but in the Fifties and Sixties he was a well-known sculptor. Then, in '68, he initiated the whole anti-museum, anti-gallery movement. He was the first artist of any importance to withdraw from the system and stop making art. He staged noisy, confrontational sit-ins at the Museum of Modern Art, pouring blood on the Mirós. He's become quite self-destructive lately, though, my dear. I don't think he eats at all. He never leaves his loft. His life has become the most super-exclusive of performances.

Twenty-four hours a day, an ongoing installation with him at the center of it. But only a few people are aware of what he's doing these days. He's become a living anachronism."

We went to a rundown building on Grand Street east of the Bowery, and climbed stairs covered with plaster dust to a door on the fourth floor. The door was unlocked, and as we pushed our way inside past mounds of trash we were assaulted by the gut-wrenching smells of urine and shit. In the middle of the room sat a shrunken, middle-aged man with matted hair and a greying beard. Cissy took my hand as we slinked along the wall and sat in a corner, instinctively making ourselves as inconspicuous as possible.

"Hello, Jack," she said meekly. There was no response, no sign that he had even seen us come in. Instead, hunched in a broken armchair, dressed in what looked like surplus bush attire from a '40s adventure movie—moth-eaten leather bomber jacket and ratty white silk scarf— he played with the dial of an old-fashioned wood console radio, rolling his eyes, saliva dripping down his chin into his beard. An unearthly light barely penetrated filthy, broken windows, and the only sound aside from the distant static coming over the radio was that of dripping in a chipped enamel sink in the corner. Underneath the sink lay a pile of rusted tools. Balsa wood model airplanes hung on wires from the ceiling, turning lazily above mounds of garbage he had arranged around himself like sandbags in a bunker. Cockroaches were everywhere in the murky light, swarming over the garbage, crawling across the furniture. Slowly Jack Rio began to moan and chirp to himself like an autistic child, swivelling his head from side to side. Grinning suddenly, grimacing, making faces, he at first whispered and then shouted the same phrase over and over again. "I carry myself around in my head," he was crying, "AROUND IN MY HEAD . . ." He gave off an air of such desolate isolation and sadness that I nearly fainted.

It was difficult to breathe in the room's overpowering stench, and after fifteen minutes we got up to go. Cissy left a handful of bills on the floor next to a dented coffee pot. I felt humbled—abashed—by Jack Rio's purity and craziness. Once we were out on the street again, perhaps to relieve the tension, Cissy wisecracked, "Well, that's what happens when you can't tell the difference between life and art." But to me, Jack Rio had been a revelation. He had brought to mind all the lost souls I'd seen in Washington Square Park and throughout the city. And the only way he'd been able to do that was by risking himself, perhaps destroying himself. His integrity was beyond question.

"Jack Rio's a saint," I replied vehemently. "The lost hermit-saint of SoHo . . ." Cissy started to laugh, but then she looked at me and changed her mind.

Cissy decided that we should proceed by videotaping my performances—documentation, she called it—and she introduced me to Jerry Arnold, her "porta-pak man," a twenty-two-year-old NYU film major. "No color," she admonished. "Forget color. It's too expensive and we don't need it. Black and white's fine. After we have a record of three or four performances we can see what sort of style you're developing and take it from there . . ."

But I had no intention of developing a style. Maybe I needed Cissy's money; however, having a cameraman follow me around was out of the question. I explained to her that anybody standing nearby, recording what I did, would only violate the space, turning whatever went on into no more than an art event.

"I'm going after more than that, Cissy, but I need time to develop my ideas. Having Jerry tag along would only be an intrusion, it would make me self-conscious. Give me a week or two alone, OK? I'll have a friend take some photographs. Does that satisfy you?"

Perhaps thinking of her three hundred dollars, she glared at me resentfully, clenching and unclenching her fists to keep from erupting. She said in a measured voice, "I don't have time to argue. I can't force you to do anything. However, we're going to need more than a few snapshots . . . At least promise me you'll keep a written record of whatever you do—dates, locations, descriptions, diagrams—anything to establish what takes place."

"Absolutely," I said.

"But I'll tell you one thing, Roy . . . You can't be shy in this business, there's too much competition out there. Performing means *performing*, not hanging back. Do you follow me? This isn't the right historical moment for being fastidious and coy. It won't hold water."

I smiled—and held that smile until, looking at me, she grew uncomfortable. "Trust me, Cissy," I said.

The next day, May 17th it was—a Friday, rainy and overcast—I took the subway up to Grand Central Station. I wanted to start in midtown, around 42nd Street. Sooner or later, I told myself, Hartwell or some of his cronies would make their presence known again by some act. And right away I wondered about that: *His cronies . . .* Who might they be? What made me assume such people even existed? But why bother writing DEATH TO THE SPROUTS around the city if not to communicate a message of encouragement, if not to pass on the word? Because I had come upon that same graffiti again several days before, on the white tiles of the 23rd Street IRT station, above a long wooden bench. DEATH TO THE SPROUTS in black magic marker, already smeared, the words DEATH TO almost obliterated by SAL 135 and MOOCHIE. And late on the night before my conversation with Cissy concerning how we should proceed, I saw it scrawled at the top of an old shattered kitchen door which had been nailed into the temporary walls surrounding a construction site near Union Square.

I parked myself on a bench in Grand Central and waited, just looked and waited. I had a spiral notebook in which I was going to keep a record of whatever I noticed, whatever anybody said to me. I opened it to the first page and wrote PATIENCE, in capital letters, at the top. Then I lit a cigarette—I was smoking again now—and leaned against the bench. People streamed past in the milky, diffuse light of the station. It was ten-thirty A.M.

During the next two weeks I covered a lot of ground, wandering through deserted parts of the city at night, but always returning during the day to the area around 42nd Street, between Grand Central and Times Square. Bryant Park, behind the Public Library, had been virtually abandoned to the junkies and dealers of nickel bags, a shadow marketplace always ready to dissolve at the first sight of a cop. But in those days, the police rarely bothered to patrol the park, and the ambience there—right in the middle of the city, surrounded by businesses and skyscrapers—was sepulchral and venal, a landscaped extension of Times Square. Much shouting, insults, knives being pulled. Junkies nodding out on benches, containers of coffee growing cold in their hands. Stirring themselves in slow-motion from their nods like statues painfully coming to life. And, spilling over from the surrounding side-walks, some of the large number of crazies drawn to midtown by the ongoing excitement of the big crowds.

Grand Central Station, on the other hand, was more the province of homeless shopping bag ladies and a variety of destitute men who lived in the steam tunnels underneath the tracks. In the waiting rooms were a cast of regulars I came to know by sight, many of them women, who existed on handouts and the remains of travellers' snacks scavenged from trash cans, hoarding brown paper bags of crumbled cookies or half-eaten cheese crackers. Some were too proud or frightened to ac-cept money from strangers, like the two elderly sisters who, all day long, alternated making the rounds of the pay phones in half-hour shifts. One stayed with their bags of belongings while the other me-thodically entered one booth after another. Pale and thin, carrying themselves with a frayed dignity, dressed in identical shapeless cloth coats, shy and uncommunicative, they reminded me of an ancient lady from whom I had taken lugubrious lessons in ballroom dancing back in Ohio, when I was twelve years old. I couldn't look at them without hearing ghostly strains of "The Tennessee Waltz" in my head, and more than once I tried to strike up a conversation, offering to buy them coffee and sandwiches, but whenever I approached they turned away, and if I persisted they began to tremble disconsolately like rain-soaked birds.

Every afternoon I bought the newspapers and would sit in Bryant Park looking through them for reports of incidents like the ones I'd seen and read about before. However, except for a shopping bag filled with explosives found in a uptown subway station, there was nothing. And obviously that could have been left there by anybody. The "shop-ping bag murders," as the *Daily News* and the *Post* had labelled them, seemed to have stopped, and as May turned into June I began to won-der if I wasn't pursuing phantoms after all. Day after day I sat on a bench in the balmy late spring weather, fending off the junkies while, on the sidewalks beyond the park's perimeter, normal life continued in all its dazzling inconsequentiality—girls in T-shirts or colorful summer dresses, salesmen lugging sample cases and staring down at their shoes, tourists filing by, heads tilted up at the skyscrapers. I began to feel I was no more than an aimless outcast myself.

I was no better than the emaciated little man who appeared across from me one afternoon in early June, carrying on a spirited conversation with himself in chirping bird language. Tucking his feet under his body like a roosting chicken, he sat down against a tree and began furiously smoking a joint by inserting it in one nostril, closing the other, and then snorting non-stop. As soon as the first was finished he produced another which he smoked in the same fashion, then another, and another, until after the eighth marijuana cigarette I lost count.

Getting up to leave, I was accosted by a nervous, scrawny white guy in his thirties, his face covered with eczema, who had been standing nearby. At first I thought he wanted money but when he came closer I saw the singular light in his eyes, the glance conveying dramas too compelling to be kept secret.

"Did ya hear about infrasound yet?" he asked, giving me a meaningful stare. As he spoke he looked off abruptly in various directions, always coming back to me with unexpected suddenness.

"I can't stay long, I gotta go. As soon as they find out I'm talking to somebody they'll be here in a flash, turn on the power, I'll be down on my knees clutching my head. *Like this . . .*" He fell to the ground, holding his hands to his ears, grinning up at me. Then his expression changed, his face becoming painfully serious as he stood up.

"What can I do?" I asked. "Would you like something to eat? Can I give you a dollar?"

"Shut up!" he screamed. His eyes, whose troubled glow had been focused on me the moment before, now appeared opalescent as he stared off behind me toward Fifth Avenue. Then they swerved toward me again. "I can't talk now," he said in an anguished voice. "I gotta tell you. People are dying, *everywhere people are dying.* Every day it's infrasound but people don't know it. Because the ones who control it are very clever. Very softly they turn it on and very slowly you don't feel right anymore. You don't *hear* infrasound, you *notice* it. Three and a half vibrations. Nothing heard directly but notice it. Nothing heard but notice. Notice, notice. All other sounds take on a pulsing quality, everything vibrates, that's how you know it's there. That's how I know they're coming. That's how I know when they turn it on. I have to listen now. Shut up. Shut up!"

Desperately intent, he cocked his head toward 41st Street, bringing his hand to his ear and cupping it, listening. Then he started to sob, the tears rolling down his cheeks, his chest heaving. "Oh God, they're not here yet but they're coming for me. It's all my fault. Now it's too late. Now it's infrasound."

Staring off into the trees, after a moment he said softly, "You heard about infrasound yet? They got a machine . . ."

I couldn't take it anymore. Anxious and depressed, I pushed past him and out of the park. For the first time I despaired of ever finding Oliver Hartwell. I was afraid of sinking into the hopeless oblivion of the streets. But I forced myself not to give in to weakness and negativity, I knew he was out there. I insisted on the necessity of having faith in what I knew, what I'd seen.

Buying the day's papers I walked several blocks to a restaurant off Sixth Avenue to have lunch. It was an old Jewish deli with faded photos on the walls of stars from the Forties and Fifties—Randolph Scott, Ginger Rogers, Ethel Merman, John Garfield—smiling and manicured, freshly shaved and coiffed, staring down with easy confidence from a double-breasted, boutonniered, satin-gowned past, at the eaters of matzo ball soup and kreplach, the pinkie-ringed devourers of pastrami and corned beef, who sat around me joking with one another.

I ordered a sandwich, took a sip of coffee, and looked down at the newspaper.

SON OF SAM WRITES BRESLIN

Hello from the gutters of NYC which are filled with dog manure, vomit, stale wine, urine and blood. Hello from the sewers which swallow up these delicacies when they are washed away by the sweeper trucks. Hello from the cracks in the sidewalks of NYC and from the ants that dwell in these cracks and on the dried blood of the dead that has settled into the cracks.

. . . You can forget about me if you like because I don't care for publicity. However, you must not forget Donna Lauria. She was a very sweet girl but Sam's a thirsty lad and he won't let me stop killing until he gets his fill of blood. No, Mr. Breslin, sir, don't think because you haven't heard from me for a while that I went to sleep. No, rather, I am still here. Like a spirit roaming the night. Thirsty, hungry, seldom stopping to rest; anxious to please Sam. I love my work. Now, the void has been filled.

Perhaps we shall meet face to face someday or perhaps I will be blown away by the cops with smoking .38's. Not knowing what the future holds I shall say farewell and I will see you at the next job. Or should I say you will see my handiwork at the next job? Remember Ms. Lauria. Thank you.

In their blood and From the Gutter, Sam's Creation .44

P.S.—Please inform all detectives on the slayings that I wish them the best of luck. Keep em digging, drive on, think positive, get off yr butts, knock on coffins, etc.

Son of Sam

"What's this city coming to?" complained a man at the next table, gesturing at the paper which lay open before me.

"I have two teenage daughters, my wife and I are afraid to let them out of the house. We live in Queens where this maniac's struck five times already. And as if we don't have enough heartache, my daughters hate us now because we won't let them out weekends with this guy running around loose. They're always figuring out ways to sneak off anyway, just to make my life miserable. I hope they catch this fairy soon and cut his balls off with rusty scissors . . ."

Ending his peroration, he sat there, slowly munching on corned beef and eyeing me quizzically.

"He could be anyone, that's the trouble," he mused. "Even a Jewish boy, God forbid . . . Who's to know?" He studied my hands, my clothes, my clean-shaven face, and sighed.

I pushed away the other papers and looked at the front page of the *Times*: voters in Miami rescinded an ordinance prohibiting discrimination against homosexuals after Anita Bryant's campaign to revoke it; Seattle Slew won the Triple Crown at Belmont; Julie Harris and Al Pacino won this year's Tony Awards.

Turning the pages, I came to a halt at a brief article buried at the back of the business section. Sitting up straight, my breath coming in short gasps, I read, SCIENTIST VANISHES IN MARYLAND:

> Dr. Maisume Iremuro, associate director of the Gerontology Research Institute in Baltimore, disappeared while on his way to work this morning. His late-model car was found by police at the side of the road just outside Baltimore city limits. Dr. Iremuro, who has lived in this country since 1964, is an internationally recognized figure in recombinant DNA research. Recently, he had begun a project on the genetic factors responsible for human aging. Police have no explanation for his disappearance, and his wife, Marjorie Iremuro of suburban Catonsville, refused to talk with reporters.

The police may have been unable to explain what happened, but I certainly could. Oliver Hartwell was behind this, nothing could be more clear. I saw now that he was at the helm of an organized movement of geriatric revenge, and had kidnapped Dr. Iremuro in order to learn what he knew about the biology of human aging. I remembered how the topic had obsessed him during our interview and the passionate determination with which he had vowed to find a way to outsmart death . . . *Outsmart death*—hadn't he used that very phrase?

I couldn't touch the bulging egg salad sandwich I had ordered. It sat there in front of me like some terrible yellow mistake, a moist explosion barely contained by its plate, enough to feed at least two people. Lighting a cigarette, bolting down the rest of the coffee in my cup, I felt a surge of nervous energy as I paid the bill and rushed out into the street.

I walked along Sixth Avenue, back toward Bryant Park. When I reached the corner of 41st I saw, ahead of me, a crowd gathered under the rows of sycamore trees in the southwest corner. I bounded up the steps thinking of the infrasound guy. He'd been so shaky and vulnerable anything could have happened to him. I pushed through the knot of people surrounding two cops bent over a body on the flagstone path.

"All right, everybody," one of the cops announced as he straightened up, "this ain't a circus. Back off." An ambulance could be heard cutting through the midtown traffic, getting louder. The crowd wavered momentarily but in the end nobody left. The second cop stood up as well, and a sigh escaped from the man standing next to me as, for the first time, we all could see clearly. It was the body of a boy not more than fourteen, his mouth frozen open, his eyes glassy, staring up at the sky.

"Here we go again," I said aloud to myself. "My God."

Looking down at the boy I noticed a series of gashes which ran from one side of the forehead to the other, disfiguring it. Blood from the cuts had congealed on his cheeks and neck.

"What happened?" I asked nobody in particular.

"It's terrible," the man next to me—a vigorous, athletic-looking fellow—was saying. "But this poor kid was looking for trouble. I don't know why the city doesn't spend some money to train these delinquents for some kind of work. As it is, they have no future. They're running around loose with nothing to do but victimize the elderly. He got what he deserved, but all the same it's such a waste."

Victimize the elderly . . . I turned to him and asked, "But what did he do?"

"I got here just before you did," the man replied gruffly. "They say this kid was ripping some old guy off and the guy turned on him. 'Course that's just a few junkies talking, so who knows? The kid's dead as can be, though, that's for sure."

People were shoving at me from behind as the two cops tried to clear the area. The siren had stopped and two attendants ran toward us past the big stone fountain, carrying a stretcher, but when I glanced down again everything else faded away. All I saw was that forehead. Then the adrenalin surged through me like an electrical storm.

"Look!" I barked, involuntarily taking hold of the stranger's sleeve in my excitement. "Look at his forehead. Tell me what you see."

"What I see?"

"Yes." I was sure of it now. "Don't you notice anything written there? Doesn't it spell anything to you?"

"*Spell* anything," he repeated, pulling his sleeve out of my grasp.

"What're you, bullshitting me?" He laughed disparagingly then added, "What do *you* see?"

I bristled. "I see the letters OPW, that's what I see."

"Letters? . . . OPW?" We both stared down for a last time at the body, just before the attendants bundled it onto the stretcher. The cuts were deep, like hash marks or chevrons, but they began to the left with a circle, the round flap of flesh almost entirely pulled away from the skull, white bone showing underneath. "It's as plain as day," I said. "Look!" It was important to me for somebody else to corroborate what I saw, but the man beside me would have none of it. Not even bothering to reply, he had turned to face me with a disbelieving, supercilious expression which infuriated me. By now the crowd had dispersed and the body was being loaded into the ambulance on Sixth Avenue, the cops standing beside it.

I remembered later it was precisely at this point that his manner had changed, shifting from disdain to a kind of clinical interest. He was coolly checking me out now, but I was too agitated to notice.

"For your information," I said heatedly, "I'm a lot less crazy than you think. I don't know what those letters mean, but I've seen them before."

"You've seen them before, have you?" he replied in that gruff, contemptuous voice.

In his mid-forties, he was dressed in a blue work shirt and worn khaki trousers, his full head of curly black hair greying at the temples. If it hadn't been for the intelligent, analytical cast to his eyes, I would have taken him for a construction worker. His burly, thick-set body was in prime condition. But that mocking voice—who was this guy to doubt what I knew?

"You're serious, aren't you?" he asked.

"You're damn right I'm serious. And I've seen a lot more too." Babbling now, not thinking, I went on about the punks who'd been killed the same way this one had, about the murder I'd witnessed under the West Side Highway, about the missing Japanese scientist, about the graffiti I'd seen.

"Graffiti? Which graffiti?"

"Death to the sprouts," I replied. "What's more, I believe they're a part of some conspiracy, some organized movement of revenge against these kids who've been victimizing the elderly, as you put it. How do you like that?"

Something was wrong. I expected a derisive laugh, but instead he was examining me with those gimlet eyes, an expression of fierce inquiry which seemed to bore into me.

"Sprouts," he echoed in a flat, dull voice. "That's very interesting."

"But you wouldn't know anything about that," I said ironically, with less challenge in my voice than I'd wanted.

"Oh, really?" Still looking directly into my eyes, pondering something, absentmindedly he lifted his left hand to his mouth and bit the inside of his thumb.

The inside of his thumb . . . Instantly I was terrified. My body went numb, I found it impossible to breathe, and helplessly I watched as, letting his hand fall, he stepped forward. A distant smile played on his lips, his eyes becoming cold and hard, as vacant as the eyes of a hawk.

"Raptor," I said to myself, "bird of prey," as I tried to scream, to call for help, but I couldn't. Briefly he glanced behind me, just a flick of the eyes, a trembling of the eyebrows, nothing at all, but it was the last thing I remembered.

"Hey, my man, you all right? You still with us?"

A voice floated down from above and I opened my eyes to see an immense, bearded black man, a leather cowboy hat on his head, a gold earring in one ear. He must have weighed three hundred pounds. As he leaned over me I thought that if he fell I would be crushed to death, and instinctively I tried to move away. Somebody else was holding my feet, however, and a third person was going through my pockets. I tried to shout but the big one clamped a meaty hand over my mouth and nose. Giggling, a look of disappointment in his eyes, he said, "It's just like a white boy, Robert, don't you think? Here we saved this motherfucker's life and he's right away coming back at us with some jive attitude. What's a nigger to do? . . . Maybe we shoulda just let them dudes as was after you have their way. They hammered you to the ground and was fixin' to cut you into little cubes like a piece of motherfuckin' *cheese* before we stepped in. Don't that mean nothin' to you? You rather be dead?"

"Got it now," another voice said. "This boy's the cautious type. He done stuck his moneybag up his ass or something, took me all day."

The big one released his hand from my mouth and said, "We gone stroll off down the park, now, whitey, and if you so much as breathe too hard we gone finish up what them other folks started. You read me? *Comprende, señor?*"

Chuckling softly as he backed off, his middle covered with an ornate hammered silver buckle, his huge legs sheathed in black leather, he turned and left me lying there on the grass, looking up at the sky.

I watched the clouds go by until my heart stopped pounding, then staggered to my feet, my head aching and my lips bloody, and left the park. I walked along 42nd Street and down Fifth Avenue past the entrance to the Public Library . . . I recalled the sound of his voice but it didn't remind me of Hartwell's. Was it possible I'd forgotten the sound of his voice? Can a person change his voice so it's no longer recognizable? I tried to remember this man's eyes. Hartwell's had been brown too. But most people have brown eyes. And what about the wire-rimmed glasses he used to wear? Was he using contact lenses now? The fact remained, I hadn't recognized him. He had looked so young. It was impossible, yet who else could he have been? He had gnawed at his thumb in exactly the same way Hartwell did during our interview. Some things you just don't forget.

Had he discovered a fountain of youth, then, a means of rejuvenation so effective that nothing but a few especially stubborn habits remained? Did lamb fetus injections accomplish this? Pills of some sort? Exercises? Was he a master of disguises, then? Impossible. And yet he'd known exactly what I was talking about, I'd seen it in his eyes.

I stumbled down Fifth Avenue, shuddering as I remembered his raptor stare—that same searching look as in Washington Square Park, there was no doubt about it. And I'd been hit from behind again, like when I'd come up the stairs to my apartment.

So now I knew the score. I began trotting downtown. As I ran I felt unfazed, unafraid. A steely recklessness overcame me. *Like a spirit roaming the night.* Climbing the steps to my apartment, opening the door, I remembered the gun I'd kept all this time. Now I had a use for it.

FIFTEEN

I'd been carrying with me in Bryant Park what was left of Cissy's advance—about eighty dollars—so I was flat broke now. Somehow or other I was going to have to convince her to give me more money. But first there was one thing I needed to check up on, a hunch which began to possess me as I went through the drawers in my desk, scraping together enough change for the subway. Separating the nickels and dimes from the pennies . . . I'd done that before too. Everything was coming full circle.

I found the little black .25-caliber automatic in the chest of drawers where I'd hidden it under some clothes. I cradled it in my hand, succumbing once again to its snug fit inside my palm, its snub nose protruding from the space between my thumb and forefinger. I put the gun in my knapsack along with my camera, then I called the Phalanx Gallery. Instantly Cissy was on the line, testy and impatient.

"Where have you been, Roy? I've been trying to reach you for days. What work have you done so far? We're putting together the fall schedule for the gallery and I want to start letting everyone know who you are, do you understand? The critics have to be told about you so they can see what you're doing. I'll need to see those photographs your friend's been taking, but if you continue to perform on the street you're going to have to accept the idea of an audience, not to mention videotaping everything. There's no other way."

I'd forgotten how hooked into her world Cissy was. She sounded almost frantic, and yet I knew that as soon as we hung up she'd be on the phone to somebody else with that same note of urgency in her voice.

"I—uh—I've been busy performing," I said. "I'll show you what I've got tomorrow. Can we meet for lunch? There's something I have to do today."

"Lunch is no good," she replied, "tomorrow's Saturday and I'm having *two* lunches, for gosh sakes, can you believe it? At this rate, soon size twelve will be a memory. Some people refuse to do business with you unless you feed them first. Come to the gallery after that—say three o'clock, OK? And don't leave if I'm not here. I'll positively be back by three-thirty, I've got a very important call coming in from Zurich then . . ."

"All right," I said. "I'll be there."

It had been four months since I'd visited Grandma Bessie and Ed Reed at Sunset Towers. Two women I didn't know were in Bessie's room, and when I returned to the reception desk I had difficulty prying her new room number from the nurse on duty. An icy, colorless blond woman with narrow lips and a forced smile, wearing a thick red sweater over her uniform in spite of the season, she crossly demanded to know why I hadn't checked in at the desk beforehand, and then claimed that visiting rights were restricted to members of the family. If I wanted to see Mrs. Goldman I would have to apply, in advance, to the Administrator of Sunset Towers.

"We don't allow strangers to wander in off the street," she sniffed, and then added, "If certain parties refuse to behave themselves they must suffer the consequences. Sunset Towers is a nursing home, not a detention center . . ."

"But this is absurd," I said. "I've been visiting Mrs. Goldman for more than a year now with no trouble whatsoever."

When she disdained to reply, officiously returning to her paperwork while a security guard left his post at the entrance and approached, I lost my temper. Earlier, I had waited outside until he'd momentarily been occupied with something else and then walked right past his turned back. I hadn't wanted him examining my knapsack then and I certainly didn't want him to do so now. It was absolutely necessary for me to see Bessie and Ed, but I hadn't felt safe travelling in the city without the pistol.

"Listen, madam," I almost shouted, "I'm only going to say this once.

I happen to be married to Mrs. Goldman's granddaughter, I'm part of the family, and if you don't tell me where she is immediately I'll call the Millers and report this to them. We can always transfer her to another institution, you know. There are plenty of them out there."

Narrowing her lips even more so that the sigh escaping them became a hiss, she wrote the room number on a slip of paper and, waving off the guard, replied, "That might not be such a bad idea, young man. If any other home would take her, that is . . ."

Sunset Towers was larger than I thought, and I wandered the hallways for a good ten minutes, past shrunken, disabled people in walkers who stood here and there like sentinels, eyeing me mournfully, until I found Bessie's room. It was in the basement, and the only light came from two barred windows near the ceiling. She lay in bed reading a looseleaf manuscript. As soon as she saw me, she buried it beneath the covers and quickly got up, walking toward me with a smile. She embraced me energetically, planting a wet kiss on my cheek, and stood there, beaming and vivacious, totally unlike the person I'd left in February.

I knew it, I said to myself.

"You look wonderful, Mrs. Goldman."

"Please call me Bessie," she said in a forceful voice. "After all, we're friends, Roy . . . Why should we stand on ceremony? It's so good to see you. I knew you'd return, in fact I bet Ed five dollars you would, and now here you are. You're just in time, too . . ."

She stepped back, grinning at me with affection, as if I were her own grandson. And she was no longer addressing me as Marshall.

"Just in time? What do you mean?"

She laughed. "We'll get to that in a moment. I look better, don't you think? I *feel* better, like a new person, and I want to thank you for your concern the last time you were here. It meant so much to me, even if I appeared unable to register what you were saying. Ed and I are both grateful to you. In my old age I seem to be making not only new friends but new family as well. Who would have thought such a thing possible? Certainly if I depended on my own family I'd have no one now. Even my Dana no longer comes, but I don't let it bother me."

Bessie seemed quiet energetic, but what impressed me most was her change in attitude. I'd never seen her as she was now, radiant and self-assured. I noticed that when she walked it was without a limp.

"I'm sorry I haven't been to see you before this," I said "but all sorts of crazy things kept cropping up. However, I brought my camera with me, Bessie, I want to have a picture of you both and I won't take no for an answer. I have to see you two together."

She reddened. "That's sweet of you, but Ed can't always get away now. I'm sure he knows you're here, word travels quickly in this place. But the problem is they're watching us all the time. Especially Ed—I don't even know what room they have him in. They decided he was a troublemaker after he helped me stop taking those awful pills. And when he refused to participate in their round-robin shuffleboard tournaments—you should have been here, what a scene he caused!—they used that as an excuse to take away his privileges."

She grimaced and looked away. "Mine too. This room is no better than a fancy prison cell. And the worst part is, the other *alta kochers* here don't understand us at all. 'The gerries,' Ed calls them. The only thing they're upset about is being too ill to get on the plane to Miami Beach any more. They have no conception of what's happening to them. They refuse to admit there's an old people's war going on."

"For God's sake, Bessie, that's outrageous. Why don't you just leave Sunset Towers? Nobody's stopping you."

She groaned. "You're so naive. To the contrary, my dear boy, many people are stopping us. You keep forgetting our situation. My darling daughter and her husband have full legal control over me, just as Ed's family has over him. We can't make a move without their consent. You simply are not aware of the degree to which our wonderful democratic society is set up to take advantage of the elderly. Lou and Sibyl are like Cossacks—my own flesh and blood! I'm not exaggerating! They control my assets and my freedom of movement, while a crook like Bernard Bergman—have you been reading the papers?—while that *momser* who has caused so much suffering gets out of jail after serving only four months. If you read the papers, you must also be aware of all those innocent people dying from the swine-flu inoculations last winter, every one of them over sixty. Like laboratory animals.

But don't feel sorry for us. Ed and I have our ways of dealing with it all, believe me. However, I wouldn't hold my breath today, if I were you. He's been acting up lately and I'm sure they won't let you see him. I wish you could, though," she said, her eyes brimming with pride. "He looks not a day over fifty-five. No trouble with his knee anymore. He's as full of spunk and sass as ever. You should hear him. Nobody talks back to Ed Reed, of that I can assure you."

Sitting on the edge of her bed she said, her voice soft but full of conviction, "I owe my life to that Irishman. He saved me from myself; he showed me the way."

Showed me the way . . .

I paced around, beside myself with impatience and irritation. I doubted I'd be able to find Ed Reed in the welter of room at Sunset Towers, much less get in to see him. Bessie noticed the state I was in and said, "Please, Roy, don't be upset. It won't do you any good. You'll see Ed another day. In the meantime, I have something for you. A gift, you might say, although Ed insists you won't be interested. 'Don't make the boy feel guilty if he doesn't want it,' he said."

She opened a drawer on the table beside her bed and produced a large photo album bound in worn brown leather with faded gothic script across the top. Turning its pages carefully, with obvious affection—the album looked as if it were about to fall apart in her hands—she sighed as she said to me, "I would like to entrust this to your safe-keeping. It contains pictures of Avram and me when we were young, old photographs of my family in Europe, and of Avram's mother, as well. You should see her, what a wonderful woman she was, proud and strong, so unlike my husband . . . Somehow I felt you would appreciate it, you would understand. I've turned over a new leaf, my dear boy. I won't need this where I'm going, but I couldn't bring myself to throw it away, and I remembered you seemed interested in my stories of the old days. You put up with listening to an old woman's memories . . ."

Electrified, I exclaimed, "You and Ed are running away!"

Her face clouded over and she snapped, "What are you, *meshuggah?* Will you please control yourself? You're behaving like a child. I'm giving you an album of photographs, nothing more. I'm an old woman about to die, and I have no family. Who said anything about running away? I thought you might be interested—and I must admit I have an ulterior motive as well . . . The last time you were here—or rather, later, when I was thinking about why you bothered to visit an old woman like me—I realized that you were Jewish. Somehow it never occurred to me before. You *are* Jewish, aren't you?"

I was certain she and Ed were planning to escape from Sunset Towers, and it was all I could do to contain my irritation at her diversionary tactics.

"Yes, of course," I replied. "I mean, I suppose . . ."

"Exactly. That's exactly what you mean. You are and you aren't. Like so many Jewish children raised in this country, you're neither fish nor fowl. You walk around acting like the *goyim*, talking like the *goyim*, eating their food, buying Christmas presents, and yet wondering why, in spite of all that—and even without experiencing overt anti-Semitism—you feel as if you don't belong. You're cut off from your own tradition, you never go to *shul*, you're ignorant of the Hebrew language. The holidays your own people have celebrated since time immemorial mean nothing to you."

I sighed with exasperation. The last thing I needed was a lecture on the state of my Jewishness.

"Am I right or wrong? What about your parents, my darling? Do they keep a kosher home? How much of your family's history do you know? Because without that you are no one. Just another half-breed American . . . All the time I was involved with the Party in the Thirties, I never gave up on my religion. Maybe that was why I finally quit. The Communists weren't interested in Jews, only in more Communists."

"Look, Bessie," I said, picking up the album and putting it in my knapsack, then eyeing the clock on her dresser, "I'll be happy to keep this for you but I don't have the time or the inclination to get into a debate about my lack of Judaism. It's almost six o'clock, visiting hours are over in ten minutes and I still haven't seen Ed or even taken your picture."

She looked at me with a resigned expression and said, "All right already, take the picture, take it. Why not? Soon it will be sunset anyway, sunset in Sunset Towers, and then I wouldn't let you. Not on *shabbes.*"

Feeling edgy, fumbling with the camera I hadn't used in nearly a year, I turned on all the lights and took several shots of her smiling fixedly into the lens, a green shawl around her shoulders and her white hair coiled into a bun. Even as I was taking them, however, I knew they wouldn't convey the rejuvenation I saw, the renewed vitality. I'd end up with a few murky snapshots.

"For posterity," she remarked ironically. "For the kosher time capsule. This will be the final picture in that album."

"Bessie," I said, "time's running out and I have something important to ask you. I hope you don't mind. Just one question. Does the name Oliver Hartwell mean anything to you?"

I was staring at her as closely as I could, glaring at her even, determined not to miss a move, a quickened breath, a blink of her eyes. And she flinched, didn't she? Her mouth trembled slightly. Chills ran up my back.

"Oliver Hartwell? No, I'm afraid it doesn't. I've never heard of him."

I didn't buy her answer for a second. I was so indignant that I blurted out, "You're not telling me the truth, Bessie."

She drew herself up. "What did you say?" she spat angrily, adding a string of Yiddish and ending with, "You're doubting my word now? It's too much . . ."

At that moment the door opened. The nurse in red stood there and behind her were two security guards.

"Personnel informs me that we forgot to search your bag, young man," she said. "Please let me see it. Don't cause trouble, either. Regulations permit—"

I stood up, throwing the camera into my sack on top of the photo album and the gun, and interrupting her.

"Oh, yeah? Well for your information I'm not one of your patients. So stuff your regulations up your ass."

Brushing past her as the guards tried to get their hands on me, I shouted over my shoulder, "Mayor Beame will hear about this!" In spite of themselves the two men laughed. I ran down the hallway and up some stairs leading to an emergency exit, half-heartedly pursued by the guards, all three of us laughing now as I kept repeating, "Abe Beame will hear about this! He's a close friend of my uncle's!"

Old people's war, Bessie had said . . . OPW . . . How fantastic . . . The phrase had lodged in my head as soon as I heard it, but not until I was riding home on the subway did I figure it out, and by the time I got to St. Mark's Place I was shaking again. I spent that evening first in the bathtub, then stretched out on the living room floor, trying to relax.

It got very late, past three in the morning, but I couldn't sleep. Friday nights on St. Mark's Place were noisier in the summer. I needed to smoke some grass but there wasn't any in the house. I hadn't been stoned since November and hadn't wanted to be until now . . . OPW . . . Hartwell was out there somewhere. I couldn't get over what he was doing. I had to find him and for that I needed money. I felt confident. I wasn't scared of him at all but nevertheless I couldn't calm down, my heart was racing, and I was jumpy as hell.

Finally I lay in bed under the reading lamp, Bessie's family album spread out on my lap. It was a peculiar sensation ending up with somebody else's past after having jettisoned my own. The album began with a small collection of wrinkled, stained studio portraits from the nineteenth century, respectable couples stiffly posed before backdrops of waterfalls and fountains. There were also sepia prints of solitary children—mysterious and unsettling, with long hair and shining eyes—standing erect against the same little column, holding an open book, peering distrustfully into the lens. And a family scene, an entire tribe of booted and spurred men wearing Russian shirts, and women dressed in crinolines. But otherwise the pictures were of middle-aged, curiously complacent couples dressed in their finest clothes, proudly uncomfortable. Perhaps they had assumed these poses of unassailable respectability in keeping with an idea of the occasion's solemnity. But whatever the reason, except for the haunted, solitary children, nobody interested me. There were no raving beauties marooned in small town Eastern Europe, no misfits, no alcoholics, no madmen.

Then I reached the pages with Bessie and Avram. Innumerable photos, beginning with an adolescent Bessie glowing with youth, her long, thick, loosely plaited hair cascading down her back. This had me sitting bolt-upright in bed, nervously lighting a cigarette. She looked exactly like Dana. There were other portraits of her at around the same age, but none of them captured the uncanny likeness of this picture. If I hadn't seen it I would have thought untrue the stories in the Miller family of Dana's close resemblance to Bessie in her youth. But this was something else. I couldn't take my eyes off her. Dana was in the room with me, only a sort of proto-Dana, an essence of Dana I'd intuited many time but never seen before.

Bessie possessed a fiery quality then, she had character. In comparison to her, Avram was quite handsome and often wore a complex expression on his face, a kind of sad self-consciousness. Yet he seemed hesitant, as if unwilling to reveal himself to the camera. By the time they had gotten older, and family portraits including a roly-poly blond little Sibyl had shown up, I felt the vice of unhappiness closing around them. So many photos, color as well as black and white, blurry, over- and underexposed. So many falsely grinning heads, desultory outings, cryptic displays of empty backyards. I threw the album on the floor, turning out the light, and lay there in the dark thinking of my own parents.

They had escaped from the Nazis with no more than a suitcase of clothes apiece, and I'd never known my grandparents as more than names connected to vague stories. One grandfather had been a cantor in a village synagogue. The other, from a larger town, had owned a dry goods store. Both had perished in the war, along with their families, except for two distant cousins of my father who had made it to Israel. In spite of my parents' intense Jewishness, a personal past hardly existed for us. This lack of relation to actual people placed Judaism in a vacuum for me. It didn't stand a chance of resisting the pull of American culture in which I grew up. And, although perhaps more extreme, my experience was no different from that of many other Jews I'd met after leaving Plainview. I remember being struck by the lack of extended family history for many, even for those who denied it. A few generations and that was it. Grandparents, great-grandparents. A few names, occupations, stories. Before that, nothing. Loss of memory. Amnesia, stretching back into the night, generation after unknown generation, in Eastern Europe, Turkey, the Near East, in who knew where. Converging from all directions toward the distant past, like tunnels to the center of the earth. But the same held true for everybody, no matter what their race or religion, no matter how exclusive their pedigree. Sooner or later the line stopped, the string ran out. The tunnels dropped down into time, pristine and silent, nameless, faceless.

Perspiring, her cheeks flushed, Cissy was sitting behind the reception desk just inside the front door of the gallery, eating a tuna fish sandwich cradled in tinfoil. Dressed in a linen suit and a silk T-shirt, she glowered at me, explaining she was in a very bad mood and felt like locking up, going home, and getting drunk, even though she couldn't because it was Saturday and streams of art tourists were pouring through the door.

". . . So forgive me, my dear, if I don't sound gracious. *Both* of my lunches cancelled, and one of them—that godawful limey bastard Richard Coburn, I hope I never see his face again—didn't even call to inform me, I'm sitting in this restaurant all alone, starving, aggravated, waiting 'til two-thirty, for gosh sakes. No one does that to me! I'm so pissed I could explode!"

She lapsed into moody silence, chewing on her sandwich. Overdressed women from the outer suburbs crowded around the desk in twos and threes, asking the prices of Ed Mull's paintings as if they were grapefruit. Cissy swore under the breath, "I don't know why I let Carole take a lunch break, now I'm trapped." But soon Carole Levy walked in. Cissy instantly stood up and told me to follow her into the small back office/storeroom, filled with stacks of paintings, where she heaved a sigh of relief and shut the door. She sat down at a little table covered with papers and stared at her sandwich. Then she looked at me.

"What's been happening, Roy? What have you been doing all this time?"

"I've been working hard, Cissy, but I don't know if you'll be interested. Above everything else, I've been *looking*."

She sat there eyeing me expectantly and when I didn't add anything further she blinked and said, "Looking? What do you mean, looking? Looking at what? Haven't you been freaking out on the street? My memory of you up at Central Park is still so fresh! All I have to do is close my eyes. It was so incisive."

She closed her eyes for a second, then opened them and frowned. "Where are the photos you promised? Let's get down to business."

"Listen, Cissy," I replied, "my record of what's been taking place is contained in these journals. They tell the whole story."

From my knapsack I produced the spiral notebook, filled by now with scrupulously detailed entries of incidents, and culminating in the killing at Bryant Park, which I related without including the meaning of the letters "OPW" or any discussion of Oliver Hartwell. The journals also contained brief descriptions of people I'd seen in Grand Central, on the streets, in the subways and parks. Cissy opened the notebook and began turning the pages. Not five minutes went by before she said, in a voice brittle with irony, "Why, this is extremely interesting, Roy, really quite unusual . . ." Then she erupted.

"All I'm looking at is a list of crazy people and a few snippets of overheard conversation! And what is this stuff about a knifing in Bryant Park, for gosh sakes? You go on and on about it. What are you *doing* to me, Roy? Why haven't you been going into trances out there on the street? You're wasting my money and my time. I can't believe it. What do you expect me to do with this?" she shrieked, seething mad, pitching the journals against the wall.

"We live in a *visual age*, my dear, need I remind you? We must have pictures, verification, *reality*. Not entries in a log, like Thomas Merton or something. I'm not in the book business. Do you understand me? Am I making myself perfectly clear?"

Her patronizing, sarcastic whine set my teeth on edge.

"Jesus, Cissy, what's eating you? I explained already I can't have cameras around. I'm onto something really big, and the last thing I need is Jerry Arnold trailing after me—or anybody else, for that matter. I do what I want with my life. You don't control it. And as you said that first day—maybe this won't work out between us. Maybe we're not compatible. I don't owe you anything."

"Oh, yes you do, buster," she shot back, her eyes flashing. "You owe me three hundred dollars!"

We glared at each other. I was thinking I'd be washing dishes again soon even though it was the last thing in the world I wanted to do now, when the phone rang.

Cissy held up her hand, signalling me not to talk. "This must be Zurich," she said before she took the call. She listened in silence for a minute. The color drained from her face as she softly replaced the receiver. "Oh, shit," she whispered—her voice breaking, her eyes red, she was crying, I'd never seen Cissy cry before—"Jack Rio's dead."

I was stunned. I felt the tears start up in my eyes, and a disabling sadness overtook me. Jack Rio meant more to me than I realized. Cissy seemed to recover quickly, however. "This is it," she said to herself, setting her jaw, "it's now or never . . ." She made a phone call and when nobody answered she became very agitated, deciding she had to go immediately to Jack Rio's loft—"I'll force the door open if necessary, after all, I'm his de facto dealer"—and take possession of his archives. She knew exactly where they were.

"You'll have to come with me. Because Jack kept everything of importance in two trunks, and they're heavy—I know, I've tried lifting them. Come on," she said, jumping to her feet, "let's get out of here!"

I could hardly believe my ears. I was too broken up by the news of his death to go carting off his effects. It seemed a positively ghoulish thing to do, and I told her so. "I'm way too depressed to run over there now, Cissy. The least you can to is respect my feelings."

"Respect your feelings! What is that, an insult? How do you think I feel? But I'm damned if I'm going to let someone else get their hands on those archives after all the trouble I've gone to, after all that cash I laid out. I'll do a better job perpetuating his memory than any other gallery, I can tell you that—I loved Jack Rio. I supported him. The people in the art world who tomorrow morning will bemoan his death the loudest ignored him while he was alive. He wasn't hip anymore. Besides, you don't realize what's involved. If I can lay claim to those

archives then I'll be a long way toward having legal status as his dealer.
Do you know what that means to me? . . . So save your indignation for
someone worthy of it, my dear. If you won't come along now, at least
stay here and keep an eye on the gallery. I can't just close the place, it's
full of people. I'll take Carole with me, I won't be able to carry those
trunks by myself. And above all, please do me the favor of answering
the phone, ok? I'm expecting a very important call from a man named
Gunther in Zurich, so you'll have to *apologize* for me, can you do that?
Tell him there's been an emergency, say whatever you like. Tell him
my mother died!"

The gallery cleared out temporarily after Cissy and Carole left, and
for a while I was alone. I felt desolated by Jack's death. The art scene in
SoHo seemed phony and denatured in comparison to him. His death
was wrong, a waste. I couldn't assimilate it.

Two well-heeled couples from the suburbs walked in, the men in
sockless Gucci loafers and snowy linen pants, the women dressed in
silk. They were in their late forties, and underneath their sleekly in-
souciant exteriors, you could sense they resented that fact. It implied
an end, somewhere down the line, to their self-indulgence and fatuous
preening. It was obvious they collected art. They sailed around the
room making deprecating remarks about Ed Mull's paintings, dropping names, cracking little jokes. Their very presence in front of me—
not to mention the predominance of others like them outside on the
streets of SoHo—made it seem as if Jack Rio's death had been in vain,
and I hated them for that. The longer they stayed, the more I fell prey
to an unreasoning rage, until I was quivering in my seat, digging my
fists into my lap in an effort to keep from jumping up and punching
one of the men—the one with the mole beside his nose, and the
slicked-back strands of hair—right in the face. Finally they left, I
could hear bursts of laughter as they walked down the stairs, and I sat
there, impotently fuming, unable to look up as several more people
arrived.

About fifteen minutes later, Cissy and Carole returned. Downcast
and subdued, Cissy related that they had been too late; they'd missed
out on the archives.

244 :: MICHAEL BROWNSTEIN

"In a way, I'm glad. I don't think I could have dealt with that scene for a second longer. Sarah Baker was the one who called me before. She said they had found Jack face down in his own vomit, and I couldn't get the image out of my mind. I couldn't even look around the loft, I made a beeline with my head down to where the trunks should have been and when they weren't there, we split. Ask Carole . . ."

Carole Levy, thin and small, appeared shaken. "I don't want to talk about it. It was awful," she said.

I thought Cissy had told me all this because of how she'd acted earlier, and for the first time since I'd known Cissy Wyatt I felt warmly towards her.

"It's ok, Cissy. I understand."

More vulgarites crowded through the door of the gallery. Cissy and I retreated to the back room. Pages from my journals lay scattered around the floor and she apologized for losing her temper. She started to pick them up.

"Don't worry about it," I said. Actually, I hardly heard her speak, I had become so preoccupied.

"I want to do something for Jack," I announced.

"Do something for him?"

"Yes, I want to dedicate a work to his memory, Cissy. I have an idea. A great idea. And we're going to make it happen together."

I paused. "I'm going to take somebody hostage."

"What do you mean?"

"Just what I said. I'll go out on the street and grab somebody—somebody as creepy as the people who've been coming in here all afternoon—and, in memory of Jack Rio, I'll abduct them."

She eyes me quizzically. "*Abduct*, for gosh sakes. . . . First you don't want anybody even knowing what you're doing, now you're going to inflict violence on some innocent person?"

I was looking steadily at her now. I could feel the seriousness in my face, my jaw muscles set. My indignation at Jack's death hadn't subsided in the least.

"Right," I said. "Just grab somebody, any of the assholes who are overrunning the area will do, they've got to be made to understand what Jack Rio stood for . . . It'll be a sort of enforced education. A mandatory lecture on the state of the art world in 1977, like the Maoist thing, what do they call it? Self-criticism? Struggle session? After you and Carole left, some people came into the gallery, I can't tell you how they disgusted me, Cissy. It was a physical response. I've got to do something so Jack's death doesn't remain a meaningless farce. And once I choose somebody and abduct them—"

"But how?"

I thought for a moment. "The pistol. I have a gun, Cissy, I carry it for self-defense . . ." I opened my knapsack and pulled out the Baretta, placing it on the table in front of her. "That's how," I said. "It's beautiful, isn't it? It's an automatic. Don't worry, the safety catch is on. Do you want to see the clip filled with bullets? It ejects from the handle, here, I'll show you."

She blanched, stealing a glance in my direction. "Of course I don't want to see the clip! What are you *doing* with that weapon, Roy?"

When I offered no explanation she said, "Please put it away now, I can't stand looking at it, it's—it's so *small*." She paused and then sniffed disapprovingly, "This isn't like your other art. It's so aggressive . . ."

"I'll go up to some aging vulgarite princess in the street—the Saturday afternoon art crowd of bridge and tunnel ladies, one of the bitches with the fur jackets and the leather pants—and I'll just stick this in her ribs. I'll bring her up here."

"Where?"

"Up here to the gallery. And we'll videotape it."

"Videotape *what*, for gosh sakes! I don't get it."

"Videotape me talking to her, explaining why she's been kidnapped, that she's being held hostage for the future of art, so Jack Rio will not have died in vain. I'll explain to her how downtown has been transformed into a distorted, ersatz version of itself which she and her friends and their husbands have created. They've thrown their money at it, inflating the market, creating a monster of art as high-powered manipulation. I'll tell her they don't know what they're doing, she and her friends, they're destroying what they want to possess, they're throwing their money at nothing, but ignorance is no excuse, lack of taste is no excuse. I'll tell her she has no taste, that she and others like her are the ones bankrolling all these new galleries showing phony art, forcing up the rents and driving the artists out, replacing art with junk, forcing artists to become caricatures of themselves in order to survive. She and her friends have mixed up the real with the bullshit, they can't tell the difference, but since they have so much money nobody's able to resist them, so nobody cares anymore, not even the artists, not even the real artists—who can turn down serious cash on the barrelhead, after all? But Jack Rio cared, he sacrificed his life to this idea, and *I* care, even if simply aesthetically. My sensibilities are offended. I'm forced to initiate this revolutionary action in order to clear the air . . . I insist on my constitutional right to clear the air . . ."

I loved looking directly into Cissy's eyes and not flinching, not even blinking. She refused to be stared down, however. Clearing her throat she said, "But what if this woman resists? What if she screams for help?"

"I'll take care of that, Cissy, it'll all work out. Trust me." And I did feel it would work out. I had an absolutely clear sense of what I was going to do, and with that attitude I knew I could meet any contingency head-on.

Cissy looked at me, not seeing me, her eyes abstracted, glazed. Thinking hard. A crazy half-smile on her lips which she tried to suppress, but trembling with it nonetheless, trembling with excitement. "There are all these problems, Roy," she said, "for one thing—"

But I wasn't listening.

"And there'll be this great *scene* taking place here when my lady and I arrive," I said. "Jerry Arnold will be taping it, and the poor gal will be trembling in her boots, while all the time I'm talking to her, patiently elucidating why she's standing here with a pistol against her ear. I'll be trying to *convert* her, Cissy, don't you see, to open her eyes to the nature of the life she's leading with the lunches and the clothes and the cars, the vacations to nowhere and the loads of expensive art on the wall at home. And I can come across in all sorts of ways saying this, speaking my piece. I can sound violent and partisan—or crazy, distant, gone. I can be calm and deliberate, sympathetic, reasonable. Any of those voices will do, because they'll all call forth disturbing responses from her as a result of the situation she's in. I can play her like a fucking flute, making sure she doesn't go over the edge, making sure she doesn't completely fall apart ... And she'll be scared, of course she'll be scared, she'll be freaking out, and I can do whatever I want with that, I can take it to the limit 'til she thinks she won't survive, or I can turn it into a fantastic joke—an art work, an elegant piece of irony—because all this time the camera's going and I'll point that out to her. She'll see she's part of a work of art, her dream come true. I'll tell her she's becoming famous overnight. She'll be a celebrity! Her face will be available for rental, the videotape will be reviewed in *The Village Voice*, everybody will be talking about it, she'll get invited to all the right parties! At last!"

We were both laughing now, Cissy guffawing with that loud whinny she had which could silence a crowded restaurant. Laughing so hard, tears were in our eyes.

"She'll end up loving it," I said, "unless I pick a dud ... But see, that's the point, Cissy, these are real chances I'm taking. It's up to me to see clearly, to choose the right person. That's what the work's all about. There's a definite risk involved. Otherwise it wouldn't be worthy of association with Jack's name."

"And we'll have an *audience* here when you arrive," Cissy blurted out in an inspired voice, "everybody who's anybody downtown will want to come but we'll keep it select, *crème de la crème*, no riff-raff. Just twenty or thirty people, by invitation only. Behind a scrim, we'll be as quiet as mice, you'll never know we're here. All she'll see will be you and Jerry Arnold, and as far as she knows he's taping the whole thing to send to her family for ransom, right? So she thinks she's alone with two mani-acs. And then, after she's peeing in her pants for real, after you've had your say and we've got a videotape—then we pull back the scrim and there's people like Leo and Andy and Larry Rivers. Laurie Anderson. Lauren Hutton. Robert Wilson. John Cage. Sitting quietly in little rows, sipping their wine. She'll be absolutely floored! All her heroes! It's perfect!"

"Like 'Candid Camera,'" I said, and we both laughed.

I replaced the pistol in my knapsack while Cissy started pacing around the cramped space, nervously kicking at the walls as if testing them. Several minutes went by.

"It's far out," I finally remarked.

"I think so, Roy . . . I think so. I'm stretching my brain in all directions, but it looks good. Of course, I'll have to check with my lawyers . . ."

I flipped out. "Goddamn it, Cissy, fuck your lawyers! I'm serious about this. The uncertainty is the most challenging element, it's what gives the work integrity. On every level. I'll be embracing the unknown, I can't explain it better than that. I'll be riding the edge. And you don't have to worry, I'll take full responsibility for whatever happens, but I refuse to clear this with lawyers first. I refuse to compromise my vision. There's not a lawyer on the globe who would go for this, anyway. The point is to circumvent that kind of caution, that kind of thinking. I'm not even sure I want an audience . . ."

"But listen, Roy, the audience is essential! Because otherwise we won't have any witnesses, don't you see? A videotape can be faked. We could have hired an actress. But when you come through that door with her, everybody will be sitting there seeing it all, they'll know it's for real. Besides, I'm going to need some instant verification that this is a work of art, in case anything goes wrong. I could be sent to jail for aiding and abetting a kidnapping, for gosh sakes. *You* may be willing to risk this thing backfiring, but I'm not. I've got a gallery to run."

Smiling to herself, she sat down, hoisted her heels onto the table and exclaimed, "Wait until Gunther hears about this!"

Cissy wanted to do HOSTAGE FOR JACK as soon as possible—before the Fourth of July, when summer started in earnest and everybody would be out of town—and that was fine with me; the sooner the better, in fact. We settled on six P.M. the following Saturday, exactly a week away. She needed at least a week to get everything ready, to let the right people know, to rent the scrim and test it, to line up Jerry Arnold's services. At the last minute she had second thoughts about doing it on a Saturday because it might conflict with other artists' openings. But we both knew that Saturdays were when my lady and her friends always came to town, and upon checking a *Gallery Guide* she decided it would be OK after all—nobody important was showing, the spring season had ended.

"You'll have to sign an artist's release," she informed me, "absolving the gallery of responsibility for injury and so forth, and giving us the right to market the video. Why don't we do that now, I have the forms here somewhere . . . And hopefully, Roy, we'll be able to get our abductee to sign something as well, after it's over—that would be optimal. Then I won't have to worry. People get the oddest ideas when they smell money, I can't tell you. It's always unpredictable, I learned that working for Leo. Best to cover all the bases beforehand."

Cissy directed me to jot down ideas now for the abduction. "Anything, it doesn't have to be an essay—in fact, little notes to yourself would be perfect, as if you thought it up in that fashion, though, do you understand? With a few diagrams. Then the notes become the *source* of your art. If this thing really works, we do a limited edition— no more than twelve reproductions, signed and stamped—and sell them for whatever the market will bear, and who knows what we'll get until we try, if not now then next year. I'm in no hurry . . . that income will be in addition to the rental of the video, of course, plus any other little extras I can think up . . . And by the way, Roy, I hope we're straight on the economics here. A contract isn't necessary at this point, but the standard breakdown will apply. Sixty-forty . . . Phalanx Gallery is sixty and you're forty . . . All right?"

"Sixty-forty? What about fifty-fifty? It's my idea, for Christ's sake. I'm the one who'll be carrying it out."

She grimaced. "Roy, sixty-forty's standard, it's only utterly famous artists like Jasper Johns who get a better percentage. Don't forget, without Phalanx you would have no way to implement this, no one would hear about it, nothing would happen. Besides, my dear, I literally found you in the gutter, did I not? Please show some appreciation."

She had been talking faster and faster toward the end, as if running out of patience with me. I mentioned that I needed money and without batting an eyelash she reached into her purse and pulled out three hundreds again. "You always seem to catch me at the right time," she said. "Let's see where we stand a week from now. This ought to carry you through 'til then, no?"

I was outraged by the condescending note in her voice and muttered, "Fuck you, too—*my dear*."

Her face stiffened. Instantly the mood between us changed. "You'd better go now, Roy, and commune with your god or whatever. I have plenty of work to do," she said frostily. But then the phone rang and at the very same moment we both exclaimed, "Zurich calling!" and looked at each other. I raised my closed fist in a salute as I left the little office, and, lifting hers in response and shaking it, she smiled.

I walked up Wooster toward Houston, past the metal doors of the loft buildings. Reaching Prince, I looked across the corner at FOOD, which a few scant years before had been started by artists to have someplace to eat in the wilderness of SoHo, and was now thronged with art tourists. Perhaps my lady was inside there right now, talking about how *famished* she was as she dug into an oversized shrimp salad plate with her friends. Complaining that Roslyn was so far away from anything interesting, although of course on the other hand it was the perfect place to live and bring up the kids. Complaining about her husband's forthright philistinism: he never wants to come to the city and look at paintings, although, on the other hand again, that leaves us free of men for one afternoon, doesn't it, so it's just as well. And all sorts of cute new shops are opening around here, it's exciting. After the Jennifer Bartlett show we can look for clothes. I'm sure the salesgirls here will be more polite—at least for a while—than those bitches up at Bergdorf's. Who ever let them get so snobby? Sometimes I wonder if they realize *we're* the ones with the money. If it weren't for us, they'd be out on the *street* . . .

During the next week I wandered around the city, not concerning myself with the abduction at all. I had decided not to think about it until I showed up in SoHo on Saturday. I knew this was the way to proceed, that what I said to my lady had to be spontaneous, unrehearsed. Any sort of preparation would only serve to stifle what I felt in my heart.

Summer was in full swing now, the steamy streets crawling with people until late at night, but I came upon no sign of Hartwell, no graffiti, no incidents. Then, on Friday afternoon, the day before the big event, I walked around in midtown until the weather got to me. It was very hot and muggy, a foretaste of what was to come in July and August, and, not wanting to tire myself out in expectation of the next day's exertions, I decided to go home and rest.

I went into the subway station at Times Square and entered the downtown BMT platform. I leaned against one of the girders, looking absently at the grimy, graffiti-covered wall across from me and at the tracks below, covered with garbage. The airless atmosphere underground was oppressive. Everybody looked as if they were at the end of their tethers, except for one rosy-cheeked old guy with a halo of snow-white hair, who stood nearby, cheerfully smiling. The train was late. Periodically people approached the edge of the platform and peered north into the darkness. I did so as well. And then, as the lights flashed in the tunnel and the local roared into the station, I heard somebody saying, as clear as day, "Sticks and stones will break your bones . . ." and I felt hands in the small of my back, below the knapsack. Before I could react I was pushed—clean and hard—off the platform, falling onto the tracks, landing on my hands and knees, the deafening blast of the horn, the headlights aiming right at me, bearing down, closing in on me, and at the last second, seeing everything perfectly, my heart racing in my chest in spite of the detachment I felt, as if this were happening to somebody else, as if I could see myself down there far below on the tracks—at the last moment I remembered the live third rail and hurtled over it, tumbling onto the second set of tracks on the other side as the train screeched to a halt beside me. I was beyond terrified now: I felt superprescient, aware of every last little detail. I knew where I'd seen the rosy-cheeked man before—in Washington Square Park the same afternoon Hartwell had humiliated me. It was the white-haired old guy who'd been involved in a discussion about his wife with a younger black man. "She never comes out in weather like this," he had said, and the black man had responded, "She's got sense." I had asked him for a cigarette and he didn't smoke, but he had offered me a swig from his flask. "Sticks and stones will break your bones . . ." I remembered that too, remembered it quite well . . . There was a big commotion on the platform, I couldn't see it because the train was in the way, but somehow I knew they hadn't caught the man who pushed me. Three Transit Authority workers wriggled between the cars and stepped onto the tracks where I stood, amazed to see I was unhurt. They were dressed in galoshes and orange slickers and carried flashlights.

"Are you OK?" one of them asked. All three looked like big stuffed toys. I felt myself getting hysterical at the prospect of responding to them. But something told me to play along, something told me that if I didn't they would *requisition* me, I could see it in their eyes. I would be taken to a hospital, I would have to see a doctor. I saw the scenario unfolding and I knew I had to avoid it at all costs. I had to get out of the station immediately, before the police showed up, before their questions.

"I feel great," I said. Did I sound natural? Was I making sense?

"The guy got away," one of them said. "Another psycho, the subway's full of 'em. But the cops will catch him, don't you worry. He won't get far."

I laughed woodenly. "That's what you think," I shot back. "You happen to be wrong. The cops don't stand a chance."

They glanced at one another. "Just follow us off the tracks," the same man said. "Don't worry, the power's been turned off. We've got an office, you can lay down on a cot until they get here, we'll give you some coffee . . ."

I started laughing again, I couldn't control it, and sounding more insane than I would have thought possible—because inside I still felt completely calm—I replied in a brittle shout, "That's really funny, because it would be absurd to drink coffee now, totally absurd. I mean, how wired do you want me to get!"

They gave one another embarrassed, sorrowful looks, but by then I was running as fast as I could down the tracks to the front of the train, hoisting myself onto the platform, hightailing it through the crowd and out of the station, certain I was no longer being pursued.

SIXTEEN

I didn't really expect any mention in the papers of my brush with death, so I got a kick out of reading about myself the next morning, even though the *Times* article—NEAR FATALITY IN SUBWAY—was only three sentences long, at the back of the second section. But I liked the last sentence a lot: "Police were at a loss to explain the victim's sudden disappearance and believe the incident was drug-related."

Police were at a loss . . . The phrase gave me a charge of adrenalin. I said it to myself as I made breakfast. I wondered if the monstrous crimes committed by a person like Son of Sam arose out of little more than the thrill of evading authority, the satisfaction gotten from looking over somebody's shoulder on a bus and reading, "Police were at a loss . . ." *That's me*, Son of Sam would say to himself and smile, and when his exploits were in danger of fading into oblivion, he would dare to kill again.

However, in this case I definitely remained the victim and not the perpetrator, although, paradoxically, while I'd almost died on the tracks the previous day, I had never felt so alive. By the time I'd gotten home, all I could think about was stimulating the same mechanism again by putting my life in danger. When I'd fallen onto the tracks and turned to see the train I'd been absolutely center stage. It was like the rush Bobby Addison had described, up in front of the audience with his band. Except, on my hands and knees on the tracks, I had felt like all of creation was staring at me.

Before I left the apartment I took out the pistol and checked to make sure it was loaded. I practised in front of the mirror releasing the safety catch and cocking back the hammer.

Cissy called, assuring me in a businesslike voice that everything was set, the audience would be in their seats by five-fifty sharp, latecomers not allowed. "*Some* people don't know what they'll be missing," she remarked crossly, by which I inferred that certain luminaries weren't coming, but I could have cared less about that. "See you soon," I said.

Then late in the afternoon I went down to SoHo. It had been muggy and very hot all day and by the time I left it was raining, but there were quite a few people on the streets anyway. I stood in the doorway out of the rain, looking for the right lady, hoping I wouldn't see her too soon. Cissy had told me that on no account was I to show up at the gallery before six, and I had every intention of following instructions, although I knew if I saw the right one that would be it, I wasn't going to let her get away.

I stood in the doorway of a cardboard factory on Mercer, half a block up from Fanelli's Bar. The gun was in my pocket now, my empty knapsack on my back. I dropped my umbrella in the doorway, I didn't want to juggle two things at once. In spite of the steady rain, Fanelli's was crowded, the front door opening every minute or so, people coming and going. And every one of them members of the Saturday generation. They all seemed to be touching base there that day. I saw many people I could have taken—men as well as women—but I didn't see *her*, and I'd long before gotten it into my head that I'd recognize her immediately, there would be no question, we were fated to cross paths. And then it happened, just after I asked somebody the time. "Ten of six," he said, and it was as if a signal had gone off, he'd been a very small guy faultlessly dressed in beautiful black leather—black leather cowboy boots, too—with a thin silver bracelet on his wrist, right above his watch, and I was looking at the bracelet and the watch together when he told me the time, they were so elegant together like that. As soon as he said "Ten of six" I looked across the street and saw her, she was standing under a big rose-colored umbrella at the edge of the sidewalk with two friends, the neon from Fanelli's sign liquid on the cobblestones at her feet. And just then I heard her say—she must have been quite pissed because her words carried half a block up Mercer—"Well, you can go if you want to, but I'm fed up. This afternoon has been a joke! I'll wait in the car, just do me a favor and don't take all evening . . ." And she turned on her heel and walked south, down Mercer, while her friends headed toward West Broadway. I moved quickly across the street and fell in behind her, drawing close as we came to the center of the block. Nobody else was around, although I didn't look that carefully, I didn't feel the need to. Stepping abreast of her, the rain against my face and dripping down through my hair, I turned my head and said loudly and distinctly, "You're coming with me."

She heard me, there was no way she couldn't have, but it didn't make sense to her. She wanted it to fit into some category of come-on or insult or solicitation, and it wouldn't.

"What did you say?"

The irritation in her voice was unmistakable, but she'd paused momentarily to voice it and I had her, my forearm under her chin taking her into the wall behind her, my other hand coming up with the Baretta, showing it to her and sticking it into her open linen jacket, right into her gut, but looking at her reassuringly, even tenderly, which, however, made no impression on her, because already she was terrified, she felt the metal against her skin and opened her mouth.

"Don't," I said.

She tried to break free, dropping her umbrella, lifting her leg as if to knee me in the groin or push my body away, but soon it was over because she kept feeling the gun.

"It's for real, the gun's for real," I said, and she sighed.

"What are you doing to me?" she whispered, "what do you want?"

I nearly had my face buried in her neck by now, I didn't want any distance between us, and I could smell her perfume, overpoweringly sweet, sickly sweet, and underneath that I smelled her fear. And with my lips beside her ear I started talking.

"This'll be over in an hour, I promise, so don't worry, just do what I say. I guarantee you won't get hurt unless you resist. But, I swear to God, I'll kill you if I have to . . ."

She still was squirming, I kept having to press the gun deeper to remind her it was there. ". . . You won't get hurt, and believe it or not you're going to *enjoy* this, all you have to do is let go, I want to tell you a few things about art . . . I'm an artist and I'm taking you to my gallery, it's only around the corner."

She looked at me in disbelief and now her lips were trembling, at last she knew whom she was dealing with—a homicidal maniac. This was the crucial point for me. I knew there was no way to explain what was really going to happen, the moment was too explosive, I simply had to make her come with me.

"I swear on my life you'll come to no harm. But I can't talk anymore, you've got to start moving. *Now*, we're going to walk together, you and I, my arm around you, my hand inside your coat—like this—and we'll be there inside of five minutes. You're taking part in a work of art now, be grateful . . . An homage to Jack Rio . . ." We were walking already as I said this, her umbrella abandoned on the sidewalk, both of us getting soaked, and in spite of how wired I was I had a hard time suppressing a smile, because I knew—I could feel it communicate itself from her body to mine—that the word "art" had gotten to her. She relaxed a little, I noticed it in her walk. I didn't have to drag her along anymore, finally we were moving together. And if I had any doubts, they dissolved after we'd gone along Prince and turned the corner into Wooster, because by then she was angry. Angry about my violence, angry about her clothes getting ruined in the rain.

"You're a pig," she said acidly and, seeming to forget again about the gun, she added, "When we get to wherever we're going you'll have hell to pay. Do you hear me? My husband's a lawyer. Bernard Katz. I suppose that name doesn't mean anything to you?" She delivered this last with stinging sarcasm. When I failed to respond, however, she reverted to hysteria. "What do you want from me?" she wailed, her mane of red hair completely deflated by the drenching rain. We must have looked a sight, the two of us, but I never took my eyes off the entrance to the Phalanx Gallery, I watched it draw closer and closer, hypnotized by it. And there was Carole Levy, standing by the door under an umbrella, peering up and down the block. As soon as she spotted us she disappeared.

"Keep quiet," I said. "We're almost there."

"Why are you torturing me? What did I ever do to you?"

* * *

We hiked up the two flights of stairs.

"Remember Jack Rio!" I shouted as we came through the door, the floodlights blazing brightly, blinding me momentarily. Jerry Arnold stood behind his tripod, as serious as an undertaker. The moment he saw me he moved behind us and, dead-bolting shut the door, turned and pointed to the far end of the room where, in front of the bare white wall, stood one wooden stool. I steered her over to it and sat her down. Aside from Jerry and us the gallery was empty and for a moment I became disoriented. Nobody else was here. Somehow the whole thing had fallen through; Cissy was gone. Then I noticed where Jerry was standing in relation to the size of the room, the wall behind him much too close to us. It was perfect.

We faced the camera, a puddle of water expanding at our feet. My lady looked simply terrible, like she'd fallen into the pool at a garden party. I waved the pistol around once or twice, I couldn't resist it, I felt really pumped up, omnipotent; *I* was the art terrorist now, as Jack Rio once had been. In spite of the moment's drama—the risk of violence, the select audience invisible behind the scrim—I didn't feel nervous. To the contrary, I was loose, in control. I remembered in years past having been envious of the musicians in the bands I saw. Now I knew why: performing was a stone gas.

In addition to being soaked from the rain, perspiration poured from our faces now from stress and exertion, and from the lights. It seemed to be over a hundred degrees in the room, as sultry as the tropics, and I wondered if Cissy had switched off the air conditioner on purpose. Why would she do that? The sweat in my eyes got so bad I could hardly see, but Jerry spurred me on, he waved one arm in a circle—*get going*—and I put the pistol back into my pocket and started in.

I asked if she'd ever heard of Jack Rio and she hadn't, so I related Jack's story, his trajectory from mid-Sixties sculptor, through art activist and pioneer of performance art to the uncompromising hero of recent years, who had ended his life in thrall to artistic vision. I explained to her that the crux of the story was his attitude toward money, toward art as a commodity, his opposition to the artist as trinket-maker for the well-to-do. "Jack sacrificed his life to this idea, and that's why you're here," I said, "to learn what his death meant."

Her eyes blinked while she listened to me, the puzzled look on her face never deserting her, but at least she no longer seemed terrified. After all, we were in an art gallery now, just as I'd promised; how could anything life-threatening occur in a gallery? But, still, she was unable to make sense out of it all, she wasn't really interested in Jack Rio's self-sacrifice, she couldn't understand it, and the fact that I was delivering what I had to say with fiery conviction only confused her further. She really didn't see why I was getting so wrought up. The more I exposed the corrosive nature of the changes which had taken place in the art world, the more I could see that my point about the triumph of commodity culture passed right through her without leaving a trace. My indignation missed its mark.

"But, excuse me," she finally interrupted. "What are you carrying on about? Nothing is more obvious than that paintings are objects. They sell for money. What's wrong with that? I don't think it has anything to do with an artist's integrity, one way or the other . . . *the artist's integrity*: you sound like you're lecturing me."

I was taken aback and, thrown on the defensive, insisted that she and her friends wouldn't recognize artistic integrity if it bit them in the ass, because they were smothering it with their money, their bad taste, their chatchka-consciousness.

"*Chatchka-consciousness?* What are you doing, trying to insult me? Who are *you*, anyway? Gandhi with a gun?"

A strangled sound of suppressed laughter came from behind the scrim but my lady didn't appear to notice. She was too pleased with herself for having torpedoed my attempt at making her feel any connection to Jack Rio's death or the state of the downtown art scene.

"I don't see where destroying yourself qualifies as art," she said. "It sounds to me like this Mr. Rio had a few problems, he should have gone to see an analyst." She smiled smugly, and suddenly I was struck by her uncanny resemblance to Dana's mother, so much so that I stopped short and asked where she lived. It may seem incredible, but I'd chosen her purely on the basis of what she represented to me when I saw her on the street, and so I hadn't noticed the resemblance, at least not consciously, until this very moment. But it was undeniable. Except for her red hair, she could have been Sibyl's younger sister, and not only in a physical sense. There was a self-assertive brassiness, a certain toughness, which they shared.

"I live in Scarsdale," she replied.

"Scarsdale!" Sibyl and Lou were from Scarsdale. "And what's your name, dear," I insisted, "better late than never. You have to tell us who you are." I waved vaguely around the room. I wished I'd been holding a microphone—Cissy and I hadn't discussed that—but apparently Jerry's equipment picked up everything we were saying. Whenever I glanced at him he gave me the thumbs-up sign.

She cleared her throat and said, "Miriam Katz."

We'd been there in front of the camera for at least fifteen minutes, but now for the first time she played directly to it, delivering her name with a big show-biz smile. It was obvious that she was spoiled and indulged, that she lived well and was used to getting her way, but Miriam Katz also had strength of character, she had a resilient intelligence which made her amount to more than the greedy, vindictive child Sibyl Miller was. I wondered if they knew each other. I kept feeling like baiting her, provoking her. I never stopped to question the validity of my animosity toward her.

"And you and your husband—Bernard, you said?—I'll bet you have an art collection, right, Miriam? Or surprise me. Go ahead. Tell me you live in spartan surroundings, wanting nothing for yourselves . . ."

She bristled at my tone of voice and refused to answer. Somehow the fact that—again, in comparison to Sibyl Miller—she was a relatively sensitive, cultivated person, only increased my outrage. The image of Jack Rio lying face down in his vomit kept assailing me. If *she* couldn't see what I'd been talking about then his death really had been in vain.

"What sort of art do you like? Who are your favorite painters? Whose work do you and your husband have in your collection?"

She got that irritated, superior look on her face again—the one she'd been wearing when I had approached her on the street. She understood now that this was some sort of art event, perhaps even thinking she could simply get up off the stool on which she was perched in her wet peach linen suit and her red heels, and walk out of the gallery, nobody would stop her. She kept eyeing the door with a smirk and just sat there. This infuriated me. I pulled the little automatic out of my pocket and began waving it around, shouting that if she didn't answer she'd be sorry. "I'll blow your fucking head off, you candy-assed cunt! Now speak up!" Instantly she was whimpering, pleading for me not to kill her—which indeed I felt capable of doing.

"Just speak up, for Christ's sake! Listen, Miriam, the sooner you say something, the sooner we're finished, and you can go home to Bernie. Now, answer my question."

"Oh, God," she whispered, "I can't take this . . ." Pulling herself together, she finally said in a small, shaken voice, "We have lots of paintings. We—we collect mostly southwestern things—Navajo painters—we have one of the largest private collections of R. C. Gorman on the East Coast," she said, her voice firmer, on surer ground now that she had something to boast about.

"Fantastic," I said, "R. C. Gorman. Who else?" I had put the gun away again, not wanting to upset her with the sight of it if I didn't need to.

Her face brightened. "Well, we have some lithographs by Dubuffet, and—and a Rauschenberg collage—I talked my husband into that, he didn't want it, but I think Bob Rauschenberg's so *cute* . . . Now there's a real artist . . . And—oh! I almost forgot, how could I?—the year before last, we commissioned Alex Katz to do a big portrait of me, it's so beautiful, it looks just like me! We have it hanging in the living room right above the sofa. My husband says it shows that more than one Katz has taste . . . And, let's see. We've gotten rid of a lot of things recently, the market was good, and frankly we made the inevitable mistakes one makes while learning. Some of the things we bought were absurd—this huge Al Held, like a big spider's web. It gave me a headache every time I looked at it. And the very first thing we acquired, I know it had sentimental value for my husband—a little Rothko—but I made him sell it, it reminded me of sitting in a dentist's office, you know? Like those crocheted wall hangings?"

"Indeed I do know," I said. "And what about Andy Warhol, Mrs. Katz. Do you like his work?"

"Oh, I *adore* Andy Warhol!" she exclaimed, and there were titters from the other end of the room. "Bernard does too, he . . ." She trailed off, squinting into the lights. I was so angry I almost fired the gun into the scrim behind Jerry Arnold. The spell had been broken. Suddenly Miriam Katz erupted.

"What's going on? Who's back there? Do you call that art? Terrorizing an innocent woman, dragging me up here to make fun of me? How do you think I feel, you bastard . . . And look at me! I'm soaked to the skin, it's like an oven in here, my hair's a mess. This suit cost me eight hundred dollars, it's ruined now. I suppose you like that, it fits in with your idea of artistic integrity—brutalizing somebody!"

She had exhausted herself with these words and slumped back on the stool. I felt drained myself, my clothes were soaked, my throat was dry, I couldn't think of anything more to say. I turned and looked inquiringly at Jerry Arnold. He was giving me another one of his thumbs-up signs in which, by now, I had lost faith. He drew his finger across his throat, smiling—what was that supposed to mean?—and then walked to the door and unlocked it, letting some air into the room. (I learned later that the air conditioner had, in fact, broken down that afternoon.) Then the floodlights were cut and suddenly the scrim behind him, which in the glare of the light had looked like another bare wall, rolled up to reveal rows of people, smiling and applauding, applauding steadily, enthusiastically. Off to the side I saw Cissy, sitting on an upturned box, still so intent on what had happened that she was sucking her thumb. Taking her hand away from her mouth she looked me directly in the eyes, fastening on me with all her attention, I could feel it from across the room. Raising her arm, shaking her closed fist. Smiling.

Now the gallery was filled with heavily perspiring people. Carole Levy stood behind a card table pouring wine. Everybody was talking and laughing, that excited but ambiguous, slightly mocking New York laughter which can set your teeth on edge. In the midst of it I felt a curious bond with Miriam Katz, we stood off to the side dazed by the noise. Somebody handed us glasses of wine. Jerry Arnold wheeled his camera over to us and continued shooting while we talked. She asked me, "You mean you made a movie of this?"

"Video," I croaked, my throat raw. I took a gulp of the wine. "You're going to be a star, Mrs. Katz. Everybody will know who you are. You won't be able to walk around SoHo without being besieged for autographs. I told you everything would turn out all right, didn't I?"

She was extremely nervous. Looking around the room she recognized several faces of dealers and artists and she began smiling, luxuriating in her newfound celebrity. "I love this!" she exclaimed. She was the center of attention, everybody staring at her. But after a while she picked up on the mocking tone of the conversations going on around her. People she knew were smiling unpleasantly, even I could see that, and before I realized what was happening, before I could react, she began crying. She threw her wine glass to the floor. The sound of it shattering brought immediate silence to the room, and she screamed, "This is an outrage! You're going to rot in jail for this, you son of a bitch. You made a fool of me!" Before I could stop her she was striding across the room to the door, her awful weeping accompanied by Cissy's oddly matter-of-fact voice as she scampered alongside holding a piece of paper and a pen, saying, "Please sign this, Mrs. Katz, it's just a formality. An artist's release . . ." But Miriam Katz brushed Cissy aside and was gone, we could hear her high heels clattering down the stairs.

Her exit left a sour taste behind. For a minute there was dead silence, everybody glancing apprehensively at one another. Then the silence broke. People I didn't know were crowding around me, full of congratulations. I felt weak and distant, as if somebody else were being praised, as if we were play-acting, except I knew we weren't, people's eyes wouldn't let me think that. Everybody was looking at me differently than I'd ever been looked at before. Volatile expressions of envy and admiration, begrudging enthusiasm and resentment. Isolating, calculating, worshipping . . . "It was great," somebody said, and a strikingly elegant woman I vaguely recognized swooped over to me and crowed fiercely, "Jack would be proud of you!" then she giggled and added, with the lightest touch of dismissive sarcasm, "It was something that just *had* to be said!"

Cissy, her face rosy with pleasure, came up and embraced me. "Two critics from the *Voice* are here . . . I'm very excited . . . You don't know what this means to me. This is putting me on the map; I'm very grateful." She looked at me with tender affection, leaning over and kissing me on the ear. "Thanks, Roy . . ."

I felt confused. The mix of sarcastic comments and fawning attention was impossible for me to sort out. I became aware of a discrepancy: *I* thought I'd been trying to enlighten Miriam Katz. The audience, on the other hand, had been more than content simply to experience the difference between the two of us. They had revelled in that difference, in the vacuum created by my earnest attempt to convert, and her implacable refusal to be moved. They hadn't expected her to change and wouldn't have wanted her to. Secretly, most of them agreed with Mrs. Katz' assessment: Jack *should* have seen a shrink—I mean, my dear, he *never got the point*: SoHo has changed, the world has changed . . . But they couldn't say that out loud, of course. Officially, the art world was in mourning over Jack's death, and so my performance served as a commemoration, although what legitimized it was its violence. One person after another told me they loved my performance above all for the risk I'd taken, for the fact that I'd actually abducted her and was waving a real gun around. Apparently what I'd done was all the more impressive because it had stood no chance of succeeding—Miriam Katz would go on being exactly who she was, and so would I. That was the beauty of it, the delicious irony, they said—that I'd put my future on the line for the sake of an impossibility . . . The only trouble with all this was, my efforts had *not* been ironic— the idea of risking my neck for a Duchampian joke didn't appeal to me in the least. I had been perfectly sincere.

"I want to introduce you to Gunther," Cissy was saying, pointing out a thin, suave, intelligent-looking man dressed entirely in black, with closely cropped sandy gray hair, who was approaching us. But I had to get outside and breathe fresh air; I felt as if I were suffocating. And I was paranoid. She'd see me rot in jail, she said. I wanted to get rid of the gun immediately.

"Call me tomorrow," I whispered to Cissy, "I've got to go home and crash."

Outside the rain had stopped, it was misty and still very hot, dusk was just beginning. Being alone now felt like a balm, and I savored the anonymous, steamy silence of the streets as I walked west toward the Hudson. My idea was to throw the pistol into the river but when I arrived at the piers I realized how exposed they were out over the water. I couldn't be certain I wasn't being seen. I turned and walked back, north and then east, into the Village. And on Charles Street, at the kitchen door of a restaurant whose entrance was on Eighth Avenue, after wiping my prints from the gun with a rag I found on the sidewalk, I buried it in a trash container.

I spent the next few days at home, exhausted from everything that had happened and unwilling, for the time being, to step outside and risk getting assaulted again. Now that I'd been forced to get rid of the gun, I had no way to protect myself. After being shoved onto the train tracks I'd felt invulnerable, but actually I was being hunted, and my life was at stake. I'd been avoiding the fact that it was simply a matter of time before the OPW got to me. Instead of admitting this to myself, I'd taken out my rage and resentment on Miriam Katz. My thing with the gun, waving it in her face, taunting her with it—what was happening to me?

Then on Wednesday, June 29th, *The Village Voice* appeared. One of their art columnists mentioned the hostage performance in glowing terms, and there on the centerfold page, staring at me in blown-up black and white, was a frame from the videotape, a head shot of Miriam Katz, her eyes full of fear, raising her arm protectively as if to ward off a blow. Below this, under the title ART HOSTAGE, were fulsome sentences about the new performance artist in town who confronts the rising bourgeois menace head-on, regardless of personal risk. Jack Rio's name wasn't mentioned more than once, although mine was.

That morning I'd been across the street at Gem's Spa picking up the daily papers—I was still combing them for mention of the OPW—when I spotted my name in a ribbon of letters running across the top of the *Voice*'s front page, like seeing it in a dream. By the time I got back upstairs and finished reading the article and looking at the centerfold, the phone was ringing. I answered the call, somebody from the *Voice* checking to make sure they had the correct phone number, saying they'd get back to me. Then the phone rang again. It didn't stop ringing all day. Luckily, the ninth or tenth call came from Cissy, who excitedly informed me that ART HOSTAGE—she hoped I didn't mind that she'd changed the title—had caught fire. "Have you seen the *Voice*?" she asked.

"My phone's been ringing off the hook, Cissy. What's going on? Yeah, I've seen the *Voice*. Jack's name was only mentioned once."

"That's not the point, Roy. Anybody who sees the tape will get an earful about Jack Rio, and plenty of people are going to see it . . . You wouldn't believe the calls I've been getting. I'll go into that later. I'm too busy to talk, really. I'm going to have to get back to you."

"Cissy, wait a second, listen to me. The strangest people have been calling. It's so weird. They all say they want to interview me and then they tell me they'll call back, just like you. Even Margo Kopperman from *The New Jag* called. Margo Kopperman! Claiming I owe her an exclusive interview!"

"*Owe* her? Who is *she*, for gosh sakes! Listen, Roy, we've got to play our cards right with this, things are moving quickly. I suggest you let me handle the details. We should be paid for any interviews we do. It's a question of controlling the situation. Suddenly everyone wants to find out about you. An editor from *The New York Times* was just on the line with me, my dear. They want to see the tape, we're having a special screening for the press tomorrow afternoon—the national news magazines, the *Times*, *Vogue*, everyone wants to check it out. I suggest *you* don't come, though, if that's all right with you. Let them wonder about you, let the suspense build. Our strategy's changed now, Roy, you've got to play hard to get. Do you understand? The more demanding you are, the more people want you," she concluded gloatingly.

"But Cissy, I have no desire to come to the screening."

"Good. Perfect. Phalanx will take care of everything. Just lay low . . . Look, I have to get off now. I'll call you back with any new developments. I think we should set up a signal, so you'll know it's me. Whenever I call I'll ring three times, hang up, then ring again. OK? Got it?"

It wasn't until Saturday that Cissy called again. In the meantime the ringing slackened off and then stopped altogether. It was if I'd passed through an electrical storm. Obviously Cissy had taken over, as she'd said. The irony of Margo Kopperman now wanting to interview me didn't offset my uneasiness. Hadn't I kidnapped somebody, pure and simple? What would the police have to say about that? I found myself hoping the whole thing would just blow over. Then, on Saturday, July 2nd, came the picture of Mrs. Katz and me on the front page of the *Post*, under the headline ARTIST TOOK WOMAN HOSTAGE. Miriam looked terrified, naturally, while, my face contorted, I seemed to be threatening her. Inside, the *Post*'s art critic accused me of "hoodlum sensationalism," claiming I'd brought the currently bankrupt art scene to a new low. I was the first punk performance artist, totally lacking in scruples, no better than the sleazy rock and roll bands coming over from England now. "The Manhattan District Attorney's office is the only proper audience for this sort of criminal behavior," she concluded.

My picture on the front page of the *New York Post* . . . All I could think of was Oliver Hartwell seeing the paper, holding it in his hands, studying my face. Talk about being a sitting duck. My sudden notoriety only made me more of a target than ever. Even before Saturday, in fact, I'd half expected him to break my door down. He knew where I lived. And when he did show up I wanted to face him person-to-person. He had to see me as a human being, he had to understand that I meant the OPW no harm. I wasn't interested in exposing their activities, I only wanted to survive.

As soon as the *Post* came out, the situation changed dramatically. The doorbell started ringing. I couldn't go to the window without seeing men in natty seersucker suits, usually in teams of three, staring up at the building. Some had video cameras and porta-paks.

In addition, another electrical storm moved in. The phone rang and rang, but I refused to take it off the hook. Without the constant ringing I might have been seduced into believing everything would return to normal, that my life would be the same as before. But my life wasn't going to be the same, the telephone crying out nonstop told me that.

Finally the three rings and the pause came. And then Cissy's voice was on the line.

"OK, Roy," she said breathlessly, "here's what's happening. You've seen the *Post*, I presume? I'm totally pissed at those bastards, they weren't supposed to do that until after tonight's TV news, we had an agreement. But I guess they just couldn't wait. And, boy, did they drop a brick on us. It's been quite insane here. Ever since the paper came out, the gallery's been getting all sorts of abusive phone calls. These animals ring up and threaten Carole, when they hear a woman's voice they immediately get obscene. She's very upset. We're going to have to close early, it's impossible to do business. But what I'm really calling you about is this TV thing. The anchorman on the local network news tonight, the six-thirty news, Channel Four, I don't know which way he's gonna go. But I'm expecting the worst, frankly, and I want you to be prepared. Things may get nasty, although my lawyers insist we'll squeak through. It doesn't affect you, anyway. You lucked out, my dear. I'll explain everything when I see you tonight. Because there's this party I think you should attend. Gunther will be there, other people you should meet as well, people who missed the performance—Andy, Larry Rivers . . . Everyone's buzzing about ART HOSTAGE, it's topic number one down here. The party's at Debbie Cowan's loft, the clothes designer, you know? I'll come pick you up in a taxi about ten o'clock, OK? Your building has a buzzer system, doesn't it? Same signal, then, three rings and a pause. And you'll have to get an unlisted phone number, my dear, that's obvious . . ."

"Wait a minute, Cissy. What's this about television? What do you mean you're expecting the worst? I'm totally in the dark, for shit's sake, you just can't hang up."

She gave a big, theatrical sigh and paused. "All right, Roy. I'm slowing down. I'm breathing deeply, I'm starting to relax . . . We'll talk . . . I have plenty to tell you . . . First off, though, please remember to watch the six-thirty news tonight. It's amazing how closed-minded the establishment media has been. It's as if we were back in the Sixties—or the Fifties, even. Getting up on their high horses and *preaching* to me. The screening on Thursday was quite a scene, my dear. I felt as if I were back in grammar school, being taken to the principal's office. Your teacher dragging you down the hall by your *ear*, do you know? That's why you should be prepared for the worst, there's no telling what this straight arrow may say. Everyone above 14th Street's decided you're some sort of inhuman punk, and I'm an ogre out of late Roman history or something, simply for handling your work. I don't know *where* these people have been all this time . . ."

"But what are you talking about, Cissy? How did all this happen?"

"Well, I hardly know where to start, although I suppose the best place is with that *woman* you picked. Why'd you have to choose a lawyer's wife, for gosh sakes? It looks like we'll have some legal fees to pay before this is over, although Gunther has offered to help me with that, thank God. Apparently, dear Miriam's husband is set to climb all over us. He's going to sue the gallery because we own the videotape, we've been showing it for a profit, we've been making copies of it. My lawyers say he simply wants money—lots of it, of course. It's tricky, but I think we'll be all right, because, so far, apparently, Miriam K. herself has resisted pressing charges against you, or us . . . The most inspired thing I've ever done in my life was—right after the performance—sitting down and writing out a check for a thousand dollars to cover the damage to her wardrobe. I sent that to her along with a letter profusely apologizing for any pain she may have suffered, stressing over and over how proud I was of her, thanking her for honoring Jack's memory in this way, going on about what a serious artist you were. And, you see, *she cashed the check*, so I think it did the trick, at least for the time being. Although I *won't* consider withdrawing the tape from circulation, which is the first demand her husband made. At least there's not a warrant out for your arrest, though, my dear. You don't know how lucky you are. My lawyers tell me that, because she changed her tune in midstream—'I love this,' she said, remember?—Katz would have a hard time making anything stand up against you in court. We've scrutinized the tape dozens of times, and it's impossible to tell that's a real gun you're holding, you see. So it's her word against yours . . . You *did* get rid of that weapon, didn't you?"

"Of course," I replied glumly.

"Well then . . . And listen to this, I have *great news*! I wanted to save it 'til tonight when we could celebrate but I may as well tell you now.

I've already sold eight facsimiles of your notes for the abduction—at five grand apiece—and the other four will be going soon, no doubt about it. Isn't that *fabulous*?"

My silence must have disappointed her, because she sounded hurt and supercilious when she resumed talking. "Did you hear me? That's forty thousand bucks, my dear, of which you get forty percent. Isn't that good enough for you? Or perhaps you think the money's tainted or something. That would be just like you, I must say . . . *Roy*?"

I didn't know how to respond. I was feeling withdrawn, unsure of what it all meant. Everything was happening so quickly I had trouble holding on. Within the space of a week I'd gone from ex-journalist and unemployed dishwasher to notorious performance artist, complete with forged art school background and an imprimatur of approval bestowed on me by the leading lights of the downtown art world—all in recognition of the job I'd done keeping alive Jack Rio's name.

"It is good news, Cissy, I'm sorry—"

"You're darn right, buster." Then she loosened up and added, "I've got a check here made out in your name for sixteen thousand dollars. And this is just the beginning. Think about it—next week you can go up to Sak's and buy out the entire men's department!"

"—But I don't want to go to the party. I'd rather stay home, all right?"

"Roy, are you kidding me? Gunther wants to meet you. He's impressed by how sophisticated your performance was, operating on several levels at once, including the criminal. *He wants to collect you . . .*"

Her voice was filled with awe as she emphasized the rarity of this development, but to me the phrase sounded positively cannibalistic.

"And who *is* Gunther, anyway," I asked, "your *eminence grise*? Doesn't he have a last name like other people?"

"Gunther Hebel," she replied haughtily, "not that it would make any difference to you. You don't deserve the man's attention, but for your information he's the most important collector of contemporary art in Europe. Being represented in Gunther's collection is tantamount to instant credibility. You should recognize this opportunity for what it is and go for it."

"What opportunity—to meet the guy?"

"He wants to *collect* you, Roy, how many times do I have to tell you!"

"So let him buy one of the notebook facsimiles." The idea that this person—whoever he was—seemed to count for so much in Cissy's estimation made me suspicious. Plenty of people collected art, after all. What made him so special?

"You don't understand," she said in an exasperated voice. "You're hot right now—really hot. You're also a completely unknown commodity. The combination of these two factors . . . I mean, otherwise Gunther wouldn't have time for you. He has a huge collection, lots of artists. Obviously you're not aware of the scale on which he operates. Anyone Gunther's really interested in he *supports*. He subsidizes what you do. He's not simply another collector, my dear. It's more a form of long-term speculation, taking the chance that in the long run your work will prove important. He hasn't decided on anything yet, of course—how could he, he hasn't even *met* you—and these things take place with a certain amount of discretion. If confronted directly, he'd probably deny being interested. This isn't like going to the corner for a quart of milk. I mean, who knows, maybe nothing will come of it. But even the *possibility* . . . I can't understand you. Any other artist would jump at the chance. You'd get a monthly check in the mail. Do you follow me? And in return, Gunther owns any work you produce during the period of the agreement—in your case not the performances you do, of course, but any documentation arising from them. Oh, he doesn't necessarily *own* it—let's just say he gets first crack at it, he has the option to take it. It's a complicated situation, I don't want to bore you with the details, but believe me when I say that having Gunther Hebel interested in you at this juncture is the best thing that could happen. If he were to take you on—and as long as you continue to turn out work of measurable interest—the development of your career is guaranteed. Are you listening to what I'm saying, Roy? . . . *You are hot*—this is now a fact of life. All bets are off when that happens. All *my* options have changed, for sure. Last week I was set to sign you up in a share deal with the Donegal Gallery—they have the best video stable in New York—but now I'm glad I didn't. The very fact that

Gunther came to your first performance . . . I mean, he's only in the city for eight weeks out of fifty-two, my dear, and during that time absolutely everyone has their hooks in him. It was a stroke of luck—a blessing—that he came. Gunther likes me, he likes my spunk, he's liked it since he met me at Leo's, but still I never expected him to show up, much less that he'd be interested in you . . ."

She was gushing on and on, I had to say it twice to bring her to a halt. "What are you, his slave?"

"I beg your pardon?"

"I said, are you his slave? And who made you my agent, anyway? You keep saying *you* can take me to Donegal, *you* can get me this contract. When do I get to say what I want?"

There was a long silence.

"My dear, I'm insulted. I'm your dealer, why must I keep reminding you? Without the gallery you wouldn't have abducted that woman, you never would have heard of Gunther much less gotten him interested in your work. We're *partners*, Roy . . . I feel as if I'm talking to a *hayseed*, for gosh sakes."

"OK, Cissy," I said, "pipe down. But why can't you bring him here to my apartment? The artist's studio, right? Why do I have to go to this party?"

A big consideration of mine was not stepping out the door until Oliver Hartwell himself showed up and I had a chance to talk to him.

She exploded, screaming into the receiver. "*What is* this Greta Garbo number? I don't get it! This is your career we're talking about. You should be *dying* to go. It's not a church social I'm taking you to, you know—some of the most important collectors in New York will be there. Lots of other folks, too—artists, musicians . . . Everyone's going out of town soon, this is the last party, everyone wants to meet you—you can't bail out on me now!"

I sighed. "All right, I'll be ready at ten. Have the taxi wait, though, when you get out to ring my buzzer. And please, Cissy, do me a big favor—stop off someplace first and buy me a pair of sunglasses, OK? It's very important."

SEVENTEEN

The Fourth of July weekend had begun, and, for a Saturday night, Manhattan was nearly deserted. The madness hadn't begun quite yet, but at every red light, if you peered down a side street you could see the flashes of firecrackers in the air, and clouds of smoke drifting under the streetlights. The taxi driver, a young unemployed actor who cheerfully rattled off a list of productions he'd auditioned for that week, had the radio tuned, full blast, to Brian Ferry singing "Love Is the Drug." Driving down Second Avenue, across town on Houston and then south on Varick into TriBeCa—the new neighborhood, already on the verge of becoming exorbitantly pricey—I remembered the Fourth of July a year before, the Bicentennial weekend. It seemed like a century had gone by, so much had changed. Then I'd been scuffling and unhappy, scheming to interview Oliver Hartwell, hoping the money I made would take Dana and me far enough away from the city to save our relationship. Now, wearing cheap drugstore sunglasses, I sat in the back seat of a taxi next to Cissy Wyatt while nighttime New York flew by and she fretted at me.

She was aghast at the fact that I hadn't watched the six-thirty news and couldn't believe I no longer owned a television set. To her it was an unthinkable deprivation. She kept insisting she'd buy me one.

"Although I don't know why I feel the need to display such generosity. As soon as you cash this check, you can line the walls of your apartment with TVs!" She reached into her bag and, with a flourish, handed it to me, waiting for a show of enthusiasm. The first money I'd earned as an artist! Sixteen thousand dollars! When I said nothing, simply folding the check and putting it in my pocket, she moaned like a parent to an ungrateful child, "I just don't understand you. So, all right, you have no TV. Doesn't this interest you enough to watch it at a friend's house? You could have gone down the block to a bar. This is your life, Roy—the most important moment in your life. And instead of watching it you stay at home doing God knows what. Sulking in the dark, probably."

"Cissy, I'll bet you sixteen thousand dollars I know what that anchorman's message was. You yourself said the establishment media was against me. How could this guy be any worse than the lady in the *Post*? So first they show an excerpt from the tape—no doubt the part where Miriam refuses to talk and I whip out the gun and terrorize her—and then the guy's face fills the screen and he says sanctimoniously, 'In our fair city a week ago today, under the pretext of honoring a fellow artist recently passed away, an obscure figure from the SoHo subculture, desperate for attention, kidnapped an innocent woman . . . If we, as responsible citizens, allow such an outrage to pass by without protest, what can we expect to happen next? Whatever that may be, we'll have only ourselves to blame, because in a civilized society, art cannot be above the law . . .' "

I turned to her and smiled. "Is that about it?"

She grimaced, squirming on the seat. "Wise guy, aren't you? Such hot shit . . . Well, for your information, he wasn't as tiresomely pontifical as that, my dear; he got to the point a lot quicker."

Then, her face flushing with anger, she spat out, "Of course he lambasted you—and the Phalanx Gallery—as well he should have! That's what I understood for the first time when I was watching it, that's what made it so exciting. He was playing his role—and happily, too, unambiguously, because of the extremity to which you yourself had gone in playing yours. Don't you see? *That's* why the establishment media waxes indignant at what we do—because they're the establishment. Somehow I hadn't realized that before, I kept expecting them to get the point. But, my dear, they *did* get the point. Their values were being attacked on that videotape. I mean, you couldn't watch Mrs. Katz' face without feeling disgusted—a helpless woman . . . I'll tell you though, Roy," she said, becoming enthusiastic again in spite of her frustration with me, "the beauty of that performance was in everything else that came across besides her victimization . . . Your commitment to Jack, for example . . . Your—dare I say—almost *quaint* purity."

I was sure she meant to wound me with this last remark but when I failed to respond she added, not missing a beat, "At any rate—yes, he condemned you in no uncertain terms, the good monkey waving his finger at the bad monkey, but any publicity is good publicity, my dear, even if we have to hire security guards for the gallery. The important thing is that they ran a full ninety seconds from the tape. Ninety seconds—on local network news!" She looked at me, her eyes shining. "You're over the top now, Roy . . . You're a success. I only hope you don't let this slip through your fingers—for my sake as well as yours."

Debbie Cowan's loft—spacious and elegant, overlooking the Hudson River from Duane Street—was crowded with people, every one of whom pretended at first not to notice us, talking louder and more animatedly, resisting, if even for a short while, their inevitable capitulation to celebrity. My celebrity. But they couldn't help themselves. One after another started giving me *the look*—envy combining with anticipation in an effort to suck out my magnetism. As I glanced around nervously, wishing I had a drink—and the stronger the better—Cissy whispered in my ear, "You'll have to learn to deal with resentment, that's the hardest part—or so the famous people I know tell me. Everyone will resent the shit out of you!"

Andy Warhol was there, and he made straight for me, snapping Polaroids as he approached, his silver hair catching the light. He held out his hand. "Terrific," he said, "Sensational . . . You have to meet Fred, he's here somewhere. We want to do a thing with you for *Interview*. Take off the shades for a second, Roy, I want to see the eyes . . . You're cute, too, that's great!"

I put the sunglasses in my shirt pocket and Cissy and I worked our way over to the bar, Cissy wearing an ear-to-ear smile and talking non-stop, forcing everyone she came across to acknowledge our presence, introducing me to people, one after the other, as if I were running for office. "This is the one and only Henry Geldzahler, Roy . . .

We're having a special showing of the tape for him next Wednesday . . . This is Harry Mamoulian, he runs the Frankel Gallery. This is Ed Mull, you know his work . . . This is Annette Ferrara, she's a painter too . . . This is Joey Blank, he's with that great new band, you know, the Tonguetwisters . . ."

She introduced me to some guy, whispering a name I didn't catch, explaining he was an important performance artist too, and suddenly the animosity became palpable. "Your hostage thing was *very* interesting," he said with a sardonic smile, "but it wasn't art, of course. More like street theater—agitprop, you know? Straight out of the 1930s." He had been standing with three or four other men and they all sneered at this remark, turning their backs to me. Cissy was unfazed, still smiling as she pulled me along into the center of the room. Before I'd been at the party for half an hour people were offering me coke, giving me invitations to openings, handing me slips of paper with their phone numbers on them. "You have to meet our hostess," Cissy said, and dragged me away from a lovely, black-haired Eurasian girl who had introduced herself as Arabella. She was dressed in a glittering, exquisitely embroidered cocktail dress and had been telling me, "I'm a performance artist too—but I do installations. Rooms filled with astonishing objects."

We found Debbie Cowan over by the windows in a blue silk kimono, super animated, rubbing her nose and chattering to a guy holding a little gold spoon. I complimented her on the view—you could see clear across to New Jersey, the reflections of the factories lambent on the water—and she made a face and began complaining about the landfill.

"Which landfill?"

"They're going to build a *huge* housing complex right there, right where you're looking. Soon I won't be able to see anything but little balconies with hibachis on them. But the neighborhood's mobilizing to fight it. It'll be like the Sixties all over again," she said with a loud, metallic laugh.

I wanted to be the fly on the wall and listen anonymously to some of the conversations going on, but it was impossible. Everybody stopped talking as soon as I approached, and, depending on who they were either looked away or stared at me, tongue-tied. Cissy introduced me to various artists, all of whom seemed to be discussing their summer places. They informed me—as if I had a summer place too—why they still happened to be in the city at this late date, asking if I thought they should leave for the Hamptons tomorrow, braving the holiday traffic, or wait until after the Fourth. "The traffic's hideous all this weekend, don't you think?" a faultlessly groomed woman said to me earnestly. "We always prefer waiting 'til after. There's so much to do in the city anyway, don't you agree? It's so difficult to tear oneself away." Then, staring at me with clinical thoroughness, she blithely remarked, "You don't *look* like an anarchist. Somehow I expected, you know, a shaved head and pimples . . . The scruffy rebel look." Bluntly she added, as she turned away, "If you got a decent haircut you might even be good-looking."

"I don't know why Gunther isn't here," Cissy was saying anxiously, peering around the room. "He promised me he would be, we've got so much to discuss. Maybe it's still too early, he'll show up soon. Still, that's not like him. He likes to get to bed before midnight. I wonder if something came up."

She made me promise to wait while she went off in search of him, and finding myself backed up against a sofa full of people, I squeezed in beside it, next to one arm on which two people were sitting, and sank down to the floor. Nobody noticed me, nobody was paying attention to me for the moment, and I listened as an almost hysterical female voice said, "Oh Jonathan, what are you *talking* about? How can you call her a good person—you don't know what she's done to me! She's so incredibly snobby, she's a bitch. It's like if you don't have money you simply can't be interesting. I mean, that attitude is *so New York*—I can't *wait* to get out of here, Jonathan, I really need to get away for a while. The city's doing something bad to my head. Sometimes it seems like a demonic beehive, an after-death state, where time doesn't exist, the rest of the globe doesn't exist, you're just doing your work, competing with one person after another, going up and down the endless corridor of your career, clearing it of all obstructions 'til it shines. And then, *well*—if you haven't made it, people manipulate you, they put you down. And when you do make it, then they're treacherous, they can't wait to cut you down to size. First they ignore you, then they resent you—what kind of a deal is that?"

Her voice, shaky and full of hurt, sounded so miserable I wanted to comfort her, but her companion took care of that. Matter-of-factly he announced, "There are losers and there are winners. That's all there is to it, Sharon. Be thankful you're among the latter. I can assure you the opposite condition is infinitely worse."

"But, Jonathan," she replied, sounding a bit mollified nonetheless, "it's so crazy. After engaging in cut-throat activities with people all year, you get invited to their summer places in the Hamptons or Martha's Vineyard for a weekend and they revert to these amazingly open, friendly, even childlike versions of themselves. Suddenly you find yourself picking vegetables with them in the garden. I mean, after a while it gets so I don't know what to think. Other people are as enigmatic as outer space."

Jonathan chuckled approvingly at this remark.

I wandered around. People continued coming up to me, fingering the sleeves of my shirt, peering into my eyes, handing me joints. I wanted to leave now. I was sick of this party. I felt trapped by my notoriety, all these smiling faces eager to ingratiate themselves with me where two weeks before they would have stared right through me. If I bought into this scene, soon I'd do anything—even market Jack Rio T-shirts—to stay in the limelight.

I looked for Cissy and finally saw her standing in the doorway leading to the kitchen, talking animatedly, the receiver of a wall phone in her hand. It suddenly occurred to me there was no reason in the world for me to remain in New York. I had a check for sixteen thousand dollars in my pocket. I could cash it and get out of the city, far away from Oliver Hartwell. It was time for me to disappear while I was still in one piece.

Excitedly I thought of flying to Mexico. I'd never been there but always wanted to go, and now I knew I could do it. Alone down there with no attachments, no responsibilities, I'd have the time to get my-self together, to read and write. I would go to someplace on the Pacific coast. I'd heard stories about Puerto Escondido, how cheap and beau-tiful it was, with few tourists or hotels. I'd leave most of this money in the bank in New York and come back to ten thousand bucks a year or two from now when everything's cooled down, when I don't have to wake up every morning wondering whether Miriam Katz has changed her mind and I'll need to hire an expensive lawyer just to stay out of jail. Wondering whether Hartwell was coming after me today, if the next knock on the door would be his.

Someone tapped me on the shoulder and I nearly jumped out of my skin. Without saying goodbye to Cissy I fairly ran toward the door, pushing people out of my way. I looked over at Cissy as I left, her mouth still moving, talking into the phone while her eyes followed me across the room.

Monday was July Fourth and the banks were closed, so it would be Tuesday morning before I could cash the check. All sorts of contradic-tory thoughts were running through my head. I couldn't wait to leave the city. I knew if I stayed Cissy would draw me into an endless round of interviews and appearances, doing her utmost to make me her art star. There would be parties and more parties. On top of that, she'd pressure me to create more performances, whereas the entire thing had only been a way for me to support myself while I looked for the OPW. But I was finished with that, those days were over, I wanted out.

Early Tuesday morning I was awakened by Cissy's three rings.

"Forgive me, my dear, I know it's only eight A.M. and I probably wrenched you away from your dreams, but I just had to call you."

I didn't reply.

"Are you awake, Roy? I would've called on Sunday but I decided to give you some time to yourself. Obviously the performance was a drain on your energy . . . *Roy?*"

I sighed. "What the fuck do you want, Cissy? It so happens I *was* sleeping."

"You needn't be rude with me, for gosh sakes, I'm not calling for the fun of it, you know. I've got something important to tell you. But I must say, I'm also concerned about you. What was wrong with you Saturday night? You bolted from the party with no explanation. It looked so strange. Everybody was asking me about it and I didn't know what to say. What happened?"

"You wouldn't understand," I snapped.

"Oh, please, spare me your condescension, Roy. If you were playing hard to get, Saturday night was the wrong occasion. I'm not in this business for the exercise, you know. I mean, was that some new performance of yours, leaving without a word to anyone? If so, please clue me in, would you? *I'm* the one left having to contextualize your behavior and, frankly, I'd rather not try. I'm sure to miss the subtleties involved," she concluded sarcastically. "But just between us, why *did* you leave?"

"I don't know . . ." I responded, trailing off.

"For gosh sakes, Roy, pull yourself together! We have lots of work to do. But I called you early this morning because I wanted to save you any disappointment if you were planning to cash that check for sixteen thousand today. You see, certain people have been delinquent with me and I've had to temporarily stop payment. Sorry about that, but it's just 'til next Monday—the eleventh—OK? I promise. If you need a small advance 'til then, just come by the gallery . . . You know, I'm writing out checks all the time and there's a cash flow problem if people who owe me don't cough up when they say they will. Some collectors are so perverse, Roy. The more money they have, the more games they play with you. Even a man like Gunther Hebel," she remarked crossly. "Not only didn't he show up at the party, he's not taking my calls for some reason. I just *hate* it when people get cagey with me!"

I couldn't believe she was telling me this.

"You've got to be joking," I said angrily. "What are you trying to pull? I put my life on the line for that performance, I can't even leave my apartment anymore because all sorts of people are after me. I need to cash that check and I won't wait until next Monday, Cissy, do you hear me?"

There was an extended silence. Finally she replied, "Listen, I'm not sure if I appreciate your insinuation at all, my dear. I'm not cheating you, but running a gallery isn't like pressing a button. Unforeseen contingencies arise, everything takes time. Why do you suddenly want the whole lump now, anyway? You didn't seem in such a terrible hurry when I gave you the check, if you remember," she said, the faintest note of reproach in her voice. "Just keep your shirt on, will you? We have more important things to discuss. Your next performance, for example. And I've finally lined up that article with *Vogue*, have I mentioned that to you yet? There'll be a photographer coming down at the end of the week, so please answer when I call, all right? The same signal as before . . . And what do you mean you can't leave your apartment? What on earth are you talking about?"

"I don't want to die, Cissy, damn it, can't you understand?" I shouted, and slammed down the receiver. I was furious. I didn't believe her story, it seemed much more likely that Cissy was toying with me, withholding the money as retaliation for my lack of gratitude. More than once while she had been talking I thought I'd detected in her voice the aggrieved tone of the wounded lover. As if I owed her or anybody else an explanation for leaving the party. I couldn't wait until I laid my hands on that money, I'd be free then, they could all go fuck themselves.

All that week I brooded. Why hadn't Hartwell come for me? Why was he torturing me like this? If only he'd listen to me, if only he'd give me a chance to explain myself. I wanted to talk to him, I had so many questions to ask. I like looking into your face, Oliver Hartwell. You can look into mine anytime you want, it's right here staring back at you. I miss you.

I'd been given several joints at Debbie Cowan's party and I started smoking grass again, venturing out onto the street late one night to buy more. I was horny as hell, and in between sessions of exercising on the floor in front of the mirror in my bare living room, I sat at the window and began fastening my eyes on the passersby. I fantasized about them, masturbating to the cast of their faces in the light, their cheekbones and lips, their shoulders and asses, the movement of their legs as they walked. Men and women, boys and girls, I wasn't particular, I wanted them all. I consumed everybody I laid eyes on, making no distinctions, running my tongue over their hips, their breasts, their necks. I licked their cocks and pussies until they moaned. I carried them with me as I moved to the floor.

"I'm famous," I said, stroking myself in the half light, lying in front of the mirror, repeatedly bringing myself to the edge of orgasm and then stopping. I watched my cock soften and shrink, then began again, luxuriating in the challenge, losing myself in it, standing up to observe my stiff cock nod its head as I posed.

I stayed hard for hours, never coming. On the floor was a magazine, I saw a lingerie ad. A simple black and white photo in which the model, a dark-haired girl in a silky camisole, stood with one knee raised as she leaned against an upholstered chair, running her fingers through the ends of her hair. The camisole came to the top of her thighs, it was creased where her left leg lifted up onto the seat of the chair. Hungrily I caressed her legs and ankles, lingering on the shape her ass made inside the camisole. I'll take her to Mexico with me. We can leave on Monday as soon as I cash that check, I won't take no for an answer. She'll be glad to come with me when she finds out who I am.

"Maybe you've heard about me. The art hostage thing, remember? It was in all the papers. It's gotten so I can't even go out to eat in this town, people interrupt me asking for my autograph, a soiled napkin, anything."

But maybe Mexico isn't right at all. What happens when she drowns in a boating accident and I'm left down there alone, succumbing to some insidious tropical disease? How stupid of me to even think of Mexico, I don't need to travel that far in order to start over again. I can go out west instead, rent an apartment somewhere, build a new career. Yeah, and make new friends. There's no friends in Mexico, man, you're a gringo down there surrounded by hostile natives, the only other Americans are hippie deadbeats and I've had enough of them right here in New York City. I want to work for a living, I want other people, I'm fucking sick of being alone.

On Saturday I spent the whole day in front of the mirror, staring fixedly at my face. My eyes began to rotate in tiny circles like stars do when you stare at them. At one point I thought I'd been making faces at myself but I didn't know for sure, my eyes were wide open and I refused to let my gaze wander. I was finished with that, I was fed up with looking down or up or sideways, it only brought on more details, each as inconsequential as the last, the endless details of life that never amount to anything more than a snare and a delusion. My eyes danced like live coals in the failing light. I knew dusk was approaching and I wondered if I'd still be able to see my own eyes after it got dark. Or would I be staring into nothing?

The phone rang, three rings followed by a pause.

"*For gosh sakes*," Cissy shouted in a rage, "I can't believe you don't have a television! Who do you think you are? You—no, damn it, Roy, you're missing it, it's too late. It's almost over. The newscaster of ABC. Wait, I'm turning up the sound . . ."

I lay on the living room floor, flat on my back, staring up at the ceiling as a male voice came on the line: "—at one P.M. today. Police believe the gunman fired from the roof of one of the surrounding loft buildings. Commissioner Michael J. Codd, in a statement at Police Headquarters, said no effort would be spared to track down the killer."

Then I heard nothing. "Cissy, what is this, what's going on?"

In a hushed voice she said, speaking slowly and deliberately, "This old lady, Roy . . . She was seventy-eight years old, it's just too awful. She must have been the only woman in all of SoHo wearing a fur coat today, with the weather like it's been . . . She steps out of a gallery on West Broadway and is shot in the back, *shot in the back*. There was a terrible scene, people weeping, the police. I didn't see it, of course, but Betsy Summers was right across the street when it happened. She says it was the most horrible thing, a person—frail as a bird—collapsing on the sidewalk, the holes in her coat, the blood. I can't understand why this maniac picked on someone so old, he must have been shooting at her from pretty far away, maybe she was just a brown speck in his rifle sights, or whatever . . . God . . . Everyone's really upset down here, all the stores on West Broadway have closed early."

Cissy paused. Seventy-eight years old, I thought. I started getting nervous.

"And then—this is the thing, Roy," she said, her voice thickening, "ABC gets a phone call from a guy an hour later saying he shot a woman on West Broadway in SoHo—'an artshopper,' he called her. They played a tape of the phone call on TV, you can't imagine how menacing it sounded . . . Shot her as a form of protest, 'an ironical comment,' he said, can you believe it? A form of protest against ART HOSTAGE, Roy, that's the thing . . . Over the phone he delivered this sarcastic, hate-filled *manifesto*, this insane outraged protest against your performance, using it as an excuse, a precedent, a source of inspiration. Do you follow me? The guy's actually saying, 'If that bastard can get away with it, why shouldn't I? I'll show those phonies in SoHo what art is really all about. Jack Rio was a phony too. Long live art!' And he laughed! . . . I'm telling you, Roy, I'm scared. That mocking voice revelling in the fact that he'd finally put something over on everybody. I mean, seeing that poor woman being loaded into an ambulance, her coat dragging on the sidewalk, while over that you heard *this voice*. It was the creepiest feeling, listening to him, one of these *exultant psychos*, do you know? I kept wondering if I recognized his voice. Like, have I ever heard it before? Has he come around the gallery? Was he some kind of disgruntled artist gone off the deep end? Because he knew exactly what he was doing to you, the damage he was causing. He was out to ruin you, Roy, that's why he did it."

"Damage," I repeated tonelessly.

"Roy, maybe you don't get the picture. There's been a big uproar, this vendetta atmosphere has developed. The Archbishop of New York, Cardinal Cooke—I don't know where they found him, suddenly he's standing there in his vestments, they must have pulled him right out of some service. I kept trying to tear myself away from the set for a second to call you but I just couldn't . . . The Archbishop appears on the screen and condemns you by name, referring to your 'notorious art performance,' saying the fact you could get away with such amoral behavior, simply to draw attention to yourself, is indicative of a total breakdown in Western values. Because it was you who awakened the unspeakably sick violence seen on the streets of New York today . . . Those were his exact words . . . Nobody but you, he said, is responsible for that monstrous crime. Now do you see what I mean? *Time* and *Newsweek* are calling. The networks are on their way down here right now with camera crews, they're demanding a statement from you. They say you have to talk to them. What should we do?"

In all the time I'd known her, Cissy had never asked me that before. She'd always had the answers.

"I don't know," I replied, then I hung up the phone and went to the window. Several men were standing on the sidewalk. They looked like media people to me, however—no OPW, as far as I could tell. A seventy-eight year old woman shot in the back . . . Then across the street I saw an old black man, rooting through the garbage cans on the sidewalk, raising his head now and then, looking toward my window. The phone was ringing again. I changed into a T-shirt and shorts, grabbed my knapsack and, remembering the sunglasses at the last moment, jammed them onto my face as I left. I crept down the stairs and out the rear of the building, scaling the cinderblock wall there into the ailanthus-filled backyard. Climbing a fence, eventually I came out of a building on Ninth Street. The first thing I saw was a taxi, which I hailed and took to Central Park.

It took us forever to reach 59th Street and Fifth Avenue in the rush-hour traffic, but I was in no hurry. If Oliver Hartwell blamed me for the old woman's death then I was finished. He wouldn't give me a chance to explain myself. Every vagrant, every wino and shopping bag lady I saw as we drove uptown filled me with dread. But I refused to stay at home any longer, a helpless target.

I walked along the paths in Central Park parallel to 59th Street. The rain had stopped by now. It was a hazy overcast evening, muggy and hot, with hardly any wind. When I reached Seventh Avenue I began trotting slowly downtown, enveloped in heat and car exhaust, navigating through traffic and crowds of pedestrians I barely noticed. As I ran I tried to master my fear, to block it out. Running was all that remained and I had to be perfect at it.

Eventually I slowed down and began walking, this time wandering north. Soon I arrived at Sheridan Square. It was teeming on this hot Saturday night. Hundreds of gay men were out cruising. I sat in the back of a coffee shop, eating and stoking up on coffee.

I stared at myself in the smoky mirror on the wall behind the counter at the coffee shop. The shades I was wearing didn't hide my hair, in fact they didn't amount to much camouflage at all, so after I finished eating I went into the all-night pharmacy on Sheridan Square and bought a box of yellow hair dye. Returning to the coffee shop I locked myself in the bathroom and opened the package, massaging the contents into my scalp. The directions said to wait for twenty minutes and I stood there, looking into the smudged mirror, my head covered with mustard-colored lather, while people approached the door and knocked, timidly at first, then with mounting urgency. Finally somebody started hammering, shaking the door on its hinges.

"What's doing there fella? This is management. Open up!"

"Just a minute," I shouted.

I rinsed off the solution in the sink and had time to register my striking new head of ash blond hair—compromised by dark eyebrows—when the door started rattling again and I unlocked it and stepped out. "You were too much time," a perspiring Greek in an apron remonstrated, but I said nothing, pushing past him and out into the street.

I crossed Sheridan Square again, this time to the cigar store on the corner, and bought cigarettes. And that's when I met Alastair. As I turned from the counter he was entering the store and he gave me a searching look, then meaningfully eyed my crotch. There was something comical about his big, dramatic eyes, as if he were only teasing me by being so forward, and when I was outside again I decided to wait for him. I saw what I had to do, it was going to be the luck of the draw. I'll be fucked if I'm going to spend the night out on the streets, waiting to be assaulted. I desperately needed somebody to talk to. I needed not to be alone for a while.

He saw me as soon as he came out of the store, those exaggeratedly cavernous eyes of his fastening on me with undisguised delight, and instantly he was standing by my side.

"What's your name?" he demanded, flashing a quick, skeptical smile.

"Tommy. What's yours?"

"*Alastair*," he announced, lovingly drawing out the name in a bogus English accent, caressing the word to show how much he liked it.

He looked me up and down—my still-wet blond hair, my white T-shirt and shorts, my knapsack—and said, again with that sarcastic leer, as if anything I told him had to be of questionable veracity, "You just get out of the shower, Tommy?"

I laughed but didn't reply and we eyed each other. Alastair's face had a pale, ravaged look, a sort of *fin-de-siècle* pallor. Perhaps the circles under his eyes resulted from cosmetics? He wore an earring in one ear and deeply hennaed hair slicked back Rudolph Valentino style, gleaming with red highlights. There was something innocently mischievous about Alastair, as if he enjoyed laughing at his own jokes. This made me think he couldn't be dangerous. Because, dressed entirely in black, he cultivated a sepulchral presence that otherwise might have given me pause.

"Well, Tommy," he said with mock-stern impatience. "Are you coming along with me or not? You don't have to answer, I'll figure it out by your actions . . ." Giggling, rolling his eyes, puffing away at an Egyptian cigarette. "Personally, I *prefer* the silent type, so—so far so good. Silent types give me more room to be myself, do you know what I mean? And furthermore I-want-to-suck-your-cock."

"I beg your pardon?"

He said it so quickly I didn't know exactly what I heard. He burst out laughing then, pleased with himself, and also pleased I hadn't turned and walked away.

Alastair was a lot younger than he looked, twenty-two, he said. He claimed he was a painter. He lived in an old-time Lower East Side apartment on Christie Street below Delancey, a tiny place with an ancient sink, a tub in the kitchen, grimy narrow windows covered with old sheets, holes in the ceiling, and no hot water. The Chinese were spreading out from Chinatown, taking over buildings—they'd just bought his building—and Alastair figured he'd be out on the street within six months. "They only want their own here, they're kicking everybody else out," he said fatalistically. But he paid only forty dollars a month rent.

The apartment, one narrow room with a kitchen alcove, had a mattress on the floor and a second-hand coffee table on which stood a collection of what looked like voodoo artifacts: African death skulls with cowrie shell eyes, beaded Haitian icons, bowls filled with seeds. He told me, rolling his eyes sarcastically so I couldn't tell if he was joking or not, that he'd been an adept—a practitioner of Santeriá—since the age of sixteen, when he'd run away from home. On the night of the full moon he would sacrifice a chicken and leave a cup of its blood on the roof of his building. "Everybody has to participate in ritual of some kind, don't you agree? Otherwise they're nothing."

Above the two broken-down armchairs in which we sat was an enormous painting, the only one in the room, of Brian Jones dead in an empty swimming pool. It was painted in weird, lurid mega-realism, with spotlights on Brian's body, his cock hanging loose, and pills spilled all around him. I immediately asked Alastair about the painting, one could hardly ignore it. Refusing to admit he'd painted it himself, he said in a hushed, conspiratorial voice that Brian Jones' death was still a mystery. Alastair himself had been only fourteen when it happened, he'd hardly known who the Rolling Stones were, but still, it had changed his life. It had made him more aware of a hidden meaning in everything, the fact that the truth of any matter was always disguised, always suppressed.

"All those deaths, man, every one of them were suspicious. All the rock stars—Jim Morrison, Jimi Hendrix, Janis Joplin, Gram Parsons . . . And as for Brian Jones, the Rolling Stones had discovered a formula for cranking out hits by 1969, they were in a groove, they hadn't any further use for Brian Jones—the most original musician among them, the one who took them to Morocco, who exposed them to Joujouka, opened up the whole world to them if they'd only been willing to listen."

I laughed. "But are you claiming the Stones did Brian Jones in? That's preposterous!"

He rolled his eyes. "*You* said it, Tommy, not me. Just between the two of us, speaking strictly confidentially, I haven't the *faintest* idea what you're talking about."

We laughed uproariously. By then we'd taken some speed, little yellow Desoxyn of which he seemed to have a jarful, and we were sailing. We stayed up all night, Alastair playing records on his battered old KLH, principally every David Bowie album ever released, one after the other. Alastair worshiped David Bowie.

Alastair talked to me about his childhood for hours: his deceased alcoholic father, his mother and sisters in Bridgeport, the momentous discovery of his homosexuality in a locker room in the seventh grade. Wired by the speed as I was, I couldn't contain my impatience and soon I was talking nonstop too, we went at it simultaneously, two conversational strands swinging in the room like live wires, now closer, now further away from each other, but touching only by chance. He laid out his family history while I went on about Hartwell and the OPW, starting from the very beginning. I hadn't taken speed in years and I was jumping out of my skin, my heart racing, my mouth motoring uncontrollably.

Finally, after what seemed like hours, I got his attention and he stopped talking.

"There's a conspiracy out on the streets, Alastair. This is serious, you better listen hard. Nobody knows about it but me. What do you think OPW stand for, anyway? Are you trying to kid me? Old people's war! The old people are taking over and I've met their leader. He's extraordinary, unstoppable, you can be standing right in front of him but you don't recognize him. He's a master of disguise, so gutsy, so smart, nobody can touch him, I know that for a fact. Alastair, you've got to listen to me, the OPW's dangerous, they don't fool around, they've kidnapped people and engaged in all sorts of experiments, lamb fetus injections, BHT supplements, weird exercises, and surgery. I'm the only one who knows about them, the only one who is able to betray them. They don't trust me. They want to kill me, Alastair, I have to get away! I don't want to die!"

Alastair eyed me uneasily. His mouth twitched as he said, "I think you'd better leave now, Tommy, I don't like the smell of this. One never knows *what* one will pick up on the street these days. You looked good to me and I thought we could get together tonight but believe me, I'm not into fucking an insane person. I'd rather—"

I was furious, the speed working away at me as I jumped up and smacked him in the side of the head with my open palm.

"Fuck you," I said. "If you come near me I'll kill you. My skin's crawling. What's in those pills, anyway?"

He smirked, rubbing his cheek and then saying frostily, "Don't worry, Tommy, it was pure amphetamine, I use nothing else . . . God, this is all so tiresome. Somehow, with that absurd tint job on your hair and all, I assumed you'd be different."

The fright in his eyes was gone by now. Instead they flashed peevishly as he added, "What I *don't* understand is why you came home with me in the first place."

"I needed a place to stay tonight. I wanted to talk to somebody."

"Well, thanks loads, Tommy, but this isn't summer camp and I'm not a counselor. Am I making myself quite clear? If you can't get it up for me, why don't you just leave?"

His derisive tone instantly had me raving. "For your information I can stay hard for hours if I want, Alastair—for hours! But I choose not to. Not with a scumbag like you. So eat your heart out!"

"Your hair color is a scream," he whispered acidly. "I'm sure your mysterious *man friend* won't recognize you now, so don't worry, sweetie. I won't tell."

I drew back my fist to punch him. At the last second, my heart pounding in my ears, I stopped myself and abruptly walked out the door.

Outside it was still dark. Christie Street seemed deserted, but as soon as I broke into a trot I saw spectral figures ducking out of sight in the shrubbery of the woebegone strip of trees between Christie and Forsythe. I saw them peering from behind walls down every side street. Terrified, I ran through the pre-dawn silence, staring straight ahead, until I reached St. Mark's Place. I slipped unnoticed up the stairs. Barbra Streisand's voice wafted down from above and I laughed aloud, the sweat pouring off my body.

"I wonder who lives here now?" I asked, apologetically at first. Then I said it more and more sharply, more and more insistently, making no effort to disguise the tension inside me, my jaws aching from the speed to the point that I could barely open and close them. Although that didn't stop me from shouting it over and over, "I wonder who lives here now!" until upstairs Barbra stopped her singing to listen, and the birds outside which had just begun to chirp were silent too, while underneath me the gypsies stirred in their beds, complaining about the noise. "That guy has a lot of nerve," I heard a muffled voice say as I went on at the top of my lungs, pausing only to draw breath.

EIGHTEEN

I collapsed in a vacant state but couldn't fall asleep, I just lay on the bed clenching and unclenching my teeth. The next thing I knew it was six P.M. and I was awake, standing in the kitchen drinking glass after glass of water and wondering how I could have slept through the ringing of the telephone. It rang now, six or seven times, followed a few minutes later by another call. I had difficulty remembering what day it was but when I did I ran into the living room and, finding my wallet, opened it and took out Cissy's check. I still had it, I hadn't lost it. All I needed to do was get through one more night.

The phone rang again. This time I answered it.

"Hello?"

Silence. I heard breathing, relaxed and deep and, faintly in the distance, what sounded like an appliance humming, or the buzz of a fluorescent light. Some sort of machine. But not loud enough to block out the breathing.

"Who is this?"

When there was no reply I started to shake. I became furious with myself for losing control. Why was I falling to pieces over some crank caller reacting to the murder? But I knew it wasn't a crank caller.

"Mr. Hartwell? *Oliver* Hartwell? Asshole chickenshit crazy killer Hartwell, is that you? You think I care? You think you're scaring me? Well, fuck you. I'm not interested in betraying the OPW but you won't believe me. And I'm not responsible for that woman's death in SoHo but you won't believe that, either. It would be too much trouble for you, right? Just push me into the path of a speeding train instead . . . And I wanted to talk to you, that's the shame of it. I missed you, I wanted so much to see you again. But you're too paranoid, isn't that it? You're afraid to trust me and you're going to kill me out of fear instead. And what can I do about that, *Mister* Hartwell? Do you know? Well, I'll tell you what I can do. I can make myself scarce, just like you. I can disappear. You understand? I can get lost! I'm going far away . . ."

There was no response.

"Goddamn you motherfucking soul-eater," I said, pulling the cord out of the wall and throwing the phone across the room. I wasn't running from him anymore, where could I go anyway? I would wait right here until nine A.M. and if he hadn't come by then I was cashing that check and going to Mexico. Mexico was the right choice after all, I was sure of it now, but it didn't really matter because I knew he was coming for me tonight, I was positive of it. The fact that I alone knew his true identity was too much for him to risk.

But Hartwell didn't come that night. I fell asleep, bewildered and still wasted from the speed, and woke the next morning past eleven, bathed in sweat. It was another hot, humid day. I left the apartment without my knapsack, I'd return and pack a suitcase after cashing the check. Two men in pin-striped suits, perspiring and looking unhappy, were ringing my bell when I eased past them in my shades and yellow hair. One of them held a copy of the *Post*: ART MURDER, the headline screamed.

"The guy's long gone," the one holding the *Post* said to the other. "Maybe that killer got him too, Frank, whaddya think?"

"I think he left town for a while. You know, go lay on the beach somewhere. I'm sure he figures memories are short. He'll be back."

"In time for the next art season, you mean," the first replied, and they guffawed.

Out on the street I heard the beating of a big bass drum. From Third Avenue along the opposite sidewalk came a group of young demonstrators, pushing against the noise of pedestrians and traffic. "No more dope," they chanted. They were accompanied by an escort of policemen, and two of them held a banner which proclaimed PUNKS AGAINST JUNK. They chanted as they made their way down the sidewalk, spilling onto the curb, attracting the attention of passersby. But minutes later, after they'd turned the corner of St. Mark's and Second, the sidewalk was filled with people walking back and forth who had no notion of what had just taken place. Standing on the north side of the street in the sunshine, looking across at the other side, I was stunned by the momentary nature of what I'd seen. It was as if the demonstrators had never been there at all. No matter what they did, they were no more than brief figures gone in minutes, leaving no trace. Suddenly I had the sensation of being underwater—Dana and I once had gone to the Virgin Islands where I'd snorkeled—and now I was expecting to see the people on the sidewalk disappear right before my eyes, just like the fish had, gobbled up by other fish.

"One second they're here," I said aloud, "and the next second they're gone, it's not even noticed that they're gone because their places are instantly taken by others. The sidewalk is always full. Even if only three people are walking along there's no room for another until one of them disappears."

Somebody was standing next to me on the sidewalk listening to me say this, I felt his body next to mine but I didn't want to turn, I knew full well who it was. He hadn't come for me the night before so I'd been right all along, he didn't want to talk, all he wanted was to kill me. I knew that as soon as I turned to look at him I'd be gone, too. Neutralized in a puff of smoke, liquidated, forgotten, just like the PUNKS AGAINST JUNK. I began running west as fast as I could, toward the wide sidewalks of lower Broadway, where I finally slowed my pace as I turned downtown.

Cissy's bank, on the corner of Spring and Broadway, was a large old-fashioned building with a cavernous central chamber and lots of mahogany, hushed and monumental the way banks used to be. The tellers weren't insulated behind a plastic shield but faced you across a long marble counter. Sacks of money stood on metal carts behind them, while up above everything in the vaulted ceiling, one huge chandelier swayed ever so slightly. Surrounding the chandelier was a dim mural from the Thirties that appeared to show the construction of the Empire State Building, with shirtless workers teetering high above the city on precarious catwalks and girders. The line to the third teller wasn't long and soon I stood facing a short gray-haired woman, slack-jawed and sallow. She wore large oval eyeglasses fastened to a chain around her neck. I endorsed the check and handed it to her.

"I'd like to cash this."

She looked at it, then up at me. I took off my sunglasses.

"Identification?"

I handed her my driver's license.

"You don't have an account here?"

"No."

She returned the check and license. "I'm afraid we can't cash this check unless you have an account with us."

"But I don't understand. The person who made out the check—it's her account. I mean, the account of the gallery, Phalanx Gallery."

"Yes sir, I know that, but you have to deposit the check in your own account, at your own bank. Not here."

"But Cissy's account is here," I said. "The money's here."

She frowned and said, rather impatiently I thought, "I just explained to you that our bank's policy, like most banks, does not allow us to handle this for you. You must go to your own bank."

"Why? Because it's for sixteen thousand dollars? I mean, if I came in here with a check for ten dollars, certainly you'd cash it for me. I have identification and it's *your* check."

"Sir," she replied resolutely, twisting in her seat, "we would not cash it, no matter what the amount."

"But this is absurd. I always thought—"

"It doesn't matter what you thought," she interrupted in a disparaging voice, probably not meaning to, and then stared at me hatefully, knowing she had provoked me.

"Don't talk to me like that!" I shouted. "I'm a customer here and I demand to be treated with respect. You can't insult me!"

She sighed in exasperation, her eyes widening behind the big frames. "Excuse me, sir, but I did not insult you. I merely said—"

"I know what you said, and I'm also aware of the way in which you said it. So don't feed me any bullshit. You're trying to get rid of me because you don't want to take responsibility for cashing such a large amount of money. So why don't you just blow it out your ass!"

She stood up and shrieked, her voice carrying around the big room and bringing everything to a halt, "How dare you curse me! You have no right!" Her arms began to windmill in the air and instantly we were surrounded, she by a covey of solicitous tellers, me by two burly security guards who pinned me against the counter.

"Take your hands off me," I said. "I demand to see an officer of the bank."

A thin, balding man in a three-piece suit appeared beside me, motioning to the guards to release me and asking what was the matter.

The teller interjected from behind the counter. "This man started cursing me after I explained to him the bank could not cash his check because he doesn't have an account here. I refuse to put up with such abuse!"

Her fellow tellers eyed me resentfully and comforted her with little pats on the back. The officer studied me for a moment, his eyes intent behind delicate wire-rimmed glasses, and said, "May I see the check please?"

I handed it to him.

"Please have a seat in there," he said, pointing toward a cubicle at the front of the bank. "I'll be with you in a minute." As I walked away I heard him say to the teller, "It's all in a day's work, Eleanor. Sticks and stones may break your bones, but names will never hurt you."

Sticks and stones . . . I sat in his cubicle on a leather armchair, shivering, trying to figure out how Hartwell had done it. He knew I was coming here to cash Cissy's check and somebody from the OPW was waiting for me, impersonating an officer of the bank. I couldn't stop shaking. This officer was going to do away with me in some fiendishly unnoticeable fashion right here in a bank filled with people. "What a way to go," I moaned, wringing my hands. Suddenly he was standing in front of me, the faintest grin on his narrow face. I noticed with grim satisfaction that his putty-colored suit was drab and cheaply made. "Officer my ass," I muttered under my breath.

Maybe they were planning to kill me later, and this imposter was here only to keep track of me.

"I'm sorry, sir," he said briskly, with no trace of emotion, "but I'm afraid this check is no good. At least I've saved you the trouble of going with it to your own bank."

"What do you mean, no good?"

"Phalanx Gallery's account has been overdrawn for some time. Ms. Wyatt is fully aware of the situation, several checks have bounced already and yet she persists in writing them. If this keeps up we'll have to close the account."

He paused, on the verge of adding more, then simply handed me the check and sat down behind his desk. His telephone rang and he picked it up, allowing himself a shrug of commiseration and the briefest possible sympathetic eye contact.

"You'll excuse me," he said, and turned his attention to the phone. "Mr. Barnes speaking."

I sat there dumbfounded, looking down at the check. I thought of calling Cissy but what was the point? She'd merely fill my ear with excuses, not to mention managing to bawl me out for hanging up on her on Saturday. And she'd insist I show up for some interview or photo session, anything to gain publicity for Phalanx Gallery while she allowed me to be condemned in the public eye and bought me off with a couple hundred bucks again. I doubted she'd sold those facsimiles, and even if she had, she still could camouflage the situation so I'd never know to what extent she'd been paid for them. What was I going to do, demand to see her books? I'd have no idea what I was looking at. Besides, I didn't want to see her books, I didn't want to talk to Cissy, I wanted nothing more to do with her. I was finished with all that.

I tore the check into little pieces and stood up, grinning fixedly at Mr. Barnes, whose head was lowered as he talked into the phone. Finally he looked up and his face blanched. I was grinning from ear to ear, I could feel the tension in my mouth as I held it in a frozen smile. Slowly he replaced the receiver, beads of sweat appearing on his forehead.

"Finally got your attention, huh, baldy?"

His chair was on casters and he rolled it away from his desk, allowing himself room for escape.

"Finally got your fucking attention, huh? Give Hartwell my compliments, OK? Tell him, JOB WELL DONE!" I was shouting now, shouting and laughing, and then I turned abruptly and left the bank running, somebody was just entering one of the big brass doors as I sailed out, the timing was perfect, I didn't even have to break my stride.

In no time at all I had run down the sidewalks of Broadway, past Canal Street, past dark Trinity Church with its yard of wafer-thin gravestones, past the Customs House into Battery Park, past Castle Clinton to my power spot by the sea. The weather was hot and hazy. I stood there at the bottom of the island, my body soaked with sweat, and looked out over the water at Staten Island and the Statue of Liberty, a vague slate-blue figure in the distance. Directly above the statue the afternoon sun cut through the haze making it impossible to see clearly. I could just make out the torch and, raising my own arm high, fist clenched, I sang out the same refrain over and over until I was chanting it, suffusing myself with it, growing strong.

"You can't burn my bones . . ."

I must have chanted this for an hour. People strolling past me on the promenade gave me curious stares but nobody approached me, nobody interfered, and I felt invulnerable. Nothing could touch me now.

I pulled my wallet from the back pocket of my shorts and tossed it as far as I could out into the water. I was free now. I was nowhere, I had nothing, I was nobody.

"You can't burn my bones."

Eyes closed to slits until all I saw was the moiré pattern—the endless reticulation—of the surface of the sea, I stood there inhaling the smell of salt water and chanting for hours, until the sun had gone down and the air around me filled with violet-blue dusk. Then I turned and started trotting uptown.

I fell into loping strides, my gaze fixed on the middle distance, my heart beating slowly. Occasionally as I ran I raised my closed right fist in triumph. I moved at a slow trot, feeling no exhaustion, skimming above the sidewalks, my eyes nearly closed. Red lights and traffic didn't faze me, I could sense where the cars were, where the knots of people were, nobody had to tell me.

"It's better than before," I kept saying, "better than the first time."

Around midnight I found myself outside the Skyline Motor Inn on Tenth Avenue. As cars pulled up to the entrance I stuck out my hand. "I need something to eat," I said, glassy-eyed, distant, covered with perspiration in the steamy light. I made nearly four dollars before being chased away by two cops. "Get lost, monkey face," one of them snarled, "or we'll bust your ass into the Tombs."

Shivering in the glacial air conditioning, I ate at a diner on Twelfth Avenue in the thirties, over by the river. It was a shiny place, like a refrigerated boxcar packed with people, in which dozens of cab drivers ate shimmering wedges of lemon meringue pie. I left all the money I had on the counter when I was done eating, then I walked around the piers for a while. A huge freighter, shining and immaculate, a world to itself, lay berthed beside a long warehouse painted battleship gray. Both warehouse and freighter were lit up by spotlights on surrounding stanchions and both were deserted. I stared at them, entranced. Eventually I began trotting down Twelfth Avenue beside the West Side Highway, down Eleventh Avenue and West Street into the Village, across Houston into SoHo, up the Bowery and Third Avenue to Thirty-Fourth Street, across Thirty-Fourth to Eighth Avenue where I turned north. And as I ran I heard his voice. I couldn't make out what he was saying at first. I begged him to confide in me. I wouldn't tell a soul.

And he said, "I'm glad you didn't give up, Sprout, because we believe in you now. You're finally alone, everyone you knew is gone, only this is real . . . The OPW, as you may have guessed, is growing by leaps and bounds. I'm so proud of our people, they've accomplished so much already. We have a base camp under the city, our headquarters. I'll find you soon, Sprout, I'll take you down. I'll show you everything, the laboratories and experiments. I'll show you people whose lives were lost, who were human junk waiting for the death pile. Depressed, crippled, mute. I'll show them to you as they are now, finally free . . .

"We've worked so hard all these months, I can't begin to tell you how much we've learned. The aging process *can* be controlled. This has been a very emotional time for me. Our movement is developing in ways I hadn't anticipated, and of course there have been casualties and false starts. Fear is enormous and disabling in some people, like a glacier, impossible to dislodge. And what do you do with those who are unable to cross over? After everything we've revealed to them? That's the thorniest problem of all, because we shall not be denied. What we've started won't be stopped.

"Meanwhile, we've decided to go underground for now, violence and confrontation are counterproductive at this stage. There's too much at stake for us to engage in foolhardy acts of vengeance. But there's been a big struggle within our movement about this, it hasn't been easy for me, Sprout. People resent you and work against you simply because you're the leader. But the main thing is to decide whether to accept death willingly or stand up against it . . . And you know this already or you wouldn't be hearing my voice . . . You're running close to me, Sprout, I can feel it, but you have to keep going, you mustn't stop, you mustn't give in . . ."

NINETEEN

I slept somewhere that night, probably in Central Park, because that's where I found myself about noon the following day, squinting into the sun, my sunglasses gone, my body rank with perspiration. I stood on a path just below 79th Street on the East Side, my palm outstretched, panhandling. I knew I should eat but I had no appetite, I felt wired and the weather was sultry, in the mid-nineties. I bought an ice cream sandwich from a vendor on Fifth Avenue and left him all the change I'd collected, grinning into his face at his look of surprise. I wandered south through the park, eavesdropping on nonsensical conversations, raising one fist high in warning whenever anybody approached. I daydreamed under the big old trees. Most of the people I saw were nodding out on the grass, little cups of methadone beside them. I stared into faces, looking right through them until they disappeared. But I had to restrain myself with the young blacks, glowering defiantly while they cradled ghetto blasters beside their ears. They wouldn't tolerate eye-contact. Once a knife was pulled on me but I chanted loudly in a bell-clear voice until my tormentor was gone. Late in the afternoon I left the park. It was still too hot to run. I wandered down Eighth Avenue past the massage parlors and shish kebab counters, past the junkies. And the prostitutes, mostly black, some of them tricked out in elaborate vinyl and leather outfits in spite of the heat, black mesh stockings and spiked heels, wigs of all colors that shimmered in the haze. Each side street clogged with shabby storefronts wavered like a mirage. The muggy air made it difficult to breathe and weighed down on everybody, fraying tempers, fueling sudden fights. People were sullen and despairing, weeks of oppressive heat had brought all that to the surface. Faces glared at me as if the first wrong move on my part would bring confrontation. And high above all this, on the billboards, brazen images of success: bronzed women in bikinis, palm-lined beaches, watches, cameras, televisions, clothing.

About six o'clock, when the worst of the heat was over, I began to run, slowly at first, getting used to the parched furnace in my face, breathing the junk in the air, beginning to float again, skimming along block after block. By the time it was dark I had slipped into a state of oblivion, my mind cool, bright, and quiet. I don't know where I went or what I did, aside from now and then being aware of people talk-ing—a cryptic lingo spoken into walkie-talkies, into microphones hidden on shirt collars, whispered into shirtsleeves, wailed down ele-vator shafts, vomited into trash barrels, toilet bowels, sewer gratings in the streets. I ran and ran and the next thing I knew it was morning again and Hartwell still hadn't come for me. I was famished, weak and hungry as I'd never been before, asking people for change. But I couldn't stop grinning, the beautiful grin spread across my face was uncontrollable now and nobody was able to deal with it, they quick-ened their pace and skittered around me like centipedes. I was in mid-town again, there was a pain in my side and I felt dizzy. Freshly bar-bered men in crisp summer suits, their ties glowing—crazy paisleys, bold silk stripes, rampant checks. I held out my hand but I was slumped against a building now, a figure crouched and mumbling, "You can't burn my bones," without the energy to project myself into their world. Three days' growth of beard, the same T-shirt, under-pants, socks. My sweat-stained running shoes. Whatever was left of my ash-blond hair. I struggled to my feet, determined to get to Central Park where at least I could collapse in peace. I started laughing, my chin and lips were numb now, I couldn't say anything more. I lay slumped against a wall again—a different one—staring straight ahead at knee level, past the pedestrians into the abruptly shifting patterns of traffic on the street, all the cars going west, I knew that much. I knew I was near Sixth Avenue in the fifties. You can sense those huge build-ings without even being next to them, much less seeing them. And now I was staring at the ledge on which I sat, I was no longer on the sidewalk, instead I was slumped over against a little row of ornamental bushes, staring at the gray-green flecks in the granite visible between my legs, singing wordlessly to myself, my eyes stinging from the dust in the air, the grime on the sidewalk below me glistening like nuclear fallout. My granite perch was above the sidewalk, on the border of a plaza in front of one of the big buildings. I was definitely on Sixth Avenue now. The people passing by no longer did so at knee level but presented me, one after the other, with their preoccupied faces. Until finally one of them stopped. She came close to me and stood smiling and humming to herself, exuding the musky perfume of her unwashed body, her milk chocolate skin swathed in layers of silks and satins like a queen, her arms covered with wristwatches, her hair thick and matted, spattered and snarled with little trinkets and snatches of brightly colored wool, her neck wrapped in garlands, her forehead, so close to me I could reach out and kiss it, covered in sweat, her smile, her faraway eyes. Slowly the tambarina lady's eyes focused on me with complicity and respect as if I'd just told her a story, relating exploits of which she hadn't thought me capable. "We certainly keeping a place open for you . . . Light as day, black as night . . . Only place left and it belong to you, oily tambarina . . . And I know you be there, too, white folks always on time," she said, chuckling and speaking all at once. Then she strolled off down the sidewalk. I longed to be cradled in her arms but I could hardly move, she was gone before I had a chance to stop her. I looked down and saw a paper bag next to me on the ledge. Inside was half a shrimp salad sandwich, cold and fresh, which I devoured. "I need more food," I said, clearing my throat, the sandwich giving me just enough strength to say that forcefully to the faces sliding past me. Soon a pile of change accumulated and I bought a shish kebab and a soda. Now I saw people around me in the late afternoon shadows. Waves of office workers were pouring onto the plazas and sidewalks. I got up and walked through the stifling heat. I crossed Central Park South into the park, found a bench, and slept. A deep dreamless sleep, the sleep of the crocodiles. Bobby Addison, Dana Miller, Oliver Hartwell, Quemoy Sheridan—what has become of you, what are you doing? Tomorrow I'm going to have your names inscribed on a sheet of blue paper in letters of gold. How I miss you! You can look but you probably won't find me, neither tomorrow nor at any other time. I ride on numberless yielding threads. They hum past my ears in the cool, nourishing night. Fresh, like a ship, huge and metallic. From an infinite distance I hear myself saying, "I looked around then and saw the trees, the traffic going by." On the bench beside me was a copy of the *Post* dated July 13, 1977 . . . AMIN TELLS OF PLOT TO ASSASSINATE HIM . . . Merrily, merrily, merrily, merrily, life is but a dream. I walked into the grass, limbering up, doing stretches under the trees. By the time I was running, dusk had set in. In spite of the sweltering evening the city looked beautiful. As I loped down Seventh Avenue toward Times Square, the lights of the stores and signs intensified as the evening faded. I ran on and on, finding my stride again, my legs and heart pumping evenly, losing all sense of my surroundings, making countless ninety degree turns on the grid of the streets, up and down the avenues, crosstown from left to right, right to left. Running with one arm raised high, "You can't burn my bones . . ."

And that's when it happened, the most fabulous thing—all at once the glittering nighttime skyline of Manhattan vanished. I didn't become aware of it for a few seconds. I was seeing it happen but it didn't register, the past forcing itself into the present for a while longer. But the present wouldn't be denied. All the lights disappeared. I looked up and down the streets. Lines of dark buildings, no streetlights, no neon, no moon, the headlights of the cars the only illumination. I don't know where I was, somewhere on the Upper East Side in the nineties, almost into Spanish Harlem, high up on Madison maybe, but I was surrounded by tenements and stores, all of them dark. Crowds of people poured into the streets, jubilant, ecstatic. Word spread quickly that there had been a power failure throughout the city, a blackout which was expected to last all night. Mayor Beame had declared a state of emergency. People of all races surrounded me, and there was an explosive generosity in the streets now. People spontaneously helped each other out of darkened restaurants, they materialized with flashlights to direct traffic. But soon pandemonium took over. Manic groups of teenagers roamed around snatching purses. Then gangs of thirty or forty people formed in front of all the stores—the jewelry shops, supermarkets, furniture and liquor stores—heaving bricks through windows, tearing down gates, urging one another on, "Let's do it! Let's do it!" A tow truck appeared and tore the gates away from an appliance showroom. A woman stood beside me holding a TV, announcing triumphantly, "Shopping without money required." The sound of breaking glass, of shouts and sirens, was soon joined by the crackle of gunfire, people screaming now while I stood rooted to the spot under a storefront awning. The plate glass window of the shoe store across the street broke with a crash and clouds of children clambered inside, emerging holding stacks of boxes, shoes strung around their necks, shoes stuck in pockets. The sound of gunfire intensified. In spite of the fact that blaring portable radios and sirens and people shouting and arguing in Spanish and English were all much louder, I listened for those popping sounds. A police car appeared at the corner, lights flashing, and then a brick thrown from the roofs hit the windshield, shattering it. I ran south. The closer I got to midtown the more thrilling everything became, empty skyscraper windows like thousands of vanished thoughts soaring up into the night, the metropolis losing its memory. Squadrons of police surrounded the big department stores. I ran east toward the river. Here no looting was taking place, instead a festive air prevailed. One woman in a long gown staggered drunkenly down the center of 57th Street, a champagne glass in her hand. The flickering of candlelight appeared here and there in apartment windows. I turned down First Avenue, trotting slowly along looking at the buildings, so mysterious in their blackout massiveness, a city under the sea lit only by the nervously pointing fingers of the automobiles. And then I saw a figure illuminated by headlights, standing on the sidewalk beckoning to me, smiling, not threatening. "Is that you?" I shouted, but he turned and started to trot, keeping half a block ahead of me but looking back occasionally to make sure I was following him. Suddenly the apartment buildings on the left side of First Avenue gave way and I saw the cobalt slab of the United Nations and, behind it, the trembling lights of traffic on the East River Drive. We ran below 42nd Street and then Hartwell turned left beside the playground there and onto 41st, continuing to a ramp just above the highway where there was a small triangular patch of ground between intersecting ribbons of asphalt. He waited for me, crouched low, and as soon as I drew up to him he motioned for me to get down. The guard rails of one of the ramps leading off the highway was just above our heads, and in the space between that and the ground, not more than three feet, in the middle of that rising little section of concrete wall, was a metal grate. "It *is* you, isn't it," I said, my heart pounding, knowing it was, but still taken aback by the complete transformation of this man who not only no longer wore glasses or had gray hair but looked younger than ever— younger even than me, now—vital and well-preserved, with skin like porcelain. "You can look into my face if you want," I whispered, but he didn't respond to that. Instead, in a reassuring, affectionate voice he said, "We know we can trust you. No one outside our movement has seen this, but you're beginning a new life, just as we are. You have many perilous adventures ahead of you. Don't lose heart!" I saw his lips moving as he talked but it was like his voice came from somewhere inside my head and I yelled, "Look at me! I have to see your eyes," but he didn't look at me. Instead he said, "We have to be quick, we mustn't be seen. As soon as this next car goes by we'll make our move, it'll be dark inside at first." And the next second he was pulling the grate away from the wall and we were clambering inside, first me, then Hartwell, repositioning the grate behind him. For a moment I panicked. It was pitch black and there was barely room to crawl. "Keep going, Roy," he said, and eventually we squeezed into a passageway, a tunnel about eight feet high of white enameled brick, lit by mesh-covered bulbs set every ten yards or so in the ceiling. The walls were perfect, cold, and white. The contrast between the hot, dark streets outside and the bright, cool tunnel, with its rush of lovely, moisture-laden air, invigorated me. I felt a surge of joyful anticipation. Soon we were trotting steadily, both of us laughing like children in that restorative air. We talked as we ran, together at last, following the tunnel as it twisted, first this way then that, mile after mile, clean and bright